PATHS OF T

Jason Born

COPYRIGHT

DEDICATION

Grandparents

Thank you for living a life worth modeling

ACKNOWLEDGEMENTS

Getting a work of fiction published involves more than just a writer writing. As such, I have some folks to thank for their partnership, expertise, and friendship.

For the cover I again partnered with Michael Calandra in Sylvania, Ohio. With just a couple minutes of background, he works hard and accurately captures the spirit of Halldorr, the Norseman. His expertise and abilities make it so that I consider no others for painting the third cover as well. Sorry Michael, but you'll be busy again!

I did the work on the maps for *The Norseman* on my own. That was not a wise idea and so with the lesson learned I found someone with a far more practiced hand and eye than myself. Thanks to Mike Brogan for lending his electronic drawing world and bringing the lands traversed by Halldorr and his Viking pals to life. I know whenever I read a work of historical fiction, looking at the battles and villages from a bird's eye view always helps me visualize events, large and small.

Finally, because I so thoroughly abused my last editor with constant badgering, I had to find someone else this time. I thank Kirk Ross, himself the author of the soon-to-be-published, *The Last McKenzie*, for invading his writing and family time to read and punctuate my work. He did so even after I candidly admitted that I had no intention of doing the same for him, nor would he want me to.

Thanks to you all and thank you readers for giving me another chance at storytelling!

PROLOGUE

Destiny must be seized, of that much I am certain; won by savage force of will and body. I had no appreciation for this when I was a youth or even a young man because my fate was thrust upon me. I undoubtedly had to exact grim force throughout my life, but the situations more often than not came to me. I did not seek them – until now.

The treachery of which I had learned near the end of my last tale helped teach me the primal importance of yearning in action. I have said I longed for peace and quiet. I have said that I wanted a soft woman in my bed with our children scurrying about a longhouse like mice in a rich man's granary. For a brief instant, I had the love of a woman and for an even shorter time, the flicker of an eye, had a son. They were gone, and with all the rage and sorrow in my heart, I sought one man on whom I could lay the blame for my ills. I ignored the fact that without him and his lies, I never would have known my now-dead wife. He was responsible for deaths, the deaths of Norsemen and women, and for my wrongful exile. He would die. By my hand and by the One God I swore, he would die.

NORSE LANDS 1,000 A.D.

PART I - Revenge!

1,000 – 1,001 A.D.

CHAPTER 1

The westerly headwind into which we sailed made the going slow. Men leaned back while tugging oars with powerful arms as the blades pitched us through the waters. Their calloused hands gripped the pine handles worn smooth from countless repetitions of the same pattern. The hands dipped, the blades rose, torsos leaned forward, all to take another bite out of the sea, to propel us further west from Norway.

Leif was at the helm pushing against the raw power of the sea with the stout rudder of his longboat *Dragon Skull*. I had known him for most of my life since his father, Erik, had adopted me following the murder of my own father. He had grown into a strong, wise, and moderate man from the scrawny, yet certain, youth I once knew. And I had grown to love him, doing his will – all the while believing I served myself.

We hadn't seen Erik, my second father, in thirteen years, not since we were banished from Greenland for the deaths of thirteen fellow Norse – ten men, two women, and one child. One year for every death, we were banished by Erik himself because he saw no other way to punish us for the killing. We didn't kill them, of course. The skraelings did that nasty business when they attacked during our Thing, or assembly. Everyone, including Leif, was convinced that he and I had invited the attack, however, when we confronted and killed several skraeling men days before.

For years I had suffered under the curse of a fate spun by the three norns who lived at the foot of the Yggdrasil Tree. My mother disappeared after my birth. My father, who never spoke of her, was killed when I was a child. I was exiled from the home of my second father, Erik, for crimes I didn't commit. Freydis, my one-time betrothed, cursed me and went off to the beds of other men to spite me, groaning loudly as they plowed her like the spring soil. My one true love and wife, Kenna, died just days after giving birth to our

---

son, little Olaf. Little Olaf died days later. Just weeks ago at the Battle of Swoldr, though, I learned that much of my fate was a consequence of a single act of treachery. At Swoldr, we fought mightily against overwhelming odds. Only three of us survived. One, Einar, fled with his family to the far reaches of Norway. The second, Olaf, former king and my third father, fled with men aboard my ship, *Charging Boar*, to the Holy Land. The third, I, Halldorr Olefsson, did not flee. With purpose I ran headlong into battle, toward revenge. Toward Greenland.

When that arrow pierced Cnute's lung on the steering deck aboard *Long Serpent* at Swoldr, he and I both knew he would die. Through spattering, gurgling blood and amidst the chaos of war he gave me the secret he had carried for thirteen years since he left with us on our exile. Bjarni Herjolfsson lied all those years ago. There were no other skraelings skulking about who had witnessed our first confrontation. Our Greenland settlement would have been secure had Bjarni not deepened his betrayal. But he approached the skraeling village and instructed them when and where to attack our own people. He knew we would have no weapons at the Thing, so the skraeling warriors stayed hidden amongst the rocks until the time was right and the killing harvest began. We were exiled following the attack. Bjarni simply profited, I was sure. He had been safe, fat, and warm for thirteen years. Soon he would find that he was secure no more.

It had been six days since we left the Fjord at Agdenes in Norway and I had parted ways with King Olaf. We did not see any land in all that time and I realized that for as many years as I had been at sea, my whole life, that was the longest I had ever gone without seeing the forests or mountains or rocks that sprouted from the shores. The breeze which blew at our stern the first night of our escape quickly gave way and we rowed as I have already said. We took turns at the benches of *Dragon Skull* for though we were young and fit, hours of the toilsome labor at a single stretch took its toll on our shoulders and backs. Leif decided to avoid the first two stops normally made on the trip west across the Norwegian Sea. He was anxious to return to his father and mother in order show off his own family; Thorgunna, his tall, striking wife with her wheat colored hair, and Thorgils, his five year old, red-haired son. So we passed by the Norse occupied Hetland Islands and the Faeroe Islands with their scattered, celibate Irish monk communities and prolific sheep populations.

I had just finished a turn at the oars and walked back to Leif to speak. "Despite the recent slow going, we should be at Iceland sometime tomorrow." Thorgunna and Thorgils both slept at Leif's feet in animal skin sacs called hudfats which were usually used to store equipment. Other women and men, including the priest King Olaf sent with us, called Torleik, were scattered about the boat sleeping on the raised deck of the prow, or in the hold, or even between the rowing benches, so we whispered.

"We should see the shores tomorrow, but I don't mean to come ashore."

"Why wouldn't we pause?" I asked, leaning on the gunwale, listening to the light splashing of the oars.

"Why would we?" he retorted. "We have plenty of provisions, strong backs, and good sailors."

He was right, of course. The only reason we had to stop in Iceland was for supplies, but since we had no need, the only rationale for the stop now would be, well, tradition. It was late in the season for our trip, so the sooner we arrived in Eriksfjord, the safer we would be from foul weather. I shrugged saying, "Sounds good."

The new moon came and went in the past several days and now I looked up at the sliver which grew larger by the night. Except for the rare gray-black cloud the sky was clear, which meant it was cold at this time of year. I remained silent while the men continued their grinding, grate-slap at the oars. My thirty-four year old back was sore from the rowing and so I stretched it by twisting at my waist. After a time Leif asked, "Why did you come back with us, Halldorr?"

Good question. I wouldn't answer it directly today. Leif didn't know about Bjarni's deceit nor my plan for revenge and wouldn't for now. I had told Leif in the spring past that I would serve Olaf for as long as he lived. "In a way, Olaf is dead," I said cryptically. Then I added, "At least the world thinks he is dead."

"Aye, there's truth in that. Not the whole truth, I know, but you've decided not to share it with me. You loved the man like he was your father and he loved you like a son. You wouldn't abandon him so readily if not for something else."

"I didn't abandon him!" I answered with raised voice, anger flashing. Leif hissed slightly at my loud voice, indicating with his head that his family slept.

Ever since I knew the man, Leif had been good at seeing truth lying in the shadows or tucked between the lies. He had become adept even at seeing the future following his sleepless night atop a barrow mound. Leif knew there would be blood at the Thing alongside Fridr Rock. He knew fate would bring me back to Greenland. Did he know that it was the chance for revenge that brought me back now?

I continued with more control, "I didn't abandon him, Leif. Don't say that. I did love the man as my third father. He had no use for Berserkers any longer and what am I, if not an instrument of death?" I had been among Olaf's most trusted bodyguards, named after the Berserkers of legends. At last, I added, "Remember I love your father, my second father, and plan on rejoicing when I see him once again."

"You're right, friend. I'm sorry for suggesting you abandoned anyone. I know you are the most loyal friend, son, or husband anyone could hope to have." The first breeze in days tussled his thick, red hair for an instant. We both involuntarily looked into the direction from which the wind had come. There was nothing to see in the black night in the open sea. "What will you do when you see Freydis?"

Freydis? His sister, my enchantress. My once-betrothed, who now hated me for a senseless reason. The woman who found another man's longhouse immediately after she gave up on me. The woman who I spent years pushing out of my mind and then at last succeeded when I met, loved, and married Kenna. I imagined Freydis now. I hadn't seen her in thirteen years and so I thought of her as I had last seen her – long, fiery red hair cascading down to her rounded ample breasts with a seat to match. I thought I loved her then. The sickly-thin Kenna taught me otherwise. The brilliant, engaging, beautiful Kenna taught me that I lusted after Freydis, but never knew love with her. Kenna, who instructed me in the art of language and writing and true love, was the mother of my son, Olaf – both dead. Freydis? "I hope to ignore her."

That comment made Leif laugh a belly laugh. He doubled over while holding the rudder, guffawing. The men, who faced us on their benches, just looked at us in the dark with expressions of puzzlement. Tyrkr, the thrall whom Erik gifted to Leif who became the thrall who bought his own freedom using plunder from our raids, sat at the nearest bench and said in his German-accented Norse, "I hope to plow her!" Leif thought this was funny too and continued laughing. I thought it was uproarious, because it reminded me of a conversation Tyrkr and I had many years before. I joined into the laughter and soon it was like one of the evil spirits which cause sickness. Tyrkr laughed. Haki, the Scottish thrall on the bench next to Tyrkr, laughed. Soon the entire fleet of men rowing their oars laughed, though most just laughed at their comrades for they couldn't have heard what we said. Haekja, Haki's sister, woke up from the noise. Other women stirred. Thorgunna awoke and sat up shaking her head, feigning disgust at her husband and the rest of his men.

The laughter slowly died away as the very first suggestion of an approaching dawn appeared on the eastern horizon, to our rear. The women on board began to awaken more thoroughly and stretch their stiff limbs. In their own ritual they went to the hold and peeled away tarpaulins to reveal bundles of salted pork and hard bread for breakfast. Several wooden dishes were unstowed and groups of men were served breakfast while the rest continued their work at the oars.

A breeze from the fore rose again to ruffle the hairs on our heads. The true seafarers among us noted it immediately. This wind was cooler than the air around us and carried the smell of a storm, maybe the first winter storm of the season. The relatively insignificant light from our stern showed that clouds sat and swirled and billowed several miles to the west. They were low with more shades of gray and black and dark blues or violets than I am able to adequately describe.

Tyrkr looked over his shoulder at the storm into which we rowed and said with relief, "If we pull hard, maybe we can at least put to shore on Iceland's lee side before taking on too much of the storm." Most of the Norse settlements of Iceland were on the more habitable and fertile western shores, but Tyrkr was proposing to land at the nearest point of land to wait out the storm. Grunts of approval from the other men and women rippled out from Tyrkr like a stone had been tossed into still water. They all knew that storms this time of year can be treacherous and last for days.

This time, however, I had no reason for worry because fate was on my side. Months ago Leif had seen in a vision that we would return to Greenland when I thought there was no way for that to happen. I responded to Tyrkr, "We needn't put ashore. We've excellent sailors on board and plenty of supplies." Any other time I would have spoken up as to how foolish this plan was, but not today.

Leif and I had built so much trust among these men over the years that they accepted the folly without protest. In their hearts they had to worry, but the commander's word was final. Some even had to remember Bjarni's fateful voyage fourteen years before where Arne the navigator was but the first to die from a terrible, early winter storm. Many more died the following days due to Bjarni's dismal leadership. I justified my belief that such events wouldn't occur on this voyage, because Leif saw our safe return beforehand.

We rowed for two more hours as the day broke, but the light never came. It was gradually snuffed out by the clouds brought toward us by the quickly stiffening, sharp wind. The calm sea was transforming from a waveless platter into slowly rolling swells. Soon those swells would have caps of white tumbling down toward us. Depending on the height of the waves, five or more men would have to unfasten some of the planking from the deck, bailing water from the bilge, so now women calmly went about tying the buckets in place. Rigging was fastened and any loose items stowed.

I had taken the rudder from Leif so he could see that the ship was adequately prepared to receive the tempest. He had Thorgils retrieve several of the men's axes from the baggage in case the air turned cold and ice began forming on the hull or deck. The only way to clear the instantly forming ice was to hack it away. While they scurried about like rats in the bilge, I steered us so that we scaled a swell and then slid down the other side at a right angle to its path. Ahead past the dragon-headed prow, a darker mass on the horizon told me that Iceland was there receiving the storm first. Sparsely scattered snow flakes gently floated down around us to disappear into the sea.

We had a choice to make: progress directly into the storm by moving around the island's south side or let the island absorb some of the gale's force and curve to the north. It sounds as if the choice were a simple one, but to those experienced in the mysteries of the sea, especially the frigid northern seas, there were other factors to consider. Our forefathers quickly learned that the southeastern coast of Iceland received a warm water current from some unknown world to the south. This current meant that there would rarely be any ice to contend with taking a southern route. The northern side of the island was filled with peril. It was early in the winter for floating ice packs, but the summer had been somewhat cool in Europe. Perhaps we would find icebergs if we went north away from the storm. One brush with an iceberg would likely mean that we would be lost. But then, as I calculated our odds, I gained confidence. I couldn't die on this voyage, I reminded myself, the norns showed it to be so. Without consulting anyone, I turned the rudder and pointed the ship northwest.

After three hours more of hard rowing and hard steering we passed the easternmost shores of Iceland. We were finally out of the terrific wind and so the seas were calmer. Despite the small, welcome respite, I could feel that the arctic air was colder, much colder than the air we just left. It was snowing quite heavily. The wind was such that we decided to chance the sail and make time. Once it was raised we cut through the cold waters swiftly. Snow piled on the cold deck planks, making the footing questionable at best. Thorgils took the opportunity to pelt, first his father, then me, then all the men, with snowballs. When Leif cuffed his head and we sent our own snow missiles to him in return, he quickly lost interest in the game.

The storm raged to the south and west with a tar black sky occasionally illuminated by the out-of-place lightning. Several small icebergs bounced in the waves one or two miles to the north. Our trip around the Iceland's north coast was uneventful for many hours.

By the middle of the following day we came to the northwestern-most corner of Iceland. This fjord-laden outcropping of land would be our last chance to find a suitable place to make shore before we sailed once again into the raging storm. The weather ahead looked like a wall. The frigid air in which we sailed crashed headlong into the warmer, eruptive air to the island's west. The seas were higher and had menacing caps of white. As we approached, the snowfall turned to icy rain. For the sake of the sail, Leif ordered that it be brought in. Cold men grumbled, but quickly found their rowing benches after taking a final draught of ale. The holes were unplugged and the oars threaded through with some difficulty due to the pitching seas. We wouldn't be stopping; Leif was determined to be the first man to cross the seas without a single landfall pause.

Leif and his thrall Haki began hacking with their axes at the ice building up on the decks and gunwale. The women and children looked miserable, huddling in their hudfats to find whatever warmth or dryness they could. Inside one sac Haekja held her long black hair away from her mouth as she vomited onto the planking from the rough seas. The vomit mixed with the ice and water and ran down between the planks into the bilge. Several men stood in that bilge in the freezing water baling bucket after bucket over the sides to keep us afloat. The priest, Torleik, kneeled in his wet robes, using his hands to balance himself whenever a particularly rough wave crossed beneath the ship, praying in Latin for safe passage through the storm.

Visibility was terrible. Driving freezing rain, a black sky, and black seas were all I could see while I fought with the steering oar. That is, until two massive icebergs appeared to starboard as if conjured by the old gods. One spun on an invisible vertical axis as it rose and dipped its way toward us. The other, more massive iceberg moved with purpose on what looked like an intercept course toward *Dragon Skull*. Icebergs are not stationary fence posts avoided by a touch to a horse's reins. No, they're tricky, always searching the seas for unwary travelers. Though King Olaf saw that we were all converted to the One True God, I still often thought of the old gods and old ways and said a prayer to both Thor and Frey that day. Since I wore my cross tunic which I received as a gift from Olaf, I prayed to the One God as well.

The action I am about to describe will take longer to read than it did to occur. The smaller, spinning iceberg came along the length of our starboard hull and snapped off each man's oar as it undulated on its sea path. I tried to shout a warning but my screams were swallowed by the storm. The backward facing men were all surprised by the force and each received a blow to the chest from their now bladeless oar handles. Many of them toppled off their benches to hit the man or bench to the fore. The berg would pass by so close that I could have reached out and touched it had I not needed both hands on the jostling rudder. As it approached the stern I shrieked to Leif and Tyrkr, who hacked at ice nearby to drop their axes and grab the heavy iron anchor immediately and throw it at the spinning mass of ice. To Thorgunna nestled in a nearby hudfat, I yelled to shorten the anchor's line to twenty or thirty feet by tying it off. Thankfully, all listened without question or I would not be here writing my tale this day.

Because even though the direct danger was the iceberg tearing our oars just inches from the hull, my attention focused on the second. I had turned *Dragon Skull's* course to port by struggling with my feet on the icy deck to lean against the steering oar, but it appeared to me that the second, enormous iceberg corrected its own route to again intercept us as a sentient being would have done. We had mere moments before a collision sent us to the icy depths of Hel. Maneuvering in the stirring sea was made more difficult by our lack of starboard oars while those men strained to regain their feet and retrieve the spare set of oars from the T-shaped rack at the center of the ship.

Within ten seconds Thorgunna had a strong seafarer's knot and Leif and Tyrkr heaved the anchor. We had only one chance for my ridiculous plan to work, but I knew it would when the sharp prongs of the anchor caught in the whirling ice. The slack in the rope wound around it for a half a turn as the mass of ice moved past us still swirling. As much as I thought I was prepared for the jolt, I found I was not. When the thick rope pulled taut, both the iceberg and the longboat snapped toward one another. Each of us aboard that day tumbled to the deck with many bruises showing later as proof. I scampered back to my feet grabbing Tyrkr's axe and swung the brutal instrument with maddening force at the anchor's rope stretched over the gunwale. The tense rope sprung away toward the iceberg while the blade of the axe became embedded in the ship's hull. I looked over my shoulder just as the enormous second iceberg passed across the front of our path. We had slowed *Skull* just enough to avoid the deadly collision, but I would have to buy Leif a new anchor.

We rowed west and south for many more hours, gradually moving out of the storm. As the next day dawned a little more brightly than what we had seen in recent days we moved into the strong, cold current that marches southward down the east coast of Greenland and were able to stow the oars and take advantage of a frigid wind blowing from the north into our full sail. We rested and tried to warm ourselves, with clapping hands and songs.

Torleik was leading a mass from the prow, praising the One God for our miraculous passing when I saw a most unexpected sight. Ahead to starboard, sitting atop a lone, jagged crag jutting from the sea was a collection of shivering men. One of them managed to gain the presence of mind or the strength, I don't know which, to stand and wave to us. Spray from the crashing sea rose to blanket the men every few moments. I interrupted Torleik in mid-sentence by saying, "Father, God has given us more miracles to perform this day." The perturbed priest, first looked at me and then to where I pointed.

The rescue was not much of an affair, but is significant for its later impact on the events following in Greenland. While the men pulled on the *Skull's* oars to maintain the longboat's position, I went with a row boat to retrieve the stranded souls. Because of the rough water, we dared not get close so we yelled to the miserable lot to make a flying jump one at a time. This was a long process. Each one grabbed the rope we threw to them and were so frozen by the time we hauled their dripping forms into the boat that they said nothing. Their beards were decorated with icicles which danced as their teeth chattered behind blue lips. We saved six men that day.

Three of the men would lose a little finger or part of their ears to frostbite, but all-in-all it was a success. Another night and morning brought us within sight of Greenland. Soon we rounded the southern tip and by the next evening we entered Eriksfjord and pushed to Eystribyggo and Erik's estate, Brattahlid. We were the first ship to ever pilot across all the northern seas without a single stop along the way!

. . .

Over two thousand Norsemen and women now inhabited Greenland; more than two times what was there when we were banished. I think that in the weeks since our return, Erik took us to visit nearly half of them. He was demonstrably proud of Leif and his lovely Thorgunna. Erik took to being a grandfather to Thorgils as I would have expected, with vigor. He traipsed us over ice and snow from estate to estate and in and out of longhouses to show what he deemed as our jubilant return. Old Sindri had passed away, but his widow, a woman he married several years after his first wife was murdered at Fridr Rock, yet lived in his old longhouse. She seemed to remember Leif and me, but I did not recall her face at all. According to Erik, the old widow raised goats that gave the finest milk in all of Eystribyggo. It was like that day after day. Slogging through the weather and visiting neighbors, catching up on the mundane details of life in this, our isolated Norse settlement.

Erik and Thorgils seemed to love the adventure. He would ride on his grandfather's shoulders as we walked or sometimes even as we rode horses from farm to farm. Leif and Thorgunna seemed at ease, effortlessly accepting their new roles as son and daughter-in-law to the jarl of Greenland. For my part, I was shocked again at the lack of trees and the rocks, rocks, rocks that littered the landscape. Darkness stole most of the day.

I loved Erik as a second father, but missed my third father, Olaf. I missed the excitement of the sea. I missed the trees and glens of Europe. When I thought of trees I thought of the two straight years I searched the woods with Thorberg Skaffhog for the right lumber for the two great longboats I built for my king in our new capital city of Kaupangen.

I was welcomed there in Eystribyggo as a son, but felt out of place. Leif knew from a vision that I would return to this forbidding land, but that did not mean I would stay. As we climbed another rise and the wind bit into my cheeks like a thrall's cooking knife I resolved to complete the duty I assigned to myself, to kill Bjarni for the wickedness and massacre he wrought. He would die by my hand, perhaps with a swing of my sword or the quick thrust of my saex. Then after the spring equinox I would leave my second father again, seeking my fortune elsewhere. I was a different man than I was when I left Greenland whimpering like a child for being separated from my second father. That morning I cried like a baby searching for his mother's warm breast and the life it brought. Since then, I had fought in great battles, giving death. I now read and spoke several languages. Perhaps I would sail to Europe again. I had friends in Dyflin and likely still had a hoard of hacksilver buried beneath my home there. Maybe I would find my way to the Holy Land to locate Olaf, again serving him as Berserker and adopted son. The only thing of which I was certain at that moment was that I would leave Greenland in the spring.

After our reintroduction to the Greenlander society, we settled into Brattahlid for the long winter. I stayed in the main longhouse with Erik and his wife Thjordhildr. It was still the largest, most impressive residence in the settlement. He and Thjordhildr were warm and caring as I remembered them, but carried an unspoken sadness that I did not recall seeing when I left. I supposed it was the sadness that came with age as a result of the harshness of the life we all find ourselves living. Leif and his family stayed in my old longhouse across the pasture until they could build their own when the weather turned. My old house now belonged to Freydis and her husband, Torvard. They had added significant space to the house, though they had no children with which to fill it.

The Yule approached and Leif, in cahoots with Torleik, who was still bent on carrying out King Olaf's demand to bring Christianity to Greenland, requested that Erik hold a feast at

Brattahlid for those near enough to make the cold journey. All men see the same event differently and this was no exception. Erik saw another opportunity to command an audience, to keep his power, and so gladly accepted. Leif saw an opportunity to plead the case for the One God to that same captive audience. I saw an opportunity to lay my eyes upon Bjarni again and plan the method of my retribution.

The Yule would be a three day celebration with drinking, feasting, and sacrifices. Erik would offer toasts and skalds would tell of the legends through verse. During the short daylight of the first day of feasting, the men of Erik's family went out into the unwelcoming weather to make the sacrifices. Leif declined to enlist in the ritual, saying that he was unwell. I knew the real reason was that he thought it was wrong to profess the new faith and still practice the old ways. I was not so certain about such rules so I joined Erik, Thorvald, and Tyrkr, who despite being a freeman, made his bed among the thralls in their tiny home on Brattahlid.

Thorvald, Leif's older brother, lived in Eriksfjord on a rocky farm closer to the sea, but within riding distance. Out of Erik's three sons, Thorvald was most like Erik in personality –gregarious, ready to laugh, and he happily organized his mind to avoid any complex thought. For better or worse, he acted. Thorvald did not discuss. He was married to a woman who emigrated from Iceland in the years I was gone. She was called Gro and was a plain woman with thin, dirty blond hair. Gro was the second wife of Thorvald. By all accounts his first was a pretty, quick-witted woman who died after she slipped on ice and fell against jagged rocks, eventually tumbling into the fjord one spring morning several years earlier. Thorvald had no children by either woman.

Young Thorstein, the youngest brother of Leif, did not join us for the sacrifices. Apart from Leif, he was the most successful of Erik's children. The boy who played warrior with wooden sticks when I last saw him had become the chief of the western Norse settlement called Vestribyggo. Thorstein was not with us this day, for making the journey so late in the year would be near suicide. He was considered a wise, just ruler and I was told he had a lovely Icelandic bride named Gudrid. She was purported to have thick golden blonde hair that was straight like a tall forest pine, though it was now wound tightly in the braids expected of a married woman. In past years Thorstein led expeditions to Europe, even travelling to Ireland for a time. When I learned of his adventures, I decided I would ask him what he thought of my old town, Dyflin.

The four of us – Erik, Thorvald, Tyrkr, and I – led several thralls into the barn which housed the livestock during the winter. In the old country we would sometimes be able to perform the sacrificial ceremonies in the open forest or glades. But here the cold was deepening by the day; and none of us had the intention of standing in the stinging wind unless necessary. Since Erik didn't see fit to build a temple to the gods, the barn would serve in its place. Two of the young thralls brought a fine chestnut stallion from its place to the center of the barn. We stood around the horse which was held in place by reins extending from its rope bridle. I hobbled the horse by tying two of its legs together with rope.

Erik said to me, "You ought to do this. We've all had the honor for years, but you've been gone. And it sounds like this Olaf had you stuck with the boring Christian God." I looked to Thorvald to make sure he wasn't offended that an adopted son performed a duty rightly completed by the family, but he indicated with his hand that I should go ahead. Erik's old bones were getting cold already so he spoke the words for Thorvald, "Get on with it!"

I pulled my saex, the only item I inherited from my real father, from my belt and walked to the horse's neck. I slapped the animal's front quarter and gave him a soft murmur as I drove the blade into the beast's neck. His nostrils flared and his black eyes widened with fright while he reared. Blood spurted all over me and sprayed as a pulsating mist over the barn floor. His fore legs rose and he clawed the air with his hooves until he planted them back on the ground, landing with a crash. He repeated this three times while the thralls held tightly to the reins for control. On the third trip back down to the earthen floor all four of his legs crumpled beneath him and he sprawled onto his left side. Erik handed me a bowl and I bent down to the dying animal's neck to fill it with the hlaut, or sacrificial blood. When the vessel was full I walked to Erik, handing it to him. He produced a hlautteinar, or sacrificial twig, dipped it into the blood, and used it to sprinkle the hlaut on me, then Thorvald, then Tyrkr.

We repeated this process several times with goats and sheep and then left the butchering to the thralls. The sacrificed animals' meat would be boiled in colossal pots suspended from the rafters or roasted on spits above the great hearth in Brattahlid's hall for the coming feasts. The bowl containing any excess hlaut would be carried around the hearth several times tonight and Erik, our chief, would offer a prayer to the gods, specifically Odin. How all of our old rituals – heathen rituals many of Olaf's priests would have called them – would help Leif plead the cause of the One God escaped me.

. . .

Villagers began arriving in the hall from the neighboring estates shortly after we finished our sacrifices. We did not clean the hlaut from our bodies as we wanted the blood from our noble sacrifices to bring us the life power it once gave them. The guests all anticipated that while Erik circled the hearth with the blood-filled bowl, he would use the hlautteinar to cover them with the blood as well.

The first visitor to appear was Thorhall the Huntsman. He was a bachelor who was old when we were banished and looked like the oldest man I had ever seen by the time of our return. Despite the deep furrows which crossed his face he was an extraordinary specimen. He had a dark complexion and was tall and gaunt. But Thorhall was a spry, active hunter and fishermen. He accompanied Erik, still, on his many expeditions into the sea for narwhal and walruses. The Huntsman was known to be temperamental and overbearing with a melancholy disposition at even the most festive times. Despite these traits, Erik was fond of him as the two men shared stories of youthful adventures in Norway. As the sullen man shook off the cold, I thought that Thorhall would likely remind me of my old friend Thorberg, the master shipwright, so I looked forward to becoming reacquainted with him.

Erik sat on a bench near the door which was situated in the gable end of the longhouse. He used this position to great all the celebrants, but his aging body did not like the cold wind when the door was opened so he clutched a musk ox blanket that was tightly wrapped about his shoulders overtop his brown woolen cloak covering, yet another layer, his tunic. Thorhall now sat next to him with a large cup of ale. I saw that Erik had given him one of his fine silver cups indicating he did indeed like Thorhall very much.

The curtains which separated the house into multiple rooms were pulled to the sides creating a large hall. From my vantage point across the room, I saw many others come through the door bringing gasps of the blustering snow with them each time. Thorbjorn, Gudrid's father; Holmgeirr; Anundr; and countless others came.

Then I saw him. He wore a broad, tooth-filled smile. His finely combed hair appeared perfectly placed despite the wind whistling over the hills. He was adorned in the finery associated with a rich merchant; silver and gold ring pins for his cloak, rings upon several fingers, and an excellent, never-used sword strapped about his waist. Bjarni took Erik's extended hand, shook it, and greeted the jarl warmly, even giving him a slight bow of the head. I recognized many of his men as they filed in behind him all paying their respects to Erik.

Bjarni made his way into the crowd acknowledging many by name and slapping numerous backs. When he came to a clearing in the room he snatched a cup of ale from a table and paused for a drink. He then scanned the room with a serious expression partially hidden behind his long beard. His gaze fell upon Leif, who was wrestling with Thorgils and several other boys, visiting from outlying farms. Bjarni gave a menacing stare through Leif's back then continued to scan the hall. Finally our eyes met and I didn't wait to receive his loathsome stare, sending him a look of absolute boiling hatred. He was surprised that I was already staring at him so Bjarni tried his best to look relaxed, raising his eyebrows with a nod. I surprised him further when I changed my countenance to a wicked smile and tapped first my saex with one hand then the hilt of my sword with the other. The saex was the very same I had used to repel his blow when he tried to strike down Leif years before. The coward couldn't take it any longer and returned to a cluster of his men, speaking in hushed tones. They took turns peeking around their master to steal glances at me. In turn, I gave each an overly joyous wave.

I sat in my corner drinking bits of ale, feeding my anger, letting it simmer inside. I had all winter to exact my revenge and I was not certain how I would kill him yet, but I would.

Musicians somewhere in the hall played traditional music honoring one of the old gods. Two of them had wind instruments; the first playing a gemshorn, or hollowed out cow horn with a wooden plug in the wide end and five holes bored along one side, the second playing a wooden panpipe. A third musician played a hand-drum, with a quick rumbling beat. The music and ale mixed to stir me. I closed my eyes and leaned back against the cold, earthen wall. I could feel the wind tearing outside at the turf wall despite its thickness. Several men began singing in low-pitched growls, almost groans, representing the voices of the gods.

My mind swam. The small amount of ale on which I sipped warmed my chest and belly, sending tingles out to my limbs. It flooded my head. I sat there in my hlaut-stained clothes and had visions. Not visions like those of Leif where he saw a clear future. My visions were of the past. I saw my true father smiling and singing songs to the old gods as he sowed wheat on our farm long ago. I saw Erik and remembered him singing songs to the old gods as we crossed the sea to Iceland when he and his father were exiled from Norway. He did the same when he sailed to and discovered Greenland after his exile from Iceland. I remembered Erling, the man whose fingers I sawed off in Norway's first church. Erling sang to Frey as he planted his field of rye on the Isle of Most. I remembered all the songs we sang to the gods as we felled the countless trees around Kaupangen to build *Crane* and *Long Serpent*. It was suddenly clear to me that although I was a Christian, owned a trunk with Christian markings upon it, had a sword with the same markings, wore a medallion with a cross, and had a red warrior's tunic with a white cross emblazoned across the front and back, the moments of perfect clarity in my life were when I honored the old gods. I was a Berserker after all! It was Olaf who made me both a Christian and Berserker. I would stay a Christian to honor my third father. But I would resume my Berserker role to exact my revenge.

I opened my eyes just as a woman of about thirty, or ten years Bjarni's junior, came up to him and grasped his hand. I didn't recognize her from before I left though she must certainly be his wife now for a boy of about nine who looked just like Bjarni followed after her. I was struck by something evil. A thought so wonderfully evil in its symmetry, that it made me shudder. I quickly closed my eyes and thought of the day of the massacre at Fridr Rock. The images came so quickly and exactly, it was like they were painted in my mind. There was Bjarni standing in his bright blue cloak next to Fridr Rock, Peace Rock, surrounded by his men. How many men stood around him that day? One, two, three . . . nine. Plus Bjarni. That's ten. I opened my eyes again, still sitting in my corner and counted the men standing there. Nine plus Bjarni! I looked at his wife and his son. It all made sense. I had decided how I would obtain revenge for Greenland and for myself.

Shushing from several women interrupted my thoughts and I turned to see Erik standing at the hearth with the hlaut-filled vessel raised above his head. The blood inside the bowl was kept wet for the past several hours with the occasional addition of water. He shouted as the last of the songs, music, and conversation died away, "We honor the gods tonight!" His face still wore the blood from the sacrifices earlier in the day. He reminded me of men, dead and living, following the carnage of battle. Erik began to stride around the hearth and continued, "We honor them for they provide and will provide. They've turned the sun once more so that the days again grow longer so that, in turn, we may plant and reap and eat. The men of my family who are with us tonight have already received the power of the hlaut and I will give the same to all of you." He overlooked the fact that Leif stood pristine in his clothing next to Thorgunna and Thorgils. Erik brought down the vessel and said, "Odin, mighty father of Thor, inventor of war, we ask for victory over our enemies in the coming year. We ask that King Olaf, who my son Leif and our Halldorr served so honorably, may rise again to claim the throne of Norway. We ask Frey to sail his ship, *Skidbladnr*, across the skies and bring us sun, rain, and wind to grow our food." Tyrkr handed Erik the hlautteinar. He dipped it into the bowl and with a flick of his wrist, began sprinkling red droplets of blood on his subjects. We stood silently as he slowly made his way around the room. Freydis and Torvard received their dousing. Thorhall the Huntsman received his spray. The children in the crowd especially loved to have the jarl pay them attention and flip the red liquid across their faces or clothes. However, one baby, in particular, who was held tightly in his mother's arms, erupted into a mind-splitting wail when the chilly liquid struck his face. The crowd laughed as Erik roughly patted the boy on his belly until the child, at last, ceased his terrorized crying.

Erik had finally reached Leif and his family. He did not hesitate, but dipped the hlautteinar into the dish for a quick soak then lifted his hand to toss the droplets onto Leif. Nor did Leif hesitate, but caught his father's hand in his own and asked, "May I, father?" Erik was surprised, but, thinking that Leif was asking for the honor to cover his own family, readily gave the instruments to his son.

Without a word, the two men switched positions, Leif in the center of the room, Erik in the crowd. Here was Leif's chance to preach the gospel as he promised Olaf he would. It was his chance to bring Christianity to Greenland; to turn the Yule into Christmas, the spring equinox into Easter.

"Sacrifice and blood," Leif called to the gathering. "Our men killed excellent livestock this day so that we may receive their life-blood, their power. Every Yule we cover ourselves in the hlaut. This year Halldorr looks as though he has bathed in it!" A few chuckles came at my expense. "I know men who burn the Yule log. We have all taken a part in eating the Yule goat. Yet amidst all this tradition, I ask questions. Is it not even more excellent when a man, rather than a horse or goat or sheep, will suffer and die to save a friend's life?" He was quickly losing them, but several grunts and nods from the crowd kept Leif going. "What about a man who is willing to die to save a stranger? How mighty would it be if one sacrifice could provide enough blood for all time?"

Someone interrupted him, "That's a lot of blood!" A round of laughter came and the crowd took the opportunity to down ale. Erik looked like he would strangle Leif but let the scene play out, keeping silent and still.

"It's actually no more blood than any man carries in his body. I know of such a man. A man who gave his life while in its prime so that others, all of us really, may live. His blood was sacrifice enough for all time, so that we never have to offer a sacrifice again. And remember the story of Thor's goats, Tanngrisnir and Tanngnjostr? Thor killed then cooked them for sustenance for himself and his guests. You know what happened next! Thor used his hammer to raise the goats from the dead so they could again pull his chariot. The man of whom I speak, was dead for three days, yet had the power to resurrect himself. He needed neither Thor nor his hammer. All that is required of us is to believe!"

"Who is this man?" asked Thjordhildr, Leif's mother. Erik looked aghast at his wife, then back to Leif.

Thorhall the Huntsman shouted, "He talks of the Christian god. We let him spend too much time with the Europeans so that we must deal with a convert!"

Leif tried to swing the discussion in his favor, "Aye, Thorhall, I am a convert to the One True God. So is your rightful king, Olaf."

Thorhall wouldn't be beaten that easily, "Yes, but you said so yourself that Olaf was beaten. What kind of super god is that, who cannot save his righteous follower?"

"He is the kind of God who gives his people true freedom. He is the kind of God that allows you your own choices to fail or succeed. To lose or to triumph. To love or to hate. It's up to you. Halldorr will tell you that it was man's betrayal that brought about Olaf's defeat, not God. But I've let a dour man cause me to avoid answering my mother's question. I speak of Jesus, the son of God. You see, God gave his only son as a sacrifice to the Romans, the gods of this earth in their time. God allowed them to kill Jesus so that for all time and throughout the world we would no longer be required to shed blood to satisfy God's bloodlust. Look at me today. Pure and clean! No blood! Look at my family, pure and clean, no blood. We are atoned for – without the blood of a horse. We are strong because of our faith in the man-God, not because of a horse!"

The crowd was completely confused, fidgeting while looking around the great hall.

Torleik stepped forward taking up the charge, "I am a stranger to most of you, but I need to share something about this man, Leif. I will call him Leif the Lucky from now on." Then the priest pointed his young hand to the six men we rescued from the rock. "Certainly, these men will call him Leif the Lucky because he saved them from a certain icy death in the sea. But I stand here tonight to tell you that the One God gave Leif power and vision to cross the wide sea without pause in order to save these men so that they can be a further testimony to God's power!" Nods from the six shipwreck survivors told the crowd that the strange priest told the truth.

Leif continued, "Olaf sent two Scottish thralls who were gifted with swift feet to spread this good news. I will send them to Vestribyggo in the spring, but their conversions of our brothers and sisters will be much easier when they can say all of Eystribyggo has already done so." I didn't think mass conversions likely, given the rather poor reception to his speech. He was a gifted leader and good speechmaker, but he missed the mark that night. He finally ended with, "Mother, would you please be the first in all of Greenland to receive the One God?"

There was a brief pause and so Erik opened his mouth to stop Leif, but Thjordhildr beat him to it with a simple, "Yes." Erik's mouth gaped open without uttering a sound and he stared in disbelief at his wife who crouched to her knees and bowed her head. Torleik sent Thorgils to get a snowball from outside. When he returned with it, the young priest tossed it into an empty pot, melted it over the hearth, and used it to baptize Thjordhildr on the spot. What happened next reminded me of the mass conversions I had seen while working with Olaf in the fjords and islands of Norway. Only now there was no threat of violence for not converting. Over the next several heartbeats a full three-quarters of the hall converted to the One True God. Notably absent from converting were Erik, Thorhall, Bjarni, and several other men and women. I was surprised to see both Freydis and her husband Torvard converted as did Thorvald and Gro.

When all who wanted to receive the Christ had done so, Leif announced, "Now sing songs, make music, dance, and drink ale because tonight we do not celebrate the Yule, but the birth of the man-God, Jesus. It's Christmas and we will rejoice in it every year at this time. We can burn the log and feast on goat and be merry!"

The men and women cheered with random shouts until one man began to chant, "Leif the Lucky! Leif the Lucky!" It was infectious. Leif had been given a new nickname.

Leif held his hands to quiet us saying, "One last item before we return to our winter revelry. I want Halldorr, who, with Olaf, spent more time converting men and women to the One God than anyone, to share a few stories of the miracles he witnessed."

Shit, I thought. I was more concerned with plotting deaths than with sharing stories. The men and women gathered here wanted to drink lots of ale and nestle next to someone under blankets before falling asleep for the long night. But I soon found my legs and rose to my full height in front of the crowd. I cleared my throat to delay for time but it didn't help, so I just started, "Thank you, Leif. He's right, while he was busying furrowing Thorgunna and then raising the resulting spring calf," this time I got a laugh at Leif's expense, which simply delighted Leif, "I was fighting and killing for the King of Norway." I paused and looked down for a moment and saw the tattoo of the charging boar on my left forearm and it inspired my speech. Holding up my arm I said, "What Leif talks about is represented by this boar. You see I met a man who was a stranger to me at first. But he fought for me and protected me and then he died next to me while in my arms, blood pouring from his wounds. He had the same tattoo on his forearm, for though we were once strangers, we became brothers. Some of you knew the man of whom I speak. Bjarni, I believe the man, Cnute, was a part of your crew when you first arrived here in Greenland on your successful journey." Bjarni scowled at the last for his first journey was anything but successful. I continued, "This man embodies what it is to give a life and sacrifice for another, more noble, man or more noble cause. Cnute died in my arms, but before he did, and Bjarni you'll find this amazing, he spoke to me about you. He mentioned you by name and confessed that he thought of you and your leadership every day. The rest of what he confessed is not appropriate for the whole of Eystribyggo, but I shall share it with you in private." Bjarni grabbed his wife's hand and dragged her to the back of the hall away from prying, confused glances. Everyone else, including Leif, was bewildered from my rambling talk, waiting expectantly for me to continue. When I did not they slowly resumed their merriment. I shrugged to myself and returned to my lonely seat, pleased that I had at last threatened Bjarni.

CHAPTER 2

The rest of the three-day festival I sat, sang, and visited with old friends. I had a genuinely good time that Yule, or Christmas as I would now call it, but I worked the entire time. Whenever I could, I prodded the Greenlanders for information about Bjarni and his men, where they lived, when they may leave for trading in the spring, and many other general questions, still careful not to arouse suspicion.

On the last night, after countless toasts to the One God in place of all those for Odin or Frey, the hall lay quiet. Men and women crowded as close as possible to the hearth and each other for warmth, nearly piling on top of one another likes pigs in a sty. Children and dogs lay scattered about in ale-induced sleep seemingly oblivious to the cold which stealthily crawled into the longhouse like a burglar in the night. The blankets of the children were haphazardly covering a foot here or an arm there.

I was awake staring at the smoke-blackened rafters which were illuminated by the flicker of light from the dying central fire. The cold penetrated to my soul since I did not claim a spot near the hearth early enough in the evening by passing out as most of the party-goers had done. Pulling my wool blanket up a little higher, I thought of the life I had for a time. My wife Kenna was a slight woman who generated almost no heat for our bed in winter, but I missed her dearly that night, her demure smile, her discerning, piercing intellect, her tiny breasts in my hand.

Nearby, a figure rose from the huddled throng between the stone hearth and me. Though I could not see her face in the dark, from her mass of curls and her still shapely body, I knew it was Freydis stirring. Like Freya, our Norse goddess of love and beauty, she raised, almost levitated, to her feet. Silently, Freydis stepped away from her slumbering husband, Torvard. He took advantage of the additional room under their blanket, by pulling more of it over himself. Other than that slight movement, the ale kept him sedated. She stood over me with her feet next to my arm. Her face was still obscured by the dark because the fire was at her back, but she could certainly see mine, though I am not sure what my expression portrayed other than the confusion I felt. For an uncomfortable moment we looked at each other before I asked quietly, "What is it you want?"

In a single movement her tunic and dress fell to her bare feet, revealing her sumptuous, naked body. Her breasts remained round and firm despite her years, because a child never suckled on them. I looked away only briefly to see that the brooches for which I paid most of my wealth before exile, had clanged to the ground. Without a word, she reached down and pulled my blanket back and climbed under it with me. I could feel the heat of her body, the warmth of her breast against my arm. She moved my long hair that covered my ear and began gnawing on its battle scars. At last Freydis thought fit to answer my question, "I want a real man inside me with the seed of a mighty warrior to give me offspring. I want the father of my child to be a man who has done more than raise goats and fill me with weak seed." She immediately returned her lips and teeth to my ear while her hand plunged between my legs and my growing manhood. I rolled to face her and kissed her hard on the mouth and put my own hand on her magnificent breasts, squeezing harder than I ought.

Then I pushed away from her and climbed to my feet. With efficiency of movement I fastened my belt and swords to my waist, retrieved my bow from a corner, and grabbed my own musk ox coat, adding Erik's coat on top for good measure against the cold. I did not look back to see the reaction on Freydis' face. Instead, I unlatched the door in the gable end of the house and slammed it behind which caused a dog near the exit to growl and no doubt roll over upon a slumbering child. I marched into the frigid, moon-filled night to what end I did not know.

· · ·

If I could have left Greenland that night, I would have. I would have left without revenge just to run away from reminders and pain and anger. All the frustrations of my life were embodied in Freydis' naked, lonely form under my blanket in the hall. I was resigned to never love again after losing Kenna. To be clear I wanted to rut with Freydis out of lust, but still felt loyalty to my late wife. I had loved her so. Happiness in my adult life was so fleeting.

It came in waves. But like waves, it quickly spent its energy, bouncing over the pebbles of the shore, and slipped back to the sea only to be replaced by the dreariness of existence.

There were some times I didn't view life as a matter of base survival. Of course, meeting and sharing a short life with Kenna was one. Serving Olaf, raiding, sailing all seemed fulfilling while I was in their midst, but now I felt empty. But for the first time in my life, I refused Freydis and the temporary pleasures she gave. Of that much, perhaps I could be proud.

Dreary or not, I stood outside with the dancing northern lights partially obscured by the shining moon. Since my true father told me those lights were the resting place for dead, unmarried women, I had at one time wondered if Freydis would ever be found there. Now I knew she would not be, of course, married as she was to the dull-witted Torvard. I wondered if my mother, whom I never knew, was there now. Would she know me if she saw me standing out in the cold like a great bear covered in the fur of a musk ox? I pulled back the hoods of the coats I wore so she could see me and find me, maybe even guide me.

Foolishness. I didn't even know her name. How would she be able to identify me since she hadn't seen me since the day of my birth? I didn't even know if she was dead or alive. But a large, dark cloud briefly obscured the moonlight and I saw the northern lights more clearly. Their irregular pattern mesmerized me for a moment and then I was certain that they brightened to a blue-green while narrowing as a hand pointing me the way. As swiftly as it came, the map was gone. But I noted where it had pointed and marched off atop the frozen snow pack.

I pulled on the woolen mittens and tight fitting cap from the inside pocket of my musk ox coat as I passed Erik's empty pasture. The livestock were all safely stowed away in the barn to keep whatever warmth they could. Some would die this winter as some always did when the sun hid itself. It was cold that night, though with the snow, the plethora of rocks was at least enshrouded under a white blanket. I walked and walked further away from civilization. On several occasions my foot broke through the icy cap of the snow, which made me stumble forward headlong onto my hands. The going was tough, but I moved with purpose toward a goal I didn't comprehend. In hindsight, I realize as I write this that it never occurred to me that I could freeze to death while following a sign from the dead spinsters in the sky.

Fridr Rock was already behind me and I was making my way down a prominent rise out of sight of the village which slept at Brattahlid when my foot crashed through another weak spot in the ice covered snow. This time, however, the snow did not come to my knee level, or to my waist level, or to my chest level. No, I fell into a snow cave that was well over my head and at thirty-four years old, I was still over a fadmr tall! I crashed onto the hard rocky earth with my ass and it hurt mightily. My back fell against the snow walls of the cave so that I landed in a sitting position. I sat for a moment swearing to myself in a fit of mumbles and grumbles that the lights led me to a cold, deep hole. Tipping back, I noted it would be a challenge to scramble out of the slick-walled cavity.

Then the wind changed from a constant howling above to a growl, a low, rumbling growl. In the shadowy darkness in front of me I saw movement. The walls of the cave gathered together and formed a single object which rose tall above me. Then the wind changed from a low growl to an outright roar. Standing before me at over eight feet tall was a mother polar bear. Huddled behind her were two cubs. They must have only been about one month old since their hair was just coming in and they were only the size of a small dog. They bleated like lost goats behind their angry mother.

I would have liked to get a couple arrows into her from a distance before I had to engage her directly, but my bow stave was unstrung next to me on the cave floor. I had one choice. Grabbing the saex from my belt, I jumped to my feet and ran at the beast. With my weapon raised, I lunged for her neck, but her vast, claw-wielding paw swatted me away like a mosquito. I smacked into the ice packed walls and bounced, then slid back toward her rear feet. She looked down into my eyes and raised her paw again to swipe at me. I took the opportunity afforded by the delay to roll away. She missed with this second blow. But now, on all fours, the bear reached out her strong flat head and latched onto my furry coats with her teeth. She dragged me back and shook me violently. My body smashed back and forth against the walls or the ground or both, I don't know which. The coats strained against my neck and I believe I was about to pass out when the clasps on the coats gave way. Momentum carried me to one wall, which I struck and again slid down to the center of the cave. Mother bear still shook the coats with all her might while I gained the strength and resolve for one last attack. But I chose trickery instead. While she finished killing the long dead musk ox coats, I pulled my saex onto my chest, lying on my back with my head closest to the bear. When she realized that she was the only movement in the cave other than the panicked cubs, she stopped her attack and dropped the coats. She sniffed the air and took a cautious step toward my silent, unmoving body. I tried not to breathe, but failed miserably as my brain and muscles demanded air. Her nose was only about one ell from the top of my reclined head, sniffing. Then her nose was at my hair, sniffing. She took a half-hearted bite at my hair and caught a portion of my scalp between her sharp teeth. Her fetid, warm breath scaled down my head to my nostrils. I wanted to scream in pain as the creature lifted my head off the ground, but I remained quiet. Then she dropped my head from her grasp and it slammed into the ground. I may have lost consciousness for a second, since I felt a wave of nausea come, but swallowed the urge and half-digested, regurgitated ale. At last she moved her nose to the blade of my saex which reflected the moonlight from above. Without delay I used every bit of strength I had left and drove the short blade up into the soft flesh behind her jaw. About eight inches of the blade became buried in the now howling beast. She rose again to her full height and promptly fell over onto her back, nearly landing on her cubs in the process. Her back feet flailed and she gurgled. I would live.

. . .

After killing her cubs, I skinned the polar bear right there in the den that night. I also took the skins from the cubs to make a pair of luxurious shoes from the soft leather. To climb out of the massive hollow, I drove my bow stave into the snow packed wall at shoulder height under the hole into which I fell and climbed onto it like a step.

When I was out I simply rested on my belly, retrieving it. The northern lights' guiding hand was long gone and so I made my way back toward the village. But the walk was not wasted since, while I skinned the animals, I decided how exactly, I would punish Bjarni's men.

Despite being gone for several hours, the scene in Erik's hall was nearly identical to what I had left with the exception of Freydis. She did not remain under my blanket. She did not return to her own place, next to her husband, Torvard. Instead she wrangled around naked under the blanket of Tyrkr while he went about her body with his own plowing. Her eyes saw mine as I walked by, and without a word, she told me she hated me. Tyrkr momentarily hit her pleasure spot and her eyes closed while she barred her teeth like a wolf from the forest.

I hid my prizes in my baggage, threw wood onto the hearth, moved my own blanket next to Torvard since it was closer to the fire, and went to sleep to warm up from my trip.

. . .

Within two weeks of my encounter in the polar bear cave, the days were slowly gaining length, but the forbidding cold still bit hard. It was so frigid the snow was like dry sand and did not crunch beneath my heavy boots, but seemed to silently rustle around my foot with each step. The night was black and moonless. Even my constant companion, the northern lights, seemed dim as I made my way over the harsh, treeless landscape.

Several hours before, I had retired to my sleeping platform at Brattahlid earlier than normal with a feigned illness. When I was certain that the master and mistress of the house, Erik and Thjordhildr, were sleeping, I would leave on my errand. However, it was taking Erik longer and longer to fall asleep as the days went by because Thjordhildr had denied him the pleasures of marriage since she converted to the One God and he did not. Following his lack of intercourse and sleep, Erik was soon even lacking in his normal jovial mood. In private conversations I found myself agreeing with the household thralls that he should convert soon, or we would be stuck with his negative disposition for the entire winter. But eventually he did fall asleep that night for his snoring from behind the drawn curtain told me so.

I quietly rose and put on two pairs of the heaviest trousers I had and two pairs of woolen socks under my boots. Over top of several shirts and chain mail, I strapped my belt with my sword and saex. I pinned a cloak over my shoulders and then pulled two bear hides from my baggage. The first was the brown hide that Olaf gave me when he named me one of his Berserkers. The second hide was from the polar bear I killed in the cave. They may be cumbersome, but I would need neither speed nor agility while I was walking into the night. I pinned the brown pelt over my cloak and then the white one over that. To protect my face from the biting cold, I scooped some seal grease out of a pot and onto my cheeks. After donning woolen gloves and a cap, I stealthily left the longhouse to begin to exact my own personal blood feud.

Two hours of walking brought me to an isolated longhouse next to what would be a flowing brook in the summer. Now the brook was nonexistent and all was quiet. Smoke from the hearth seemed to breathe in and out of the smoke hole at the top of the gable with the blustering wind. Three of Bjarni's men shared this house when they were in Greenland because, I learned, he didn't pay them enough to live on their own or to take brides. They lived off the land by hunting or fishing when they were not sailing with Bjarni. I chose them as my first victims because they were remote. If I could survive attacking three grown men, the rest would prove to be easy.

I immediately put my simple plan in motion by walking down to the door. Unlike my long walk, for the attack phase, speed and agility were necessary so I paused outside the door to remove my heavy, warm bear hides. Just as I raised my hands to unclip the polar bear fur, one of the men burst out the door. He had only a light shirt and boots on, no pants. He stepped past me without taking notice and started pissing next to a wood pile. He groaned as he relieved himself, while the white skin of his bare legs turned red in the cold and the stream of urine sent steam away on the breeze. A female's voice from inside yelled, "Dagr, you fool! Shut the door!"

"Shut up woman or I'll send you out into the night to find some other man willing to share his bed with an old maid," shouted Dagr. That brought amused chuckles from his two comrades inside the house.

I froze. I thought waiting until they all fell asleep might be my best course, so I moved back a silent step and tried to make myself small. The hide from the polar bear's head acted like a hood and flopped down over my head as I shrunk into the shadows. Dagr finished his business with a high-pitched hoot against the cold, grabbed several logs, and turned to re-enter the house.

I was not small enough. From beneath my hood, I saw his ale-hazed eyes widen and brighten in an instant. Dagr dropped all the logs save one which he swung at me. I ducked and, using my instincts, pulled my sword from its fleece-lined scabbard and chopped off his arm with one motion. He fell face forward into the house shouting with madness, "Bear, bear, bear," then screamed in agony as he finally felt the pain.

The woman screamed while the men shouted. One of them had his hands on Dagr's shoulders to drag him all the way into the small longhouse when I burst across the threshold. The hero craned his head back to look at me and shouted, "It's a . . ." before I ran my blade straight into his neck. The other man had procured an ax. He held it in two hands and bounded across the single room toward me, screaming. The weight of the hero falling forward on my blade made it temporarily impossible to dislodge it from his neck so I let the sword go as the third man swung the ax down at me. I easily avoided the blow with a sidestep while digging under my hides for my father's saex. Out of the corner of my eye, I saw a completely naked woman jump from a sleeping platform and grab an unstrung bow.

The third man stepped on Dagr's back to swing again with the ax. This was a wild sideways swat and I leaned back to watch the ax miss my face by less than half an ell. My right hand finally had the handle of the saex so I pulled it out from my belt and went on the offensive. It was not an evenly matched fight once I regained a weapon. I had spent thirteen years mastering sword and shield in magnificent battles while this man rowed an oar for Bjarni since their betrayal of the village. With two hands he made a mad swing from his left side. I raised my right hand and allowed the ax handle to strike my mailed arm. That was a foolish thing to do because he could have broken my arm. It hurt terribly but my bones were strong. Without hesitation, I gripped my saex more tightly and slid my arm down his outstretched arms. The short blade struck home on his right shoulder and removed a section of his jerkin and his muscle the size of a reindeer steak.

The man dropped the ax while he staggered back two steps. I pressed the attack, running the blade into his soft belly. He looked at my shadowed face under my hood. His eyes said he did not recognize me. I pulled the blade free while the man looked sleepy and fell to his knees. When he toppled to his face I wiped my blade across his back and panting from the skirmish, faced the woman. I recognized her from before my exile. Her breasts were large and pendulous, but they hung lower than all those years ago. It was Tofa, the woman known to share many men's beds throughout the long winter. She was too old for a husband before we left and now she had no chance. It was amazing she still found a man to take her in, but I supposed that she had acquired a certain skill set from her years of humping men.

Tofa screamed and babbled out of terror at what she expected to come next. She still struggled to bend the strong bow to receive its string. I was in no danger for even if she did get it strung, she would never be able to draw the cord back. I went to the hero who lay dead next to Dagr and pulled out my blade. Bending, I slit Dagr's panting throat to end his misery. Then I faced the naked Tofa with my massive polar bear hide splattered with the blood of three of the conspirators. I held a blade in each hand, rolled my shoulders and head forward, and roared beneath my polar bear hood. During the howl I spit out the words, "Revenge. Thirteen." I was again a Berserker, or an Odin-inspired warrior who wore a bear shirt into battle.

I left Tofa sobbing in the longhouse. I could hear her cries above the wind while I began my long walk back to Brattahlid. Ten to go.

...

After sleeping most of the day, the next night began in a similar fashion. I ate great quantities of salted meat for energy and then invented a sickness to retire to sleep early. After listening to Erik try to coax Thjordhildr to spread her legs and receive him and then her firm, but loving rejection, I eventually did fall asleep again. The long hikes and skirmish of the previous frigid evening had exhausted me. I dreamt of Kenna and Norway. The short months spent with her were the happiest in my life. I wanted to remain in that moment but, a terrific snore from Erik startled me back to my reality in icy Greenland.

Without giving my dream a second thought, I dressed myself as I had the last night. This time, however, my polar bear hide had the unmistakable stains of blood. Closing the door silently behind me, I walked into the night. I planned to attack two separate homes as they were closer to Brattahlid and each other.

I passed around the inland-most tip of Eriksfjord, past Fridr Rock. Of course, it was the site of the skraeling attack where thirteen of my countrymen were killed. The attack was orchestrated by Bjarni and his men, although no one knew it but me. Leif and I had been punished, but now I was the dispenser of righteous justice.

Soon I came to the farm of the one of those on my list that night. Except for a lone sheep bleating in a modest barn, it was quiet and I passed it by. It was the neighbor who was to be my first visit.

A half hour walk brought me to that neighbor. Jormungandr lived on the next farm with his wife and three children. He was Bjarni's second in command and had profited handsomely over the years. His farm was on a steep hillside facing the fjord. The structures were ill-placed on the northern slope and so didn't get the benefit of the southern sun and its needed assistance for warmth. It didn't matter tonight. The traitor would die, cold or not.

I wanted to be quick with dispatching Jormungandr. His oldest son was about eleven years old and would no doubt try to help his father during the attack. I did not want to have to defend against a boy, because I knew only one type of defense, offense. The boy would die if he approached me. Jormungandr was also wealthy enough to have a barn full of sleeping thralls. Although the wind howled that night, too long attacking their screaming master and mistress would bring the slaves into the fight as well.

I went to the longhouse and knelt next to it listening. My lesson was learned last night, I would not approach the door until I had completed at least a basic reconnoiter. Listening for several minutes, I heard no laughter, no conversation, no humping. I nodded to no one and then tossed the polar bear's head over my own and took on the persona of the vicious redeemer, the Berserker, the crazed warrior.

To prepare myself for what would come, I thought about treachery and lies. My anger boiled again. The rage coursed through my veins and hit my muscles. They tensed and I drew both blades while kicking open the door. Jormungandr's wife sat up with a start while he sat up with a confused, but benign look on his face. Their bed was at the far end of the hall past the blazing hearth. Shouting, I ran past the children who bunked together for warmth. The oldest was starting to climb up so I thumped his head with the extra large pommel of my sword. He crumpled onto his younger siblings.

By now Jormungandr realized the danger and stood with his sword blocking my path to his plump wife. I halted at the end of the hearth nearest the married couple and sheathed my saex. I grabbed one of the heavy black iron pots that hung from the rafters and hurled it at Jormungandr. He covered his face, blocking it with his forearms. Satisfied by his response, I snatched another heavy pot and heaved it at him while moving forward myself. When he instinctively blocked the pot again, I swung my sword at him with terrific force. It caught his left elbow and then slashed across his chest creating a debilitating gash. He crashed back into a post of the bed. His wife was screaming uncontrollably now. I took the last step to him, feigned a copy of my first sword-strike, and when he moved to block it, snuck my blade between the ribs of his right side. I gave it a sharp twist and felt the scraping of the blade on bone as it withdrew. He fell down onto all fours and I struck the top of his head with the sharpened edge of my sword. Jormungandr slumped to the floor. I spit on him and wiped his blood on his terrified wife's nightgown. I ran for the door just as three puzzled thralls came into view. I picked up a short three-legged wooden stool then jammed it into the first man's chest to knock him down. The next two stood in the center of the threshold and I ran at them with full strength. We all fell headlong into the snow, but I jumped to my feet and ran south, up and over the slope so as to confuse the direction of any pursuit.

It never came.

Running, I cut a rounded path back to the first farm with the bleating sheep. I was tired so I invented a new tactic for this killing. After listening at the wall, I pulled out my saex and noiselessly opened the unlocked main door. This man and his family were all sleeping. Their peaceful sounds gave me a tinge of regret for what I was doing. I pushed away those feelings and crept to the back of the house. This man's two children were younger, both under five. As I snuck past them the youngest opened her wide blue eyes and stared at me. I froze in place and held a single finger up to the polar bear nose indicating she should be quiet. She nodded and then rolled over and closed her eyes.

I stood there for many minutes to be sure she slept. When her breathing was again relaxed and regular, I finished my path to the master's bed. He lay with his back to me with one arm slung over his wife. Placing one knee on the ground I cupped a hand over his mouth while forcing the saex up into his lung from beneath his ribcage. His arm left his wife and flailed behind to me, but his strength lasted only seconds. When he was completely melted back into the bedding, I withdrew my blade and wiped it on his wife's clean white nightgown. The touch made her adjust her position, but she returned to a deep sleep immediately.

While I passed the hearth toward the door, I saw some cheese and soft bread left over from supper. I put it into my coat pocket for the walk home and silently opened the door. When I was safely outside in the Arctic night, I slammed the door to make a loud crash. As I hiked over a jagged rock toward Brattahlid, I broke out the cheese, and then heard the first shrieks of the man's horrified woman. Eight more were yet to receive my judgment.

· · ·

The next day the sun would likely shine for about five hours and I planned to sleep through all of it. These arrangements were spoiled when a thundering series of knocks sounded at the door. While I still lay curled under a blanket, Erik invited Tofa, along with two men, in from the cold. They had come to see the jarl about the killings. Erik encouraged them all to sit at his table.

The promiscuous woman still wore a shaken countenance. Tofa's pudgy hands trembled while she sipped a warm broth Thjordhildr served her. Below her disheveled hair, her nose and cheeks were bright red from the trip across the bitter land to Brattahlid. Her eyes looked wild, far away.

Erik asked, "What is going on?"

One of the men, Skari the Seagull, who was a member of Bjarni's crew and therefore sentenced to death, spoke first. "Three men are dead." He let it hang for a moment before continuing. "She says she knows who did it."

I panicked on the inside but remained still. I was certain she did not see my face two nights earlier. Perhaps Tofa recognized something I wore. My sword and saex were both within reach if I needed it to fight the visitors. Erik could be reasoned with, I was sure, if it came to that.

"Well, out with it then. What did you see? And who is dead?"

Tofa set the bowl of steaming broth down onto the heavy wooden table. Her hands bounced quickly which she seemed not to notice. Tofa looked at Erik, then to Skari, then to the second man, Yngvarr, whom I had condemned to death as well. She was uncertain and it appeared that her mind was elsewhere so Yngvarr started her out, "Three of our seafaring crew were killed two nights ago. Torir, Tollakr, and Dagr." At the mention of the last, Tofa burst into tears from her puffy red eyes. They streamed down her face and joined similarly streaming snot to coalesce above her lip. She paid the mess no attention while her hands continued to quake on the table.

Turning to Yngvarr, Erik asked, "Are those the men who live farther out of the fjord, by the creek?"

"Yes. That's the group."

"Skraelings?" asked Erik.

"She says no," indicated Skari with a thumb. "She came to my wife and me late yesterday with the tale and we let her stay. We picked up Yngvarr on the way here for added protection."

"Protection from whom?" asked Erik with anger. Greenland was a safe settlement for the most part.

"You mean from what," spoke Tofa for the first time. Her hands stopped vibrating and she put one on Thjordhildr's, squeezing.

Erik looked incredulously back and forth between Yngvarr and Skari. He shook his head saying, "Men, you know that if a polar bear got them, the beasts will run from you in daylight if you make enough noise. And if you are scared of a fox or stoat, it would be best if you returned home to your wives for protection."

"It was a polar bear," said Tofa.

"There. You see. Nothing to worry about. Thankfully, those men had no families so I don't have to worry about feeding more mouths," answered Erik. He rapped his knuckles on the table as if proclaiming the meeting complete, but Thjordhildr cleared her throat and indicated the frazzled Tofa with a nod of her head. Erik considered Tofa for a moment then added, "Yet, it was tragic to witness, I am sure."

"It was a brown bear," said Tofa.

"You're just confused, Tofa. There are no brown bears in Greenland. You just said it was a polar bear," said Erik in an understanding voice.

"It was a man," continued Tofa. Now Erik was confused and looked at Yngvarr again, who nodded. Tofa went on, "We were up late enjoying each other's company when Dagr went out to piss. He returned just a moment later missing part of his arm screaming, "Bear!" Then the creature came in the door after him. It had the head and body of a polar bear, the stomach of a brown bear, and the legs and arms of a man. It carried two swords, one small, one long." I looked at my belt with its scabbards for my sword and saex and cringed. "The beast killed all three men, then it roared like a bear, and shouted like a man before it left."

Except for kitchen thralls preparing the next meal, all was quiet in the hall as Erik digested the story. At last he said, "And you two believe this story? How much ale have you been drinking?"

The men never had a chance to respond because another series of forceful knocks came at the door. Erik huffed and yelled to one of the thralls, "Alverad, see to the door!" Without hesitation the slave woman ran to the door and let in the two widows I created last night. They brought their children with them and two more men who served on Bjarni's ship, *Thor's Treasure*. The men wore serious expressions, while the women looked like Tofa – crazed, fearful. Erik was exasperated, "What's this emergency about?" Then in partial jest, "I suppose you have seen a bear-man too!"

Eyes widened in shock that the jarl knew of their problem. The young girl I had shushed the night before was bundled in hides and toddled over to Erik. He picked her up to place her on his lap. While tugging his red and white beard she said, "Yes, I saw the bear-man. He helped put me to sleep; then I think he killed my father. When do you think papa will wake again?"

Jormungandr's widow, Nessa, described the horrific scene she had witness the night before, ending with how I cleaned my blade across the nightgown she wore. Then she said, "And the sword was unique." Nessa searched for words to describe it. "It had intricate pictures running the entire length of the blade."

"Pictures?" asked Thjordhildr.

"Yes. They were pictures of fish and men. One of the men on the sword was a giant compared to the rest," answered Nessa. Thankfully, I had not had the occasion to show my sword to anyone since I left Norway. Neither Leif nor Tyrkr had seen it and so I thought I was safe from discovery for, at least, a time.

"Is this punishment from the gods?" asked Erik.

"For what?" asked Yngvarr.

Shrugs all around gave me the chance to sit up where I lay and address the group. Most hadn't even noticed I was there so they turned in surprise when I spoke. "I think Erik is right. We must assume it is punishment. But it is not punishment for all of us."

"What do you mean?" asked Erik.

"Ask yourself who is dead. Dagr, Jormungandr, Torir, Tollakr, and this woman's husband were killed by a bear-man carrying a distinctive sword. They are all members of the same merchant's crew; they are Bjarni's men. It sounds like all the gods and the One God are conspiring against them for something they harbor, some evil they've done. Think about it. The old gods send a Berserker to exact retribution, but he uses a sword with fish, men, and a giant emblazoned across it. These are clearly stories from the word of the One God." I paused for effect. "Bjarni's men are condemned to death."

Angry shouts erupted around the room. Bjarni's men shouting at me and one another while Erik tried to calm them down, waving his hands in the air. "We must consider what Halldorr says is true!" exclaimed Erik above the rest. The room settled, and so Erik continued, "We must make certain that we protect ourselves. Families should group together for protection until we can kill this beast."

"Or until it satisfies its bloodlust," I added matter-of-factly to the displeasure of all in the house.

Erik gave me a reproving look and continued, "Sick or not, Halldorr will go out with the remaining daylight and gather houses together. Stay with them if you must, Halldorr. I'll also send Leif, Thorvald, Tyrkr, and others to spread the word." Then he indicated to Bjarni's men, "And you men, I want you to boil the dead down to the bones so that we have something to bury in the spring. I don't want bloated bodies in my village for months at a time."

. . .

I spent three weeks sleeping in various longhouses throughout Eriksfjord, careful not to alarm the populace, making my announcements with relaxed conversation that the gods had sent a beast to carry out revenge on Bjarni's men. I assured my hosts and their neighbors they were safe. And, of course, they were. It happened that for those three weeks even Bjarni's men were safe, for the beast did not return in all that time.

But human beings are forgetful. We soon find ourselves occupied with the drudgery of daily life. At first, men would return to their farms while the sun shone in order to tend livestock by breaking the layer of ice from their water troughs. Then some men spent an evening at home. By the end of the third week, with no trouble reported anywhere in the fjord, men were inviting their families back home. The panic was over; except for the widows and their families, normal life resumed. And I was happy because the darkness of the new moon returned.

I was glad to traipse into the frigid night again. I felt alone and liked it. My thoughts could wander wherever they wished and no one would know by my expression. Memories of love, lust, revenge, hatred could stir from within and follow whatever path they wished. In one recurring thought I saw my dead wife's sister, Thordis. She had been married to my close friend and fellow Berserker, Einar, but in my retelling of history, she had chosen me, and I was next to her now in Norway making baby after baby to go out and see the world. I sighed because I didn't really want any of that anymore. I wanted Kenna. I wanted my woman with her big thoughts and small breasts. My blood-fueled frenzy against Bjarni's men would not bring her back. It would not bring Cnute back. What would come of it?

But it didn't matter what came of my actions, I thought. These men had the blood of thirteen Norsemen and women on their hands and I would see that justice was served. Bjarni manipulated the shocked elders fourteen years ago. I would not let any of my own thoughts manipulate me into forgoing what must be. As I hopped atop a large boulder typical of the Greenland landscape and peered down at the quiet longhouse of Bjarni, I once again resolved to see that he meet his end tonight.

About one hour would bring with it the dawn; I was exhausted. I had traversed much of the hills surrounding Eriksfjord and I had already killed five more men that night. Skari the Seagull, Yngvarr, and the final three crew members who were complicit in Bjarni's treachery met the One God with blood-soiled clothes, piss in their breeches. They died in similar fashion to their brethren; at the hands of a bear-man in complete view of their horrified families.

I needed to complete my work that night because my victims' homes would certainly be reinforced once news of more deaths spread.

Bjarni Herjolfsson was to be the last to die in my feud. With purpose I jumped off my perch on the rock and ran down the slope across the snow. I tried the door, but it was barred so I just thumped hard with the side of my fist. Nothing. I pounded again. This time a groggy voice, yelled, "What is it?"

"Halldorr Olefsson," I said with no need to hide it anymore. "I'm here with a message of grave importance. Please let me in."

"Give me your message and be gone!" shouted Bjarni from the opposite side of his sturdy door.

Thinking quickly I said, "I must see you for the message is long and it's frigid this morning."

"Well then come back later! Why are you out so early?" shouted an increasingly distrusting Bjarni.

"I already told you that the message is literally of grave importance." Then I added the first thing I thought of, "It's from Sindri Sindrisson and his wife; the message comes from the grave." Sindri's wife had been killed at Fridr Rock in the skraeling attack. A long, long pause came in the conversation until I asked, "Did you hear me?"

At last Bjarni's voice indicated interest. Quieter, this time, he asked, "Are you alone?"

"I am."

"Then back your bastard self away from my door and shout back when you are at least twenty ells away."

I did so, and the door opened just enough for Bjarni to emerge. It slammed shut again and I heard a heavy bar crashed home by his wife or son. He had put on a coat of mail in pristine condition. Obviously, he purchased it on a trip to Europe, but never had the need to use it in battle. In his right hand he carried a finely decorated sword, though it looked like the blade's weight was too large for the pommel. He stood there letting his eyes adjust to the dark. At last he must have noticed the polar bear hide strapped around my shoulders was splattered in various shades of red from fresh, dried, and frozen blood because he gave a start. I said nothing.

"So you are the bear-man, come to exact revenge on me for the exile of you and that confident son of a bitch, Leif?" mocked Bjarni.

"I am, indeed, a Berserker to the king! I have come seeking revenge, but not for my exile. Bjarni, the One God, whom you did not accept at Christmas, has a saying that goes like this; what you intended for evil, he can work out for good, for his purposes. You meant for us to be killed in the skraeling attack. Then when that didn't work, you meant for us to disappear forever, maybe killed in faraway lands. But Leif found love, as did I. I found the fatherly love of a man who converted thousands to the One God. I also found the love of a woman. For these things, I am grateful to you."

"My life has never been my own. Fate rules me. But today, for this moment, I am seizing my destiny as the dispenser of justice, not for my wrongful exile, but for the thirteen deaths directly caused by your treachery."

"Are you finished with your speech-making?"

"I am finished speaking, but I think you know I have work to do."

"You are alone and I have a sturdy longhouse. I will simply retreat into the warm indoors and outwait you sitting on your cold ass in the snow."

He already had his hand on the door when I said, "Aye, you could retreat. But I won't wait. I will merely walk to Erik and confess my killings while telling him of your betrayal. I will be punished, but I've already said my fate is not my concern. You too will be punished, probably killed. Your only chance is to fight me now, win, and become the hero who killed the mad bear-man, returned from the outcast world."

The dawn began to break behind the snow-capped mountains to the east. It spread just enough light so that we could see each other's faces more clearly. Mine showed certainty. Behind my blood-streaked beard I smiled. He was worried. That was good. Frightened men make poor, impetuous decisions. He closed his eyes in resignation and removed his hand from the door, gripping the hilt of his sword with both hands. When Bjarni opened his eyes again they looked confident, prepared.

He shouted and ran to me with sword raised. Without drawing my sword I stepped to the side to avoid his strike and kicked him in the back. He fell to all fours, rolled up to his feet quickly. His face was not so confident. Bjarni whitened his grip on the sword and moved his feet beneath him into a stable position. I was overconfident, foolish really. I stood before him wearing an amused expression, with my weapons still sheathed. This angered Bjarni so he screamed, "I'll not fight an unarmed man!"

"Yet you have no problem encouraging foreigners to attack unarmed women and children. You are more complex than I thought; a riddle really. But it will be as you wish." I drew my father's saex from my belt. It was foolish to fight with it, but I was sure of victory.

He quickly lashed out, but was careful not to show his back this time. I simply leaned out of the way while his sword whooshed in front of me. My arrogant attitude infuriated him, so he screamed yet again and ran with the point of his sword aimed at my belly. I parlayed the blow with my saex and let him crash into me. Both or our blades pierced the snow several feet behind where he had been standing. He was a soft, wealthy merchant; I had been fighting for fourteen years. I would win even without the weapon. But as we tumbled backward my head struck a rock jutting up from the hard snow. I saw lights like the mid-day sun before my clenched eyes while grabbing the wound which spilled blood into my hand. Bjarni rose to sit on my chest and he began rapidly striking my face with a balled fist. I put my forearms in his way to deflect the blows while he shouted, "Bergljot! Bergljot, help me!"

The bar promptly scratched open. The door flung wide, and light from the hearth spilled out the door onto the snow. His wife, Bergljot, and their son ran out in file. Bjarni screamed to them, "Get the blades! They're somewhere in the snow behind me!" They ran to where we dropped them while I managed to shove Bjarni off me. I was on my knees ready to fall upon him when a sharp pain shot into my back. I screamed, turned, and saw his horrified boy holding his father's sword with my blood on the tip. The polar bear hide and my chain mail prevented his weak thrust from doing more damage. I reached for the sword, but Bjarni's blows started again on the wound on my head. I hit the snow on my belly while he repeatedly drove the palm of his hand onto the back of my head. He paused for a moment and I rolled to my back, only to face Bergljot pointing my saex at my eye and Bjarni holding his sword in a similar menacing fashion. The boy sucked a ball of snot from the back of his nose and spit it into my still face. I rested.

"You bastard!" screamed Bergljot. "Bjarni told me of you and you're worse than even he said. You come and attack *my* husband? But what should I expect from a bastard son of a village whore!"

I looked at her in total confusion. I had never seen this woman until the Yule and yet she supposed to know about my mother. Bjarni could have told her something from Norway, but he was only several years older than I. He had no reason to know anything about my past.

Bjarni laughed merrily. I could have tried to attack him at that moment, but I was still processing his wife's insults. "You don't even know why I hate you and that bastard Erik Thorvaldsson, do you?" asked Bjarni derisively.

"You took Leif's childish confrontation and my protection of him when you first came here as an insult," I answered.

He doubled over as he cackled. This was my chance to escape from beneath the blades, but I did not take it. I wanted an explanation. "You are a bigger fool than I thought," he said. "You may even be a bigger fool than your father!" His insult to me was immediately forgotten, but when he mentioned my father a new rage poured into my veins, feeding and bringing new life to my muscles.

I calmed myself asking, "Then why is it that you hate us so?" The blood flowing from the gash in my head was slowing since I rested it on the freezing cold snow.

Bjarni stepped on my right hand and indicated that both Bergljot and the boy were to do the same on my left. I did not fight them. He bent down and said, "It will be fun to tell you and then watch you die. You see, as Bergljot has said, your mother was a whore. She was pregnant with you, you little bastard. I don't know who the father was. Maybe it was my father, maybe it was a town drunk, or maybe it was a goat. I don't know. But she was fat with child and your foolish, impotent father agreed to marry the woman. Can you believe it? Such a fool."

"So the whore was parading alone in the fjords of Rogaland one day when she came upon my uncle and asked him if he wanted to rut in the woods. Though she was a whore, I've heard your mother was pretty, so he said yes and pushed her onto all fours and made his way inside her. So your mother, I think I mentioned she was a whore, changes her mind and starts yelping. My uncle was intent on finishing what was rightfully his and did so. Just as my uncle finished, your limp father came along, saw the whore laying in the leaves crying with blood coming from her ass, and my uncle pulling up his trousers. Your foolish, weak father killed him by thrusting a dirty old saex into his back."

This was crazy. He was just trying to torture me. Yet I asked, "How do you know all this?"

He gave another wicked laugh. "Because I was with my uncle that day. I must have been about six years old and watched the whole thing from the bilberry bushes. The whore died right there in front of me while she gave birth to you in the woods like an animal. I was very frightened that day, but, you'll like this. When I was older I swore a blood feud on your cowardly family. By the time I was twelve, I killed your father and was pleased when Erik and his father, Thorvald, thought it was someone else. Erik and your father, Olef, had sworn a blood oath with one another so Erik and Thorvald killed the men they thought responsible and were banished from Norway before I had a chance to kill you, but now here you are." He smiled broadly and the boy spit on my face again.

When I thought I could not take any more from a past I did not know, Bergljot screamed, "And I'll see to it that Erik, your beloved adopted father, dies! He began a war with my family in Iceland and again was exiled before my family could do anything about it." This was a contortion of the truth for, though Erik committed an awful mistake, I was old enough to remember what happened in Iceland. "Then when Erik and his family are dead, my husband will become jarl of Greenland."

The boy sucked a third ball of snot from the back of his nose, but before he had a chance to spit it on my face I pulled both of my hands free by sliding out of the mittens I wore. I used the mail on my forearms to knock the blades away from my face and rolled backward onto my feet. My striking sword was in my hand before any of them reacted. Immediately its point was driven deep between Bergljot's ribs while the boy crawled up my left arm like a wild animal. He pulled my hair and scratched at my eyes. With great force I struck him in the side of his head with the pommel of my sword as I withdrew it from his mother's slumping body. The boy crashed to the snow on his back swearing all the while, "Bastard! Son of a whore!" I said a brief prayer of forgiveness in Latin that I remembered from my book and stabbed my sword into the boy and through to the snow underneath him, silencing his shouts all the while Bjarni stood looking like a dumbstruck oaf.

I left my sword quivering back and forth in the boy's body, trudged to Bergljot, and picked up my saex but didn't have a chance to use it. Bjarni's eyes widened, then he ran for his door. I sprinted after him, tackling the man headlong into the sod wall of his house. I punched him several times in the face before he finally passed out, after which I continued punching him while the sun's first direct beams rose behind me.

. . .

Bjarni awoke hours later with his hands tied to a post behind his back. His swollen eyes stopped bleeding long ago but now looked like slits while he used his wobbly head to peer around his longhouse. I stood over a large iron kettle of boiling water above the hearth. When his eyes locked on mine, I smiled and used wooden tongs to pull out a bone from his wife which had the flesh cooked completely off.

After tossing it back into the pot I went to Bjarni with my saex. "I assure you that this blade has killed many men. Most by my hand, but the most justified killing it has ever done was in the hands of my father when it slipped into your uncle, the rapist." Two of his teeth spit out at me while he tried to fashion a rebuttal. The words turned to screams as I pushed the blade into his thigh. He was still screaming while I slapped the side of the saex across his head. Then I punched him several more times until he passed out.

I stood and walked to Bjarni's sleeping platform where I had thrown the polar bear hide. I held the fur in my hands. It was drenched with blood. For a moment I thought it was blood spilled out of justice, but then I cried. I had killed many men in battle or on the strandhogg, but never in cold blood like I had during those weeks. I felt angry and weak, not in any way vindicated. I gripped the fur tightly in my hands and some of the blood from last night's killings was wrung out onto the floor. The fat, deep red droplets splashed into the hard-packed dirt and pooled in isolated semicircles. At last, I took the hide and threw it into the fire under the bubbling kettle. The melted snow amongst its hair sputtered from the heat while the drier parts immediately captured flame. I watched as it billowed smoke into the entire room, slowly curling and shrinking away into the fire.

The smoke made Bjarni cough awake again. I wanted to torture him for the rest of the day and through the next night, but instead I drew the saex again. I grabbed Bjarni by the messed hair on top of his head and jammed his head into the pole. With my nose pressing against his own, I said, "This is the end of your blood feud." I slipped the saex under his mail shirt into his chest. He gasped quietly while kicking his legs behind me, then died.

I spent the rest of the day and night boiling away the flesh from his bones. Using my saex I etched Norse runes into the blackened timbers above his hearth:

"Thirteen dead for thirteen dead. The bear-man has perished."

I didn't know what else to write so stopped there. When the sun again was ready to pop above the horizon I left the Herjolfsson farm behind, walking to Erik's Brattahlid. My mind was empty. I had been awake for two days and was ready for sleep. I felt nothing. No anger. No pain. No joy. No relief. Nothing.

As I walked past the slave house where the thralls and Tyrkr slept tightly packed inside, I saw Freydis emerge affixing one of her brooches at the shoulder of her tunic. She saw me, but paid me no attention and skittered off to my old house and to her husband. I again resolved to leave Greenland once the equinox came as I watched her sneak silently into her home.

Raised voices told me visitors were in Erik's great longhouse, but I didn't care, bursting in through the door. All eyes turned to see who walked in at this hour of the morning. Those eyes belonged to Erik, Thjordhildr, Thorhall, several other men, and the widows of the five men I killed two nights ago. Thorhall the Huntsman sized my wounds up quickly, "What happened to you?"

Before I answered, Erik added on, "And where have you been? We've had more attacks from the bear-man."

"I killed him," I said.

"Who?" asked Erik.

"Bjarni and his family are dead, but so is the bear-man. I laid him to rest." None of what I just said was really a lie, but lies would come. "Two nights ago I had a vision that I should go out into the night alone. While I was out I found the bear-man. I followed him and when I reached him he was finishing the killing of Bjarni and his family. In fact, he was already boiling the bodies. I fought him for hours that seemed like days. He finally jumped atop Bjarni's hearth and my sword found a home buried in the beast's belly. Instantly the beast disappeared except for his hide which fluttered into the flames and except for his sword with the markings on the blade which now sat in my hand. I looked around and I saw some runes had magically been written in the timbers above the hearth, but couldn't read them."

Thorhall scoffed, "Halldorr, that's quite a tale, but we have tragedy going on around us. These women have lost husbands. It's not something to joke about." Erik scowled and nodded his head in agreement.

"I can prove it," and pulled my blade, the bear-man's blade, from its scabbard. Everyone in the hall looked on in astonishment as I held the distinct blade described by all the witnesses under their noses.

"How do we know you're not the bear-man just trying to exact revenge for Bjarni's part in encouraging your exile for your invitation of the skraeling attack?" asked a disbelieving Thorhall.

Thjordhildr came to my aid, "It couldn't be Halldorr. He was ill for all of the first attacks last month."

"He's not sick now though is he?" asked Thorhall rhetorically.

"Thorhall, you're right that I have reason to hate Bjarni. But you have no idea why. If you'd like to blame me for his death or the death of his men, I do not care, an assembly can decide. It was Bjarni who killed my father and now that he is dead, I can revel in the payment of vengeance."

Erik was frustrated now, "Halldorr, you must be dazed. Bjarni would have only been about twelve years old when your father was killed. I already avenged your father, my friend Olef's death. Now quit talking nonsense and let's go to Bjarni's farm and see if what Halldorr says is true." While the group draped their coats over their shoulders, I collapsed onto my bed and fell asleep.

CHAPTER 3

By the spring equinox Freydis was, at last, with child. Her oblivious husband, Torvard, was pleased that a son could soon be his. My pity went out to the man. I and the thralls, who were forced to listen to her lust-filled moaning beside them at night, suspected the baby would resemble Tyrkr. I remember wondering for a moment if, when the baby spoke its first words, he would have a German accent like his true father. The thought made me chuckle then as it still does today.

Early that spring Leif and Thorgils were out hunting beyond Fridr Rock when they came upon the rotting body of a polar bear stripped of its hide. Leif swore that the beast appeared to be part human and even had two dead cubs with it, also stripped of their hides. To eliminate all vestiges of the old gods and their retribution, whatever it was for, from Greenland, the two burnt the remains on the spot. So the last strip of evidence that could implicate me in the winter killings was gone.

Leif was busy carrying out the promise he made to King Olaf. He would see to it that the rest of the Norse men and women began to receive and accept the new faith this year. The Eastern Settlement, Eystribyggo, where we all lived had come to believe in the One God at Yule with Leif's and Torleik's speeches and his mother's consent. As soon as the waters again became navigable, Leif sent out Haki and Haekja, the Scottish thralls, with several of the more zealous converts from our settlement to the Western Settlement, Vestribyggo, where young Thorstein ruled with his wife Gudrid. I had served Olaf so long and observed his more forceful method of converting the populace that I questioned the wisdom of Leif's passive approach then. Now as an old man, I acknowledge his good judgment. Olaf had been motivated by speed and action – by converting massive numbers quickly. It worked to some extent, but he didn't have their hearts. Leif was going for the heart.

Erik's wife, Thjordhildr, was busy that spring as well. She had become so infected with the new faith that she demanded her husband build a church on his estate. The two still had not reconciled their differences enough for her to allow Erik the pleasures of her body, but he did begrudgingly agree to the project. He was fervently opposed to the new faith for himself. I think, however, that allowing the church was his way to demonstrate to Thjordhildr his commitment to her. He did love the woman, despite his past transgressions. Erik also desperately wanted to be allowed beneath her dress once again.

The structure of Greenland's first church was tiny; eight feet wide by twelve feet long. To protect against the bitter cold in winter, the walls were made of stacked turf. At the base of each long wall, the turf was about two ells wide, slowly tapering until the short wall met the roof. For the supporting walls inside the turf and for the roof we used split wood that was imported from Norway's thick forests the previous year. The planks on the roof were finished by covering them with a layer of turf so that from the outside of the church the only wood that could be seen was the vertical siding on either end.

Erik hired a skilled craftsman from the fjord to carve animal designs in two long planks which crossed each other on each end of the roof as they extended past the peak. Reindeer, bear, and whales danced their way across the timbers. The ends of these planks which reached toward the sky were shaped to look like horns so that the tips pointed toward the heavens. Beneath them, the same woodworker fashioned a simple cross with bell-shaped or flared ends that was affixed above a short door. The frame around the door received a similar set of carvings as those on the roof edge. With all the laborers from Brattahlid working on the tiny project, it was completed in just two weeks.

I was most interested in the first burials in what would become the cemetery at Thjordhildr's church. We considered it a good winter as only two of the oldest members of Eystribyggo died of illness – a husband and wife who happened to be the parents of Gudrid, Thorstein's wife. They would need to be buried; so too would the remains of Bjarni and his crew.

When the earth had finally thawed then dried enough to dig graves, we held all the ceremonies, such as they were, on a single day. In a show of defiance to the new faith, Erik stayed inside his longhouse buried beneath a thick blanket next to his roaring hearth.

Gudrid's parents were old and did not have many family or friends so only a handful of villagers gathered to watch the proceedings. I think most of these had come to find out what a Christian funeral would look like. Thorstein and Gudrid ruled in Vestribyggo and were not even aware of the deaths in order to make the special trip. Gudrid's father was buried on the south side of the church to protect his woman and the church from spirit invaders from the fjord. When we lowered his body into his resting place using long ropes, we were careful to be sure that his head pointed to the west so that he could see Christ's return in the eastern sky on Judgment Day. As the lone priest in the settlement, Torleik spoke some words at the burial of the old couple. His words must have been unremarkable, for I do not recollect them today. Then we moved to the north side of the new church and lowered the woman into her grave.

As I scooped the last dirt back over top the woman's body, Tyrkr and several thralls arrived at the church with an ox pulling a cart laden with several large baskets heaping with the boiled remains of Bjarni and the others. With our two-piece oak shovels, we began digging a single large hole immediately adjacent to the southern wall of Thjordhildr's church that would receive all the remains at once. The widows and their children still held a look of shock as the mass grave deepened one shovel full at a time. Life in Greenland was harsh. Life in Greenland without a husband would likely prove to be crueler still. I thought they would be better off selling their husband's lands to any bidder, leaving to find new husbands in Iceland or Norway.

When the hole was to the bedrock and the ground above was level with my chest, I and the other laborers threw our shovels out. I stayed in the pit while the laborers scampered up to stand amongst the widows and gathered family. Tyrkr then began tossing the skulls to me one by one. Out of respect to the grieving women, I saw to it that the skulls were lined up along the west end of the grave facing up. It was easy to tell the boy's and his mother's skulls from the rest, for his was smaller and hers had finer features, especially the brows. The skulls of the eleven men, I could not tell apart. Each one of these I set down, I wondered if it was Bjarni who looked up at me with the hollow, empty eyes. I didn't grieve or worry for my own soul. Surely the One True God would understand the need to rid the earth of these men. The blood feud Bjarni began was done; a thing of the past.

With an extended arm, Leif pulled me out after I set the last skull down while Tyrkr and Thorvald took the remaining baskets of assorted bones and dumped them in a massive pile on the eastern end of the grave. Leif offered some assurances about the dead and the afterlife then also about the charity of the now-Christian community for needs of the living. His talk ended quickly and with nothing more to keep them at the new churchyard, those gathered began to disperse to carry on whatever business they must to survive. The onlookers' faces seemed to say they were disappointed at the ceremony for the dead in their new faith. Torleik hiked up his robes so that he could flee the scene and return to the farm where he made his temporary home.

When we were done filling in the large grave so that it now appeared like a grand mound of loose dirt, I leaned on the turf wall of the church to rest. Tyrkr and Leif joined me, while Thorvald went off to his plain wife, Gro, and the thralls from Brattahlid went back to their own meager existences.

The three of us sat there looking out across the fjord with its waters littered with icebergs, big and small. The spring thaw brought them calving from the glaciers which stretched from the inland elevations down to Eriksfjord. Sunlight glinted off the ice chunks and water so that I had to squint to take in the sight. Water lapped repetitively at the shingle. It was a rare beautiful day in rocky, treeless Greenland.

After a time, Leif spoke. "You're not at home here with my family any longer, are you Halldorr?"

"How can you say that? Your family is my family. I love you all," I retorted.

He turned to face me with a sad smile, "I know you speak the truth. I know you love Erik and his. But I also know you mean to leave us." He had done this to me since our friendship began. He was more right about my thoughts than I was. "You've finished your revenge on Bjarni and mean to return to Europe."

So Leif knew. I looked at Tyrkr to see if he caught the revelation. If he had, he did not betray any special concern. Leif continued, "But what is there for you? Olaf is gone to the Holy Land. Will you return to Dyflin and pillage for the remainder of your days, landing on a foreign beach using your sword as a cane? Will you be celibate like some old monk forever? Nothing is there for you."

I was angry. "Dyflin was a fine place. I still have treasure hidden under my home there. I can return and buy my own ship and live a profitable life. That's all life is anyway; profit or death. I can find a woman and rut and lick her tits, too. What do you know of what I will do?" The last was the wrong question to ask Leif, who always knew what I would do.

"Do you remember the feast Olaf held in his hall after I came to Kaupangen last year?" Leif asked.

"Of course, I do. I stopped drinking so much ale by then," I answered, confused by his change of tack.

"Before the speeches, ale, and banquet began, we talked at the end of the hall. Do you remember what we talked about?"

I was exasperated, "Yes. You told me I'd come back to Greenland with you, but you didn't know how that would happen. Well, almost everyone I cared about is now dead and those who yet live are in hiding. Are you happy that I could come?"

Leif looked like at me like I was a confused child. He remained calm, almost soothing trying to coax me to understand what he was saying. "Halldorr, I am happy you've come back with us, but it saddens me deeply that so many close to you were killed." He paused as several puffins swooped in close, caught a draft of air, then swung back out over the fjord to fish. Tyrkr carelessly tossed a stray stone in their direction, missing widely. "I also told you then that I would buy *Thor's Treasure* from Bjarni to explore the lands he skipped when he first came to Greenland. Now I don't even have to buy the boat as it has no owner. I want you to come with me to explore the lands Bjarni saw."

My mind turned on the idea. New lands? I listed the kingdoms I had visited so far in my life. I had already seen Iceland, Norway, Sweden, Denmark, Wendland, Frankia, Ireland, England,

Scotland, and Wales. What did they have to offer me? A new adventure could be what my mind needed to see the world fresh again. Going back to Europe, no matter how rich I became, would take my thoughts to a perpetual frozen Hel. Kenna's death. Olaf's defeat. My despair. "Aye, I'm going with you, but there are conditions."

"Name them, and they'll be so," said Leif.

"No women."

Tyrkr frowned and crossed his arms across his chest making a displeased harrumph sound. Leif smiled broadly and said, "Done. What else?"

"You'll still buy Bjarni's boat. If you need money, I'll give you some for the purchase. You should also buy the supplies and see that all the money for both the knarr and supplies goes to the widows of his crew members."

Leif eyed me uncertainly, but his smile returned shortly, and he said, while shaking his head, "I don't need your money, but thank you for the offer. You are a complicated man, Halldorr. First you kill Bjarni and his men, then you want to make sure their women are all taken care of. I'll do it."

Tyrkr's frown turned to a look of surprise with wide eyes. In his German-accented Norse he said, "What are you talking about Leif? It was a bear-man! Have you had too much ale this morning?"

Leif and I looked at one another, then back to Tyrkr. We both erupted in laughter as we rose to walk back to Erik's longhouse to make the plans for our next journey.

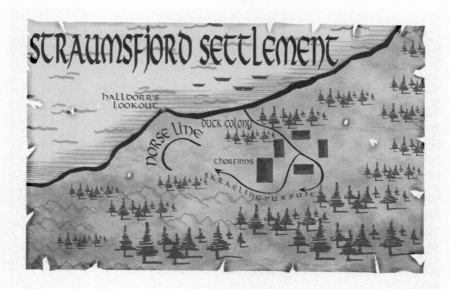

PART II – Explorers!

1,001 – 1,006 A.D.

CHAPTER 4

The year of the bear-man was a difficult one for Gudrid. As I have shared, her parents both found their way into the new Christian graveyard in Eriksfjord. They were aged, every bit of fifty, so had they been the only deaths she had to endure, she would likely have recovered quickly. But they weren't the only deaths from sickness that year. In Vestribyggo, where she lived, over sixty people died. Among them was Leif's youngest brother and Gudrid's young, adventurous husband, Thorstein.

He became ill in late winter and died in the spring, shortly after the Scots arrived with news of the One Faith. Thorstein accepted the One God with exceptional vigor given his weakened condition and saw to it that Haki and Haekja spread the word throughout the fjords under his leadership. He himself converted while reclined in a lake of his own sweat, bedridden, after the thralls told of King Olaf's conversion to the faith on Scilly. If he thought the conversion would save him from his illness, he was mistaken.

Even though the last time I had seen him, Thorstein was but a boy, I knew I would miss Thorstein, the man, greatly. He was intelligent and quick-witted as a youth, and I expected those traits became enhanced as he matured. All who spoke of him, spoke highly.

Those of us in Eystribyggo were made aware of the news when a knarr, laden with walrus tusks and whale blubber for lamps, from the Western Settlement stopped in on its way to Iceland. The commander of the ship brought Gudrid with him so that she could stay with her parents. Instead, she would stay with Erik's family because her father's farm, known as Stokknes, was now desolate.

Erik and Thjordhildr took the widow in with welcome arms. Erik offered to see to it that Stokknes was well-tended so that any livestock or crop production went for her benefit. Thjordhildr, upon hearing the news of her youngest son's death fell deeper into her newfound faith in the True God. She often went to the church which bore her name to quietly sit upon the hard wooden benches and pray. Women from neighboring farms came to sit and grieve with her. Torleik would come by the church in the afternoons and read a Psalm in Latin from his Bible. He then said a Latin prayer to Mother Mary. No one in attendance could understand it. I was most likely the only other person in all of Greenland who could comprehend the foreign tongue.

Erik fell into a deep depression, withdrawing from those he loved. That spring he did not go hunting with Thorhall the Huntsman. Nor did he lead a fishing expedition to the icy northern waters as he had every year before. Thorstein's death even drove a more profound wedge between Erik and Thjordhildr. She had her faith, but he was even more unwilling to discuss the One God with her than before the news from the Vestribyggo arrived. Erik would meander around the house, mumbling to Thor under his breath. His normal gregarious nature seemed to be replaced by a quickened ill-temper.

All this went on while Leif and I simultaneously prepared to go a-Viking once again and built a longhouse for him and his family. As we had discussed, Leif purchased *Thor's Treasure* by giving a fair price to the widows of Bjarni's crewmen. He also made sure to buy supplies and even a couple of horses from their farms, even though we had plenty from Brattahlid.

One evening Leif and I returned to Erik's home from our work on the longhouse. Thjordhildr had not returned from her church, yet. Gudrid was visiting the pregnant Freydis, next door. Erik sat grumbling on a short stool next to the hearth. Two young women who were owned by Erik, one German, Alverad, one a Frank, I forget her name, prepared a simple meal for the family. Normally Erik would have taken the opportunity to slip a hand under one of their dresses or, at the very least, steal a lecherous glance. Not now. He stared at the skipping flames with a blanket pulled around his shoulders. Back then, I felt it was much too mild to sit that way, but approaching one hundred years on this earth, I have known for some time that the bones ache with the slightest of chills.

We walked to a basin filled with water in order to rinse off the grime for the evening meal. While dipping his hands in the basin, Leif said, "Halldorr, I think adventure is the purest form of living."

He said no more and so I replied, "That's likely." Looking back, I should have had a better response – perhaps disagreeing and then saying something about furrowing his sister or killing a man in battle as examples of pure living.

But I didn't, so he continued, "Adventure acts like a balm. It keeps a man young or takes an aged man back to his youth. It even takes away pains of the heart. A man should go exploring when he feels he has lost his way."

"Hmm," huffed Erik, without looking away from his flames.

Leif flashed me a smile because he now knew Erik was listening. Finally understanding Leif's intention, I took up the charge, "You're right! Once the exploits of youth creep into a man's blood, they aren't easily removed. I think a man who discovers new lands, fights to settle them, and then leads people to them, must eventually find his way to new discoveries. If not, he is doomed to while away like a toothless old woman in the confines of a longhouse. If an adventurer found himself doing such a thing, it would be better for him to be dead."

With the last, I took it too far. Now that I am truly aged, about twice as old as Erik was at the time, I sit wrapped in a blanket in my lodge for days at a time. I pray for death. It doesn't come. Nonetheless, when I finished speaking, Erik demonstrated the fire for which he was known. He flung the blanket from his shoulders. When he stood the stool tipped over backward and bounced across the hard-packed earthen floor to settle against the wall. Erik shouted, "You boys think I don't know what you're doing! I'm not going on your damned adventure out of shame from you two women! But I will go on your damned journey and, no doubt, teach you a thing or two about the subject!" He finished his thoughts by spitting at the fire.

The thralls had stopped their work to stare at Erik and one another during his outburst. Erik turned his head to look at them and smacked the Frank on her ass, shouting, "Get on with it!" They immediately returned to preparing the meal while Erik brushed past us to the door. "I'm going to the barns to prepare my hudfat." He nearly ran over Gudrid as she walked in the door. Erik said nothing to her, but, instead, slammed the door behind him.

To Leif and me, Gudrid asked, "What's come over him? I haven't seen him move like that since I returned."

Leif gave a hearty laugh and said, "He has decided to return to the seas." Leif then followed his father's example and walked to the door saying, "I've decided I'll eat with my family and my sister's family tonight." He left Gudrid and me looking at one another.

Except for the occasional clatter from the evening meal cooking, the house was quiet for a time. Gudrid took off her light green cloak, hung it on the wall beneath some reindeer antlers, and said, "I do love those men. Erik and his sons have such passion. I hope Erik has found his again." I moved to sit at the table to await Thjordhildr, while Gudrid sat across from me. "You were raised like one of Erik's sons, Halldorr. But you seem distant, not as passionate. It's like your mind is somewhere else."

I had not really gotten to know her since her return from Vestribyggo. She was bold. That was, likely, one of the qualities her dead husband found wonderful about her. Gudrid was beautiful, too. All men noticed her thick, golden hair, but as I sat across from her while she sized me up, I became aware of her face for the first time. Her complexion was fair as I would expect. Her skin was exceptionally smooth, but not perfect for she had a small scar on her forehead. It was usually hidden behind a shock of hair, but today I saw it and wondered what put it there. Her eyes were pale blue. They were cheery, but I knew that behind them was a genuine sadness from losing her husband and parents in a single year.

I thought about how to respond to her accusation and decided to be honest. "I think you misperceive me." Pointing to my chest I said, "My passions are in here. They are not for anyone else. I happen to be selfish that way. I love adventure in the salty air of the sea. I love speaking with friends in Latin or Gaelic or Swedish or other languages." I held up the medallion Kenna gave me to use as Olaf's official seal then said, "I love reading and writing. I've done so for kings, you know." For some reason my ardor grew as I spoke, so I added, "I also love rutting women like the stag of the forest does a helpless doe."

Except for a slight widening of her eyes at the last, my outburst brought no indignation from Gudrid. She reached across the table, putting her hand atop mine, saying, "Halldorr, I meant no offense. I've heard you lost a wife and still grieve." Her hand lingered while the silence between us resumed. Then she added, "You can read and write all those languages? How?"

My mind bubbled like a hot spring along a mountain pass. Thoughts and feelings of the past years rushed to my consciousness. Then I shared my story with her. Of course, I kept the details of Bjarni's role in my life to myself, but I did share Freydis' part. I talked about my fathers, Olef, Erik, Olaf. I spoke of Dyflin. I talked of Maldon and London. She learned how I built ships and about how Crevan the old Irish priest taught me my first letters. We talked for a long while. She shared with me details of her life, her father and mother, her love for Thorstein. I told her stories I recalled from Thorstein's youth that made her laugh to tears of joy. They quickly turned to tears of sadness and it was my turn to reach across the table to put my hand upon hers. We sat quietly like that until I, at last, related tales of my too-brief time with Kenna.

When Thjordhildr returned from her church vigil we abruptly finished our talk. Like embarrassed youths nearly caught in the act, we grew silent and distant when the lady of the house walked in through the door. She set down whatever baggage she carried and washed in the basin that was newly warmed by Alverad, the household thrall. I welcomed Thjordhildr, but excused myself, saying I would not eat with them that night and went into the still-light evening. I was not ten steps from the longhouse, when Alverad came out calling after me.

"What is it?" I asked the girl.

She was young and pretty, with a nose that went to a narrow point, but I never spoke to her other than single word phrases in the normal course of living with Erik and his family. She was from lands similar to Tyrkr and even had a like accent. Alverad struggled more with the words as she tried to speak, so I asked her if she would do better in a Danish dialect. My hunch was correct. The

Danes were very proficient traders, especially in the trade of slaves. After her initial capture, she spent several years with them before being sold off to the Norse.

Now in Danish she answered. "I do not know exactly what you and Gudrid spoke of in the house tonight, but you two should marry." Why she seemed so certain as to what I should do was beyond me. When I didn't immediately respond the young woman continued, "She has been very sad in the weeks since her arrival. For the first time I saw a brightness in her eyes while you spoke. Women notice such things. You are a widower and she is a widow. You will make a good match. You can work her father's land."

The thrall woman was right. I have told you again and again that except for the occasional summer a-Viking, all I ever wanted was to be a farmer with a good woman nestled under my covers. Here was my chance. I could be near my second father. My goals were finally within my reach. I think that if I was given the chance to stand there again today, I would march right back into that longhouse and propose a union. No delay. I have had some good times since then, but I think that marrying Gudrid that summer would have made me a happy man.

Instead I said, "What do you know about me? You're a thrall and should act as such. Maybe I'll just have you and be done with it."

She was stubborn, but not overly so. A worried look flashed across her face that perhaps I would see a punishment sent her way. It was very common for female thralls to be used by their masters for pleasure. Since Erik had lost all interest in such things recently, Alverad would have feared me coming to her sleeping place in the night. Yet with as much courage as she could muster, she said, "I am sorry for noticing, but I think I have been told enough about you. Tyrkr shares stories with us sometimes. I think you are gentle and noble. I know you want a wife and farm." Then she finished, "I did not mean to speak out of turn. I thought I helped."

Tyrkr and his flapping German lips! I would need to talk with him sometime. But, as I said, the woman was right. While I stood there, I resolved to marry Gudrid upon my return in the autumn from our adventure to the lands Bjarni ignored. More gently this time I said, "You were right to tell me. Thank you, Alverad. Now please go back and attend to Thjordhildr and Gudrid." She nodded with a slight smile, heading off into the house.

I walked to Fridr Rock to spend the night staring up at the stars and think about what might be.

. . .

Bjarni's ship, *Thor's Treasure*, hadn't looked that seaworthy in years. I saw to it that we employed freemen and their horses to pull the longboat onto land. Thralls then scampered over its walls and decks to recaulk the strakes with tar-soaked wool or to swab another coat of pine tar over any exposed wooden surfaces. Bjarni had a partially finished sail in his home that Leif bought from the crew's widows. He hired women from neighboring estates to finish the cloth in a matter of weeks. It was handsome indeed, with alternating blue and white vertical stripes.

The boat was pushed back into the waters of Eriksfjord. A long plank was set, leading from the gunwale to the shingle so that provisions could be easily loaded. It was stocked with plentiful food such as salted mutton and smoked fish. Four large casks of ale were rolled up the gangplank to be stowed in the cavernous hold of the knarr. The old sail was stowed away in the event inclement weather came upon us. We could stretch it over the length of the ship like a tent to protect us from the elements. As I stuffed it into the hold, I remember wishing we had something similar on our trip from Norway to Greenland the previous autumn. But if we had, we would have seen neither the icebergs coming toward us nor the stranded crew. I shrugged and thought that these things usually work out right.

We planned to leave for our adventure on the summer solstice. The sun was terrific with not a cloud in the blue sky. A good omen, I thought. For its part, the sun would set for a mere two or three hours this time of year so we should be able to make efficient time toward whatever land we sailed. Most of the crew, including my old friend Tyrkr, was already aboard. I lingered on the stones scattered about the shore, trying to think of more reasons to talk with Gudrid, who was kind enough to walk with me that morning. I told her I waited for Leif and Erik to arrive. They had taken their horses to make last minute governing plans with Thorvald, who would serve as leader while Erik was away.

"But why must you go?" Gudrid asked while the soft waves from the fjord lapped the shore.

It was a good question. I've stewed myself to anger and despair over my lack of a home and woman. If I asked for the woman before me to be mine, I would have her. I knew it. I would just tell Leif I changed my mind; that I would stay and help Gudrid run Stokknes. We could rut under the covers all winter, then she could give birth to the first of our children while I worked and hunted outside in the summer. We would repeat this as many years as we could. But my plans weren't so easily achieved. "I gave my word to Leif that I would go a-Viking with him."

She wasn't impressed with my logic, "So tell him that circumstances have changed." Gudrid was opinionated. I found that captivating.

I gently touched her arm while saying, "Giving my word isn't the whole truth. All my life, I have told others I wanted to find a good woman and work the earth. And that's true. But something changed in me while I was serving Olaf all those years." I hesitated because I was afraid that speaking my thoughts out loud would make them so and, therefore, change who I was. But I was already a different man. So I said, "I have come to yearn for adventure. I still want a good woman. I still want to build an estate, but something pulls me to the sea, to adventure."

Gudrid nodded quietly with a quivering smile. Tears pooled in the corners of her eyes. Then she sniffled out, "Halldorr, you are so much like my Thorstein. He wanted two lives. He wanted to see the world and so he travelled to Ireland and back. But he also wanted to be firmly planted and rule with honor in both his home and the Western Settlement. He was honorable. I was proud to call him my husband."

A great shout echoed over the hills to the southwest, interrupting our conversation. We both turned to see Erik and Leif cresting the hill atop their galloping horses. The beasts' thundering hooves kicked up dirt, grass, and rocks while their riders whipped the horses' rumps, driving them ever faster. I instinctively pushed Gudrid behind me and put my hand to my sword hilt to prepare for the trouble that must pursue my friends. But then I heard the laughter and taunting of men racing.

Both men rode medium sized palfreys. Erik's was a dappled grey, while Leif's was light brown with one white sock. The palfrey was generally a fine horse, and Erik had imported several over the years. They did not trot, but by their nature had a smooth, ambling gait. The horses were superb for the rocky, uneven terrain of Greenland.

Leif led his father by two horse lengths, but Erik gave a shrill scream and jammed his spurs further into the creature's sides. The grey's eyes widened while, like its rider, it gave a shrill neigh of its own. Erik's face was livelier than I had seen it since we heard of Thorstein's death. His forehead was furrowed with intensity. His teeth gritted behind his smile. Wild red hair flew behind him while the tips of his beard blew up to obscure his view. Erik looked like Erik once again. His horse began to pull closer.

The men onboard *Thor's Treasure* heard the commotion and all moved to starboard to cheer on their leaders. I snuck a glance back to Gudrid who stood with a broad smile, our serious conversation forgotten. Turning toward the racers, I shouted my encouragement to them both.

I could now hear Leif's baiting, "How do you expect to embark on a journey when you can't even get your horse to budge? Maybe the beast is taking after your bowels and has decided not to move!" Erik was only a half-length behind.

With a determined smile Erik retorted, "You little bastard! When I win this race, I'll show you how fast my bowels work. You'll be in charge of the dung bucket on our journey!" Leif was surprised to now see Erik abreast of him. The grey had the momentum and would certainly win for they were a mere thirty ells from us.

Then it all changed. Erik's horse found an unexpected furrow behind a large stone. The right front leg plunged into the depression, then snapped with such a piercing sound, my ears still hear it today; my face winces as I record the event on this page. The strong chest of the palfrey smashed into the earth while Erik continued forward into the air. His horse's ass-end was already rolling over toward us by the time Erik hit the ground. My second father bounced once off his torso, rolled in the air, then bounced again. He skidded to rest against a dark brown, jagged boulder.

Leif pulled his horse to a halt, dust rising into a billowing cloud, and scampered down to his father while I set out at a sprint. The fall would surely mean the death of the horse, but did the man live? I didn't know. The rock partially obscured my view of him. His legs lay still to the left and one hand jutted out from the right. Then I heard Erik shouting a string of curses, "Thor's goat shit! By one-eyed Odin's turds! Freya's tits! Tits! Tits! Tits!" He pulled his hand back to cradle his ribs just as I rounded the rock. He looked bad, but not terrible. Erik's face was scraped with a bloody nose. His arms and legs did not appear to be broken.

"Ox shit! My ribs! I've broken my ribs. It hurts to breathe." He intentionally tried to limit the volume of his inhalations so as not to stretch his chest.

Leif and I knelt down to the man. When I touched his head with my hand he shouted, "Halldorr, this doesn't mean you can rub me like a lonely woman! Ow!"

Leif laughed, "If it's just your ribs you can rest on the ship while we sail. You'll be up before we set foot on this new land."

Gudrid slid to a stop behind us when Erik grunted out, "I'm not going anywhere."

Undaunted, Leif responded, "Then we can delay our trip by a week or two. You've broken ribs before. They heal."

"I'm not going anywhere, anytime!" Then gasping, "Shit that hurts. This is a bad omen. I'm not leaving Greenland in my lifetime. I even question whether or not you should go after this." Gudrid squeezed my shoulder. I read her thoughts. She, no doubt, hoped that I would be forced to stay with her. A part of me wanted to walk to Torleik and have him marry us on the spot, but another part craved the uncertain danger to which this omen directed.

We received our answer, "Father, you may stay here like a woman. But Halldorr and I, the adventurous sons you have remaining, are leaving." Leif jumped into his saddle, walked his horse to the shore, and shouted to several men to see to it that Erik was carted back home. I looked into Erik's eyes. He gave a half smile and shrugged.

I finally noticed the grey palfrey breathing heavily, snorting. It lay sprawled in a heap five ells from us and gave an occasional, pathetic neigh. Its broken leg was bent into several awkward directions with bloodied bones protruding from grotesque wounds. Gudrid's eyes reminded me to put the horse out of its misery, so I pulled my saex out and slit the animal's throat. After two or three gurgles of wet blood from the creature's neck, it lay motionless.

We spent another hour or two hauling the horse and Erik back to Brattahlid – one to be butchered, the other to heal. I gave Gudrid a half-hearted smile of encouragement, kissed both Thjordhildr and Erik on their foreheads, then walked alone to the shingle. The brilliant sunshine of the morning had been replaced by fog and a chilly breeze. The signs and omens were shifting. I waded into the cold fjord, walking on the uneven stones beneath the water's surface. Tyrkr offered an arm and hauled me into *Thor's Treasure*. Without fanfare or ceremony, Leif ordered the men to their oars and we started on another voyage atop the waves.

CHAPTER 5

The fog stayed with us for two days as the men strengthened their backs at the oars. We were thirty-five men, altogether. The seas were calm with no breeze. Leif was solemn since his father's accident and ardent refusal to consider joining the voyage. At the time I thought his disappointment made sense because it meant more morose inaction from Erik, but looking back on it now, I think Leif had another one of his premonitions of the near future – more on that in its proper turn. In his foul mood, Leif actually did tend the turd bucket as Erik had threatened at the end of their race, a task of penance to be sure and fitting for the man who brought Christianity to Greenland.

Most of our crew had sailed in the waters surrounding Eriksfjord for seal or fish and so those first days brought no concern from the men. Most Norse sea voyages involve an overnight stay on land, but on this trip we simply had the men sleep beneath the foggy midnight sun for several hours before resuming their rowing. We ate the smoked fish from the hold and washed it down with ale.

When I was not lending my back to the oar, I spent time in the stern staring back at the fog to an unseen Greenland. What was Gudrid doing? What was she thinking? Our round trip journey would likely last just two months if we did extensive exploring in the new lands. I could be married by the autumn harvest of the short, low-yielding barley crops grown in Eystribyggo. The thought of marriage excited me for Gudrid would make a fine wife.

The thought also brought guilt. I had not experienced such a feeling before, but it came in waves like the sea as I sat there wondering about Kenna. Was it right that I should revel in my future happiness when the woman I had loved so deeply, died so recently in an agonizingly incoherent state brought on by fever? Even now, as *Thor's Treasure* cut a path to adventure and hopefully glory, Kenna was rotting in the ground with my son, Olaf. My wife had taught me authentic love and language. I missed her companionship.

If Kenna were what are now called pagans, we would have burned her body then buried her remains with a small wagon to represent a more feminine version of Frey's ship, *Skidbladnr*. The burning and transport would have seen to it that Kenna was in paradise in the blink of an eye. But she was not pagan. She was devout in her faith to the One God, having even spent time in a nunnery before we met. How long would she tarry in this world or in-between until she found paradise? I worried that my joy would cause her profound sadness as she looked at me from the heaven of the One God or wherever she now tread.

Ignored by Leif and the men and feeling utter woe, I reached into my pack to pull out my book for the first time in many months. I carefully removed it from the thick, leather purse which had protected it since the day I stole the book from Arwel during a strandhogg in southern Wales. I ran my calloused fingers over the imprinted, three dimensional cover thinking of the times I read the book while on journeys with Olaf while missing Kenna.

Among the many animals on the cover I took particular note of the dragon this time. Thinking the dragon imprint was more pronounced than what it appeared in the past, I took it as a good omen and opened the book to a random page toward the back. The first passage I read, a Psalm of David, brought a wicked smile amongst my beard. David spoke to the Lord about a deceitful man who hated and attacked him without cause. David beseeches the One God to, "Constituet sibi resisteret malus," or "Appoint an evil man to oppose him." I thought of Bjarni, his lies, his hatred against me. I thought that I must have been the evil man appointed by the Lord at David's request. David further asks, "Ut dies eius pauci," or "May his days be few." Bjarni's certainly were, for I, the evil bear-man, saw to it.

Completely satisfied by David's and the One God's justification of my revenge, I flipped several pages more into the Psalms only to find my answer. In the middle of a Song of Ascents, Solomon writes, "Erit uxor tua sicut vitis fructifera in domo tua, filii tui sicut rami olivarum in circuitu mensae tuae. Sic benedicetur homo qui timet dominum." My heart leapt with joy and I gave a shout as I slammed the book closed with a smack. Leif gave a sideways glance from his post at the steering oar to which I returned a sheepish grin. I didn't turn around to face the men who faced me from their seats at the oars. No doubt more than one of them shook their heads at the whelping man-child aft.

But my joy was genuine and ignited a new enthusiasm for life within me. The One God sanctioned my actions against Bjarni and now He told me that I would have a wife like a fruitful vine, supplying me sons to surround my table! If that was so, he did not expect me to mourn for Kenna for the rest of my days. As much as I loved the woman, I could and would love another. I was certain that Gudrid was to be my woman. She would provide me with warmth in my bed and a host of children. I would very soon finish this adventure with Leif and return to Eystribyggo to be wed in Thjordhildr's own church.

. . .

Based upon Cnute's original telling of Bjarni's journey, we estimated that we should first find the land Bjarni had seen last within three or four days of Eriksfjord, depending on the wind. His description proved accurate in the middle of the fourth day when a stiff, cold breeze kicked up the seas white before us and blew away the fog with a frigid fury. Totally unmasked now, stood a land of mountains with immense blue and white glaciers plunging into the icy waters of the sea. While the terrain seemed forbidding to be sure, the spirits of the captain and crew of *Thor's Treasure* sprang to new heights.

Leif's pleasant smile returned while he looked on the land with anticipation. He didn't even have to call to encourage the men. Their rowing quickened into a sharp clip as everyone looked forward to discovering new worlds.

After one hour of rowing we came close enough to the rocky crags jutting from the ice and water to cast our anchor. Leif, Tyrkr, and I put out a boat with three other men and rowed ashore. After tying the boat off to a spire-like rock we scaled the dangerous shoreline to the highest nearby point. A brief survey told me that this place was no place for men. My initial elation subsided as I scanned over theses glaciers that carried huge boulders in their midst, grinding them to dust as they pushed toward their inevitable deaths in the sea. The only breaks from these lumbering ice packs were the occasional rocky masses such as the one on which we stood. Further inland was even more dreadful. Jagged mountains rose up with sharp peaks leaving no place to hunt or build or plant in between. Rocks and ice. Not that different from Erik's Greenland, yet more foreboding.

Leif seemed elated though. So much so that he slapped my back and exclaimed, "Look at it, Halldorr! Look at it!" Leif's extended arm swept out over the land and he shook his head in wonder.

"I am, and all I see is cold and death. Bjarni was wrong about much, but I think he figured this place correctly," I answered. "I say we row back to the ship and head south to find the other lands he saw."

Leif chuckled while crossing his arms to brace somewhat from the cold. "We shall, Halldorr. We shall." Now pointing to *Thor's Treasure* he said, "These men are our witnesses so that it may never be said of us as it is of Bjarni that we did not set foot upon this shore." A shock of his red hair rapped at his face from the wind which he ignored so that he could continue making his speech, "Since the discoverer of a world gets the honor of naming it, I am going to name this land Helluland." This disappointingly unoriginal name meant Rock Land.

We spent three more days following Helluland's shoreline and confirmed, as Bjarni had, that it was an island. During this time I spent time at the oar marveling at the harsh landscape and going ashore whenever a party went. Everything we saw confirmed that none of us would get fat or rich off this land. Why did the One God see fit to even construct such a place, good for nothing? With no incidents to share, our time there came to an end and we struck out south for, hopefully, further discoveries, rich, lush, and green.

On this leg of the journey our backs were rested from a warm wind. It was not necessarily a favorable wind, coming at us from the south, but it was wind nonetheless. We stowed the oars atop the T-shaped brackets in the ship's center and spent the day beating to windward. Leif found that the starboard tack was most favorable so we sailed for quite a time to the southeast before coming about for a short port tack. We then turned for a starboard tack again, repeating the process over and over again.

Since only a handful of men were required to manage the sail in a change in tack, most men found a spot onboard to catch a nap when they were not needed. I slid my whetstone slowly, deliberately over my sword's edge while watching one man, Folkvar, sleep as peacefully as if he were at home sleeping with his lips upon his mother's breast. His beard needed to be trimmed above his lip and so he sucked the coarse brown hair into his mouth when he inhaled then blew it out violently when he exhaled. He wore a saex strapped on his dry-rotted leather belt. It was not the quality of my saex blade, made in Frankia. Folkvar's saex looked like it was something he inherited from his father when he was still a youth without whiskers. Regardless of the quality of the blade, I could see it was in poor condition as it had partially slipped out of its small wooden scabbard. Orange rust blanketed the steel, slowly eating it away while he lounged. I thought of the countless strandhoggs I had been on in Europe. I thought of the many battles I had sailed to and what we did aboard our ships. We used whetstones to sharpen spears, swords, javelins, or axes. Thralls would polish our mail until their muscles were sore, sweating and burning, and the chain sparkled. Commanders would review battles plans. In short, no time was wasted. On this journey, we wasted time.

Late in the long second day, the wind shifted – a header to our starboard tack. So as the old adage goes, "Tack on a header," we came about for the now more favorable port tack. After sailing southwest for over an hour Tyrkr, one of the few men awake, shouted from the prow, "Land! Starboard!"

I jumped over the slumbering Folkvar and ran to where the German stood pointing. Tyrkr's eyes were good, for the land was just a vague darkening of the sea at the horizon, but it was land. Leif ordered that we stay on the port tack much longer so that we would work our way closer to the shores. An hour more brought us to a better vantage point to see the land Tyrkr spied. It was a group of islands each about two miles wide covered in dark green hills and trees. But they were not the only magnificent sight. For behind them lay a great, vast land of fantastic forests and lush gently sloping knolls. This land was much more thrilling to view than Helluland just two days north. This land had possibilities! In a moment, thoughts of settling this land flashed through my mind. This country must be superior to Erik's Greenland – this land was actually green!

We looped south around the group of islands then sliced north between them and a head on the mainland. A beautiful, wide harbor opened in the mainland north of the cape. We crept into it with sail lowered and our backs at the oars. The harbor was about one mile wide with the land rising smoothly from the still waters. After sailing inland for three miles the harbor turned sharply to port before ending one mile later with two curving beaches. One was scattered with grey pebbles rounded from the constant lapping of the sea. The other had fine sand. As we traversed the harbor, I thought of the Fjord at Agdenes so I instinctively looked to the hills for the mountain goats which stood watch over Agdenes, but there were none. In fact, we saw no wildlife except for several varieties of birds.

Like all areas where land and the sea meet, we saw sea gulls, some with distinct black heads. They floated on air currents above us, following our ship. Two of the boldest landed on the stern and were rewarded with chunks of stale bread from Leif for their bravery. The men laughed as Leif asked questions of the birds such as what this land was called and who led as its jarl. They laughed more when the gulls responded at the proper times with their screeching calls. Higher above the waters, a flock of twenty ducks quacked their way inland from the harbor. They seemed to be descending, so I guessed there was a river or lake nearby.

Leif ordered that we slide the keel into the soft sand of the beach, but I quietly suggested to him otherwise. We would do such a thing if we were a crew of warriors, but since we were not and since we didn't know what kind of skraeling to expect, I thought we should cast our anchor and row ashore as we had done in Helluland. Leif looked disappointed that he did not think of this action, but agreed with the prudent idea, swiftly countermanding his original order. The men held the oars stiffly so that the blades remained under the water's surface, slowing our progress. They then pulled up their dripping blades and as we slowed, Tyrkr and I heaved the mighty iron into the harbor. It plunged out of sight, quickly stretching its rope taut. *Thor's Treasure* came to a restful stop, tugging on the straining cord.

Our row boat was launched. I joined Leif, Tyrkr, Folkvar, and two other men as we made the short distance to shore. My feet splashed into the rippling water so I could help pull the boat up away from any currents, and then we struck off inland. As we entered the cover of the first set of tall pine trees Leif chuckled, "Twice in one week we have outdone Bjarni."

"Not hard to do," was my reply. Sitting in my longhouse today, I still think comparing ourselves to Bjarni was weak, at best.

"Aye, you're correct. But even so, we've now set foot upon two undiscovered lands. No Norseman, no man at all for all we know, has ever been here." Leif rapped a tree with the face of his sword which rang loudly as he made his point. "This will get us into the sagas for sure."

With a broad smile to match his immense shoulders, Tyrkr piped up as Leif finished, "Well, hopefully if there are no men here, we have good luck with the women." We all had a good laugh and marched steadily along a tiny creek. Leif and I walked next to one another and chatted about mostly nonsense. At least I recollect none of the conversation today. After one-half mile the trees opened to a small, deep blue lake. The sun was on the opposite side of the water and reflected sharply off the surface. The ducks I had seen earlier were idly floating near the opposite shore, taking turns diving for the afternoon meal, in between their quacking chatter.

I dreamed of building a longhouse on the side of the hill, next to that unnamed lake. I dreamed of exploring the forests around it for the rest of my days. I dreamed of retrieving Gudrid to my longhouse and raising a family. I silently dreamed all this and more as we walked around the water to head further inland still.

The afternoon went by quickly while we walked in the abundant lowland in the valley. We came to another lake then climbed a large knoll nearby only to see that we were still on an island. We were not on the mainland as we thought. That didn't stop Leif from claiming his right as discoverer of all these lands to again name them. Looking more like his father, Erik, than the Leif I knew, he made a little show of sweeping his sword over the land and seas, saying, "I will name these lands . . ." But he was interrupted by my snorts and giggles. The whole of the group looked at me, mostly out of the corners of their eyes. Leif looked honestly confused, "What is it Halldorr?"

I chuckled out the words, "It's nothing." Leif's face said to go ahead and say what I had to say, so I spit out, "It's just that I had one of your premonitions that you so often have."

Leif became genuinely excited and said, "Then share it with us. It must be humorous, whatever it is."

"I don't know how funny it is, but I felt as if I knew you would name this land Markland." When I finished, I laughed and laughed and laughed. I laughed so much that I leaned up against a tree while tears ran down my cheeks, wetting my beard. When I finally regained my composure, I noticed that not a single man had joined me in my fit. Only Tyrkr had a smile on his face, but his was probably from not understanding my joke more than any understanding.

Finally Leif finished, "Halldorr, you are an enigma. And you're right. We don't know how funny it is. But you're also right that this land shall be called Markland, after the forests that it offers to us." He was quite serious in this proclamation. In fact, this was likely the most obtuse I ever witnessed Leif to be in my life. But even the wise and moderate among us are occasionally at a loss. When he finished speaking, I again laughed by myself. The men grew tired of watching me so the group began its descent down to the creek to find its way back to the ship.

When they were gone several minutes, I eventually regained my composure. Being alone for the first time in days, I stood surveying Markland. I thought that we should immediately go back to Eystribyggo and tell all of Greenland that we must resettle to these new lands. Plentiful timber; harbors; game, no doubt; and the likely warmer climate made Markland a place where our displaced, fortune-seeking Norsemen could excel. I would talk to Leif about it when I went back to the ship.

As I turned to face east and the direction of the harbor, I noticed a waft of smoke some miles inland on the mainland. At first

I thought it was just fog or low hanging clouds in the distance. Then I saw that the waft of smoke was quite large and was being fed by at least a dozen small fires somewhere beneath the forest canopy. Skraelings. I ran to report my findings to my companions.

. . .

Folkvar was urinating into the harbor while the rest of the men were loitering in the row boat when I burst from the forest onto the beach. Only Leif took notice of me when I slid to a stop in the sand.

"Get in Halldorr," he said without a care in the world.

"Skraelings!" I panted while pointing back in the direction from which I had come.

"I suspected we would find some. But we're leaving when Folkvar is done defiling the seas, so I suspect wherever they are, they can't cause us much harm," replied Leif. Then with a little mockery he added, "Unless an entire tribe is chasing you."

I ignored his gibe. It took a moment for me to comprehend the rest of what Leif said, "So we're returning to Greenland already?" We spent more time rowing around the frozen Helluland than we were going to spend in this paradise? But at least I would be able to retrieve Gudrid sooner than I thought, be wed, and return here to build a life!

But Leif shook his head, "No, we're going on south. Remember, Bjarni's men spoke of a third land."

The skraelings now completely forgotten, I opened my mouth to protest, but Folkvar turned at that moment, showing me more of him than I cared to see. He cinched his trousers, took three broad steps across the sand to step into the rowboat, then all the men looked at me in anticipation. After deciding it wasn't much of a letdown, that the lands to the south may be better on which to explore and whelp children, and that Gudrid could wait, I walked to the boat and took my turn at the oar until we reached the ship. With our stern to the creek, we captured a small breeze in our cloth, and sailed out of the harbor.

I stared back at Markland, letting its image burn into my mind. I hoped to return here one day, I told myself. I hoped to bring my fine woman, Gudrid, to live in these gentle slopes, drink of the tumbling waters, fish in the sea, and, of course, furrow her like the plow does supple soil.

But that was hope. My fate has not seen fit to consider my hopes. In fact, it often seemed thoroughly opposed to my hopes, preferring to counteract whatever my wishes dreamed to be.

. . .

We spent the rest of that day and night slowly angling away from the shore headed in a generally southeast direction. I was bored with our journey so far. While I certainly didn't miss the killings that went along with the mass conversions on my expeditions with Olaf, I did miss the excitement inherent in any and all of his endeavors. For years, Olaf had led me and even Leif for a time, across the seas, conquering and subduing. Now Leif seemed to be content with briefly setting foot on new land then leaving it behind, wholly unexplored.

Leif was slowly changing, maybe maturing into a jarl while his father yet lived, before my eyes. He seemed less inquisitive, less willing to explore – even though this was an exploratory voyage – as our too-brief walk in Markland demonstrated. That night while I pushed against the quiet sea with the rudder of *Thor's Treasure*, Leif lay on the steering deck near my feet fast asleep. Early in that cloudless night, he reminded me of Vigi, Olaf's old dog, so soundly did he sleep. Yet as the night aged, his sleep became fitful. He spoke out loud incomprehensively at times. He turned over and over, nearly rolling onto the main deck below.

As the sun rose off the port bow, Leif, too, awakened. He rolled over onto his back across my feet, and I could see his hair and beard were matted with sweat despite the chilly sea air. He wore a grave expression, not unlike he did the day of the Thing at Fridr Rock all those years ago. I asked him about it at the time, but he put me off, focusing instead on the dragon-ordained, bronze wind vane which swirled at the top of the mast. "Wind shift coming," he said.

I followed his line of sight and saw that, yes, the vane seemed to be settling on a new direction, even though the square sail just below it still plumped with the breeze we had used since leaving Markland.

"Looks like we'll get a northeasterly in a few moments," I said.

"Aye," groaned Leif as he pulled himself up from his erratic rest.

Tyrkr lounged nearby, scraping the mold from our very hard bread which would serve as a breakfast for the men. We would likely have to soak it for some time in ale or seawater so that our teeth would not shatter. He finished one fist-sized loaf and carelessly tossed it back into a dark wicker basket, retrieved another, then looked out across the waves while his knife flitted across the sustenance in his hand. He tilted his head to the northeast observing, "The ripples look like the shift will be fairly strong. Should I wake the men?"

Leif and I smiled at one another. Tyrkr was not much of a sailor. A crewman I would want on any voyage, to be sure, but never captaining a ship. He was looking into the direction of the new wind and saw growing ripples atop the waves. Somewhere, someone had told him that the size of the ripples indicated the coming wind's power. It was a common misconception. But ripples always appear enormous when facing wind, new or not and always appear miniscule when facing away.

Leif just nodded saying, "That may be Tyrkr. I thank you for noticing. I think we'll just have Halldorr turn to starboard and use the full force of the gale." He said the last word with a little sarcasm that was lost on the still-smiling Tyrkr. The former thrall went back to his scraping while I changed our heading to the southwest.

I don't have anything at all to report on the next two full days and nights. The weather was ideal. The breeze was steady. We sliced through miles of water without incident, though the men began to grumble that we sailed far enough to reach the Midgard Serpent which would swallow our small ship whole.

. . .

And then I laid eyes on the land that would become my home for many years. I would know joy and sorrow, elation and depression, friends and isolation, peace and war. I would even fancy myself as jarl of this land someday, but I am getting ahead of myself in the story.

On the morning of the third day one of the men saw land and we made our way toward it, coming ashore by way of our rowboat. Like Iceland or Greenland, it was a rocky landscape with tufts of scrub grass bobbing in that day's intermittent wind. I saw no trees to speak of from my vantage point sitting in the stern of the small boat. The jagged cliffs above the sea grew while we closed in, looking for a place to land.

We found a point less forbidding and tied the boat off on a long finger-like rock. In my years since coming ashore that day, I have had the pleasure of listening to several skalds visit my longhouse and tell the story of how we discovered this land. Without variation, the songs these men sing all talk of a dew upon the grass that was sweeter than anything we had ever tasted. Supposedly we scooped our hands into the pale green blades as if they were a lake and brought up handfuls of rich, delicious water. In truth, we scaled the rocky hillside to an empty windblown meadow at the top. We walked around for several minutes, getting our feet wet from the heavy dew, and then returned to our ship.

Leif ordered the men to row *Thor's Treasure* around the headland to the west. The sun was high off the port side, much higher than it reached in the northern reaches of Greenland or even in Norway. It reminded me of Dyflin at the same time of year. Entering an area of extensive shallows, we crossed a narrow channel between a small island to the starboard and a cape to port. The tide was rapidly ebbing – so rapidly that the blade of my pine oar struck bottom once, then again. Then other men soon began shouting the same thing. Leif was sitting on the steering deck, chin in his hands, elbows on his knees. Folkvar manned the rudder and called to Leif for direction, but received none. Soon we found that the keel was resting on the muddy bottom and the boat began tipping to one side as the water slid away.

The men pulled in their oars and stacked them in the racks at the ship's center. They stood around on the slanting deck holding onto the gunwale or mast to steady themselves. When it was clear Leif wasn't going to respond to their inquiries, for he must have been having one of his visions, they turned to me. At first I shrugged, but then, pointing while clasping my belt and sword about my waist, said, "Tyrkr, pick ten men and come with me. Bring swords and spears. We'll walk to the nearest shore to the south. The rest of you will stay with the ship and with our sleepy captain." With that, I jumped over the gunwale. My feet splashed down into a deep sucking mud, not unlike the mud we encountered on Northey Island during our Maldon victory. I was halfway to the shore by the time Tyrkr and the rest of the company began jumping into the slosh. Twice I nearly lost a boot in the mud where a nearby shallow pool held a flopping fish gasping for his sea breath. It felt good to be aggressive again. It felt good to become filthy. It was as if I was campaigning again, if only for a brief time against an invisible, imaginary enemy.

I splashed ashore on a low, flat cape jutting northwest. It was covered in lush grasses which welcomed me with a continual friendly nod. Behind the waving meadow stood an old forest, greeting me with its majestic beauty. Turning about, I surveyed the area. To my rear was the stranded ship, beyond which sat the small island. In the distance, further north was a hazy indication of a large land mass. To the east of the cape was a deep bay, with its wide mouth gaping northward. Past the deep bay was the rocky land we originally set foot upon earlier. A small iceberg slammed against the rocks. I thought that it was possible it had floated all the way from Eriksfjord only to end its life upon these shores. To the west sat a shallow bay, which now consisted of a wide plain of mud from the outflow of the tide. Seagulls shrieked above while taking turns diving into the small, isolated pools of water left behind to capture their mid-day meal of the newly confined fish.

I began to follow the cape southward. To my right sandpipers teetered in pairs along the beach. They ducked their long, narrow beaks into the sand again and again to seize their modest sustenance. A forest of firs, poplars, and larches quickly closed in around me. A small, curious woodpecker with a black head and yellow crown briefly stopped his incessant tapping to look down at me. Rapidly disinterested, he returned to his work on the tree. I came to a tiny brook which wound its way into the shallow bay. Finding a large rock, I perched myself upon it to wait for the men to catch up.

A ray of sunlight fell through the trees onto my rock and so I leaned to the side, closed my eyes, and caught it on my face. The warmth was good. I thought of Kenna, but for the first time, was not immediately saddened. I smiled to myself, remembering our time together as husband and wife as a time of near perfection. A profound happiness swelled in my soul when I thought of the woman and her soft, gentle wit. I then thought of Gudrid. What a good pair she and I would make – a childless widower and a childless widow. We would be able to build a life in these new lands. Patience, I told myself.

Clattering and laughing shook me from my trance. It seemed that Arnkell was not having a good day. He lost one of his boots in the mud, but was only able to retrieve it after it was filled with muck. Arnkell then carried the boot to shore where he immediately slipped on a sharp stone, creating a bleeding gash on the bottom of his naked foot. Finally, while he sat on a rotting tree trunk to tend to his boot and foot, a curious black and yellow woodpecker swooped down and shit on his head. The telling of this tale brought us all a much needed respite. All but Arnkell laughed until our echoing snorts filled the forest. A stealthy army we were not.

After each of us crouched down and took a long draught from the creek, we split into two groups. I led one set of six following the creek inland, while Tyrkr led a group of five southward along the shoreline. We agreed to meet for an evening meal back at the ship. "Come," was all I said before plunging deeper into the trees.

The brook made a sharp turn to the south after only about ninety ells. To my left I saw a beautiful cove of mature trees covering a flat, raised expanse that I thought would make an ideal spot for the beginnings of a new settlement. It was a narrow terrace surrounded by soggy bogs that could be efficiently defended from attack. Depending on the density of Norseman who eventually tread upon these lands, we could expand the new colony out onto the cape for maximum landward protection from any skraelings. Perhaps we would build a wall like that which we built at Kaupangen, the new city across the wide sea.

The high-pitched song of a warbler pierced the otherwise quiet forest, pulling me from my military-trained thinking. Half an English-mile later, we came to a small lake where a group of mostly black ducks quacked back and forth to one another. The males had a stubby black tuft jutting out from the backs of their heads so I named the body of water Black Duck Pond – only slightly more original than the names Leif had been giving to his discoveries. Folkvar had brought a small bow with him that he used to bring down three of the fowl for a dinner treat. He tucked them into his rucksack before we struck off inland again.

The rest of the day passed uneventfully as we explored the surroundings. I kept my group away longer than necessary partly out of fear that our return would hasten Leif's command to move on. By the time we came back to the shore, the tide had lifted *Thor's Treasure* free, and Leif saw that she now rested on a more accessible part of the beach rather than stranded out in the muddy shallows. One of the men struck his jasper stones in a fluffy heap of dry grass to start a bonfire on the cape to ward off the coming darkness, and for the first time, I realized that we had come southward enough to make the daylight and nighttime hours more similar in length.

Looking around I asked, "Where's Tyrkr?"

Leif, who sat upon a gnarled driftwood log that had its origins from some distant shore, piped up, "He hasn't returned. Was he not with you?"

"We split up into two groups to cover more ground," I answered.

He stared at the lapping flames for a moment, then stood and slapped my back, "I believe he's naming this new land for me. I mean to say, that since you make light of the titles I have bestowed thus far, perhaps our friend Tyrkr will devise something more cunning. We'll wait for his return before we give this fine forest its designation." Leif flashed his smile then set the men about their tasks of preparing the night's meal and scheduling the watch.

I wasn't sure if Leif had a premonition that told him of Tyrkr's whereabouts or if he was going mad before my eyes. The safest way to interpret his actions of the past few days was to think he had lost his mind and prepare accordingly. So I told the men to double the watch in case Tyrkr had gotten into some sort of trouble that would soon find us. I also prepared to set out in the morning with Folkvar and Arnkell to go out and search for our missing party.

After sharing in the roasted duck with the men I wrapped myself in my cloak at the forest's edge to sleep. I stared up at the sky looking briefly for the unmarried old maids in the undulating lights of the heavens, but they weren't there since we travelled too far south. Instead, I watched the stars and thought happily of Gudrid before succumbing to sleep. The fair Gudrid carried herself from my thoughts and into my dreams that night. Time and again in those visions I saw her standing among these very trees carrying a bundled baby in her arms. It was my child, I knew, for he was large and strong with fair hair. In my dream she smiled and waved to me while I broadcasted a crop of wheat onto freshly turned earth. But also time and again Gudrid was carried away in the arms of a fat merchant in a wide-bodied knarr heavily laden with trading goods.

When her knarr sank below the horizon for the last time my eyes opened to the new day just before the cresting of the sun. I shook away my confused uncertainty from the nightmares, getting my head into the tasks before me. Our fire smoldered since our watch had not seen to it that it was properly fed that night. A lone orange coal sat in the midst of blackened wood remains. I pulled my chain mail from the baggage on the ship. It felt good to feel its pronounced weight on my shoulders after I slid it into place. Then, after rousing Folkvar and Arnkell with a swift kick in their asses, clasping our weapons about our waists, and informing the sleepy watch of our plan, we left.

· · ·

We quickly passed by Arnkell's shitting woodpecker, waking from its slumber and returning to its incessant tapping. Neither Folkvar nor I said a word about yesterday's incident, but a quiet chuckle from Folkvar and a grumble from Arnkell brought a smile to my lips.

I jumped over the brook where our two parties split up the day before and so began our hunt. They likely stayed several ells into the forest to avoid the briars growing near the edge in search of nourishing sunlight. Within just a moment, Arnkell announced that he found signs of Tyrkr's passing. We followed the path quickly as they had discovered a track used by animals which was worn, free from undergrowth. In no time we came to a steep sandstone ridge. Standing at the base of the ridge, the brook had curled around and was to our left. We decided that since we did not see any signs of them on our return trip yesterday, they must have scaled the bald crest.

We did likewise and used the vantage point to survey the area. Behind us we saw the cape where the ship was now hidden. Inland we saw that the wooded landscape was broken by countless lakes with no sign of humanity. We should move the whole of Greenland here, I thought at the time. Ahead, the shore curved several times making many small coves. We descended the southwest side of the ridge and again picked up their trail.

It was like that all day. We followed their sloppy trail through the forest, climbed ridges, found creeks, bogs, and ponds. Nothing. No sign of trouble. No spent arrows. Neither blood, nor bodies.

We stopped for a very late mid-day meal of smoked herring and water from another winding creek. The three of us were in the middle of throwing out rampant speculation as to what became of our friends when the unmistakable, accented shout of Tyrkr echoed through the forest.

Without a word we unsheathed our swords and plunged toward the sound. Again a high-pitched howl came. This time it was from another man in the group and ended abruptly with a sharp cracking sound. As we came closer, laughter roared, then a belch.

The three of us, Viking heroes all, emerged with a burst from the forest's undergrowth prepared to hew down any miserable skraelings who tortured our crew. Before us was a secluded meadow with wild grapes growing nearly as dense as if cultivated, their vines pulling down on the branches of nearby trees. Four of Tyrkr's men with mouths stuffed with grapes looked alarmed at our arrival. Behind them a small pond had large boulders protruding toward the sky at its shoreline. Just then a naked Tyrkr ran across the top of one of the rocks, hanging onto a grapevine he had tied to an overhanging tree. With a scream of boyish joy he swung out over the water and let go, landing with a loud crack as his white belly met the surface.

. . .

So Leif was correct. Tyrkr would end up naming the new land on which we now strode. "Vinland!" Tyrkr exclaimed when asked back at the ship. "After the vines we found," he added for unneeded justification, shoveling more grapes into his face.

Leif gave a joyous nod saying, "Excellent!" Then turning to me with a twinkle in his eye he added, "All your worries for nothing, Halldorr. Tyrkr and our men were in good health."

"Aye, that is so, but I can't say the same thing for me and my men after seeing Tyrkr's white, fleshy ass flapping over our heads like a wounded albatross. It might take a man like our old priest Crevan to drive that image from my mind." This response, of course, brought the expected laughter at Tyrkr. For his part the former thrall smiled broadly, clearly not understanding my good-hearted slight against him.

That day and for the next several months, Leif was back to his old self – moderate, strong, decisive, and good natured. He seemed to leave the moody despondency from our time on the ship behind. Today, as an old man many years and miles removed from our adventures there, I look back with fondness at the months that followed our landing at Vinland – though the first bit of news Leif shared following our return from retrieving Tyrkr initially made me quite frustrated.

We were only a few weeks removed from the summer solstice and had plenty of time to make a return trip to Greenland, but Leif announced we would be wintering here in Vinland. The men with families grumbled quietly with sideways glances at one another. I stewed to myself thinking of another year away from the woman whom I would wed. But then Leif's enthusiasm for his own idea became infectious. Soon I and the men warmed to the plan, perhaps thinking that we had a chance to seize countless acres of the choicest land on which to set up their own estates such as Erik had done at Brattahlid. Some of them may have even fancied themselves in some leadership capacity in the new colony.

Leif championed his proposal, "This land will be an important stop as more and more Norsemen come to settle this new world. You saw the treasures in Markland, just as I had seen them. You see the lands off the horizon to the northwest. You see that this land, Vinland, extends far to the south. Who knows how far? But we will find out!"

One man asked, "What of skraelings?"

"What of them?" retorted Leif. "We need to build this camp to support us and supply us as we spread over the area. If we find skraelings, so what? We trade with them. We convert them to the One God and then by definition we become brothers in Christ! It worked with Olaf and Aethelred in England. It will work here. We will be successful, and this journey will be recited by the skalds for millennia!" Looking back and knowing the history of what occurred after, I am not so sure that our travels that year warrant history, oral or written, but as I am now isolated in my old age, I do not pretend to know what others are saying.

Regardless of my doubts about whether we made history, Leif's talk persuaded me to be an enthusiastic supporter of the idea. After all, I was kept away from Kenna on a voyage with Olaf for a full year when I had intentions to marry her. In hindsight, that absence went quickly and did not reduce my passion for the woman. It worked once, it would work again. So I put my mind into the task at hand.

"Since we are few, we'll want to select a spot that can be defended from attack. I saw such a place when my group explored the surrounding terrain. It's just south of where we stand today at the base of this cape, close to the cove to the west," I piped up to support Leif.

"Excellent!" Leif exclaimed again. "Take twenty men and axes and begin clearing the area. The rest of us will bring the ship around to the western cove."

. . .

A sentry watched the unfamiliar surroundings for us as our axes sang in the forest for days. We worked shirtless in the warm summer as we brought down the tall straight fir trees from where they had stood watch for decades. The steel ax heads created flashes in the air while we heaved them toward the wood, stabbing the tree, belching out chunks of timber, only to repeat the movement again and again. Not a single one of these men were with me when we built *Long Serpent* and *The Crane* in Norway, yet the songs began spontaneously in the same fashion and were, in fact, the same songs. We sang to the old gods, the gods of my youth. I think it bothered Leif that we did this, but neither he nor we knew any working songs for the One God, so away we sang.

Since Odin had made the first man, Ask, and the first woman, Embla, from the trunks of trees like those we harvested, we started the mornings singing to him. A portion of my favorite song follows:

Odin who is wisdom and knowledge
Asgard is your home.
The trees you felled which became Norse
Provide for us still.

Our king, he is your son
As is your mighty Thor.
Thunderbolts, lightning, wind, rainstorms.
Your strength is now in us
To keep the giants at bay.

The dwarves you keep beneath us
Holding the land on which we stand.
Odin you favor us in war
And will forever more.

We snacked on grapes that Tyrkr volunteered to gather and
bring to the work area each day. Two of the men had so many
grapes those first days that they had to frequently drop their axes and
run into the forest while they tugged down their trousers before they
soiled their clothes. On one occasion one of these men and his loose
bowels did not make it to the trees, fouling his breeches before he
took a single step, creating an eye-watering stench that attacked us
all. He never did live that down, I am sure. For the rest of my time
with him, he was constantly ridiculed, often called Seeping Man.

Our evening meals were plentiful. Hunting parties brought
back all sorts of water fowl. On one occasion a party killed what
looked like the large elk that walk all over Norway. This beast,
however, had a broad, flat palm-like portion of its rear section of
antlers. I have since learned from the native population that they call
these beasts, moose, which means twig-eater. Fishing parties
brought in herring, smelt, and eel from the salty sea. Trout and some
large pike were caught in the lakes and streams of Vinland. Along
the way we began to salt or smoke much of the plenty to prepare for
the coming winter.

Stumps were cleared. Soon boards were split and frames
assembled, stone foundations laid. Turf was cut and placed. We
would all share a single longhouse that first winter. This hall was
oriented in a north-south direction to follow the raised land on which
it sat. Three rooms made up our main living and sleeping area and
were structured long-ways like our typical longhouses. Each of
these three rooms had its own central hearth. Separate enclosures on
the west side included the kitchen and a storage room. Finally to the
east was a room we called our workshop which included a forge.

When our shelter was complete we began to harvest timber to
take back to Greenland. Each year traders brought logs from
Norway, first to Iceland, then if they were adventurous or greedy for
a higher price, to Greenland. Leif was eager to transport the trees we

cut directly to Eystribyggo. The supply was closer – likely only a three or four day direct sail – and therefore, would be more inexpensive than the previous source. He certainly inherited Erik's savvy business sense.

The next task was to pull the ship ashore for winter. At high tide we used ropes wrapped around trees to act as pulleys. With all thirty-five men heaving on the tether, the keel slowly inched its way up the beach until at last the steering oar and stern were clear.

Now with the shelter built, the logs harvested, and the boat dry-docked, we awaited the inevitable, wretched winter. It came, but was nothing like the short, frigid days in Greenland. Never once did I have to crack ice from the brook to gather water for cooking, washing, or drinking. We had sleet several evenings and on occasion it snowed, but each time the sun saw to it that the ground was cleared by late morning. It was so mild the grass never withered so that any livestock that we eventually brought to the land would not require oversized stocking of forage for the winter.

One morning many days after our celebration of Christmas and burning of the Yule log, Leif and I set off to the far inland south to hunt. It was a chilly morning as indicated by our breath that led us through the forest. Leif was particularly chatty that morning, more than he had been for most of our time in Vinland so I recall it vividly. We talked in hushed tones so as not to frighten our prey. At first our conversation was harmless bordering on inane. We chuckled about Tyrkr again and marveled at the man's loyalty to his adopted people, the Norse. We reminisced about strandhoggs in Scotland and Wales – even remembering our taking of Aber Tawe and Leif's execution of the town's cowardly leader, Arwel, by the quay.

Eventually, the conversation turned to my third adopted father, Olaf. After a time I asked, "Do you think he ever made it to the Holy Land?"

With confidence Leif answered, "Absolutely, he did."

"How can you be so certain?" I asked, though I knew Leif always knew the future or what happened elsewhere through his visions.

"I've seen it," he said. We hopped over a winding creek where ankle deep water ran lazily toward the sea. Then we ascended a rise in silence. Finally, he spoke again, "I need to return to Greenland."

Thinking his timing was odd since we were still some months from when anyone could safely expect to return to the icy fjords of Eystribyggo, I jested, "Perhaps we can shove one of the logs we have stacked at the forest's edge into the sea for you to paddle home. You'll certainly have a hard time convincing any of the men to join you."

Leif smiled noncommittally at my humor then patiently said, "Not now. After the equinox, I mean."

"We all intend to sail back after the equinox, Leif." He was being obvious and obtuse, I thought. But it turns out that I was being obtuse, for he had something to tell me.

"Erik will die," said Leif with some reflection just as a majestic eagle screeched high overhead, working the air currents with its long, outstretched wings and powerful chest. I didn't know where Leif's mind was headed, so I said nothing. "I've known about it for some time, at least since we were sailing to Vinland, but my vision told me to wait until the winter passed to return."

"Is he dead already?" I asked with real concern. The man took me in, raised me as one of his own. I loved him as my second father.

"No, he is not. I'll have time to say goodbye when I return in the spring."

"Maybe we can leave earlier. With the improvements last year, the ship is in terrific shape for such a journey. We need to get back," I pleaded.

"Aye, that is the case, the ship is in fine condition. But I cannot leave early. I have to rescue more men on the return trip as we did coming from Norway. I used to think these visions came from Odin or Thor, but now I know they come from the One God. The rescue last year helped convince the men and women of Greenland to accept the One God without bloodshed. I think this next rescue will hasten the conversion of the last followers of the old gods."

At one time I thought Leif's abilities were a gift, but I now saw them as a curse. He wanted to get to his father who would soon die, but he felt obligated to shipwrecked men who perhaps didn't even think about leaving on their own voyage yet. Furthermore, he was obligated to them because of his obligation to the One God. "We can leave early for Greenland, then send out a rescue ship. Either way, all will know of the One God's power in alerting you."

Leif gave a heavy sighed as he stopped and put a hand on my shoulder. "Halldorr, it must be as I said. I am in no hurry to get home any sooner. The part I am trying to tell you, the part that is weighing heavily on my heart, is that you cannot return with us."

I blinked in disbelief at what he said. Angrily I retorted, "Leif, I am going back with you!"

"Halldorr," Leif repeated my name. "Halldorr, I wish it could be so, but it cannot. You must stay here to manage Leifsbudir." Leifsbudir was the name we gave to our one-halled village on Vinland. He gave a knowing nod and a smile. I could never stay angry at him, but this day I held onto my anger longer than normal.

"No!" I shouted. "I'll not let another father disappear without a proper goodbye. I've lost one to death and another to self-imposed exile. I must see Erik." I wanted to strike Leif and his surety down with my balled fist crashing into his cheek, but held back.

"I will pass on your feelings to him. But you must stay," he said with an understanding calm that infuriated me.

"I am a free man. I can come and go as I please!" I added still shouting, not caring if I scattered game from the whole of Vinland.

"Halldorr, you are free to travel as you wish. But if you intend on pushing this, I'll have to remind you that I own *Thor's Treasure*, and I can let whomever I choose board her."

"I have plans to marry," I added, now grasping for any reason I could to justify returning.

Leif sat down on a rotting log, indicating I should do likewise. At first I had no intention of listening to the man, but when he sat there silently picking at the ground with a stick, in time I succumbed to his quiet pressure. I sat next to him looking at the side of his bowed head which seemed focused on the earth beneath his feet.

Certainly it was only seconds that went by, but in my anger they seemed like painfully slow hours. At last I asked, "Well, what is it? Why am I now sitting next to you?"

"Halldorr, we all need patience at times when it seems we should not have to have it. Patience would not be patience if it were easy for any man to obtain."

This was more than I could take, "Leif, I am not a child and don't speak to me as such. Patience might be easy for you since you see the future, but the rest of us must live in the now. I don't know what will happen, but if you tell me I cannot go back, I don't think I can stand for it. I'll not lose another woman before I even get the chance to marry her."

He started cracking the stick into ever-smaller pieces then said, "Patience is not easy for me either. I have these visions, but I do not know what I should do about them. I do not know what I should say about them. I do not know if I should allow the future to play out or to try to change things before they happen."

My sympathy for him that morning was lacking, "Leif, I don't really care about your plight. I want to return to wed Gudrid."

He smiled again. A sad smile, but a smile, then Leif said, "You'll marry again. That is why you must stay here."

Now he was speaking convoluted goat shit. "How will I be married if I stay here? I suppose you'll tell me that Gudrid will come here."

"She is sailing here in the coming years. I've seen it as clear as if she stood amongst the trees already," he confirmed.

I took a breath, thinking about what he said. "But why can I not return in the spring? What harm would occur?"

Another sigh, "Halldorr, you must stay. I wish I could tell you more. But I don't know more. You must stay here."

We sat there silently for a long while. The only sound was the echo from the ocean slamming against a distant shore. Minutes went by. I picked up my own stick and scraped at the ground in anger, making a crude cross in the dirt. I already knew that I would accept whatever he asked of me, but at the time I turned the new information in my head over and over just for the satisfaction of feeding my anger. I thought about tumbling on top of my friend and brother to smother the life out of him so that I could command *Thor's Treasure* and return to wish my second father farewell and marry Gudrid.

But Leif's hand slowly rose to touch my arm. Turning to look at him, I saw from his eyes that he gazed down into a small ravine below us. I followed his stare and saw the largest bull-moose I had ever seen or will ever see. My frustration melted away, forgotten in the joy of the hunt. I smiled to Leif, who smiled back, nodding, and we gradually rose to pursue our prey.

. . .

We killed that moose, struggling mightily to drag his gutted carcass back to Leifsbudir. At last we rigged a platform made out of small logs to float across the lakes and ponds we came upon. This, at least, took the burden from our shoulders for a time, until we had to cross land to another lake. I still have those antlers on display in my lodge to this day. In fact, even now, I look up to them as I put my quill to the parchment. They are filthy, carrying heaps of spider webs and dust.

That winter passed by uneventfully. Leif and I never spoke of Erik or Gudrid or my predicament again. The equinox came and Leif set out with the men, leaving me to tend to Leifsbudir on my own, for all the other men were permitted to return to their homes and women. It was the last time I ever saw my dear friend, my brother, my fellow adventurer. Though he is most assuredly dead by now – I've come to believe no one has ever lived as long as I – my mind's eye still sees him in his prime as a wise leader.

CHAPTER 6

I was isolated from Norse contact for greater than a full year. At first, the time crawled by, but eventually I came to appreciate the peace. When I was not felling trees for the dual purpose of firewood and to expand our village, I spent many hours hunting, fishing, and gathering berries and grains from the uncultivated plants growing amongst the wilds. Occasionally I would travel far from my longhouse, even spending a night or two in the forest while on a hunt just to see more of Vinland. These trips helped me realize that Leifsbudir was situated at the northernmost point of a long sliver of land that extended a vast distance to the south. The peninsula was approximately thirty miles across, and on foot, I was never able to ascertain just how far south it went.

As I became more and more comfortable with my surroundings, I even took my book along with me to read by the light of a fire. It was somewhat careless to strike a fire without a proper inspection of the area, but since I had never seen another human being, I allowed myself that carelessness. I would roast a rabbit or some such quarry over the fire and lean back on my elbow paging through the book. I loved reading the psalms. David wrote most of them, Crevan always said. He was a fine writer. They told of a man of God who pleaded for strength and guidance. They told of a man who was a great leader, but was often uncertain and begged for the One God's help. I often have felt alone or rudderless in my life and wondered if the One God would guide me.

One such night as I lay under the stars, after being alone for just over one year, I prayed to the One God for discernment in my days. I asked him for leadership, a wife, and for children. I think he spoke to me that night, though in my vision he looked like the images of Thor I had seen throughout my life. We stood on opposite sides of a deep blue fjord. I stood at the shingle with smooth round pebbles littering the ground beneath my feet, the soles of my boots wet. The One True God was perched high on a lush, green hill that rose gently from the fjord. He had a deep voice that resonated across the water directly into my ear. He did not need to strain to talk with me, instead it sounded as if he were sitting next to me, speaking at the table of a desolate mead hall.

We talked for a long while about my life's actions. He nodded often and laughed. He laughed at me like I was his child who had just discovered something for the first time. But in his face, I knew he loved me, and I felt no resentment toward his laughter. Eventually, he turned to walk down the far side of the hill. The One God who looked like Thor, or maybe it was King Olaf, stopped in his tracks and pivoted on unseen feet. When he wheeled around to face me, he gave me a wink saying, "Whatever you ask of me in my name, I will do, so that the Father may be glorified in the Son." I thought of this as he disappeared beyond the green grasses. Both Crevan and Olaf had said that many times as they led prayers. I too had read it in my book in the portion written by John, only it wasn't the One God who spoke these words, but his Son, the Christ.

My eyes opened to see the rabbit was fully roasted, a bit too blackened on the bottom side. I ate of it joyfully, knowing that I asked the One God for gifts and that he would answer my prayers through his Son. Gudrid and our many future sons came to my mind. I was in my thirty-seventh year, hardly a young man to begin having sons. The now elderly Erik was my age when Leif and I were first exiled, though my age didn't bother me as I lay on a musk ox hide tearing at the succulent meat with my teeth. I still felt fit and able to hew any man who would give me trouble. Certainly I would be able to rut with my new woman and stand up to the onslaught of my own children. I would tell them stories of my adventures with the man who was once king of our homeland an ocean away. I would laugh with them about Fife, my Scottish thrall and brief friend, they would marvel at his miraculous counting ability, they would be enthralled while I told them how he helped me kill the mighty Lord Byrhtnoth. In short, my long life thus far had been filled with adventure and would bring countless hours of delight around the hearth on cold winter nights.

The rhythmic pulse of the nearby sea lulled me as a mother's beating heart soothes her infant. I went to sleep thinking pleasant thoughts. My belly was full and I slept deeply. The entire night passed as if it were but a moment.

It was such a deep slumber that the sun was quite high by the time I awakened to the sound of men's voices. Despite my lack of consciousness, I instantly knew it was an unfamiliar tongue. My hand had pulled my beautiful sword from the fleece-lined, leather scabbard before I even thought about performing the act. Momentarily the voices ceased. I took the opportunity to quickly check my fire. It had died during the night and so did not betray my position with any smoke. I rose to my feet, leaving the safety and shade of my spruce grove, silently stepping over the thick bed of needles these trees and their ancestors had shed for eons.

The spruce grew in the shape of stunted, disfigured creatures from harsh storms brought to these shores by the ruthless westerly wind. I descended a gentle slope toward the sound. Because they were more sparsely spaced than trees deeper in the forest, I crept slowly and then lightly trod, not without haste, to the next bit of cover. From the echoes, I guessed the men were on the shore, but it was still obscured by the scrubby trees. A clear voice immediately to my right froze me in my tracks.

Two men walked right past me without taking notice of me as I hid among some tall native grasses. They talked in a tongue I could not understand. They used no words from the many languages Kenna and Crevan had taught me. But my ear had been honed by their patient instruction so I listened intently.

I guessed that both men were over ten years younger than I at the time. They wore nearly identical tan clothes made from animal hides, but each had his own ornaments to designate rank or status or preference. The taller of the two men was handsome. Around his neck he wore a string necklace decorated with carved bone pendants and an enormous animal tooth that all clanged together as he walked. The shorter one did not have a necklace, but he had a distinct red paint smeared on the lower half of his face. It made him rather stern looking, though in truth, I cannot say because so obscured was his expression.

Both men had long, coal-black hair that hung midway down their backs. It was straight like a carpenter's ruler, and the sun shone off it like a jewel. The shorter one tugged at his and said something with the words "niminisisan" and "nashoqua."

The handsome one thought this was funny and laughed while he used the words "ikwe" and "segonku." Then he reached below his tunic, producing a comb made of bone. He gave it to the stern one who started passing it through his long locks while they walked. The tall one just chuckled and shook his head at his companion while he mumbled "nashoqua" several times. They rounded a tree and walked out of sight, beyond a hill. From the friendly greetings they received at the shore, it sounded as if there were a total of four men – the two companions I had seen and two more.

I quietly poked into my rucksack and pulled out my own two-sided comb made of walrus tusk ivory. I read the Norse runes on the band in the center which read, "Thor, the mighty god." Standing now, I sheathed my sword and walked confidently holding my comb. Leif said we would someday trade with these people, so I thought I might as well begin with my comb.

When I rounded the tree to see the stone-covered beach I called, "Nashoqua! Nashoqua!" twice, hoping that the comb I waved in my hand was a nashoqua.

I must have looked like a wild man to them with my fair skin and bearded face. I was larger than the largest of them. I think my shoulders alone were as wide as one and one half of their own. The handsome one was nearest to me, about ten paces, and procured a short axe from his belt, standing at the ready. The other two I had not seen earlier were behind him several ells. One of them had a stone-tipped spear with the feather of an eagle tied near the head. The other pulled a small axe from his belt, too. Finally, the stern fellow with the red face stood near a low boat made of birch bark with high, rounded ends that sat at the water's edge on the shore. He held the comb he borrowed from the handsome man frozen in mid-air while he peered at me.

The four young men looked at me with a sincere bewilderment. We stood in silence for several heartbeats. Then I said, "Nashoqua, nashoqua. Trade," indicating with the comb that I wanted to give it to them.

When I said their word again, they looked confused. The handsome one blinked several times trying to ascertain what exactly was happening. The stern man at the boat shouted something loudly with such speed I could not gather anything he said. The tall, handsome man turned quickly and hushed the vain, combing one. He turned back to me and while pointing to the comb said, "Nashoqua trade?" He looked around behind me, considering what danger might lurk there.

I smiled while nodding my head. "Yes!" I proclaimed.

"Trade? Yes?" the handsome man asked. He said the words with an air of uncertainty.

"Yes!" I said again. I made no hostile motion. I only smiled and extended my comb toward the near man.

He approached me slowly while lowering his weapon. The man looked me up and down, paying particular attention to the sword at my waist. I am certain he had never seen one before, but I am equally certain he knew it was a weapon of some kind. Still he came. When he stopped about two ells from my reaching hand, I bobbed the comb once or twice and nodded, saying, "Nashoqua, trade."

He reached his strong arm out and took hold of the comb. The handsome one studied it while turning the comb over in one hand. He slid the axe back into his belt and said, "Nashoqua," while nodding with a smile.

We studied each other for a moment. I could see in his eyes that he was intelligent, thinking. He was a good man. I decided I would like him. I pointed to my chest and said, "Halldorr."

He pointed to his chest and said, "Halldorr?"

I shook my head, "No, my name is Halldorr. Halldorr."

He smiled again, letting a small chuckle roll as naturally as if we had been friends for years and pointed to his chest saying, "Kitchi. Kitchi."

I nodded and repeated what I heard, "Kitchi Kitchi."

Kitchi laughed louder now and shook his head, "Kitchi." He pointed to me saying, "Halldorr," then back to himself, "Kitchi."

Then he turned his back to me. Kitchi spun to the other men and pointed to me while saying a host of things with my name thrown in periodically. The man with the spear and the other axe-wielding man both lowered their weapons and listened intently. But the vain man shouted an interruption over Kitchi's words.

I smiled broadly while settling my hands at my waist. Something in that motion agitated the red-faced one greatly for he immediately dropped the comb into the boat, unveiling a bow. He was fitting an arrow in one fluid motion and drawing it back to aim it in my direction. Kitchi held up both palms to stop whatever was happening. He screamed, "Megedagik!" But it was far too late.

Passions and fear overtake men. I've seen it in the shield wall. I've seen it on the floating battle platform at sea. I saw it in that red-faced man's eyes that day. The arrow sailed and I surely would have died if it wasn't for Kitchi. He stepped in front of the arrow meant for my heart and so it pierced his. The force knocked his already-dead body back into my arms.

The red man screamed a wretched scream and a string of words. The other two men sprinted in my direction. Their faces told me what they meant to do. If I had time to sigh, I would have, but events were changing far too rapidly. I set Kitchi down as gently as I dared while shouting, "No. No." The first one to reach me swung his axe down toward my skull. I still thought I could salvage this encounter for good so I did not draw my blade. Instead I caught his sinewy arm in my hand to stop the blow. We stood there, he and I, staring at one another. He was young and quite scared, I could see. I tried to tell him with my eyes and the shaking of my head that I did not intend to fight. I think he began to understand, but then I felt a terrible, searing pain in my left thigh.

I looked down to see the stone spear head buried in my leg. Blood already spilled out my torn trousers. A barbaric shriek erupted from my mouth while I shoved the axe man down to the ground. The spear thrower looked uncertain as to what to do next, so I tried to pull his weapon from my wound. It was stuck so with another loud scream I broke the wood handle short, hurling the stump of a handle at the man on the ground. Red Man screamed more instructions of encouragement to the two attackers, while staying near the boat. They gained heart and surged at me in accord. I gave a heavy sigh, partially out of pain and partially out of concern as to what I knew would come next – death, unnecessary death.

I pulled my sword, the sword I had used to kill many well-trained warriors, from its resting place. The now unarmed man checked his attack but the axe man did not. He was the first to meet the sharpened steel edge. With my left arm I deflected his powerful strike. A bright light flashed in my eyes as I felt the bone of my arm break with a pop. Still I was able to slip the blade deeply into the man's belly – so deep that it protruded a full foot from his back. He dropped the axe when I shoved him off my sword.

I wavered on my feet. If the next man was a little more patient, he could have simply waited until I keeled over from pain or the loss of blood. He was not patient, though. He was young and foolish as are all young men. He bent down, grabbing the loose axe. My head felt thick with clutter, my eyes came in and out of focus. I did not have the time to let him regain his footing. With my useless left arm dangling at my side, I swung the fierce blade in order to disable him with a single blow. His right arm was hewn at the elbow. The axe hit the ground a second time, but now still in the clutches of a body-less arm. The man clasped at his wound where blood poured out like a waterfall. He fell to his knees, crying. He slowly turned onto his side, as if he were turning in for the night, breathing shallowly.

At last I turned to the red-faced skraeling who started all this needless killing. I howled at him. I barked. I roared like my days as a Berserker. One step at a time I limped toward him, the spear stump wobbling, causing intense anguish with each footfall. I thought I would likely die when the astonished vain man remembered to launch another one of his missiles in my direction. He never did such a thing, though. He threw his bow into the boat then pushed the craft into the water. It was light and danced across the pebbles into the surf in mere moments. He ran two steps with it into the sea before jumping in on his knees and paddling away.

Unmoving, I watched him for a long time while he struggled to control the boat on his own in the unforgiving waves. After a long time he was gone, slapping a path to the south and west past an island that sat in the harbor.

When I could no longer see him I looked down at my leg. The gaping wound burned greatly. The blood-flow had slowed somewhat. It was already starting to darken to a deeper brown-red. My left hand was splattered with my own blood, dangling uselessly at my side. A congealed drop hung from my ring finger where I still wore my wedding band from Kenna. I moved the finger which sent a blinding jolt of pain throughout my arm.

I leaned heavily on my sword, using it to pivot around to walk toward the men I had fought. My movement was slow and unstable. It took several minutes just to reach the last man I killed. His face, which used to be ruddy, was now drained of color. A pool of the poor young man's blood gathered around the stub of his arm which jutted out from his shoulder.

Next I reached the man I had run my sword through. He yet lived. He cried and mumbled incomprehensible words, repeating them over and over. With great pain and effort, I knelt to him and held his hand. It occurred to me to get his axe so I rolled to where it lay, still grasped in the severed hand of his companion. The dying warrior nodded his appreciation through panting groans when I forced the weapon into his hand. He died shortly thereafter, life vanishing from his eyes.

Finally, I crawled to Kitchi. I marveled at the peaceful expression that remained on his face despite his abrupt, tragic death at the hands of his own men. Kitchi was older than I originally thought, perhaps thirty summers had passed in his life. Now there would be no more battles for him. Kitchi likely had a wife who would grieve when she heard the news of his death. He likely had children, perhaps a boy of twelve or thirteen years old who would miss his father's hunts. A tear formed in my own eye. We would have been good friends. I hoped to meet him in Valhalla or the Lord's heaven one day.

I could feel my mind slipping out of consciousness as I saw that Kitchi still held my comb tightly in his hand. I put my own hand atop his, squeezing it tightly around the ivory. The last thing I remember before passing out was the sound of voices calling. I swore they called my name.

. . .

Leif had often told me how our fight with the skraelings all those years ago in Greenland could have been avoided with intelligence or cunning. It was our own fault, he said, for not understanding how to avoid the conflict. I think Leif was wrong. Some things happen no matter how perceptive you may be.

Olaf was going to be defeated no matter what I warned him about. He grew careless when he followed the evil fork-tongued man from Wendland. Kenna would die no matter what efforts I put in, no matter how diligent Sif the midwife would be. I would kill those skraelings that day on the pebbled beach no matter what smile or comb or other gift I brought to them. The One God's Providence willed it. The three Norns spun it. Their will mattered, not mine. I needed only to accept what fate or doom struck me.

For a season, I seized upon my destiny while exacting revenge in the fjords of Greenland. But that was no longer than a moon or two. My life quickly returned to what I had grown to expect. Fate was thrust upon me.

These are the first thoughts that swam in my mind as I recovered from my wounds. My eyes fluttered open to see a roof made of wood timbers, blanketed with birch bark, and covered with sod. The wood was fresh for it did not have the distinctive black soot covering that came with the normal aging of a longhouse. I turned my head to scan the room, shaking the cobwebs from my mind. The room looked familiar, like the longhouse I helped Leif build in Leifsbudir. A fire burned quietly in the central hearth, its smoke idly creeping along the peak to find its way to freedom through the smoke hole.

Then a musical humming touched my ears. Really it touched me to the very soul often talked about by the One God. So melodious was it that I knew I would love whoever uttered the sound. The sound grew closer, and I saw Gudrid enter the room humming an old song about a woman mourning the loss of her warrior chief husband.

Surely death had claimed me. Only I was not in Valhalla, the raucous hall where men sang and drank with the one-eyed Odin. This must be Christ's heaven, his paradise. I remember thinking that I was happy with the change from my daily life as well as pleased that I would not be in the drinking hall. Oddly enough, I can almost say I was at total peace with my death. I was brought here to live with Gudrid for eternity.

Then the thought occurred to me that if I was in heaven then Gudrid, too, must be dead. I gasped audibly which caused the woman to look in my direction. She dropped the black iron kettle she carried, smiling despite the water which splashed down her red dress.

We looked at each other for a moment. Then without a word, we both moved to greet one another. I quickly discovered that I was not in heaven for the pain in my leg and arm caused me to tumble back to the bed platform, exclaiming several curses. Gudrid came to my side, and we embraced. My left arm was held in place by a splint, but still I lifted the cumbersome device from the bed and smothered the woman as we kissed.

No words passed between us as she slowly pulled my covers back while simultaneously lifting her clothing up and over her head. I was only somewhat surprised that her desire for me matched my own desire for her, such had been our connection while in Greenland. I discovered that I wore no trousers so she was able to gently lower herself onto my aroused manhood. With a hard swallow by both of us I found myself inside her.

When I made love to Kenna, I had to fight all my aggressive impulses because of her physical frailty. With Gudrid that day, it was she who fought allowing her passion to run like the wolves of the forest. Each time her movement rose to a crescendo, a small wince brought on by the pain I felt in my leg brought her back to a slow rhythmic motion. I wished that pace went on forever, but I was soon exhausted from my injuries and finished spilling my seed into her. She closed her eyes as if my seed's entry gave her additional pleasure.

I took this silent time to study the woman who would be my wife. Her golden hair was lush like a carefully tended garden. It carried more curl than I remembered it having when I last saw her. The ends of the flaxen locks turned upwards in a gentle caress of her erect nipples. Her breasts were those of the dreams of mature men. They were not the large tits like those of Freydis, for they captivated men when their whiskers were yet new. We all thought we wanted more breasts. They were not like the small firm breasts of Kenna. Gudrid's chest was ample, but fell between the two extremes. I reached up with my good arm and lightly ran a finger over one of them in a circular motion. My finger then worked its way down past her ribs and across her stomach where she had two beautiful, prominent moles that formed a line angling away from her navel.

Eventually my fingers made it to her legs where they quickly slipped between. She lifted herself off to lie next to me while I ensured that the woman had more pleasure despite my exhaustion. I had never done such a thing before, and I think Gudrid had not had this happen because at first she gave an uncertain glance. But soon those eyes quivered closed. Watching her body writhe as she experienced a last burst of ecstasy was one of the most delightful experiences of my life.

When we finished making love, we pulled the covers back over top of us and held each other. Still we spoke not. I tried to stay awake to relive the moment again and again – to dream of our future, but sleep came swiftly as if I had been on a days-long hunt, ceaselessly tracking my quarry.

By the time I awoke the sun had begun to set. The sky through the smoke hole looked like the red of dusk. To my left, I saw that Gudrid was awake watching me while leaning upon her hand. She wore only a smile of regret or sadness.

"What is it?" I asked. "Why do you stare at me?"

"You were a good husband to Kenna, I'm sure," was her answer.

I wanted to roll toward her, but my leg prevented me from doing so. Instead I reached across to her face, moving a shock of her thick hair. Afterward I set my large hand atop her temple. "And I'll make a good one to another woman soon," I said, slowly rocking her head.

"You will," she said in a far away tone.

"And I'll make certain that I spend time in the longhouse to see that children come in the springtime." I chuckled at my own joke.

Gudrid crawled out from under our cover and began to dress herself. "I'm sure you will." Tears came down her unblemished cheeks. To this day I do not understand the feelings of women. We had been separated for two full years, then upon reuniting we joined our bodies, but now she cried.

"What is it?" I asked again.

This time Gudrid ignored my question while she finished clasping her brooches at her shoulders. She then found a comb on a nearby shelf, running it though her hair.

"Gudrid," I said with slight firmness. "What is going on with you? Why do you not speak to me? After all we are to be wed soon. Without asking, I can tell you want it to be so."

It was good that Providence had given me a weak body that day. If I had been in complete health, I would have gotten up and shook the woman, she frustrated me so.

When she finished combing out her hair she began to slowly, tightly wrap it into braids. I watched her in uncomprehending silence as she tied her hair into two taut bundles which she then wound atop her crown. Gudrid then stood before me with her hands on her hips with the appearance of anger having replaced the sadness.

Astonished, I asked, "You're married?" Only untethered women wear their hair draping about their shoulders.

Gudrid gave a terse nod.

"When? To whom?"

Then her emotions which had clearly been brewing together for some time boiled into an angry spout. "Who are you to ask who I choose to marry? I did not see you for two years. What was I to do? Would you have me turn to an old maid while I wait on you? Should I have hoped that you would come running back to me so I could replace the good man Thorstein with an adopted member of Erik's family?" She remained frozen with those hands on her hips, hips which just hours ago had been atop my own. Now her foot tapped rapidly on the packed earthen floor.

I mustered a weak, "Yes, I had hoped you would wait."

Then the crying started again. Through her tears she uttered, "Well, I wanted it too. But my life is not my own. Fate constantly intervenes to give me what it will. Do you think I wanted Thorstein to die in his own sweat? Though I accept the new God of Leif and the king, I do not think he enjoys sweeping the plans of men away any less than the old gods." Gudrid plopped her behind down on the hearth, setting her face into one hand while the other hand balled into a fist and repeatedly hit the stones beneath her.

I rolled onto my back and stretched my arms toward the ceiling. My *Charging Boar* tattoo reminded me that I too was a subject of the whims of royal Fate. All I could do was sigh while I moved my hands to support my head. Not sure what to say next I said, "We are all implements – play things of the gods."

My tired platitude did nothing to improve her mood. Gudrid let out an angry shout before saying with resignation, "Last summer, the year Leif returned, a man named Thorfinn Karlsefni came to Greenland from Iceland. He's a rich merchant and well liked. Shortly after the Yule, I mean Christmas, celebration, he asked Erik for my hand in marriage. Erik agreed without consulting me."

"Why didn't you just offer up a protest? Erik is not so harsh, especially in his age, as to force a woman to marry."

"How could I do such a thing? He took me in after I could not save his son, Thorstein, from death. He became steward of my father's estate, Stokknes, when my parents died. How could I oppose the wishes of a man who had done so much for me?"

And there it was, I thought. Gudrid and I were a perfect match for one another. We were both so resigned to our obligations and the destiny which wound around them that we, she and I, were identical. But so bastardized were our fates that the perfect match made it impossible for us to find ourselves together. Shit, was all I thought next.

"You're right," I said, stating the obvious. "You had no choice. Because you are a good woman, you had no choice."

The darkness began to fill in around us so that I just saw her silhouette against the tired flames. Leif had been wrong, I thought. Staying here to mind Leifsbudir only prevented my wedding, it did not ensure it. But I had obeyed my friend and leader. My fate.

"Erik lives?" I finally asked when I accepted the fact that there was no more to say on the matter.

"No, he died some weeks ago. His health had been in decline for most of the last year. He never really came back from his tumble from the horse the day you left."

Well at least Leif was right about one thing. "Did Leif rescue more men on his return trip?"

Gudrid looked up and through the dim light I saw surprise on her face, "How did you know that?"

I huffed a chuckle, not bothering to answer. So Leif had been right about two things.

Talking and laughing from far away outside the longhouse caused me to tilt my head. Gudrid just said, "The others are returning."

"Others? By the way, how do you find yourself here alone with me?" I asked.

Gudrid rose, beginning to stoke the fire. She set about preparing the meal she was likely to have already finished. "Yes, there are many others. One hundred forty came on three ships. They've been busy adding more houses and fence to Leifsbudir since we came here over a week ago. Several men went out in search of you and came back after two days. You've been unconscious for about five days after your fight with the skraelings. I volunteered to nurse you back to health while everyone else worked on bringing down trees or hunting or fishing."

"Is Karlsefni here too?"

"Of course he is. He wouldn't miss a chance to find new trading territories. He's out with the others."

"Then how does he let you walk about with your hair spilling out like an unmarried woman?"

"He doesn't," was Gudrid's quick reply. "Each day when I was sure everyone would be gone for a time, I unbundled my hair to pretend that I was still eligible to be wooed when you awoke." Her face was illuminated by the steadily growing flames. "It was a foolish thing to do, I know."

"Perhaps it was, but I'm glad you did. It allowed us to be together at least once."

Gudrid smiled while the voices outside grew louder. Some began to head toward the cove where the ships were probably moored. Another group filed into the longhouse where Gudrid and I had spent the last few hours.

The first man through the door was unfamiliar to me. He was a beast of a man – almost as tall as I but with even broader shoulders and a belly that said he provided well for himself. He had a great mass of dusty wheat colored hair encircling his weather-worn face. His eyes were a bright green and immediately showed an adventurous side to the man. He tossed a bloodied spear into a corner with a hand as big as a shield.

"Gudrid, my dear!" he shouted. "I've killed one. I killed one of those monsters that carry antlers like those hanging there on the wall." He pointed to the moose antlers I had mounted in the home when Leif was still in Vinland. "By God that thing was fierce. But I brought it down with my spear and my spear only. None of this bow and arrow goat crap for me!"

Ignoring his boast, Gudrid said, "Thorfinn, Halldorr's awake. I think he has a lot of strength left in him!" She said the last with a twinkle in her eye that only I noticed.

Thorfinn Karlsefni turned his enormous head my way, flashing a genuine grin. His golden beard carried a single braid that was entangled with the rest of the hair dangling on his chest. The braid was adorned with a bright red bit of cloth at the end. The man marched to the platform where I lay – where his wife, Gudrid, had lain only minutes ago – and crouched to my side. He grabbed my good arm and shook it mightily saying, "I am so glad to see you awake, lad!" He said the last even though I was sure he was younger than I. He continued, "I've heard nothing but great things about you from Erik and Leif, everyone really."

"Not from me!" This was said by Erik's old sporting companion, Thorhall the Huntsman, who had just walked in.

"You never say anything nice about anyone you old shriveled tit!" retorted Thorfinn. "And I only just met you in the past year."

The Huntsman grumbled something inaudible while stowing his gear along the wall. Thorfinn returned his attention to me, "So everyone who counts spoke highly of you. But then I come here and you are nowhere to be found. I thought that was not like the descriptions of you so Thorvald and some men tracked you down.

Here you were playing dress up with some skraelings – what with your combs and everything – and things got out of hand. Did one take a dislike to you when you expressed your true feelings for him?" This last caused him to let out a jumbo laugh. The generally grumpy Huntsman snorted his approval. Gudrid smiled sweetly at her new husband.

I liked the man. And I could see he would be good with Gudrid. I felt a small pang of guilt over what she and I had just done, but decided that the past could not be unwound. I shrugged it off as Thorvald, Leif's oldest and only remaining brother, came in with some men I recognized but whose names I did not recall.

Thorfinn sprang to his feet and inquired of Gudrid as to the whereabouts of dinner. She thought quickly on her feet saying, "I was so surprised by Halldorr's recovery that I did not help with any preparations. He needed his bandages replaced." That explanation sounded reasonable to Thorfinn who shouted outside to his thralls who cleaned the moose to find some dinner for us all.

After eating a meal of fried eggs and cheese like a ravenous wolf, I propped myself up against the wall of the longhouse to hear all the news and stories about life in Greenland and Iceland since I left. After Erik's passing, Leif had assumed the role of jarl of Greenland. He was popular among those he ruled despite his past banishment. This year would be his first chance to run the Thing at Fridr Rock. I smiled as I heard stories of several of the disputes he had already been called to judge. My favorite involved a wealthy widow, a bull, and a jealous neighbor woman. One of the two people in that story ended up naked lashed atop the bull, but I forget which one.

Each year settlers continued to arrive to the frigid land my second father first discovered, sometimes two or three boats at a time. Many of the far reaches of Eystribyggo's fjords were now claimed by the existing Norse Greenlanders so Leif was sending the newcomers to Vestribyggo to further colonize that more remote settlement.

Trade with Iceland and the mother land of Norway continued to flourish. Timber of all sorts generally made the long journey from Norway to Iceland. Many enterprising merchants held back some of the stock from the Iceland market in order to continue on to the more lucrative, and desperate, Greenland market. Many men, Thorfinn among them, hoped to find a ready supply of trees to fell in closer proximity. Markland, to the north, fit that need perfectly, but for now, Thorfinn and the rest were content to spend time further exploring the new lands Leif had discovered.

When I asked if trade had been affected by Forkbeard's ruling of Norway as his vassal state, the individuals around the hearth just shrugged and tried to move on to more fun tales. However, the mentioning of Sweyn Forkbeard reminded Thorvald that he had a package from King Olaf for me. My face was incredulous, for how could the king who was hiding in the Holy Land see that a package was delivered all the way around the world to me in Vinland?

But he did send me a package along with a letter written in his own hand using the runes of our people. Thorvald went to the sleeping platform on the opposite side of the hearth, pulled a small, tightly packed hudfat from underneath, and plopped the heavy bag across my legs. I nearly jumped out of my skin from the pain, but withheld a scream, clenching my teeth. I eagerly untied the drawstring, loosening the top of the bag. Olaf's neatly folded letter toppled out first. I moved to open it for immediate reading, but the eyes of all were on me and they protested, demanding to see the gifts.

Setting the letter to the side I pulled out the pelt of a strange beast with tan fur speckled with black spots. This caused a stir among my companions as they passed it around, holding it up in the firelight. Out next, came a handsome suit of mail. Olaf remembered that I lost my brilliantly expensive chain coat in the sea battle with Sweyn. In fact, I had lost two suits while serving my king. Since then I had used the chain mail that I had carried with me for countless years, old, rusted, and sporting broken links. The new suit had long sleeves, extended to my knees, and even had a separate hood of chain to place under a helmet. It was heavy, perhaps forty-five pounds, as I held it out with my good arm. Its shine was gone from the long journey likely completed amidst rain, fog, snow, and the sea-salt air. However, a vigorous scrubbing from a thrall would have it back to perfect condition.

Out next came a small bag gathered with string, holding some gold trinkets and coins with a flowing script form of writing unknown to me stamped across them. Finally, I reached deep into the sack to pull out the last item. It was box-like and wrapped in a sturdy leather purse. Pulling back the covering revealed a book! Olaf had been the one to force me to learn my letters under Crevan's tutoring. I smiled to myself remembering how I initially bristled at the command. However, I had grown to love reading and writing, and my third father must have seen that for I never said anything to him.

This new book was written in the language of the long dead Romans, Latin. I was thankful for that had become the word in which I was most proficient. I opened the well-worn cover to reveal words closely packed on the pages. There was no artwork, other than the penmanship of the writer. It was the detailed drawing in my first book that even compelled me to keep it. Now I jumped from page to page in this book, not missing pictures in the slightest. How I had changed.

The onlookers quickly tired of me paging through the book and returned to their chattering. But Thorvald again had his simple memory jogged by a mention of Leif and reached into a pocket hidden beneath his jerkin to pull out bit of wrinkled parchment. He threw it atop the book opened on my lap saying simply, "I was to give you that too."

Leif, too, had sent me a letter. The parchment had originally been rolled up, but Thorvald had probably found it cumbersome to transport it in that manner, so I had to pick away at the creases in the letter to reveal Leif's words. They were few, and what was there was written in runes.

Halldorr, Jarl of Vinland, Good Steward of all Properties of Erik, Dear Brother, I conveyed your words to our father, Erik. He expressed his pleasure in having you as an adopted son before his passing.

I thank you for staying in Vinland. By now you know that Gudrid is wed. Please know that my vision remains true. You will wed. It was necessary that you stay in Tyrkr's land of the grapes.

Thorfinn is a good man. I like him. Please help Thorvald in all his endeavors; he will need a good advisor.

Your Brother in Christ, Leif

"I'll go farther than Leif and farther than Thorstein ever went," Thorvald was shouting as I finished Leif's note. The mention of our two brothers piqued my interest, and I returned to the conversation.

"What was that, Thorvald?" I asked.

"I said that I will explore farther from home than any of Erik's sons have before. I'm taking my ship next spring and going to claim more and better land than this!"

"Oh," was my only response.

"I was happy to serve my father for many years while on Greenland, but that place is now Leif's land. He has his son, Thorgils, to pass it onto. I do not intend to serve behind my brother and his snot-faced son. I'll claim land for us, for our new God, and bring Gro there to rule with me."

I remembered Leif's request in his letter that I was to be a helper to Thorvald. I wondered just how much of my fellow exile's appeal was part of his visions. I said, "Then count me among your crew." In many ways Thorvald had always lived in his more prominent brothers' shadows, even though he was the oldest. He had been a reliable hunter and provider to his wife and a reliable aid to his father, but Thorstein's wit and Leif's intelligence outshined any and all of Thorvald's deeds. I looked forward to helping the man, now in his late thirties, in making a name for himself, to step out from the shadows of his accomplished brothers.

Thorhall the Huntsman piped up from his place in the corner while he rocked back and forth on the legs of a short stool, "I'll be with you, Thorvald Eriksson. Even though you are even more of a turd than your father, I must go to be rid of all these women." His head pointed to Gudrid. We all, even Gudrid, laughed at the curmudgeon's words.

Karlsefni raised a mug of ale exclaiming, "To exploring a new world. May it be profitable to you, Thorvald!"

The night finished like that, much boasting and ale drinking, though as I stated in my first writing, I gave up drinking to excess following my drunkenness after Kenna's death. My awakening that day was being used as an excuse for an impromptu celebration. One by one, sleep came to the others in the longhouse. Even Thorfinn and Gudrid retired to their place next to one another on the platform. I watched them with only a tinge of regret as they snuggled. He would make a good husband, and I had to admit that, like Leif, I liked the man.

Eventually there were only two of us left with our eyes open. Thorhall the Huntsman babbled on about how he would make a name for himself one day. He speculated that he would end up taking a long journey that no one had ever before conceived. I silently looked at the old man's dark complexion and sullen expression, thinking that his time had passed long ago. But I liked him too. He was honest to his thoughts, unafraid to give his opinion, which put him in high stead in my estimation.

When the Huntsman's chin finally lay on his chest, I impatiently lifted Olaf's letter from the bench and held it in the fading firelight. I wanted it to be for me only.

Halldorr, Captain of the King's Guard, Faithful Warrior, Dear Son, I write this letter to you in my own hand mere months from my arrival in Jerusalem. I have had much regret in my heart since we were forced to part company. I fear that I was not the king the One God wished I would be. You and I led many to His Name, but my leadership ultimately failed in securing a free Norse. Now our people are subjects to the rarely sober Forkbeard. How pitiful I feel in this regard.

However, you should know that my heart also has bouts of extreme elation. I think about your service to me and the Norse. I think of your unfailing dedication to that thrall boy and how we may have won at Maldon as a result of him. You are wise beyond what you choose to exhibit, dear son. You should know that your life until now has demonstrated nothing but exceptional judgment, except perhaps your fondness for me. When you are given the opportunity to lead men, please seize it, they will be the better for it.

The One God has seen fit to present me with more than I need at this time. The Holy Land is a marvelous place with more skin colors of men than I knew existed. The hide I included in this package is from a cat-like beast called a leopard. I saw a living one at a traveling carnival just last week. It comes from the land south, beyond the Red Sea.

Unfortunately, I know you will find a good use for the coat of mail. I still laugh to myself when I think about how one of your suits nearly caused you to drown because you could not hang on to the prow of your own ship. I recall you did manage to hang on to your father's old saex which speaks volumes of your character.

As you can likely tell, the coins are of high value. They are solid gold and stamped with words in the Arabic language honoring one of their gods called Allah. They are a curious people, even claiming some of the patriarchs of the Jewish faith as their own. But despite that, they seem to exhibit open hostility toward both Jews and Christians alike. I fear I may find myself in battle against them one day.

The Holy Land is a wonderful place of learning and many books. It seems as if there are more books here than water. The people must live on the words that sprout from the vellum. This reminds me of the One God's word saying that man does not live on bread alone. Certainly, on my journey here, I needed my faith more than I needed a meal. For years, I observed your love of the written word and hope you find my gift appealing. It is the text of the One God's word before he sent his glorious Son, Jesus the Christ to us.

With Fondness, Your Father, Olaf Tryggvason

I read the letter over and over that night, parsing every word. The package took three years to reach me. The amount of time was not the surprising part; it was that the package arrived at all. It would have changed hands many times on the journey, each time a chance for thievery. I have never learned of the path my gifts from Olaf took, I only know they came and gave me a feeling of satisfaction.

When the moon was long past the smoke hole, I at last placed my head down on the platform to rest. I fell asleep that night thinking of my meeting with the One God from some days ago. I thought of my letters from Leif and Olaf. I smiled and knew with certainty that the One God would make my life my own one day.

. . .

The summer passed us by while the new arrivals to Leifsbudir expanded its boundaries by clearing trees. The clack, clack of the men's axes sang loudly. The logs they harvested were stacked in one of Thorfinn's knarrs and sent back to Greenland later that year. He had gold in his eyes each time I saw him talk of trading the logs in treeless Eystribyggo.

The newcomers even dug a shallow ditch to drain part of the surrounding area to the creek to make for a drier plain. I thought this very wise now that so many Norse were there for it would allow for a clearer field of vision to protect the village from attack. I am sure that Thorfinn just thought it would make better pasture or farmland if the bogs were gone, but I still thought like a military man. Whatever the best justification for the project, I envisioned a Leifsbudir teeming with Norse in several years. The thought seemed entirely logical at the time. After all, in my life alone, I had witnessed the expansion of a Norse population on Iceland, the founding of a Norse civilization in Greenland, and the planting of a new city in the Norwegian wilderness. I rightly thought it inevitable that Norse would cover the earth. We were warriors, merchants, sailors. Who could halt our progress?

It wasn't until very late in the autumn when I finally had the strength to move about the settlement without the aid of a crutch. My arm healed very nicely, feeling even stronger to me than before the break. However, the healing of my leg was another story altogether. It was so badly damaged following the skraeling attack that I had to retrain myself to walk, concentrating on the movement of each step. Many weeks after the wound finally closed up for good I was still weak. The left leg eventually recovered most of its strength; however I still walk with a slight limp to this day. Most people cannot tell, unless they know how tall and proud I walked before the incident.

Some of the men went exploring to the west that summer. They found more land, but the only report of any value they passed on was that they discovered a wooden grain trough on the shore of one of the lands. It had obviously been built by human hands, but they saw no other sign of skraelings.

Winter fell upon us. It was mild compared to many we had seen, but the icy wind bit. On days when the temperature varied greatly, my leg and arm throbbed somewhat, though not enough to inhibit my movement.

Christmas came and went. We all celebrated our new holiday now. Thorhall the Huntsman was the lone holdout. When we gathered for a large feast to celebrate the birth of the Christ, he stayed in another one of the newly constructed longhouses and drank until he passed out. Before-hand he even wanted to show his displeasure with the new faith so much that he went to the extent of killing his own horse and using a hlautteinar to douse himself in the animal's blood. He spoke his own words to the old gods in the outdoors just outside the main longhouse, just so that we could hear him. However, his plan failed because the bustling celebration inside deadened his calls. I only know of his attempt because I went outside to relieve myself and could only laugh at the irritable man.

As we passed the equinox, Vinland began to spring to life. Birds I had not seen since the year past returned from wherever they had gone. I helped Thorvald provision his ship for the journey of discovery we would embark on in several weeks. My old companions from Leif's original journey here, Folkvar and Arnkell, would join us. And Gudrid, who had spent the winter with an ever-growing belly, gave birth to a son. He was certainly passable for Thorfinn's boy, but his eyes and Gudrid's look told me he was mine, sprung from my seed. I now had a son – one of the joys of life I had spent years trying to bring into the world.

He was mine, but I would never be able to call him my own, of course. I soothed my feelings by thinking that one day, when he was of age, I might take him hunting with me deep into the forest and tell him the truth. I would tell him that I loved his mother. I would tell him that I loved his father, though I wasn't certain of this at the time. I would tell him that I was a part of him – that the blood of a Berserker coursed through his veins.

The boy was born large, likely weighing a fjordungr or more. He was bald except for three stray hairs that remained plastered to his shining head the first time I saw him. Thorfinn named the lad Snorri, after two men who shared the name. One man was his long dead grandfather; the other was his closest friend, Snorri the Elder, son of Thorbrand, who had come with him all the way from Iceland. In fact, the son of Thorbrand was there next to me while I looked at his namesake with pride.

"I see a tear in your eye, Halldorr," he whispered to me while Thorfinn talked with those gathered to see the baby.

Wiping it away, I confessed, "Aye, he's a strong boy. I had hoped to have my own boy by now." Gudrid and her husband Thorfinn nodded in understanding.

Snorri the Elder tapped my shoulder, "You don't want that, old man. The brats just die when they come from such seed as old as yours. And what woman young enough to bear children would have you?"

I am certain now that he meant only humor by his remark, but that day I would have none of his joke. So I created an enemy. With my fist balled into a rock-like fierceness, I cracked him on his nose without warning. Snorri the Elder fell onto his ass with blood streaming from his now broken nose. He jumped up to face me but found himself on the ground, lying on his back when I punched him again in the broken nose. When he tried to return to his feet unsuccessfully yet again, Thorfinn spoke in a matter-of-fact tone, "Snorri, friend, I think the man means for you to stay down. You would be wise to obey his commands. He is after all, the leader of this busy camp." I huffed to myself, thinking I had no more control over this camp than I did my own fate.

The bloodied Snorri just looked at me with contempt. His own tears from the tremendous pain I had administered to his face were mixed with the blood to make quite a mess. My eyes burned a hole through his face while I returned the stare. Pointing to my chest with a thumb, I said, "You would be wise to listen to this old man, you whimpering, castrated sheep!" Then I turned and gave the new parents and baby Snorri a heartfelt, "Congratulations to you all. May the boy be a blessing from the One God to you for all your days, Thorfinn." I bowed and walked away without another word.

As I limped away, I heard Thorfinn groan while he lent a hand to pull Snorri the Elder to his feet. "Snorri," said Thorfinn, "I like that man. He is wise at times and strong always, but most of all he is faithful. He is an adopted son of Erik and a brother to Leif and Thorvald. I expect no disagreements between the two of you." Snorri's attempt to protest was immediately cut off by Thorfinn, "Quiet. Now go see that a thrall tends to your face. You're dripping blood all over my wife's blanket."

A satisfied smile curled behind my blonde beard as I made my way to Thorvald's ship, *Glorious Discovery*, to finalize preparations for our voyage.

CHAPTER 7

Thorvald recently changed the name of his ship to *Glorious Discovery*. He bestowed it with the new moniker just before they came to Vinland, wanting it to convey all of his hopes and dreams for this journey, but also to express his vigorous support of the new faith in the One God. I thought the new name a bit overstated; the Huntsman absolutely despised it. I liked simple names taken from tangible goods or powerful creatures. Some of my favorites from the past were my own *Charging Boar*, Olaf's *Long Serpent* and *The Crane*, *The Goat*, et cetera. I often thought that if given the opportunity to name another vessel, I would call her *Leviathan*. Most boats should be named after an animal, and the beast from the tales of our new god seemed fitting enough. *Glorious Discovery* was originally called *Floating Louse* when he acquired it from an old settler who no longer had a need for long travels. I do not jest about its initial name. I would never have thought of such a designation myself, so I appreciate its creativity, while simultaneously cringing at the thought.

We sliced through the water with the oars stowed at mid-deck in their T-shaped rack, as the dirty blue sail billowed with invisible wind to push us on our way. Befitting the new name for his ship, Thorvald had his wife Gro and other women from the Greenland settlement sew on a black cross in the center of the sail's cloth before embarking. In a plain demonstration of the haste they must have put into the project, the cross sat a full one and one-half ells off-center. Additionally, one of the lateral arms was already pulling free, now flapping in the breeze and making a constant slapping sound that I found quite irritating. Thorvald ignored its imperfections and often looked up proudly to his wife's work. Love! Hah!

Thorfinn did not join us on this voyage. Around the mead table one night, he informed me that he would stay behind with his wife and new son. A curious decision, I thought, for I had never heard of a man staying home when the sea or adventure called, but on the deck that day while at the steering oar of *Glorious Discovery*, Thorfinn's judgment seemed sound. How many more days could I have had with my Kenna if I had just come to a similar conclusion? Would I now be married to the fair and strong Gudrid if I made the choice rather than coming with Leif to Vinland? I shrugged to myself, as I have often done when thinking of the past while questioning my actions. Such activity made no sense so I pushed it from my mind.

Thorfinn would go a-Viking, however, this very year. He told me he would sail in the opposite direction that Thorvald chose to go, but Thorfinn would leave later in the summer when he was confident all was well with Gudrid and little Snorri.

I was not certain if I would be back in Leifsbudir to see him off given my current trip. But, I was assured that Thorfinn would go west and south because Thorvald pointed *Glorious Discovery* north and east as we let the tide lift us from the sandy earth beneath the waves. That had been six days ago.

We were thirty-one men in total. The five women who now inhabited Leifsbudir had stayed behind, making Thorhall very happy indeed. He showed his joy by singing songs to the old gods while holding onto the lion figurehead on the prow as we cut through the surf. The Huntsman left his own ship sitting on the bank back at Leifsbudir, awaiting his return. The men on this particular voyage were all very close to one another, all having come from the fjords of Eystribyggo. I had known almost all of them at one time in my life, but my years of exile had made it difficult for me to relate to them. I found it difficult to relate to most men. Thorvald was very much like my own flesh and blood, so I loved him like my brother. Yet I found myself drawn to the self-isolated Thorhall as my closest friend onboard, despite the generally unkind words that he often sent in my direction.

As I have said, when we left Leifsbudir, we sailed north around the point of land where Leif and I supposedly drank the sweet dew from the grasses with our hands. Thorvald then pointed us in a southeast direction. We maintained that heading for four days, camping on land one or two of the nights, before finding that the land turned abruptly to the west. Slowly we changed our heading to keep the Vinland within eyesight so that we now sailed almost due west. After another day or two we lost sight of the land, as it fell off our starboard quarter, yet continued on our way.

On the sixth day I had been watching an ominous set of clouds rolling toward us from the southwest when Thorhall's song from the prow suddenly halted. "Land!" he shouted. "Port bow!" Squinting, I confirmed that at the horizon's edge was a dark mass that must be land. After his announcement Thorhall plopped down on the raised deck of the bow and jammed a cold piece of smoked fish into his mouth, satisfied that he had seen the new land first. I gave him a nod and smile, to which he gave a silent reply of a hand gesture considered vulgar among my people.

A flash from the clouds I was observing told me a thunderstorm was approaching. Within moments the land we had so briefly seen was enveloped by the coming weather, disappearing as if it had never been.

Thorvald shouted from the beam, "Halldorr, make your course to that land. I mean to explore it."

"We may want to lower our cloth to protect it from the storm," I yelled as the first wind from the gale smacked me in the face like a dive into the fjord.

Thorvald leaned out to look ahead to where the land was visible only moments ago. "I think not," he said. "The land was just ahead, we'll be able to beat the worst of the storm and wait it out on shore."

I merely nodded, but was forced to turn the rudder to the right then, after a time, to the left to fight the wind's new heading. Despite the excitement of navigating against the wind, a feeling of anticipation set in. When a sailor shouts, "Land," it is often tempting to think that the land is nearly upon you. However, a man's eye, even one as old as the Huntsman's eye, can see quite far. It would be several hours more before we would slide into the beach. Normally, when serving Olaf, we would have spent the time tending our weapons with a whetstone and securing our mail. There would be no time for the mind to build in expectations. Not so this day.

. . .

After two hours of cutting our zigzag path in the quickly roughening seas, Thorvald finally agreed to lower our sail. Except for more of Gro's cross tearing away, no real damage was done to the cloth up to that point. Our westward progress was simply negligible because of the need to constantly change tack in the face of the storm. The driving rain had begun; the day had become black as night. Just as the men put their backs into the first several rounds of rowing, a frightening crack sounded, not from above in the clouds, but below the waves. It was accompanied by a temporary halt in our forward progress, sending more than one man to the deck, myself included.

Then as quickly as it came, the sound and arrest in our movement passed. But I knew what happened. We had hit a rock or shoal close to the water's surface. The prow now sat at an abnormal angle to the direction we drove the ship, implying that the stem had likely been badly damaged. Within moments, I was shouting at the men fore of the mast to pull up the planking on which they stood. Doing so, they found that we were taking on seawater in the bilge.

Panic hit the men. To his credit, Thorvald remained calm, but it was clear he didn't know what we should do. A din of voices all shouting different words at the same time made understanding impossible. Luckily, Thorhall took charge of the men at the prow while I commanded those men aft, from my position at the rudder. The Huntsman screamed above the terrorized crew, naming five men to procure rope-handled wooden buckets from the hold, and begin bailing. He put two more to work at finding any cookware or the like to provide for more bailing vessels. Finally, Thorhall had two of the biggest men, Njordr and Volundr, walk shin-deep in the water spilling in to lift the large ballast stones that had been wedged between the boat's ribs at its launching many years before. These last two worked together on wavering legs in the pitching seas to lift the back-breaking rocks. One was so heavy they had to roll it slowly, one grueling step at a time, up the ribs and over the gunwale. Eventually, their concerted effort showed true progress and our bow seemed to level off, no longer plunging toward the sea's bottom.

Compared to Thorhall's fight, mine was much less difficult. I needed to shout words of instruction and encouragement to the men who remained on their aft rowing benches. The instruction was necessary as I could see the swells which came toward us while the rowers, who faced me, could not. The encouragement, of course, was needed because the men's faces told me they feared a certain death as they fought to control *Glorious Discovery* in the tossing waters.

I, too, thought we would all swallow the salty water, so I did something to take my mind off our troubles. My voice rang out above the roar of the storm to sing a rowing song we used to sing while serving Olaf. It was unfamiliar to the men so that more than a few tilted their heads, giving me a questioning glance, a unique sight among the chaos. After two rounds singing solo, first Folkvar, then Arnkell, then all the men, even those bailing with Thorhall, joined me in the song. A full hour passed while we sang the song over and again, remaining focused on our individual tasks, before we crept within sight of the dark shore.

Soon, and with little fanfare we slid into shore on a narrow beach of sand just as the storm abated. The surf still pounded the shore, but the clouds parted to reveal the sun shining brightly. I thought this a tremendous omen after what had just transpired, for we could have all perished the salty death. But now the sun told me that grand adventures were likely to be had on this new land of Thorvald's.

After exchanging uncertain peeks at one another, someone started a chuckle of relief. In short order, the hesitant laugh gained momentum, infecting all the men. Soon backs were slapped and Thorvald was congratulated on getting us to land safely. At that, Thorhall and I passed a half-smile to one another and shook our heads. Such was the life of a captain. He receives the glory for good and the doom for bad.

With the sun now out in full force causing the longboat to steam as the water burnt off her, we were now able to get a better view of the land on which we found ourselves. We sat at the very tip of a long headland extending out to sea. Within ten paces of the lapping sea a dense forest of pines started, blanketing a hillside that quickly sprouted from the beach.

Some of the men began to inspect the damage to the keel as the water leaked out onto the beach, giving them a better view. I did not need to look, for having built two longboats, great warships really, I knew what had to be done.

Picking four of the closest men I said, "You men will be sentries. One go north and one go south a good distance along the beach. You other two go into the forest, spacing yourselves, and keep watch." Without looking to the captain, they strapped their swords, such as they were, to their waists and were off. Command, I thought, when properly executed and obeyed, was quite satisfying. For the first time I was thankful for all that had happened to me in the past. My time serving Olaf, especially, gave me ample opportunity to develop my abilities to lead men. In his letter, Olaf implored me to seize leadership, so I did.

Walking to the next set of men I shouted, "You twenty take axes from the hold, as many as we brought, and begin bringing down straight trees with a diameter about the size of a single spread hand. Clean them of branches and haul the trunks to this shore. We will prepare them further once they arrive. Start with sixty trunks. Njordr will be in charge." I suppose my directions were clear because no one asked any questions. They immediately set about tearing apart the hold to get all the axes stowed there. As they then marched their way into the thick forest of pine I yelled, "And did any of you think to take whetstones to make your work easier?" When they looked sheepishly at one another, I reached into my rucksack, producing mine and my spare. I indicated that any other man with the stones on his person should give them up for the cause.

Then I turned to Thorhall. "Huntsman," I said, "Lead a hunting party to get us some game for dinner tonight." The sour Huntsman gave a curt nod then poked his finger hard into the chests of the three men he wanted to come with him. As they secured their bows and hunting knives, I rolled my eyes saying, "And I suggest you go south so that on your way you can tell that lazy sentry that he should get his fat ox-like ass off that driftwood and move further than fifty paces from the ship."

Thorhall and his group said nothing to me, but finished their preparations, soon leaving. When they were gone, Thorvald crossed his arms with visible disgust. "Halldorr, that was some commanding I just witnessed, but I want to explore. After all, we are on a ship christened *Glorious Discovery*! You've sent all my men away."

Nodding, I began fishing around in my baggage. When I didn't immediately respond Thorvald's frustration with me grew. "I am talking to you, Halldorr!"

When I recovered what I was searching for, I stood up to face Thorvald and the two men left at the ship. "Aye, brother Thorvald, you are talking, but making no sense. We stand on a pile of wood only good for a pyre. Until we get the keel repaired, we best not go poking our nose where it may not belong in case we need to flee."

I adjusted some of the luggage in the hold then plopped down upon it. After sidling my rear into a comfortable position, I leaned back and placed my feet up on a small barrel of ale. I spread my new book across my lap and began to read the text from a page I randomly selected.

"Flee? What could we possibly have to flee from?"

"Deduc me Domine in via tua iustitiae via, dirige in conspectu tuo fac me inimici mei insidiatus," was my cryptic answer.

"What is it you think you are doing?" questioned the now fully exasperated Thorvald.

I made sure to finish the sentence I was now reading silently before answering with a sweeping motion of my hand, "Dear Thorvald, I am standing watch over our very own *Glorious Discovery*."

"Your time away in exile and alone in Vinland has made you impossible to deal with sometimes. I don't understand you." I went back to my reading while Thorvald and the other two stood quietly looking down at me. One of the men became uncomfortable with the silence, so he hummed a little tune. It made me smile as I read. Thorvald told him to shut up.

Sometimes I think back to times like that and feel guilty. I loved Thorvald. He was my older brother and I wanted nothing but good for him. Yet I tortured him that day. I don't know why I did that. I think we torture those we love. At least that is what I tell myself. Eventually he erupted, "By the One God! May Christ himself smite you! What am I to do with all my men gone?"

While carefully turning a page, keeping my eyes fixed on the book, I said, "Thorvald, I do not know what you intend to do, but I do know what you ought to do if you care for a suggestion."

He sighed, "Oh, what is it? Out with it."

"Well, since we are likely to be here for a while, why don't you take these two men and make a camp, using the extra sail cloth for a cover? They can get a fire going and that way when the Huntsman returns we can prepare a feast for all the men who carried out your bidding today."

Another exasperated grunt told me his pride was hurt, but that he agreed. Soon these last three were gone and I had the boat to myself. I began by devouring the words. Within moments I was devouring page after page. Hours slipped by.

. . .

We left the boat where she lay that night. By the time everyone returned to the new camp from hunting deer or felling trees, dusk had settled in. We placed new sentries while we celebrated our safety with fresh venison steaks. Thorvald led us in a prayer of thanksgiving to the One God for delivering us from the storm, ignoring the Huntsman's role. He made many mistakes in his words since he never read anything from the One God, not having known his letters and since he rarely attended Thjordhildr's Church where Torleik the priest now faithfully served. The men did not notice his inaccuracies, however, since they were all new to the faith and also rarely attended the lone church on Greenland.

Following our make-shift feast and prayer vigil I gave instructions for the watch, found a soft patch of earth under the tarp, and slept all the way through to a brilliant morning sun cresting over the horizon atop the sea.

We were busy that day. Njordr and several others helped me cut the logs now strewn across the beach to the length I wanted while Thorhall supervised their placement to the fore of *Glorious Discovery*. We placed them perpendicular to the keel in a manner so that we could use them to roll the ship ashore. Some of the logs were cut for supports to prop her vertically while sliding across the log rollers. We had just enough of the small logs for props, chocks, and stocks to buttress our wounded boat.

Long, heavy ropes were secured to the ship in two places near the bow. We ran them up to the forest, wrapping each once around broad trees to give us the needed leverage. Then we pulled the ship ashore with the massive Njordr and Volundr acting as anchors on each of our ropes. The men dug their feet into the sand while they struggled to get her moving. Eventually she began to inch her way up the log path while I had three helpers with me to move the props as she went. The last several ells of pulling were difficult indeed for we had made a short ramp to help bring the ship up out of the sand to work. When I finally yelled, "Stop," the men had to hold the boat steady while we hurriedly set all the chocks in a more permanent place.

After pausing for a mid-day meal of dried meat and the last of the stale bread, I pointed out how I wanted the damaged portion of the keel removed. Parts of the garboards were damaged too, which would lengthen the time needed to complete the repairs.

I left Thorhall, who had a good head, behind to run this project. Meanwhile, Thorvald and several men accompanied me into the forest to select a tree to splice into our keel. Since we only needed a short section to join into the stem, we did not need to be as particular as old Thorberg Skaffhog had been when selecting trees for the long keels of Olaf's ships. However, we did a fair amount of walking before we came to a small grove of oaks tucked amidst the pines.

From Thorberg's able tutoring I could tell that any of the nearest trees would have been suitable so I did not hesitate when Thorvald slapped one of the trunks, declaring it would be our keel. Two of us worked our axes rhythmically and brought it down. Then all of us pulled out our axes to clean the branches free. Normally we would let the women and children gather these left over pieces for use in cooking fires or other sections of the ship. This time, however, we let them be.

With huge steel wedges, I halved the great tree, splitting it lengthwise. Njordr then quartered the trunk until we had logs the men could handle, while I rested, dripping sweat to the ground. Even though we did not need all of this lumber today, we decided to take it with us to the boat for future use.

Two days of shaping and fitting the replacement sections of the keel and fractured garboards, then a day of coating these new portions with a thick coat of pine tar, and we were finished. In the opposite fashion the boat was brought to shore, she was slowly set back into the sea. With a hammer I knocked the chocks which held her in place while men dug their feet into the sand holding the ropes to lower her back to her salty berth.

Without the fore ballast stones in place, *Glorious Discovery* sat at an awkward angle as she floated in the surf. I would have preferred to balance her while sitting in smooth waters, but I decided that we would do a rough job this day and be more precise in the future. I played the part of Thorberg, the old master shipwright, sending men onto the ship to set large stones amongst the ribs to balance the ship, shouting instructions as to their proper placement based upon my view of the ship.

Thorvald demanded that several of the men who were not thus occupied with any current chores dig a deep hole in the beach near our worksite. I heard their grumbling from behind me, not sure what my adopted brother was up to. When they were finished he had them drag the damaged keel into it so that the massive log stood pointing to the sky. They filled in the hole around the section of the keel and it now looked like a branchless tree growing straight out of the beach.

Thorvald smiled while admiring his commissioned artwork. Our two crews finished their work simultaneously so I walked to where he stood. Thorvald felt my presence creep up behind him. Without turning he spread his arms asking, "Magnificent is it not?"

I simply pretended that he spoke of the forest that sat majestically behind the upright keel so as not to discourage his enthusiasm. "It is. It truly is."

Thorvald turned and grabbed me at the shoulders, a joyful smile carved into his face. "I'm so glad you think so! I had the keel raised to signify our first glorious discovery in the name of the One God!"

Again looking past the damaged stick planted in the sand, "It is glorious, Thorvald! This land would support many thousands of Norseman! What will you call it?"

A look of gleeful surprise sprung onto his face for he had forgotten the right of an explorer in bestowing a name on new worlds. However, his countenance quickly shifted to one of concern as he pondered how he would signify these lands for all time. Running his hand through his thick red-brown mane which was flecked with many grey hairs now, he dropped onto the beach thinking.

I chuckled so he raised his head inquiring, "What is it? Why do you laugh?"

"You just surprise me, brother. I've never known you to worry of such details as this. You are more like your father than either of your brothers in so many ways, but even the inquisitive Leif came up with names for lands without fretting like an old maid." Thorvald, like Erik, had typically felt completely at ease allowing his instincts, right or wrong, to guide his decisions.

"You are right, but I've never before given a name to something. All my children have died in birth. I've never even bothered to name my dogs, preferring to call them dog instead." Now I rolled my eyes, which, thankfully, he did not see. I did not wish to mock him. "How do you name something?" he asked.

I felt I was surrounded by children, "Just look around you. What do you see? Name the land as such."

Thorvald peered around while his backside was still firmly in the sand. As quickly as he surveyed the land, he was immediately done. Wagging his finger at me with the broad smile returning, he said, "You are wise, Halldorr. Wiser than I have ever thought." He jumped to his feet proclaiming to the few men within earshot, "This land will forever be known by the marker we raised to the heavens today! Men, this marker will tell all future travelers, traders, or settlers that this land is called Kjalarnes!"

Now, I venture to say that anyone reading this has probably never heard of Kjalarnes, which means Keel Point. It is more likely that the splendid monument Thorvald buried in the beach that day was swept to sea during the first or second severe storm that fell upon the shore. I use the word "likely" because I only saw the buried keel one more time in my life.

We did not have time to settle Kjalarnes as my brother and I hoped. We barely had time to perform a cursory exploration of the discovery. His dreams would shortly be extinguished. For that day, the day Thorvald buried the keel in the sand, was also the day that he would direct the building of another memorial – the marker for his own grave.

. . .

After spending so much time repairing the *Glorious Discovery's* keel and garboards, our men, including Thorvald, were eager to find whatever riches awaited them in Kjalarnes. Led by their captain, they were already beginning to haphazardly disperse across the sand when I yelled, "Thorvald, don't you think we ought to have the men arm themselves, at least with some leather mail, and post a watch before we all go traipsing into this still unknown land?"

Thorvald craned his weathered neck to see that I was taking my time to dress in my new coat of mail from Olaf aboard the beached longboat. I never did have someone put a sheen on it, so the suit still looked tarnished from weather. Thorhall, too, dressed in his simple leather coat, strapping a sword to his waist afterwards. "Halldorr, you delay discovery! Yet we will wait for you if you are afraid that some skraeling woman will slit your throat."

His good-natured taunt brought an expected round of laughter from the men. I did my best to goad the men right back in order for them to choose the wisest course on their own. "It's not my throat I worry about, nor is it a skraeling woman. I think of my soft belly and how much damage a lucky spear thrust from one of their warriors will do. If I were some of these men with their women back home, I would also make sure I protected my stick. Who knows which Norseman will find his way into a woman's bed when her man has been castrated by a skraeling axe." I paused before adding, "But it's up to you, commander."

Thorvald took the hint, partially. Tossing his hands up, he said, "Whichever man wants to suit up should do so. I'll not because I am a confident leader, like my father, who trusts my men completely." I remember thinking, you'll be a dead confident leader.

A handful of our companions returned to the ship while I finished tying my belt and sword to my waist over top the thinner belt that always held my father's saex. I yanked up my shield from its place in the hold where it was stowed when we were not on a strandhogg. At last I hooked my helmet at the rear of my belt and splashed down into the shallow water next to the beach. I was glad the water slowed my precipitous drop, with the added weight of the mail coat, because that was the first time in my life I noticed a pain in my knees from the jolt. Was I so old, then?

When all were made ready, I set a watch of four men led by Njordr, who was most displeased at having to remain behind. Thorvald led our clamoring band, plunging into the forest. We quickly passed the area in the wood where we had harvested our lumber and soon found ourselves in virgin territory.

Here the forest floor was relatively clear and the sun was shaded by a massive canopy of leaves and needles above our heads. Despite our raucous march, I spied a dark brown marten with a smart looking orange throat patch chasing a red squirrel down a tree. I recall this because of how astounding it was to see the marten pursuing his prey at such speed and agility down the pine, head first. I had never seen one during the day – this marten must have been particularly hungry.

Since we were on a sharp point of land, after a time we came to another beach opposite where *Glorious Discovery* sat. The sea was calmer here because there was a small natural harbor. Dramatic rock formations rose from the sea several ells away from the shore. These rocks looked like enormous mushrooms because the working of the sea at their bases for generations had carved them narrower than the rock heads above. I thought about gathering some wild mushrooms that night for my meal.

On shore, smooth giant rocks sat strewn about. Many looked like they had been shaved from a mountain with the blade of the One

God or his son Jesus then dropped into the sand, like seed strewn by a sower. For a short time, we walked along the beach, further and further from *Glorious Discovery*, toward a particularly large heap of these boulders. I'd like to say the men trailing behind us were silent as an army in unfamiliar territory should be, but they were not. They chatted among themselves. Laughing and telling jokes at each other's expense. They were confident in their ignorance as men so often are wont to be.

I would also like to say that I acted as a leader of men that day. Men had granted me their permission to lead them at different times during my life even though, based upon our ranks in Norse society, it was Thorvald who led us. I should have seized the leadership crown bestowed upon me that day. I should have directed them more fully – even countermanding Thorvald's orders. I did not, regretting it still.

As we neared the heap of hewn boulders, we heard a hushed chattering of men's voices coming from the other side. We then heard rustling in the sand followed by a hollow thud. Silence came next.

Thorvald called to the men, "Weapons. Draw your weapons, charge over the stones and dispatch whatever it is you find."

"But . . ." was all I got out before the men did their duty and starting scampering over the rocks with their swords and spears clanging against the stones. Thorhall was shaking his head in disgust as he faithfully complied with the order, among the last to make the short trip. For a time I stood alone on the sand looking foolish, I am sure. But reluctantly I too drew my sword and joined the men's attack on what, God only knew.

When I reached the top of the rocks I saw a curious site before me. Our Norsemen were scattered over the descending side of the rocks impotently pointing their weapons in the air while Thorvald, Volundr, and Arnkell led three small groups creeping toward three hide-covered boats that were overturned on the beach. These boats were the only sign of men in our vicinity, but I quickly scanned the area from my vantage point atop the high rocks.

My eyes shot wide when I saw it sitting inland next to a quiet creek. "Thorvald, no! Retreat!"

But it was too late. Volundr was the first to reach his target. He silently reached under the overturned boat then flipped it over to reveal three unarmed skraelings cowering in the sand. They shouted in fear but their fate was written by the norns long ago. Volundr sent his sword straight into the nearest skraeling's ribs. He tried to scream, but all the air from his chest whooshed out the new hole in his side. The other two men did scream as they clawed their way through the sand away from their attackers. It was no use as the men Volundr led chopped them down with blood spattering all over their beards.

Those three hidden under the second boat died similar deaths at the hands of Arnkell's men. Only those under the third boat that Thorvald attacked had a somewhat different outcome, two of them living only moments longer. They had heard the death cries of their companions, and so the extra heartbeat it took for Thorvald to reach their boat gave them time to change tactics. When Thorvald hauled the boat over with his powerful arm, the nearest skraeling jumped at him. He punched Thorvald in the face while yanking at his beard. Thorvald was so surprised that he fell backwards. The second skraeling under the boat did likewise to another of our men, pounding his fist into the man's face again and again while letting out a high pitched shriek.

Both of these skraelings were soon hacked down by neighboring Norsemen, but their sacrifice helped the third man escape in the boat. He ran toward the water dragging the lightweight craft behind him, tossed it into the sea, finally producing a paddle. With his shoulders bulging from the effort, he stabbed the blade into the water which caused the boat to skip over the waves, picking up speed. He steered the small vessel into a small fjord heading to his village – the village no one else had seen.

I ran down to where Thorvald stood dusting himself off and wiping the skraeling blood from his face. "Success Halldorr! We met the enemy and have prevailed. Not a single loss!"

He was more like his father and grandfather than ever. After all, it was murders they had committed that got them exiled first from Norway, then Iceland. I just watched Thorvald and our men commit murder! To be sure the dead were skraelings, but in my life

I had seen the unnecessary deaths of skraelings bring undo pain to the Norse. "What are you thinking?"

"What could possibly cause you all this worry?" he said, laughing. Our men rooted through the minimal possessions of the fallen skraelings. One gave a hoot when he stood up holding some type of jewelry he stole from a man's ears. Others laughed as he danced while holding the dangling rings as if they hung from his own ears. Another waved a hollow tube that had a right angle at the end. The tube was decorated with many colorful designs and had several feathers affixed at the center.

I grabbed Thorvald's arm, "We need to gather our men and run to the ship! Trouble is coming."

"Halldorr! Why would I retreat from a victory?" Thorvald now cried so that everyone could hear him, "I came exploring to spread news of the One God! We all came to settle new lands and make ourselves into jarls like my father!" His followers gave a mighty cheer. Nothing inspires men like victory, fleeting as it may have been.

"That man who escaped will gather his village warriors! We will be outnumbered. We will die."

Thorvald had enough of me. He strode off past the boats, bodies, and blood indicating with a turn of his head for the men to follow. They did. Stubborn ox balls!

Thorhall walked up behind me saying, "He is like his father and for that I love him." Then the Huntsman looked me in the eyes before walking after Thorvald and said, "Even though he is stubborn like a constipated goat."

For the third time that day I was left standing on my own while, unbeknownst to them, they all headed toward the skraeling village I had seen from my perch on the rocks. I closed my eyes while taking a deep breath, ready to follow Thorvald. But a terrible scream halted me. A second shriek put my legs in motion over the low ridge where I saw my worst fears realized. Frighteningly red-painted men streamed out from the village. Their leaders had already engaged Thorvald, Volundr, and others at the front.

While I sprinted down to the fray, I drew both my sword and saex but left my shield clanging, strapped across my back. Before I was halfway through our men, Volundr was dead from a blow to the head from a blunt rock attached at the end of a skraeling's staff. His badly misshapen head spilled deep red blood onto the forest floor.

Two more of our men fell with spears jutting from their soft bellies as I finally slammed into my first skraeling, who had been swinging a stone axe at Thorvald. While he was looking to my brother, I lowered my shoulder, knocking him to the ground. His axe fell from his hand and as he desperately reached for it, I drove my beautiful sword into his chest. He heaved up, arching in pain so much so that my sword was briefly stuck. Another skraeling gave a war yell and bore down on me with a long spear. He held it over his head with both hands, apparently confident that my weapon was of no use to me, lodged as it was. However, he did not see my father's saex held in my left hand. I ducked to one knee so that his strike was high over my head. Then putting my right hand on the earth for leverage, I drove my saex to the hilt into his belly.

After retrieving both blades, I looked for my next kill only to see the unmistakable countenance of the vain skraeling who caused three deaths of his own people and nearly my own the previous year. The pain in my badly scarred leg howled as if to offer its agreement that it was indeed he. The man wore red paint like his companions, but I knew it to be him for the round shape of his face was permanently carved into my mind's eye. Not five paces from me, he now wildly swung a narrow-bladed axe at one of our men who effortlessly protected himself with a battered shield while jabbing his spear into another skraeling. I decided I would kill the vain one.

"Segonku!" I shouted, remembering the word I had heard Kitchi call him while they walked in Vinland. My strange pronunciation of this familiar word immediately caused him to turn toward me. His eyes told me that he recognized me and was stunned that I yet lived. Furiously I yelled, "You'll die Segonku!" before taking a step to him.

My prediction was not to be born out that day, however. Folkvar was thrust back into my path so that I had to help prevent him from falling. By the time he was righted and I looked up again, the vain Segonku had melted into the teeming mass.

It was just as well. The pause in my fighting allowed me to scan the battlefield, and what I saw disheartened me. I shouted to Thorvald, "We must retreat now! Look at all of them." So many more of the skraelings flowed from the village, that they would soon be able to envelope our feeble band of warriors.

Thorvald, swinging his own blade with two hands, cut across a skraeling arm, then repeatedly beat the man on the back of his head with his sword's heavy pommel. "Yes! To the ship!"

"Take the men! Thorhall and I will stay behind a moment to slow the attackers," I screamed.

My brother nodded just as another of our men fell at his feet. His orders were welcomed and Norsemen disengaged en masse, running back toward the beach to get their bearings for the return flight to *Glorious Discovery*. Thorvald was the first over the hill and disappeared from my sight along with the twenty or so others still living. A whiff of air from an arrow past my scarred ear pulled me back to the fight. We needed to give our fleeing companions a few extra heartbeats to safely escape.

The sinewy Huntsman wielded a skraeling spear now for he must have lost his own weapon. He stabbed a man in the neck, tearing out his windpipe. The man's organ was still stuck on the end of the chiseled stone when the Huntsman buried it deep into another man's side. The spear became lodged and I heard Thorhall swear to the old gods as he used his foot to push the dead attacker down. It still didn't come free so he broke the shaft off then started beating a young warrior away with it, quickly bruising the man's forearms.

It was time to go. The Huntsman grabbed my hair and jerked my head back the direction we had come as he led us over the hill. A brief glance over my shoulder told me that our attackers were not pursuing. A lucky break, I thought.

But as I crested the ridge back to the beach I saw that we were likely already dead. Ten more of their boats, this time covered in bark, had circled around behind us and were now approaching land. Their arrows had already started slapping into Thorvald and the others. Thankfully, most of our men used their shields wisely while they retreated over the rocks. Thorvald stood at the base of the stone slabs roaring at the men to move faster. He did not have a shield. Shit, I thought.

At this point in the battle a shield was more important than a sword, so as I dashed toward the rocks, I slid my blade into its resting place at my waist while pulling my shield from my back. We ran directly past the first of the small boats just as it scratched into the shore. In short order two loud thuds cracked into my heavy wood and iron defense nearly knocking me off my feet. Thorhall was there beside me and used his powerful grip to steady me.

When we made it to Thorvald, arrows were already slapping off the rocks around us. I held my shield in front of my brother to protect him from his own stubbornness or stupidity or both, while indicating that Thorhall should scramble over and follow the men. Then fate or Providence or both rang out. Fortuna or Deum.

An arrow struck at the very top of the iron rim which encircled my shield. It made a musical ringing sound as the stone met the metal then harmlessly careened off. But the force of the blow caused the shield to tip upward for just one brief moment. As fate often does, fate took advantage of the time it was given and assailed us. A second arrow that may have been loosed at the same time as the first, slipped just beneath the lifted shield and buried itself under Thorvald's left arm. He fell to his right against the rock face howling in pain, disbelief in his eyes.

Again I thought, shit. Thorhall was now out of sight so it would be up to me to carry Thorvald out of this mess.

Working as fast as I could now, I slammed my saex home into its short scabbard, tossed my shield across my back, and hoisted Thorvald onto my shoulder. My healed leg wound felt compelled to remind me of its presence with each arduous step up the rock formation with Thorvald's extra weight. Despite my fears of what chased after us, I did not take any time to look back at my pursuers. Their arrows hammered around me. At least two more sent splinters flying from my shield.

Then we made it over the stones. Thorhall was halfway to the trees waiting for us and swore when he saw us coming. The rest of the men had already disappeared into the forest toward our ship.

Thankfully the skraelings had enough of killing that day. They chose not to follow us past the rocks. But despite that luck, we ran with all haste to *Glorious Discovery*. With each footfall, Thorvald bounced on my shoulder, letting out a shallow, pain-filled gasp each time. During the run, I convinced myself that because he still breathed he would live.

Fate had other plans.

. . .

I was soaking wet with sweat when I finally made it back to the ship. We slapped Thorvald onto the deck just as the men used the oars to pull us free from the beach. The boat bobbed in the sea as the surf rolled into shore, and I slumped to my ass against the gunwale to catch my breath. While looking down at my waist, I saw that I was soaking wet not just from sweat, but also blood, Thorvald's blood.

Based upon the volume covering my clothes, the man couldn't have much left. It was a miracle of Jesus that he even yet lived. I knew now that he would die.

While we buffeted in the seas, I crawled over to Thorvald where Thorhall and others surrounded him. I roughly pushed them out of the way and hung my face above his own, saying, "I'll speak to my brother now!" Upon seeing his face, I gasped audibly for he was white – white like the new snow falling in winter – white like the feathers of the gull – white like the face of a dead man. "You stupid bastard," I yelled then closed my eyes as my first tear smacked into Thorvald's cheek.

The tear temporarily revived him and he weakly raised his arm toward me. His flittering eyes were glossy like those of a blind man. He looked in the wrong direction then spoke with a feeble smile, "No, Halldorr, you are the bastard." Then he gave a frail laugh. "I love you, my brother. I join my grandfather, my father, and my brother Thorstein with the One God in his hall now." More of my tears streamed onto him. "Find a fine point of land near Kjalarnes. Bury me there and put a cross at my head. Then set a cross at my feet and forever call the place Krossanes after that."

Then he died.

I rose to my feet and grabbed items from the hold, throwing them all over the ship. No one else said anything. Njordr watched silently from his place at the rudder. Thorhall leaned on the gunwale staring out to sea; he spit something from his mouth. I swore, I screamed, I swore again. I cried and cried like I was but a child. When I at last looked around the ship at the men pulling on the oars they all wept as well. We lost our commander that day, and we lost ten good men.

. . .

Njordr guided the boat south, following the land, until we were far enough from the skraeling village to be free from immediate further attacks. Unceremoniously, we crept onto a cape with a soft, sandy beach. Several of us carried Thorvald into the forest where we found a small, grassy meadow hemmed in by trees.

Using wood-bladed shovels we dug a grave for him. Carefully we lowered him with his head pointed west so that he could see Christ's return from the east. I fashioned two crosses from small pieces of wood left from the repair of our keel and, like Thorvald asked, drove them into the earth at both his head and feet.

No one wanted to say any words, but I knew we must. Without much thought I began, "The One God has seen fit to take many of his warriors to him in recent years. Of late, he has been most fond of Erik and Erik's sons." I paused, not knowing where to go with my eulogy next. While he waited for me to speak, Thorhall spat upon the cross nearest him. I cannot say I took offense, though many men would have. Faith in the One True God had brought no particular favor in the eyes of the norns. Fate looked just as capricious as it had before my conversion.

I continued, "The One God's Providence brought us to these lands where we gave and received death. But our men's and our leader's death this day do not reduce the One True God's power. His Son gave himself up for other men. Thorvald gave himself up for us." Not exactly true, but we often say things when friends die to make us all feel better. "So in that way Thorvald is like the Christ.

And if he is like the Son of God then that means perhaps we can be that way too." I was rolling now. "Like the first followers of the Christ when they received the power of the Holy Spirit, we can become powerful if we ask that part of the One God to live in the longhouse of our hearts." I am still not certain what I meant by that. I then finished, "We pray as powerful warriors for you One God; that you make our hearts strong, make our swords blazing, and make our tongues full of praise so that we may become all-powerful in you."

When I finished giving my speech, the men gave a round of applause. Even Thorhall smiled while nodding his head in my direction. Truthfully, it was the most celebratory funeral I had attended since converting to the One God. Heretofore, most of them had been melancholy to say the least.

We slowly made our way back to the beach and *Glorious Discovery*. Without hesitation, the boat was pulled out to sea, and we limped back to Leifsbudir the way we had come. The unhappy air set in like the fogs of Greenland, and I can honestly say that I have never had such a quiet sea voyage for so many days. Most of my time was spent at the steering oar with vague, indescribable thoughts. In a daze, I watched the ocean stream past our hull, not often making eye contact with the men. When I did look into their faces, without words they told me their feelings. Almost universally, enthusiasm for exploration had waned after witnessing so much death.

CHAPTER 8

Karlsefni was becoming a good father to my son, Snorri. He spoke of him often as we talked around the hearth at night now that we were back in Leifsbudir. As much as it pained me to admit, he was a good husband too. While he opined over and over again how his wife and son would see the world from the planks of a trading knarr standing next to him, Gudrid often stole fond glances at him. She was growing closer to the man; they would be good together. I would listen to Thorfinn telling the stories of little Snorri as if they already happened, but found myself watching Gudrid, wondering what might have been if I had returned to Greenland with Leif.

Usually finding no purpose in such thoughts, my mind wandered – sometimes to my own father. What had been his hopes or dreams for me? Did he want me to grow to be a Berserker? Likely not. Did he hope to watch his grandchildren grow and take brides for themselves? I do not know. Sometimes my thoughts went to Bjarni's treachery, sometimes to Olaf's defeat. I'd sip from a wooden mug of ale absent-mindedly, only laughing at the correct parts of the tales when outbursts from everyone else cued me.

Glorious Discovery was back to the banks of Leifsbudir after a voyage of just three weeks. Members of the miniature settlement were bustling about the forests when our repaired keel settled to the sand in the shallows, so no one welcomed us as we sloshed through the muck to the drier beach. When the residents did return, they could tell by our countenances that *Floating Louse* would have been a more appropriate name for the ship and expedition. Our story was told by the survivors and quickly wound its way through our camp. Several men who had remained behind had lost a brother in our battle with the skraelings. Melancholy sunk about the lot of us.

I settled into what I now call my quiet period. While never one of unnecessary speech, now I spoke to no one unless first spoken to. I didn't feel particularly angry at anyone. Rather, I was confused. The One God continuously spoke to me through my reading that he held mankind in high esteem. Yet he allowed all this death to prevail. Why couldn't I have stopped Thorvald before he attacked the hide boats? Why couldn't the skraelings have been followers of the One True God already? Maybe we all could have become brothers in the Word. That's what Olaf tried to accomplish, but he failed. Didn't the One God want Olaf to succeed?

In the end I decided that these questions had no answers. Not answers that could come from any man, anyways. So I gave them up and remained quiet.

One cool, foggy morning I left the main longhouse early with my bow to hunt. The house was quiet except for the snoring of several men along the walls and the cooing of little Snorri snuggled next to his mother's breast, so I thought I snuck away unnoticed. I was mistaken, however, because I was no more than ten paces from the threshold when the broad form of Thorfinn materialized in the fog. He leaned on his own bow, still unstrung like mine.

"I've been waiting for you," he said with good humor. "Cheese?" asked Thorfinn extending a chunk broken from a piece on which he gnawed.

Taking it, I gave a simple, "Thank you," then continued on my way past him.

Nonplussed by my disinterest, Thorfinn strode next to me with his cheese and bow. "As I said, I've been waiting for you because I want to ask you something." We walked past a man's brown and black mottled dog that was rolling in the dung heap. The man called the dog Mead because the beast could keep up with any man in the village after the drinking began around the hearth. This morning he lapped at the edge of the steaming pile which sat downwind from the houses and I thought about how the man often used his eating knife to share his mid-day meal with the animal. Shaking my head I realized that because of this familiarity, the man likely had eaten some of his own manure.

We entered the forest, walking along the brook that bubbled from Black Duck Pond down to the sea. After rounding the small lake I found a rock and sat upon it, pulling out some hard boiled eggs I had packed in my sack. I gave two to Karlsefni who ate of them gladly. We watched those handsome black ducks I had seen my first day in this land as they floated atop, then dove into the water for their own morning meal.

Some water gathered in our hands from the edge of the pond washed the breakfast down, and we set off once again. Thorfinn was quiet this entire time. I think he enjoyed the peace of the woods that morning too even though he was generally a boisterous friend to everyone. Eventually we came to a path where I had frequently taken down nice game. Leading the way step by careful step, I moved along the worn earth toward an overlook above another tiny lake.

We crawled upon our bellies for the last two fadmrs to the edge of the short cliff, sticking our eyes over the rim. Below us, scattered about the fresh water were several deer. Three does and four of their young spread out. Some were nibbling at the succulent grasses that grew nearly to the lake's border. Others waded in with their forefeet spread wide to drink the steaming, morning water. Two of the young deer had already lost their spots while the other two retained only a faint hint of the characteristic markings.

What wind existed was in our favor that morning, blowing lightly into our faces as we peered down at our prey. None of them had heard us yet as their tails wagged lazily across their backsides, showing no alarm. It would not be that easy, however. Several stout trees stood between us and the deer. The distance was not too far for my arrow to reach, but the range would likely prove difficult to maintain accuracy.

Thorfinn and I sidled back away from our vantage point and, without a word, decided upon our course of action. Before slipping noiselessly back into the woods to make our circle, though, we heaved down on our strong yew bows and restrung them.

We split up – I went to the left, he to the right. That improved the chances of at least one of us dropping our quarry in the event the skittish animals fled. Many minutes passed as I deliberately stepped from place to place – avoiding a cracked branch here or a pile of rustling leaves there. Occasionally, I caught a glimpse of the deer. Some of the older mothers sensed something strange was afoot, now holding their heads erect with ears forward. I froze. After an eternity, they resumed consuming their humble breakfasts.

At last I was perched atop a rock the size of a man hunched over on all fours. I was about three ells deep in the forest, but the rock raised me above some particularly coarse briars for a perfect shot at one of the does. She was a beautiful creature with some fat left on her haunches despite having probably nursed one or more of the fawns nearby.

While watching her I carefully nocked my arrow then patiently waited for Thorfinn to get into place. Many more minutes passed. The fog began to steadily burn off so that I could see all the way to the other side where Thorfinn should be positioned. He was not there yet, so I rolled my eyes and waited more, occasionally rocking from foot to foot, searching for a more comfortable position.

Then my target's head shot up, looking away from me. Her tail, all the beasts' tails shot upward, showing the white warning sign beneath. In unison they ran toward my hiding place, gobbling up distance by taking great bounds. Reflexively my bow was up and drawn to my cheek. My eyes took in the scene. My soul felt the deer and their leaping rhythm. For a moment I became a wolf, a bear on the hunt. For a moment I even became the deer. My timing became her timing. Nothing else existed in the world. There was no Gudrid, Snorri, or Olaf. There was neither past nor future – only the present, my present, survived. With one last spontaneous thought offering to both Thor and the One God, I loosed my missile.

The arrow and the doe met in mid air. She was just leaving her back feet for a particularly long bound when the point crushed into her strong, white chest with a loud crunch. Both had such momentum that neither the arrow, nor the deer won over. They hovered there in the air for a moment while the terrific energy from both the living creature and the inanimate object dissipated to nothingness. Then the two became one and fell straight to the ground in a heap.

The other deer and their fawns tore past me, leaving tufts of fur amongst the briars while they quickly melted into the dark forest behind. Then all was quiet.

I hopped down and picked my way through the hide-covered briars and walked the five steps to my prey. She was quiet. Her legs didn't thrash. Her nose didn't gurgle with bubbling blood. She was at peace there in the tall grass while I crouched to inspect the arrow. With my fingers I felt that the iron head had found its way between two ribs then immediately pierced the heart. There would be no additional pursuit while following a bloody trail that day. She had died instantly. I gave thanks to the One God.

With my saex, I began field dressing the animal. There was no sign of Thorfinn, but I knew he was about since he must have scared the deer in my direction.

I should have been more vigilant, however, because it was not until I finished my task that I noticed a sound on the breeze. It was a panting sound interrupted occasionally by a low moan. Thorfinn!

Plunging the saex into my belt, I nocked another arrow while running toward the noise with my limping gait, leaving my kill behind. Kitchi and his men were the only skraelings I had ever seen around Leifsbudir, nonetheless, I prepared for the worst as I ran up the gentle slope within the woods on the opposite side of the shore. I saw only Thorfinn's feet sprawled straight out across the ground behind a tree as another moan told me he yet lived. My eyes were alive with the rest of my senses looking all around for lurking danger. I heard not a sound; I saw nothing.

So I moved closer to Thorfinn, rounding the great tree. From the scratch marks on the ground, I could see that Thorfinn had dragged himself to the tree after receiving a wound from some weapon. The lower right quadrant of his stomach bled, though slowly now. No arrow or spear protruded. His head was also wet with blood, causing his blonde hair to mat to his face so that three or four stray hairs looked as if they formed a crooked hand creeping along Thorfinn's cheek. His eyes fluttered once or twice, and he moaned some incomprehensible words after sensing my presence.

I scanned the surrounding forest again. Nothing. Thorfinn must have surprised a skraeling who stabbed and hit him, then fled into the trees. Thorfinn's bow was haphazardly strewn in some bushes to the side with the arrow he had nocked now dislodged and laying nearby. He didn't even get a shot off.

Decisions needed to be made. I could pick the giant of a man up on my shoulders and carry him back for help. I could leave him and run to get more arms for additional strength. Instead, I chose to build a campfire right there using my jasper stones and tend to his wound with clean water and some bandages. After that was done and while Thorfinn slept, I walked back to my deer. Not wanting to waste my quarry, I set about drying some of the meat that day in the bright, warm sun that eventually outfought the morning fog. I roasted some of the steaks over my fire and ate heartily.

As night fell and still the man slept, I am ashamed to say that evil thoughts slithered into my mind. Terribly wounded next to me was the only man who stood between me and Gudrid and my son, Snorri. My son! I could let Thorfinn expire, or, I thought, I could help him expire. A bag over his face or my saex to his belly would end his marriage, letting me raise my own boy. I could find my way next to Gudrid's body and run my hands down her smooth, naked skin.

In the end I did what I always did, accepted my fate and helped Thorfinn restore his health.

. . .

Thorfinn was at the helm today, standing as tall and strong as ever. His fat knarr, simply called *The Merchant*, was billowing with passengers while the cloth above our heads captured ample wind, causing the ship beneath us to skip across the salty waters. The northerly wind pushed us southward with my home of nearly three years, Leifsbudir, off our port stern, shrinking in the distance.

Back in the forest one month ago, Thorfinn awakened groggily the morning after receiving his injuries. Thirst was foremost upon his lips, so he drank heavily of both water and ale. He vomited when he tried to eat small bites of the venison steaks, so we didn't try that again for some time.

It turns out that my imagination had been running wild for there were no skraelings.

"A furtive stag," was what he first said, while laying on his left side, looking at me with eyes scrunched in pain, his bit of braided beard dragging in the dirt.

"What are you talking about?"

"I was coming down to shoot one of those doe we spotted from the ridge, when an irritated snort caught me by surprise. Before I even looked to my right, antlers from the biggest deer I have ever seen were plunging into my belly. Apparently he wanted all the women for himself," Thorfinn added with a wincing chuckle.

"Why didn't you shout for help?" I asked.

"I tried, but the beast threw me down on my back and knocked the wind from me. I swung the bow to scare him off, but he caught it with his snout. I lost my grip, watching him toss it away. Angry now, he lowered his head again for another strike, but I seized his antlers in my hands to prevent another goring from the bastard. The force of his blow pushed me back again and I felt a terrific pain on the back of my head and saw flashing lights. Then the world went dark. Seeing you this morning was the next thing I remember."

I nursed him for another day before carrying him and the dried, butchered meat back to Leifsbudir. We came back to the main hall where I was welcomed as a hero by Gudrid and the rest of the village. I had also endeared myself to Thorfinn who proclaimed loudly one night around a large fire in the village, "Had it been any other man out there, I would be dead! Halldorr, as his father, Erik told me, as his brother Leif told me, as everyone says of him, is as true as a man as you could meet." I thought that most all men I knew would have done the same as I since all I did was tend to his wounds. Yet he continued, "I have heard that Halldorr even fancied himself to be married to my Gudrid. What an opportunity he had to find himself thus wed! And he took it not!"

The men around the fire that night cheered for me and my mediocrity, not knowing the very wicked thoughts that swirled in my head when Thorfinn was injured. Snorri the Elder, the man whose nose I bloodied earlier that summer, shouted "Yes, he took it not because the old man must remain celibate so that his shriveled nuts aren't scared back into his belly at the sight of a woman." This brought a lot of laughter from the others. I merely smiled while looking into my cup of ale while wishing the elder Snorri would attack me so I could just kill him and get it over with. My silence goaded this Snorri, with his now misshapen nose, to continue badgering me most of the night. The other men took this as a further sign of our friendship, that our scrap earlier in the year was forgotten. I took it as the insult he intended.

Several days after returning to the encampment I was told why Thorfinn waited for me that foggy morning. He was planning another expedition away from Leifsbudir this very year and wanted me to come with him, even though I was not beholden to him in any way, even though Leif wanted me to oversee the camp. Somehow, now after coming to his rescue, I was assured that I would travel with the man for Thorfinn saw fit to elevate me to captain of his own ship to prevent me from saying no. This rapid elevation among Thorfinn's men, of course, did nothing to enhance my already imperfect relationship with his one-time favored confidant, Snorri the Elder.

So we sailed. Leifsbudir was abandoned for now, its doors securely fastened. Not even a stray chicken remained behind; instead they pecked away in their makeshift cages made from loose kindling. The cages were stacked neatly and tied securely in the hold so that they wouldn't topple over from the boat's motion. Three curious cows sniffed at the chickens at head level, occasionally snaking a long tongue between the thin wood rails, only to be vigorously pecked for their uninvited presence.

Two of Thorfinn's knarrs sped with the wind gage that day. Like sturdy horses galloping, they strode nearly abreast of one another with the sea spray finding its way over the gunwale to thoroughly douse our passengers. We made it a game to see who could take the lead.

Thorhall the Huntsman took command of *Glorious Discovery*, though he changed the name to *Valhalla*, and she followed closely behind.

We were settlers looking for new, fertile land to explore. Thorfinn was looking for new peoples with which to trade. He had gold and silver in his eyes, but he did not expect to find the soft metals tumbling from the side of a hill. No, he expected that he would work, hunt, or trade for the stuff. His willingness to earn riches was some comfort, at least. Thorfinn did not want success handed to him, nor did he expect us to convert the skraelings to the One God. I thought about how simple life would be on this adventure without the added burden of proselytizing to whomever we met as we had to do with Olaf. This would be simple – settle, farm, hunt, and trade.

Our small flotilla camped each night along the west coast of Vinland. The second night was only a short distance south of where my fight with Kitchi and his men occurred. These nights were uneventful except for the usual stories, lies, and ale-induced fights.

During the third day, we left sight of the southwestern coast of Vinland, confirming that it was truly a large island. In short order, we passed the point of land Thorvald named Kjalarnes with the stark, broken keel from *Glorious Discovery* jutting from the sand at a sad angle acting like a solemn mark of our less than triumphant first pass at the land. I looked back to Thorhall the Huntsman to point out the marker with a wave, but he was already staring toward it as he leaned on *Valhalla's* gunwale.

Some of the other men noticed it too, but thought it best to say nothing. They again perked up their heads as we passed where Thorvald was buried. We could not see the grave or the crosses, but the landmarks of several tipping trees and the beach told me that was where we entered the forest to place his drained body into the earth to be devoured by her. If Thorfinn noticed any change in the emotions of some of us, he did not mention it. Gudrid, however, sensed something was amiss and set her hand gently atop mine as I stood in a trance, thinking of the constant death brought on in this life. Little Snorri was nestled next her chest with his eyes closed in a deep sleep aided by warm milk from his mother and the rocking motion of the ship. What will his life, my son little Snorri's, be like. Will it be harsh? Will it be peaceful? Will he love a woman? Will he serve the One God for all time? My gaze met hers, and we shared a sad smile of wonder of what was or what could have been until Thorfinn bellowed, "Halldorr, what shall we do here?"

We were passing several fingers of land extending out into the sea which created what would either be sea water fjords or perhaps even freshwater river outlets. Thorfinn was pointing to them asking me if we should enter or continue on. I thought about all the Norseman deaths just weeks ago in those forests. "There's no trading in there," I advised. "Norsemen have already been here

without much luck. You want to move further for trading riches."
He looked at me, thinking intently for a moment then nodded with
satisfaction.

With the passing of two or three more hours the land turned
abruptly to the southwest so we turned our ships to shadow it. A
night of camping on the shore was uneventful. I willed myself to
spend it in a dreamless sleep so that I could stop questioning the
point of all my service to others, the blind acceptance of my destiny.
Except for the brief moment when I took revenge upon Bjarni by
taking hold of the rudder of my life, fate continually poured over me,
drowning me beneath its might. I was unsuccessful directing my
will power, however, and tossed the whole night through.

The next morning was filled with a lonely, bright sunshine
for there were no clouds in the blue sky. After a breakfast of ale,
grapes, and fresh fish, the biggest salmon any of us had ever seen,
we allowed the tide to lift the keels from the shore where we had
camped. God provided another day of fair winds and soon our
entourage was skimming over the waves once again. The sight off
our starboard bow was magnificent though later when I spoke to
Thorhall the Huntsman about the subject he said, "The sight was
bleak." At any rate, extending for miles upon miles to the west was
a string of sand beaches. They were interrupted by the occasional
cliff or grove of deep green pines that reached directly to the sea, but
the sight of such a line of white sand was nearly as impressive as my
first view of Dover's towering white cliffs before the Battle of
Maldon many years earlier. Gudrid, demonstrating much more
originality than any of the men had during our explorations, named
the length of coastline Furdurstrandir which means "Wonder
Strand."

So immense was the Furdurstrandir that we travelled along it
for over two full days before the land, and therefore *The Merchant*,
again turned northward. Soon we came to an area of the sea with
strong, forceful currents at the mouth of a wide fjord. An island
rested just outside this fjord and so we called the island Straumsey
which simply means stream isle. I guided our small fleet into the
bay, now aptly named Straumsfjord, and found a place to rest for the
night, sliding the ship into the shore.

As we came to a halt at the shingle, we scared the nearest members of a vast colony of ducks from their own sleep so that they flapped noisily around us. Some were so confused by our presence they crashed into our sails which made it much easier for our women to grab the fowl, ringing their necks for a succulent supper later in the evening. The beasts' eggs, too, littered the shore. In fact, as we walked across the sand we could not take a step without smashing some beneath our feet.

This was to be a land of plenty.

. . .

My, that winter was harsh. Most of the cattle died from exposure to the elements shortly after our humble Christmas celebration. We immediately butchered those that died of the cold, smoking the meat, but we could not put up much because most of them died of illness. I have seen men eat of animals who died of some illnesses, and they themselves subsequently became sick or even died. After their deaths, we were left with just two bulls, two cows, and a heifer calf to provide milk or meat for nearly one hundred fifty souls. Three sheep and twenty-one chickens remained alive to supply further sustenance, but they would be gone within the week if we simply slaughtered them to feed us all.

Many of the men, especially Thorhall the Huntsman, braved the ruthless wind and snow by leaving one of the two temporary longhouses we had built before winter to hunt for wild game among the forests surrounding Straumsfjord. However, I cannot explain why, our success was severely limited. There were no deer. We killed three rabbits in three weeks. The entire colony of ducks which cluttered the beach at our landing had moved on, leaving only their droppings behind. It was as if our prey had been lifted out from among the trees so that even their tracks disappeared. Even our attempts to fish were utter failures. Poles broke, hooks were lost, nets torn. The Huntsman began to curse the One God even more than normal in new, imaginative ways in his everyday speech for allowing such a malady to befall us.

So within one moon of our Christmas merriment, we began to ration what remained of our food. The chickens were fed pebbles and some dried grasses to keep them laying eggs. This worked to a point so that three-quarters of the hens continued producing an egg every two or three days. Gudrid was given a daily cup of milk and a slice of meat because she ate for herself and for Snorri, who still nursed at her chest. Even though she received more food, Gudrid lost weight at roughly the same rate as the rest of us. Within two full moons of Christmas, or nearly one month before the equinox, our eyes were dark sunken pits, our cheeks pronounced, and our clothes several sizes too large.

All of us were concerned for our very lives by now. Each day I awoke expecting to kill a moose, but it never occurred, so Gudrid organized a mass prayer vigil in the main longhouse to ask the God to provide for us.

"One God!" declared Thorfinn, who spoke for the crowd that huddled toward the hearth as they knelt to pray. "You, like our Norse kings, are mighty. Priests have told me that if I ask you for something, you give it to me. Well damn it, I want food so that I can once again be mighty. Have you seen my wife? Her tits aren't as full as they should be. I don't want my boy to grow up to be a runt because he doesn't get the milk he needs. I have heard something about this Job character who loved you, who served you, but you saw to it that he suffered. What kind of king does that? And I have been told that you killed your own son. What kind of king does that? I say, show me that you are great and give us some food, damn it!" With that, an uncomfortable silence ensued. Most of the listeners were still new to the faith and had never seen a book, much less read the Word of God, but they were familiar enough to know that a certain reverence to the One God was expected. For my part, I was too hungry to laugh at his gross mischaracterization of the Word, so I drew my shoulders in a little closer to pray quietly.

Thorhall the Huntsman, of course, was not there and I never expected to see him at any of the other prayer vigils which followed, but by the fourth day of supplication, someone noticed that he had not been seen for many days. Since I loved that rotten malcontent I volunteered to lead a party out to find him.

In full battle dress we left the encampment within an hour while Gudrid led another prayer in the longhouse. Her words were more soothing than anything her husband had uttered the previous several meetings, so I hoped that, at least, the assembly would leave feeling better in spirit if not in stomach.

We found no trace or track of our quarry and were, therefore, forced to begin a methodical search by splitting up into three groups of three to make concentric sweeps around sleeping lodges with ever-wider diameters. This was grueling because of the fresh, deep snow and because we fatigued quickly due to lack of strength. The first night all nine of us huddled together under the bottom branches of a fir tree next to a cold, weak fire that sputtered from melting snow falling from the bowing branches above.

I awoke the next morning hugging one of the men for warmth. So weak was I that I didn't immediately move away from him, but tarried there trying to continue to steal further warmth from his body. He didn't move either for he was dead. We left him there frozen under the tree, and the eight of us continued our methodical search for the Huntsman, hoping to avoid a similar fate.

That day I killed a squirrel. Even though it was not time for a meal we abruptly struck our stones amidst some dry leaves we brought with us to start a fire to cook the meat. I am ashamed to say that our work on the fire was for naught because before the flames grew to the size of the squirrel itself, we had already eaten the animal's raw flesh. The tiny beast had warmth remaining in his muscles as the flesh slid into my belly.

Even though the quantity of meat was little to spread among eight men, we all instantly had more energy and moved quickly the rest of the day. It is truly amazing what hope men can find in the littlest success of eating raw scraps of squirrel meat.

After the sun fell and the stars shone brightly above on the cloudless night, one of our groups shouted that they found something. The rest of us ran toward the sound so that we now stood at the foot of a rise of land. There above us in the midst of the woods was a barren hill except for the silhouette of a large flat rock which was perched atop the crest like a vigilant watchman. From below where I stood, I saw what the search party pointed to. In the middle of the rock I could see two arms meandering back and forth slowly. They appeared to rise straight up from the stone like someone lay prone on it. Then I heard a quiet mumbling of nonsense in the voice of Thorhall, but using words I had never heard.

"Why did you not retrieve him?" I asked.

The men looked at me with uncertain eyes. Finally one said, "We were frightened. We were afraid he had been possessed by the One God for all his blasphemy! I'm not going up there."

"What is blasphemy you idiot? You don't even know what you are talking about." With that, I strode up the hill alone toward my friend.

I climbed up onto the rock where Thorhall lay. His eyes, mouth, and nostrils were agape. He stared at the stars as if in a trance. Thinking that being closer to him now, I would be able to decipher his words I leaned my ear down to his mouth. Alas, I could understand none of it. He took no notice of me so I shook him. Still he went on.

I spread myself out on the rock in a similar position to look up at the stars. After some time of silence he said, "I miss my friend Erik."

"As do I. He raised me."

Ignoring my comment, Thorhall continued, "He was the only one left who understood the old gods."

"I still understand the old gods," I responded.

"You? Humph!" Thorhall retorted. "You are among the worst of them with their love of the cowering god."

Changing the subject now, "What are you doing out here?"

"That's no concern of yours, Halldorr, you dry chicken turd."

I smiled at his obvious fondness for me. "It does concern me because I have been looking for you out in the snow for two days. A man died."

"No one told you to sit with me like an addled old fool. Maybe next time you'll tie me to a heavy rock like we would the village simpleton," he complained.

"Are you coming back with us?"

"Of course I am!" exclaimed an exasperated Huntsman. "But you are a dense one! Do you expect me to stay out here and freeze?"

We camped at the foot of the hill that night, trying to stay warm. Despite the men's initial fears of a devil inhabiting Thorhall, our discovery of the man renewed our spirits to make the daylight seem to come more quickly. We walked straight to the village instead of taking the zigzagging systematic route we used for our outward journey. It was time for another sparse mid-day meal when we walked into camp, but it was deserted – both houses were empty.

Then the nine of us heard a loud series of cheers and shouts down at the shore where the tide climbed and fell dramatically each day. It sounded like a celebration. With a knowing smile, Thorhall merely sat down to rest his old bones on a short stump while the others and I ran to the noise.

We burst from the trees to see nothing short of a glorious gift from God. A mass of our people teemed over a great whale that had been beached as the tide ebbed away that morning. It was wedged between two large sheets of ice that jutted vertically from the shingle, also left behind when the water fled toward the sea. Even as they butchered the beast, men and women alike greedily shoved its blubber into their mouths. More than one found the richness more than their wanting, thin bellies could handle and promptly vomited it back out. Nonetheless, I hadn't seen smiles like these in months.

While Thorhall's other rescuers began to scavenge the creature's remains for themselves, I pulled my saex and used its razor sharp Frankian blade to cut out a large steak to share with Thorhall and walked back to the camp. There he sat tilting, half asleep, on the stump when I walked by and kicked him in the leg. "By that frozen bitch Hel, what do you think you are doing?" he shouted while falling to a knee.

I merely bade him to follow me to one of the longhouses where we fried the steak in a small pan over the hearth, using its own blubber as a grease for the pot. When the meat was cooked, we sat alone on crude stools which had hastily been assembled over the winter and silently enjoyed the first real food we'd eaten in months.

"It's stifling really," he said to the floor while repeatedly licking his teeth to capture as much of the flavor and nutrition as he could. When I didn't say anything back Thorhall continued, "These people, our floating town, their faith, I mean, it's all so stifling. I need to escape. I feel hemmed in."

"Aye, but we'll likely explore again in the spring," I said, wishing I had cut off a bigger steak.

"No, since the One God came back with Leif, I don't want to be with these people," he protested.

"So?"

"So I'm escaping. I aim to return to Leifsbudir with several invited men. You may come if you like, you worthless ram nut."

I gave it honest thought for Leifsbudir was a fine place. I could lead my own small village. Thorhall would be a very reliable aid. No women would be there to further disappoint me. Yet I said, "No friend. I will go exploring as Thorfinn's captain. But I'll likely return there soon, perhaps in a couple years."

With a huff from Thorhall our conversation was done and our paths were decided.

Soon thereafter the weather broke, and all of our fortunes changed. Fish seemed to jump into our boats, we could row out to the island and gather eggs from geese, and the land-borne wildlife returned. The camp gave the credit to their consistent prayers to the One God. Thorhall swore about the Christian God and gave the credit to Red Beard, which was the name he used for Thor to whom he had prayed on his solo adventure into the snow.

· · ·

"But you're a great fighter, and I can't stand to lose these men," argued Thorfinn, pointing to the nine Greenlanders who desired to travel away to Vinland with the Huntsman as the first drops of rain began splashing onto us. Thorfinn stood on the windy beach following our first hungry winter in Straumsfjord while the Huntsman and his small crew finished packing up *Valhalla* with supplies.

The ducks were slowly returning to their place on the sand, but this time stayed some ells away from where we kept our ships. When Thorhall didn't respond to his plea, Thorfinn shook his head in disgust, but Snorri the Elder picked up a stray small speckled duck egg and threw it at *Valhalla*, shouting, "Don't you see Karlsefni? We don't need these men and their tired old Huntsman! He's a heathen anyway." In stride, Thorhall reached over the side of the ship and scraped the fracture egg debris from the strakes with his palm, then after taking a taste, wiped the rest onto his jerkin. Droplets of rain began to fall at a more pronounced angle that continually flattened as the wind picked up bringing a true, rolling storm toward us.

"Quiet down, Snorri," said Thorfinn. "These are good men, with good heads on their shoulders. They would be missed."

Ignoring his leader and friend, Snorri cried while extending a thumb in my direction, "They should take this piece of the devil's shit with him so that they can all live like the womanless hermits they are!"

"I said shut up Snorri!" yelled Thorfinn who seemed to grow a few more inches as he blustered in anger at his somewhat estranged friend. "You're acting more and more like a jealous woman than a trusted friend! So shut up!" I openly chuckled at the exchange which caused Snorri to storm off through the growing puddles like the woman he was. "You shut up too, Halldorr, you're not helping," finished Thorfinn, again shouting to be heard over the loud storm.

"I'll make you a partner in our profits if you stay with us," pleaded Thorfinn while the men aboard *Valhalla* already began threading the oars through the holes to pull the ship from its resting spot and into deeper water.

The knarr began to slip away into the growing surf of the fjord as the Huntsman said to Thorfinn, "We've made our decision, Karlsefni." Then to me he said, "See you in Vinland again someday." He turned to guide *Valhalla* through the fjord using its sturdy rudder before I was even able to give him a weak wave goodbye.

I stood there for some time watching the boat disappear into the storm after Thorfinn walked back to camp. Even though it was the middle of the morning, the darkness soon swallowed up my grumpy friend the Huntsman, or my father's friend at least, but I remained. Eventually I dropped among the pebbles and received a thoroughly wet ass for my troubles, but did not care. I felt aged as the abrupt change in the weather caused the old wound from the skraeling spear to burn in my leg.

My thoughts wandered while I tossed stones into the white-capped breakers which now collapsed around my feet. My mother was dead. I can't say that I ever even knew her name. At least I couldn't remember it. My true father, Olef, was dead. Why did I even care anymore? After all, I killed his killer, Bjarni. My second father, Erik, dead. His oldest son, Thorvald, dead. His youngest son, Thorstein, dead. Fife, the Scot, dead. Kenna, dead.

For thirty-nine years I had fought in Midgard, the realm of men. I was so old – well I thought I was old then, but now as I pen this writing, I know what old truly is. What did I have to show for any of my toiling to that point? A beautiful chest of wealth. Two books. A son who starved to death wanting for his mother's milk and her touch. Another son who may never know me as his father. Most of the people I loved were dead. Leif remained living, but ruled in far away Greenland. King Olaf lived in self-imposed exile after our thorough defeat on the seas.

Thorhall had tied me to my past due to his friendship with Erik. But now he left and I served Thorfinn, who had taken Gudrid as his wife. How would I ever find a woman now at this age? Most men had slept with a woman for over twenty years at this season in their lives. What woman would have me? No land. Though I suppose I could return to Europe and buy land, I could use my wealth to buy respect.

God, I was foolish to ask such things. Crevan, the old priest, would say, "May fides rector vos." "May faith be your guide." But after making a mistake when learning my Latin for the first time, I interpreted the saying as, "May fortune be your guide." Even now as an old man, I think my mistake carried more real-life wisdom than Crevan's wishful thought. My fortune, my fate was being spun by the three norns living among the roots beneath the Yggdrasil tree. It was clear that they too served the One God, as I now did. They simply switched their allegiance when I was forced to change my own. They chose to torture me so. Did they laugh while they did these things to me?

God, I was foolish to ask such things. An introspective Norseman? Huh! It is a dangerous thing to think! It is dangerous to question. Though I made many decisions, I had no choices in my life. Why should I believe I did? Nothing in my life thus far had shown me I retained control of anything.

Though I did have control over others occasionally, for I had been able to make a difference in someone else's life by hastening them to a shallow, too-soon grave. I controlled death. Snorri the Elder was right in so many ways. I was to be a hermit, good for nothing but killing whenever an overlord needed killing done. I would have no friends. I would have no family of my own.

. . .

Thorfinn left several Greenlanders and a few of his thralls behind in the Straumsfjord settlement to construct more permanent shelters. Like my third father selecting Brattahlid, the most productive land in Greenland, for himself before other settlers arrived, Thorfinn found a picturesque rise of land overlooking the fjord and laid claim. He directed the men to build his personal estate on the choice morsel of dirt and timber, complete with a fenced pasture, a small blacksmith shop, and a large longhouse.

The rest of us travelled in the two remaining knarrs out of the fjord to find unknown lands. We were again explorers on the move that summer. For much of the trip I piloted *The Merchant* with one hand while I picked up the now toddling little Snorri. His steps were wobbly at best while on land, but on the pitching ship, he more closely resembled a dwarf who had enjoyed his mead too much. Over and again I made a big show to reach down, picking him up by the back of his tunic, so that his feet would fly free from the deck. While letting him dangle and swing from my hand with the ship's motion, I would slowly lower him back down to his unstable footing. When he immediately fell to his backside, I repeated the process. Little Snorri found this all very enjoyable; in fact he often let out a great scream of excitement when he knew my hand was coming to pick him up once again. Gudrid and the small number of other women watched with broad smiles while they sat across baggage in the hold patching holes in a spare sail.

We sailed on and on along a coast that must have gone on forever, possibly all the way to Utgard where the giants tread. I never saw any signs of these Goliath-like men, but as we cruised, the trees changed from mostly tall, straight pines to mostly bushy oaks or maples. The coast line too changed, gradually shifting from the ruggedness to which I was accustomed to gently sloping land gracefully exiting the sea. Beaches, too, became more frequent. I was not certain how we would be able to tell when we crossed out of the land of men into the land of the giants, but was sure that the landscapes I then saw were too small for anything but men.

I say the coast must have gone on forever because after over two weeks of moving mostly southward, Thorfinn ordered our ships to tarry around a spectacular wonder before turning back northward. In all the many years I have lived, I never returned to see just how far south that coastline extended. It is something my clouded eyes still yearn to see, something my old bones long to feel.

Back to the magnificent wonder – a narrow cape, continuing for perhaps hundreds of miles curved out from the shore, creating a natural sound. Far to the south, the cape curved back toward the land to nearly seal the inland sea off entirely from the ocean. Only periodic channels connected the two bodies of water. The sound itself appeared quite shallow as did the inlets on the rougher, ocean side. The entire area had extreme tidal shifts, changing by many feet in a short time, leaving behind countless shoals. These shifting sand bars made navigating in the wind terribly difficult, as we would quickly find ourselves blown atop a mound of sand despite our shallow draft. This happened three times in the weeks we explored the area. Thankfully when it did occur, the weather was mostly agreeable so we merely had to sit and wait for the sea to lift us from where she had deposited us.

It was very hot there. The air was wet, and we sweat constantly even with the ocean breezes. My beard stuck to my chest. The men were shirtless most of the time, and we received punishing sun burns for our troubles. Thankfully, many of us had fair skin upon our backs so I was not the only one to suffer from the pain and humiliation of a peeling pink back. Just a few of the men and women with slightly darker complexions fared much better. Snorri the Elder, of course, was one such lucky soul, and he took great pleasure in ridiculing me and my fried hog skin for some time.

Days later we sailed up a shallow, winding river which emptied into the great sound. After travelling for some time, we came upon a man-made clearing filled with several large round huts. Their roofs were gently sloping and covered with dried grasses which extended out from the walls creating large eaves. A lonely boat, nothing more than a hollowed-out log, bobbed at the shore. The grounds immediately surrounding the huts were immaculately maintained with grasses kept short by a scythe or animal grazing. There were no well-worn paths between the huts, no drying hides, no smoke from fires so that the place almost looked abandoned. We saw not a soul, except a small naked skraeling boy carrying a tiny bow and arrow. His long black hair was tied into a single braid which hung lazily over one of his shoulders. A single white feather jutted from the braid and tapped his shoulder with each step. He was sneaking out of one of the houses and looked surprised when he saw us. His face said he was scared not of us, but that we caught him doing something he knew to be wrong. Without a word he ran away from the river into the far trees, quickly engulfed by the forest's darkness.

Propelled on by the wind further up-river, we saw one more skraeling. This was a man of some immense age. His thin skin sagged all over his thin body, which was covered in tattoos of black and red and even blue. The old man sat cross-legged on a large boulder at the river's edge. He held an ornately carved wooden implement that he pinched between his lips, before he blew puffy smoke trails out of his mouth. Behind him, extending for many, many ells into a pine forest was a carefully cultivated field of a plant I had never seen. It was broad-leafed, bushy and short, perhaps knee-high. The plants were spaced several feet apart with light green foliage.

We stared at him, and he at us while the ship lazily floated past. Snorri the Elder wanted to bury a javelin into his chest, but

Thorfinn thought it unnecessary, telling his friend to tend the steering oar instead.

On our return trip downriver later that day, the old man still sat on his rock, blowing billowing smoke out of his mouth, at ease, apparently still paying us no heed.

Because of the treacherous seas and since we were so far removed from other Norsemen, certainly too far for Thorfinn to trade profitably, three days later we turned our bows northward to further investigate many of the inlets we saw on our outbound trip from Straumsfjord.

Eventually we came to a fjord which narrowed to a river, before widening again to a broad, long lake or lagoon. Because it too changed with the tides we called the place, Hop, which means tidal pool. North of the pool, the land again grew closer together to form a river which extended for many miles nearly straight north. Great hills grew from the edges of the river and lagoon and continued on rolling away in all directions like the waves of the sea. By the time we reached Hop it was late autumn and the changing leaves gave the colorful swells depth and character. It was beautiful.

We decided to stay for the winter and so, like in Straumsfjord last year, we built a hasty longhouse to squeeze into to keep warm. Another simple structure was built for the thralls to share and to get their filth out from our noses. When the weather came to us, we would invite our livestock inside. Hopefully, there would be room for them in the thrall shelter so I did not have to sleep with the scent of hog shit in my nostrils.

But the winter proved to be exceptionally mild. Snow never stuck to the ground. Twice we had a light, airy flurry, but the flakes rapidly disappeared, melting on the grasses.

Going into the cold season everyone feared a repeat of the hardships last winter brought after Christmas, so Gudrid led a heart-wrenching plea to the One God before our celebration. Perhaps because of that prayer, we ate heartily all year with the lagoon providing overflowing nourishment.

At the shore where the tide rose highest, we dug pits so that when the tide fell away, halibut rested at the bottoms. These were delicious fish and each fed us for many days. At times they were enormous – one weighed as much as a man and nearly broke my leg with his powerful flapping when I went into the hole to retrieve him. In the future I would shoot an arrow into the flesh from the safety above, but that day my father's saex buried to the hilt in his eyes ended his movements. It took both Thorfinn and me to haul the beast up out of the pit and then drag it back to the longhouse.

We fished in the river and hunted the prolific game in the woods around Hop. Trees with delicious nuts like those of the walnut trees native to Tyrkr's homeland were gathered by the basket. We lived in a land of plenty and never came across a skraeling, though I found a stone-tipped arrow on one hunting trip. From its condition, I could tell it had been lost years ago.

I began to have big thoughts, and one evening as Thorfinn and I sat across from one another at a campfire a single day's walk from the settlement, I shared them with my friend, "We should carry the news of this place back to Greenland and Iceland, maybe even all the way back to Norway or our settlements in Ireland. I've lived in all those places and know from experience that both Iceland and Greenland are pitiful excuses to call them delightful."

Thorfinn sat on a log gnawing at the last bit of meat from a rabbit that we roasted. The flames lit up his curious face and he said, "And what do you think telling everyone about this place would get us?"

Thinking of my life back in Ireland many years before, I answered at first mysteriously, "Profits, dear Karlsefni, profits." Then clarifying, "Iceland and Greenland should just be resting points to bring Norsemen to Markland or Vinland and then here or beyond to settle. We have only the occasional skraeling to confront and from what I've seen, several determined Norsemen can triumph in any engagement with them."

"What do I care if Norsemen settle here or in Iceland? It would take years to bring enough of our countrymen here and I need people with which to trade. How else can a merchant make a living, but through trade?" asked Thorfinn before spitting a bit of a sharp rabbit bone out from the corner of his mouth that had clearly been bothering him.

"My friend, you are not seeing the possibilities! In only several years Erik had Greenland covered with Norse transplants – and Greenland is awful! People will clamber to get away from their new overlord Sweyn Forkbeard in Norway. They will clamber to find land on which to farm, hump their women, and whelp babies. When they do this clambering, they will need a strong leader who already knows the land. They will need a strong leader who can settle disputes at the Thing. They will need a jarl."

I let the idea hang there for a while. Thorfinn's face told me before his mouth did that he liked the idea. "You're right, you old man! We go back to Greenland and begin spreading the news that a vast new and mild world awaits them. All men want easy riches, and so they'll bring their women and come. Maybe a trip to Iceland or Norway would help build support too."

"Yes, exactly," I nodded.

"And then we are rulers of all this," he said with his large paws spread wide.

Then my military mind took over, "We must first make certain that Vinland and Straumsfjord are secure fortresses, with men under our employ to give safe haven to travelers on their way here to Hop. When they finally arrive, we rule. You rule that side of the pool, I rule this side."

He scowled at me saying, "What if I'll have this side for my rule?"

I scowled right back and hissed, "Then you'll be dead." We both laughed at our own joke, before draining two entire pots of ale and settling down to sleep. As I drifted away, I thought about how much simpler and more satisfying my life would be now that I would again focus on profits and not on the whims of love and fate.

. . .

So in the spring we set about making our plans become truth. The mild weather permitted us to break camp early, well before the equinox, and sail back to Straumsfjord. All of us returned to build the Straumsfjord camp and then Leifsbudir into permanent settlements in order for Norsemen to reach the lush, mild Hop safely.

When we arrived, we found that those left behind had indeed been busy. On the hill overlooking Straumsfjord, Thorfinn had a large longhouse in which to move. They had even managed to fit a flap-covered window into the side, overlooking the bay. His hall was surrounded by a fenced-in pasture that traversed both sides of the hill, toward the sea and away. Several of the least desirable trees were left within the pasture's borders as they would only be good for firewood someday rather than immediate ship, house, or fence building. The hut holding the livestock and thralls was on the bottom of the hill on the side of the forest.

Thorfinn set me to the task of building an easily protected village with his new home as the centerpiece. The setting was not an ideal location like Dyflin or Kaupangen with their natural winding rivers, but I was determined to make it work. In any case, his own home on the hill would serve as a good refuge in the event of an attack by skraelings.

But our first encounter with the local population occurred long before I could make adequate defensive preparations. Nine boats filled with skraeling men came into Straumsfjord early one morning. At the bow of each boat, one of the men balanced himself gracefully on his feet while the others slowed their progress by dragging their oars in the water. The standing men each held a long, narrow wooden pole and they waved it in a sun-wise manner so that we could hear the whooshing sounds they made from the shore. They said nothing, but instead, looked to us to make some type of reply to their initial foray into communication.

Thorfinn was baffled, "What do they want us to do?"

Nearby, Folkvar asked, "Should I get more men and weapons?"

"I don't think so," was Thorfinn's reply. "What do you say, Snorri?"

Snorri the Elder scrunched his forehead and said, "We should just leave them be. Let's walk back to the village and let them alone with their poles."

Thorfinn considered that for a moment before saying, "What about trading with them? I am a merchant, after all."

Now shaking his head, Snorri said, "I think that we invite trouble if we talk with them."

Folkvar remembered his last interaction with skraelings when ten men and Thorvald died, so he quickly agreed with Snorri, "Snorri's right. Let's go back and alert the village, we don't have to pick a fight, but we should warn our men."

"You're not saying anything, Halldorr," prompted Thorfinn. "What do you think they mean by this?" he said, pointing to the men in boats.

Folkvar was right to be worried, and in truth, Snorri was right; if we talked with them, they would be able to scout our village. I remembered when Leif and I had used a similar ruse to reconnoiter Aber Tawe before we sacked the town. Yet risks sometimes had to be taken, "I don't think they mean us any harm," I said, measured. "If they wanted to attack us, why come in full sun and make these motions? I think we should invite them ashore to trade with us as Thorfinn suggests."

Thorfinn nodded, "He's right. Now how do we get them here?"

"Folkvar," I said, "go to the ships and get several white shields. Since we think they show us a peaceful gesture, let's give them one of ours in return." With a nod from Thorfinn, Folkvar went to retrieve the shields. In short order he returned, carrying several of the heavy round items, while the skraelings still sat in their bark-covered boats. I took a moment to admire their low boats. They appeared to be light-weight, perhaps only two men could carry them. The bark was wrapped tightly around thin ribs of cedar, sealed with pitch. I would build one of those someday, I thought.

Each party looking at the other, our band held the white shields above our heads with two hands, waving them at the skraelings. The men who had been turning the poles immediately stopped and started talking excitedly to the others in their boats. One of those in the bow eventually shrugged his shoulders and with hesitation again swung the pole. We smiled and returned the signal with our waving shields. This went on for some time until the oarsmen were ordered to slowly push the boats to shore.

We stood there, our two groups of men, staring at one another. They had all climbed out of their boats so that we must have been surrounded by thirty or forty skraelings. The four of us still held our shields, but eventually I set mine down and walked up to one of the men who looked to be the oldest. I extended my bare hand out in greeting, but the man looked confused. He leaned to his right to see if my hand held something he could not immediately find. I smiled and nodded that he should take my hand. Eventually, he understood and grasped my hand with his own, returning a genuine smile. He had a firm grip.

As we stood there, I studied the man while he nodded to his companions. He was at least ten years older than I was at the time, though it was hard to tell since I have never been able to properly decipher the age of skraelings. His long hair was mostly white with occasional clumps of its original black interspersed. He had many black and red tattoos that started from his hands and wound all the way up his arms and across his bare chest. When the man saw my *Charging Boar* tattoo, he grabbed my forearm and remarked something to his friends about it. They all nodded their approval, I think, while one or two frowned with wrinkled brows. Ignorantly, I broadened my smile and added a vigorous head-bobbing of my own.

Thorfinn could take the waiting no longer so he huffed, "Let's take these men to the village to trade." The other three set their shields down and waved on the crowd of skraelings who eagerly followed us to the scattered longhouses just a short walk from the water's edge.

Once we crossed the narrow band of trees which separated the town from the fjord, other curious Norsemen saw our visitors, and we soon had a gaggle of admirers. We found a large, clear area and set blankets down for all the skraelings to sit upon. Thorfinn had Gudrid and the other four women of our party bring out chunks of cheese to give to our guests while we set ourselves on blankets across the way. This act proved to be fortuitous because the skraelings all smiled as they raved over the food, acting as if they had never tasted cheese before, nodding and grinning.

Because of their obvious pleasure, Thorfinn called for a large basket of cheese to be gathered from all of our possessions, brought out, and placed in front of the old skraeling with whom I shook hands. Gudrid set it down and retreated behind her husband who said, "I offer this as my first item of barter between your peoples and mine."

The skraeling seemed to instantly understand, and he directed one of his youngest men to run to the shore. While his runner was gone the good-natured old man asked of me, "Aanek azhiwasin gichi-akiwenzii danaanagidoonowin an?" His face was open, yet inquisitive and reminded me of Kitchi's face who died on the beach south of Leifsbudir several years earlier.

We all looked back and forth to one another not sure of what he asked. As the uncertain silence inched by, Thorfinn goaded me to do something, so I opened my mouth to offer some words, but was pardoned from speaking by the return of the young man from the boats. In his thin arms he carried a large mound of pelts from all kinds of creatures, beaver, marten, deer, and rabbit. As their leader directed, the runner placed the pelts in front of me as the oldest member of our contingent, assuming I must be in a leadership position.

We all nodded our approval and then, after another uncertain pause, began to cautiously rise from our seats, to indicate our meeting was over. The skraelings understood and carried their cheese basket back to their boats where it was loaded safely in the center of the old man's hold.

There were no parting speeches, no goodbyes, no waving arms, though almost the entire village watched as they paddled away toward the mouth of Straumsfjord and then circled south out of sight.

. . .

It was like that for a few months. Our new trading partners would arrive in the morning in groups of about thirty men. No women ever came with them. They paddled their low, bark-covered boats into the fjord from the sea, so I was not certain where their village was situated. I wondered if they were from the village near our battle at Kjalarnes where Thorvald died, but Straumsfjord seemed like a long distance to paddle such small boats. In any case they would arrive unannounced with the early sun, the leaders of each boat spinning their wooden staffs in a sun-wise direction. We became quite practiced at our own greeting, even having the white shields stacked at the ready next to a particularly proud larch tree, so that whoever happened to be down at the shingle would confidently signal to the new, valued customers in the fjord.

The skraelings' favorite good for which to barter was easily cheese. They devoured hunks, large and small, in front of us and, before I understood the tongue, the traders indicated with hand gestures that they desired more filled baskets to take back home. So much of our cheese did they take that the women soon complained that we would have none left for ourselves when winter came, to which Thorfinn would answer, "With all the high quality pelts we are receiving in return, you may be able to buy all the cheese in Greenland, so pipe down."

Ahanu, which was the name of the old man who seemed to be their leader, means "he laughs." I do not know if he was given the name at birth by a soothsayer or someone gave it to him later in life, but I do know that it's a name that was aptly bestowed for once he became comfortable with us, like a gift offered to a new bride, he offered his laugh frequently and with zeal. It was not the cackling whistle that emanated from the old master shipwright, Skaffhog, nor was it like the hearty guffaws men gave around the mead table as they lied their way through mug after mug. It was, rather, a gentle snicker with such a musical quality that whenever it fell upon someone's ears, that person could not help but like the man. I was one such person taken in by its charm; I liked him very much. Ahanu would, of course, laugh when expected. But he would also laugh when it was most unexpected or even inappropriate. But his giggle always brought happiness to me, even when we disagreed on some topic of importance.

After the their third or fourth trip to our growing village, Ahanu and I found time to stroll into the forest to teach one another the simplest words of our respective languages while the other men stayed behind to barter with Thorfinn and his band.

Ahanu led our discussion off by pointing to a pine tree declaring, "Zhigwaatig oog." As expected, he laughed gently while

I slaughtered his native tongue, but smiled genuinely, like my old teacher Crevan, when I finally mastered my first phrase of these Vinland peoples.

We pointed at a stream, "ziibiins," a turkey, "mizise," and even my nose, "injaanzh." It was during this walk that I recalled the word I had used to describe the vain one that caused the death of Kitchi. When I asked Ahanu about the word, segonku, he joyously laughed and bade me to follow him deeper into the forest. Despite his age and long grey hair, he was nimble with strong legs so that soon we came to a place where a small creek or "ziibiins" flowed at the bottom of a ravine then curved around a large boulder, disappearing in a cave-like mass of gnarled trees, before reappearing some ells away. With surprising agility, the old man scampered up the smooth rock, and without question I followed. When we reached the short summit, Ahanu pointed down into the thick underbrush on the other side, whispering, "Segonku." With his tattooed arms and hands silently waving me on, his face betraying nothing but excitement, I lowered myself down amongst the branches until the sun's light was almost entirely swallowed. I must admit that although I had no reason not to trust Ahanu, I blinked to get my eyes used to the shadowed darkness with ample concern, fingering the hilt of my blade. Was this segonku a claw-filled beast that would rip my arms from my body – a bear, a wolf? To be safe, I finally slid my father's saex out from its place in my belt and peered into the mangled darkness.

After an eternal moment I quietly beckoned up to the old man, "What is this segonku?" He gave me a chuckling hiss, demanding silence so I looked around again, even taking an uncertain step forward. Then I saw a small creature toddle out from a burrow that was well hidden, tucked between a large root jutting from the hillside and a partially eroded rock. Despite its small size, it initially gave me a start, quickening my pulse. But after settling down, I whispered to myself while nodding, "So you're a segonku little one? But why did Kitchi call the vain one by your name? Oh well, I think I'll make a nice warm hat from your hide."

Ahanu's laugh was quietly building now so that it was quite loud. I smiled at the thought of my new friend up above me, having me so worried over this tiny harmless creature, while taking my first rapid step toward my prey. That little segonku's response was surprising to say the least! I expected to have to cut him off before he dove into his home, but he stood his ground, unleashing a powerful spray of liquid like that from a miniature whale's blowhole.

Instantly I knew I was in trouble. I knew why Ahanu laughed while keeping a safe distance between himself and the segonku. The liquid was among the most pungent, foul smells I have ever inhaled in all my life and it now covered me, burning my eyes in the process, soaking into my beard. My surprised screams and hoots brought more, louder howls from Ahanu, who stood with tears rolling down his pronounced, handsome cheeks when I crawled out from the stinking segonku lair. While I was certainly angry with his practical joke, I must admit that it was a memorable vocabulary lesson.

. . .

We returned back to the Straumsfjord village to find an argument had broken out between the two groups of traders. Several of the younger skraeling men were demonstrably agitated, with arms flailing, while speaking at the speed of a ship under full sail in a good wind. I could not decipher their words. I did understand what our men were shouting, and it made me nervous for our immediate future with these men.

"I said no!" shouted Thorfinn. "No. No. No."

Snorri the Elder chimed in, "I don't care how much you admire our swords or how much your old man likes our old man, we'll trade neither our steel nor iron!"

The young skraelings shouted while pointing at a large pile of goods they had assembled outside Thorfinn's longhouse to offer to us in return for weapons. Among the menagerie of implements on the pile were several smartly bundled sets of arrows with brightly tipped stone points that the brave young men apparently viewed as an even exchange for a sword.

While we stood there looking at the scene, Ahanu placed his hand upon my shoulder as if to steady me from acting rashly. However, he then thought better of it, removed the hand, sniffed it, and offered one of his chuckles while wiping the now pungent hand on the skins he wore for leggings, seemingly oblivious to the growing danger not three man-lengths away.

The argument continued when Snorri stopped in mid-sentence to now say, "By the God of this earth, what is that smell?" Apparently both sides sensed my odor at the same time and paused their shouting long enough to turn to see Ahanu and me watching them. "Oh, I should have known it would be that old goat urine-smelling half-wit, Halldorr." Snorri then returned to his belligerent shouting at the skraelings.

Ahanu walked over to the party and questioned his men on the fringes of the crowd. He nodded several times, asked more questions, before nodding again. He seemed completely nonplussed by the events, as I grew frustrated by what could be a potentially dangerous situation for all of us. And so even though I agreed with Thorfinn that we should not trade away our superior weapons to these men, the situation needed to be controlled before someone, like Snorri, did something foolish.

So I did something foolish. Although even at the time I knew making Snorri my target would only make him more of an enemy, I disregarded the thought as irrelevant. I strode over to the blathering idiot, shouted, "Knife!" and used that as an excuse to tackle Snorri to shut him up. Using my knees to pin his arms to his sides, I proceeded to break his nose again with three rapid jabs to his face. By the third stroke, the already misshapen nose had turned to the consistency of cooked walrus blubber, with its oozing blood intermixed with semisolid bits of bone. He wailed mightily while I drew back for another colossal blow.

But Arnkell and Folkvar grabbed me by my shoulders, pulling me, still swinging, off Snorri's heaving chest. Now my Norse brothers were shouting at me, but I smiled as they dragged me away for my plan had worked long enough as a diversion to let the cooler head of Ahanu prevail upon his men. Our men roughly took me to the nearest maple, tossing me on its exposed roots, yet I didn't even bother to struggle under their grasp, preferring to send a wicked grimace toward elder Snorri.

In truth, I think the skraelings liked to watch the two tall light-haired strangers fall into a scuffle. But whatever their reason, soon the young men began to make signs that they would respect Thorfinn's decision to disallow trading weapons.

Instead of swords, while Snorri the Elder limped off dripping blood onto his clothing and the earth, Thorfinn, the master trader, helped the skraelings divert their focus onto some large bolts of red cloth our five women had woven the previous winter. Gudrid, in her tight braids, brought it out and now rested it atop little Snorri's head, using it like a table while the men negotiated the cloth's value as if the argument never occurred.

Ahanu came and sat in the dirt next to my stinking body and bloodied hands. Together we watched as little Snorri kept reaching his short arms up to grab the fabric from his head only to fail again and again. Undeterred he repeated the attempts, despite the fact that Gudrid tortured her son, our son, by whisking the cloth away each time his hands got close. Adding to the mayhem for poor little Snorri, while still negotiating, Thorfinn took his mighty foot and tapped the boy on his backside each time his hands went up for the cloth.

Ahanu's chuckle started and mine soon joined him. It was, after all, a joy to watch my son. But when Ahanu muttered, "Segonku," I knew he laughed not at little Snorri, but me.

And I laughed all the more, for I had a good friend.

. . .

I should have known that life would not be that pleasant for too long. After all, you know my feelings on the norns and their wicked sense of humor when it comes to laying out my path. But I was so easily drawn into thinking that my plans, made in conjunction with the successful, Thorfinn, would bring fantastic achievement. We would secure a valuable trading franchise from Greenland to Vinland and beyond to the mild lands of Hop. I would become richer, though I didn't care about the riches. I would lead a band of military men in protecting the trading lanes with our new friends, the skraelings. I would train these men to be intelligent fighters, but savagely brutal when necessary. Some, out of necessity, would be vicious or cruel even. Outside of battle, however, I knew that my role as their leader would involve using the skills they brought. Whatever their other characteristics, they would be utterly loyal to me and our way of life. I would grow old, though not too old, perhaps dying in one last great battle to protect our women and their children from evil wrought by the low serpent spoken of in the One God's book of Genesis. I contemplated all these things while we traded with the skraelings that year. I count nine "woulds" in the previous sentences; would means plan, plans have no place in my life. I should have disregarded all my thoughts as completely lunatic. I should have known that my life would soon change, in a most unexpected way.

Following the disagreement about weapons, we still traded successfully using simpler items such as cloth and the always popular, cheese. So it was of no concern to anyone when on the chilly morning of the equinox, the skraeling men with their boats came swinging the rods in the familiar way.

Ahanu was ill, coughing with snot draining from his nose, but remained his normal cheery self. His illness certainly did not impede his ability to laugh other than making the sound a touch more robust. Ahanu offered a smile of appreciation and a laugh when I pulled one of the arm rings from my bicep, giving it to him as a gift. His strong, sinewy arms were not as stout as my own and so the ring slipped down past his pronounced elbow time and again. At last I took it back, squeezing the ring between my muscled hands so that it would fit. Ahanu took the opportunity to flex one of his biceps, squeezing it with the opposite hand then comparing it with a squeeze of my own bicep. He acted very impressed by the size of my arm, chuckling merrily.

But soon he indicated his throat was sore from his ailment that day, so I mostly talked with another man called Nootau while Ahanu stood back and watched with a bright smile showing teeth worn short from years of grinding on venison and berries. Nootau seemed to be a reasonable sort of man while we chatted. We spoke for a long while about many diverse subjects. I soon learned he had a wife, four children, and six grandchildren even though he must have been about my age. He and Ahanu both looked genuinely saddened when I told them of Kenna's and little Olaf's death.

In his own tongue, Nootau offered, "Your woman, she is with the Earth Mother now. Your son, he runs in the open fields with Glooskap, the good son who would rise from the dead, killing deer with his own small hunting bow." He made some sweeping motions with his arms, palms upward facing while he spoke, making his words dramatic. As I began to translate his words then slowly comprehend them, my mouth gaped open.

"We call Glooskap by the name of Jesus," I said after a heartbeat. "He's the son of the God mother who rose from the dead, as in your story."

Ahanu and Nootau exchanged approving nods that I recognized their story of the gods, but my old friend quickly turned melancholy, offering in a deeper-than-normal, gravelly voice, "I have lost a son too, Halldorr, though he was full grown with a wife and son of his own. I know of your pain for I think of him often. No man should have to bury a son."

I put a hand on Ahanu's shoulder, "You have a grandson to look on and remember your son. I am sure you see him in the boy's eyes." He worked hard at carving a smile in his face to show he appreciated my words. "Your son, was he lost in battle?"

Father-like he patted my extended arm saying, "It is not important today how he died, though I may tell you someday." At that moment, bellowing from Thorfinn's cows echoed over the hill from their pasture. We ignored the intrusion on our conversation as the cows often made racket in the morning in order to make their presence known, trying to get a spare bit of grain put before their snouts.

"Very well, I will ask only one more question on the subject. I wish to pray to the One God about your son. What name shall I use for him when I pray? What did you call him?"

Ahanu kindly waved his fingers at me indicating he didn't want to talk about it anymore, as he sat there on a stump, but Nootau picked up the conversation, "Ahanu prefers not to talk of it, but I think he should honor his son. I know he means to in his own quiet way, but I do not have any such distaste for speaking on the subject. The boy's name means brave in our language. He would be our chief someday, but he is dead, hunting with Glooskap and little Olaf. We called him Kitchi."

The cows bawled. My ears rang. My eyes glazed. I am sure my face went completely white at the news. I felt pain flare in the place where my left arm was broken in the skirmish with Kitchi's men. Instinctively, I grasped it with my right hand, kneading it as a thrall does bread. I felt the place in my thigh where the stone spear tore my muscle and bone, nearly killing me; even now it sent fire shooting up and down my leg. Cursed, that is how I felt. The one chance I had been given for peaceful friendship with these people, and I was there when this man's son was killed. When, at last, I stumbled against the wall of the nearest longhouse, both Nootau and Ahanu moved to steady me.

"You look ill, my friend," whispered Ahanu. "Let's sit you down," and they lowered me to the stump on which he sat just a moment earlier.

"I am sorry," I started after throwing away all hope at peace and camaraderie in the future. Pulling my sword and saex from their places in my belt while teetering on my seat, I handed them to Nootau, who looked at me with surprised concern. "Nootau, you will use those on me if you must."

"Friend, I am afraid you are ill. I'll not use these weapons against you. Perhaps you have caught the spirit which has been with Ahanu," said Nootau. Ahanu nodded his agreement, giving a bewildered glance to his companion. Nootau continued, "Do you have a powerful medicine man among your people? Whom should we retrieve?"

"I am sick, though not ill."

This further mystified them, and so Nootau rose from his crouched position, taking a step to locate assistance, but I cut him off saying, "Nootau, you will halt. You must stay here and listen to what I have to say. I am not ill." The force of my voice was enough to stop him for I was coming back to my senses, blinking away the blackness of my mind. "You must know; you both must know I am sick with knowledge and fear and even self-loathing." I turned to look directly at Ahanu, his face betraying that his only concern was for my well-being. "Friend," I began. "I was there the day Kitchi died."

His friendly eyes fluttered a moment and his head tilted almost like a hound that is confused by his master's order while he took in the news. Ahanu looked away to the ground, swallowed hard, then looked back to me, saying in a tone that was both stern and sad, "Why do you say this lie? You hurt me, because I know the monster who killed my son was slain by another member of our tribe. I will continue to hope this is your illness speaking." He turned to Nootau and with a wave of his hand, dismissed him away for aid.

"Stop," I forcefully shouted. "I am not ill. Ahanu, I was there that day. You will listen to what I have to say on the matter. Kitchi was a wise, peaceful, young man – considered handsome among your people, I am sure. After meeting you, I should have seen that it was your eyes I saw in him, but did not even think it possible. Though you must know I did not raise a hand to harm your son, you may say that I had something to do with his death, so please allow Nootau to stay here with my weapons. In this way, if you wish it, he can strike me down. I'll not fight."

Looking confused and hurt, Ahanu agreed, beckoning Nootau to stand next to him. Nootau obeyed, awkwardly standing with the two blades at his side, loosening and tightening his grip in an alternating manner. "Now talk," Ahanu said with a level of seriousness I had never heard him speak. I spent the next several minutes, with the nagging cattle as background noise, explaining all the events of that terrible day from start to finish – from my late morning awakening, to my passing out, bleeding and left for dead, next to his own dead son.

When I finished Ahanu let out a heavy sigh, leaving nothing but silence in its wake. I spoke not, nor did Nootau. The air seemed thick with foreboding. I did not want to make eye contact with the men, so I stared at my feet upon the ground. We all stared at the ground. A large black carpenter ant poked his head around a bit of stray leaf stuck in the soil. At last I looked up through my wrinkled forehead to see that Ahanu rubbed his head, thinking. "Nootau, please return this man's weapons to him. Then sit down next to me so that we may talk more." When he finished speaking, Ahanu gave me a little smile. Still feeling guilty, my return smile was weak.

He continued, "Friend, I believe you have told me the things that are true. You describe my son perfectly as I remember him. You describe the other two dead men, good men, with the same exact detail, even the spear with the eagle feather. You also give a perfect description of the round, vain one you now call segonku, the only survivor of the encounter with the pale monster, which is how he described you. He said he killed you." Ahanu paused here, shaking his head, mumbling under his breath. Yet he resumed, "This segonku is a man of some importance in our village. He is likely to be chief someday as his father is the current chief."

Stunned I said, "I thought you were chief and that Kitchi was to be chief someday."

He giggled, slowly returning to his normal ways, "Oh, no, I am old, but no chief. As far as Kitchi becoming chief, we do not need to be concerned with such things anymore. Nootau likes to speak of these things. I do not. My brother is chief and even older than I. He cannot make these trips because of weakness in his legs, so I come instead. The vain one is his son."

"Then why does the segonku not come to trade with us?" I asked.

"Megedagik, you should know this segonku goes by the name Megedagik. His given name is Mukki, which means "child" and that is what he is still today, but after a hunt on which he killed several rabbits, I think it was, when he was much younger, he and his father came back proclaiming him to be Megedagik, which means "kills many." Megedagik does not come to trade with you because he says we should have nothing to do with you and the evil you people bring. After all, you did kill our men hiding under the canoes right outside our village."

They were from Kjalarnes. "That is true, it was my brother who led us on that fight. He is dead now, pierced by one of your arrows. I am truly sorry."

Ahanu didn't want to linger on those thoughts, "Yes, yes. See we have all lost family in these fights. My people like to think we are without blame in confrontations, but the hide-covered boats you found outside our village that day were stolen by warriors of our tribe from the fur-wearers who live toward the lights of the sky. We are all men, and men fight. We, the two of us, should help our peoples avoid clashes at all costs in the future, but I fear that will be difficult. You see, Megedagik complains to his father after each of our visits here. He says you will kill us, in fact, he says that is why you've come in your giant canoes. You intend to kill us and take our land."

"Canoes?" I asked.

"Yes, boats, I mean."

"Boats, I see. We come only to find empty spaces in which to live and partners with which to trade. Last year Thorfinn and I found a wonderful place many days journey from here where we plan to build a settlement. We saw no people our whole winter there. This place," I said pointing to the homes around us, "will be a safe station for our people to stop and rest on the way."

"Perhaps, if you come back with us, you can talk with our chief, my brother, and convince him of your good intentions. You make our talk very good already," Ahanu suggested.

"I'd like that very much," I said with sincerity. "However, I hate your nephew for what he did, and I am sure he hates me. Won't that become a problem with him whispering in your brother's ear?"

"Halldorr is right, Ahanu. Megedagik will just speak terrible words into the chief's ear, ruining all chances of peace," said Nootau.

"I fear you are both correct to be concerned," admitted Ahanu after a pause. "So I will go back and ask for a private audience with my brother where I will prepare him for a surprise visit from you sometime soon. I can then send Nootau back to retrieve you while I can keep my eye on Megedagik – maybe encourage a hunting trip for him." He said his nephew's name with spite then added, "My distaste for my nephew was already intense because he took Kitchi's dear widow as his wife, and as we sit here today, raises my grandson, Kitchi's son, with bitterness. It is difficult for me to say this, but I now hate my own nephew."

The cows and their bellowing grew louder – so much louder that the three of us simultaneously craned our heads in the direction of their calls. Men, Norse and skraeling alike, were already running in the direction of the commotion. Shouts, screams really, filled the air.

It was Snorri the Elder, I think, who caused all the problems that were happening at that moment. I'll go to my grave swearing it so, though subsequently, over and again he claimed that it was all the fault of a blaring cow, frightened by some unseen event and then the over-reaction of Thorfinn's youngest thrall. Maybe it was Snorri, maybe it was the cow, maybe it was the norns, by hell I cannot be expected to know all the reasons for what happens in this world. Even now as a man of ancient age, with pain in my joints holding this quill, my fist clenches with frustration at my inability to control any destiny, narrow or broad.

It was in the fading autumn grass of the pasture over Thorfinn's hill, beyond my sight, where the trouble began. The three of us abruptly rose, I shoved my blades back into my belts, and then we ran toward the cries. Though the distance was short and we made excellent time, we were among the last to crest the hill at Thorfinn's longhouse, but it was already too late.

About twenty skraelings were sprinting in our direction, some carrying weapons, some not. All of them looked frightened. Behind them were scores of our men chasing after the skraelings in a hastily assembled war party. Only some of our men were armed as well. Further behind still were at least four skraelings sprawled out on the now red-painted, brittle grass that lay bent and cracked beneath the bodies, their arms spread wide, their eyes opened wider in a permanently frozen look of pain. Scattered among those four bodies were two dead Norsemen, staring into the morning sky with no chance to ever again see its bright majesty.

We were soon enveloped by the running skraelings. Two of them decided to team up and tackled me to the ground, beating me with their balled fists. With surprising spryness, Ahanu kicked both men off me, screaming at them. They looked at the old man in anger before climbing upright and continuing their run toward the boats in the fjord.

With scratches on my face and blood draining from my lip, I rose to my elbows and saw that my Norse brothers were nearly to us. "Run," I yelled to Nootau and Ahanu in the Vinland language. They hesitated only a moment before nodding their agreement and swiftly moving to the boats. As they ran, my friend Ahanu, continued wrestling with the arm ring, sliding it back up in place after it slid down. Eventually he pulled it down his arm and over his hand, tucking it in a small pocket on his loin cloth, never breaking stride.

By the time I walked to the shores of the fjord, my friends were paddling to safety in their canoes. We did not pursue and I was glad of it, though Snorri the Elder complained unceasingly. Just one of our ships half-filled with men would have poured death down upon those skraelings, laying a blood slick upon the waters and sending them forever to the bottom of the sea.

. . .

It was a busy two weeks with many disagreements among the men and women of the village. Each day brought the fear that we would be attacked by the skraelings in retribution for their dead. Many men wanted to put an end to the waiting and attack them ourselves to avenge our own dead. Other men wanted to fortify our current surroundings for the inevitable attack from the fjord. I was the only male voice saying that we should send a mission of peace to their village, offering them gifts and apologies for the misunderstandings and death. I argued that we could end the killings right here. Gudrid was the lone female voice supporting my idea, but in the end, we were both washed away by the calls for revenge. More blood would spill.

At an impromptu Thing held along the slopes of Thorfinn's pasture where the six men lay dead not so long ago, it was decided that we would strengthen Thorfinn's home as our collective fortress. His pasture fence would be reinforced to become a wall. We would become a lone, but impenetrable, stronghold bristling with armed Norse men.

So I was forced to cast aside my woodsman axe, to set down my fisherman nets in favor of my beautiful sword with the sagas of the One God emblazoned along its length and my strong, simple saex. Thorfinn, the de facto leader in the men's eyes, was wise enough to ask me to prepare us for battle because he had never seen the sweat and death of combat. For two weeks I drilled the men, teaching them fearlessness in the shield wall, but it was not enough time. They were good men, but they were here to farm, to trade, and to lay claim to new lands. These men were not the hardened men I had with me aboard *Charging Boar* or *Dragon Skull* on our countless strandhoggs along the coasts of Scotland and Wales. These men bragged like good warriors should, but that was where the similarities ended.

"We might as well float ourselves into their village with our eyes closed if this is how you expect to fight them," I cried after one full day of a particularly pathetic effort by the men. Snorri the Elder took great pleasure in shirking any and all of my commands, even encouraging other men to do the same. Two of them were snickering back and forth to one another so without warning I raised my leg to kick the nearest man's heavy wooden shield which he held lazily in front of his chest. The force of the blow drove the iron rim hard into his mouth, causing his head to snap back, leading his instantly limp body to the ground. He lay there, unconscious and still, with four of his teeth scattered about his ears in the dust. A winding snake of blood trickled its way out of one corner of his mouth.

Snorri opened his hole to protest, but I cut him off by swinging my sword down at his head. I am truly thankful that he was fast enough to raise his shield to protect himself, because I would have killed him if he had failed to do so. I was angry and I let it take over. I was angry, not only at their performance and my inability to prepare them for war, but I was furious that I would be forced to fight good people, Ahanu's people. For the first time in my life, I had a thought that perhaps skraelings were a real people worth living and trading with. I was even outraged that I now had these thoughts. Life was simpler, decisions uncomplicated when I could kill without question. Here was the enigmatic Halldorr obscuring my own path.

Snorri thought he saw an opportunity to strike at me with his sword so he took the chance, stabbing from beneath his tilted shield with his right hand. In one fluid motion I threw my shield at his, letting it go, then grabbed his extended wrist with my now free hand. I jerked his arm while letting out a wild howl. I felt his shoulder dislocate which caused him to topple to his knees. With the flat side of my sword I then whipped him on his rear like he was an unruly child, something his father most assuredly should have done. Snorri whimpered after I hit him ten times, still pulling his arm in what had to be a most painful position. The other men had shut their mouths, staring at the scene, in frozen obedience.

"By God, Halldorr, can you not go one month without abusing that man?" shouted Thorfinn from behind. He was walking up during a break in the men's work on the fences. "Leave him be!"

He was right so I dropped the arm so that the now free Snorri rolled to his left side moaning like an expectant mother undergoing a bout of pre-birth pain. "We'll die here! Gudrid will die here and little Snorri will die here!" I growled.

"That's why you're training the men," yelled Thorfinn, not backing down from my anger. "You're the best, most experienced fighting man we've got. You'll train them well enough to beat some naked skraelings!"

"They're not just naked savages! Their stone is sharp enough to pierce even the fattest belly and drain a man of his blood! Those men could be our friends, our allies in this wild, desolate country! Ahanu is a good man, he doesn't want death." I was pleading, begging someone to show sense.

"We'll just see what a good man he is and how much death he does not want," Thorfinn said with sarcasm. "If they do not attack us, then they do not want death. In any case, you must agree that we must be ready."

"No, what I agree with is your intelligent wife who thinks we should send men and offer good will to these, our neighbors." He opened his mouth to respond, but I held up my hand to silence him. "But I know that no one else will support me in these ideas, so I am resigned to perform my part in this mess. So we will be ready, but this plan as it stands will not work," I finished, extending my empty hand and sword to the men and fence around us.

Two women had finally come to take Snorri the Elder away to tend to his wounds. I gave a nod to Arnkell to follow and use his strength to put the arm back into the socket as Thorfinn continued, "Well, if you think you've got a better idea that does not involve paddling into their village, offering ourselves up on an altar to be killed, please tell us, military genius."

I did not have a better idea, but just then another plan to save my people exploded into my mind. "You're right Thorfinn! We should offer ourselves up to be killed! And by doing so, we will kill them!" It was a plan of trickery, but it would be decisive enough to maximize our chances of victory and minimize our losses. My mind galloped like a charger hammering across a battlefield, its thundering footfalls spurring earth haphazardly in all directions. I put my friend Ahanu and his dead son, Kitchi, out of my mind and thought only of triumph.

I gathered the confused men around me and sketched my plan out in the dust.

. . .

A harsh wind cut into my face while I peered out to the fjord from my hiding place in the trees. I wore my bear skin, the gift given to me by King Olaf, to keep me warm, but also because today I was a Berserker once again, prepared to kill indiscriminately. The men had come to agree with the plan I laid out in the dirt, and that was fortuitous since already today it would play itself out. I watched the beginning of the action, but would soon return to my position to guide our battle against these people I had no reason to kill.

But I would kill them. And do not think of me as some vicious monster. What else could I do? My people were the Norse people and the One Mighty God had made me into a warrior. It must have been God or maybe it was the old god Thor, after all my name, Halldorr, means Thor's Rock in my native tongue. In either case, events in my life shaped me, chiseled me into this fighter, willing to kill when he did not want to in order to fulfill the goals or commands of others. My thoughts were beside the point. I thought not of Ahanu. I did not think of Nootau. Push them away, I did.

So I crouched there, watching. My bow resting next to my ear against the tree awaited the commands from my muscles to do its work. Boats, or canoes, as the skraelings called them, clogged the fjord, rocking amidst the waves. At least fifty birch-bark canoes ballooned with men with a single man standing in each bow, one foot resting on the short gunwale, wearing leather shoes they called makizins, waving the wooden poles as they had at each visit before. This time, however, they spun them in the opposite direction or counter-sunwise. I could not hear the familiar whooshing because the wind blew the sound away from me.

We would be outnumbered by the frightfully dressed attackers, but not badly so, perhaps nearly two to one or a little less. My counting Scotsman, Fife, would have known with exact precision. From my vantage point I saw that many of their men had shaved off most of the hair on their heads except for a long patch at the top that they somehow had stiffened with animal grease or the like, making it stand up tall like feathers on the head of a duck. Those who did not shave their heads wore their consistently black hair in braids; some then hid it under warm-looking otter skin caps. Almost all of them wore some type of single or double feather clipped in their hair. As was typical, their lower limbs were covered with hide leggings and they wore breechcloths tied at the waist. Some wore deerskin tunics, with or without sleeves, while others went shirtless despite the cool weather. Many had new tattoos with ink that seemed to shine directly to the eye, fresh, crusty scarring visible.

Turning, I flashed hand signals down the hill to Folkvar, who then passed them onto the village, indicating that I wanted twenty men to make their way to the shingle to confront the skraeling warriors. Before hand, we had held races to determine the fastest runners who were then pre-selected for this first line of men. They would need swiftness to stay alive.

Leaning back out to see our opening move in what would be a killing dance that eventually evolved into the killing song of clanging blades, twangs of bowstrings, and screams for mothers, I watched our men scramble to the water's edge. They came in twos and threes, they were confused, disorganized. They searched among storage piles for our red shields, battle shields. The men hastily strapped on their belts while forming a ramshackle line there on the beach. One struggled while wrestling his too-large bow to lace its string back on the powerful yew. In short, they were worse than the pathetic lot I had been training for several weeks. In short, they were perfect.

Then the taunting began. Every battle, small or large, in which I have ever fought, begins with taunting. I do not know if the skraelings began their battles that way before seeing us, but we mocked them that day. The twenty men stood there shaking their red shields high, shouting curses at the invaders. One man made a motion with his hands that is considered vulgar among the Norse, though I do not think it was considered much of anything by the landing party. They spat and swore; one even walked knee deep into the water and pissed at the oncoming horde. All these efforts were having the desired effect. The skraelings began shouting back, anger building, while shaking stone axes in the air. I could not hear every word because of the wind, but those I did hear and could interpret were curses indeed. One of the canoes began teetering as a single skraeling stood up to make himself heard. His movement made the man in the bow lose his balance and soon they had all fallen into the cold fjord. Excellent, I thought. My men were causing confusion, maybe even frustration. Hopefully soon we would bring death.

In Europe it was often the army which drank less ale on the morning of the battle that carried the day so I allowed only a single mug with breakfast. Today I also hoped it was the better organized, better prepared, perhaps even the more cunning army which would rule the day while spilling the other army's blood. I hoped we were the cunning band.

Two other canoes went to help their companions right their boat and pull them from the deep cold waves, delaying the progress of three boats in total – more good news. As they did this, our man who toiled so with his bow string succeed in looping it, then calmly walked to the end of our line. I admired him as he nocked the arrow, picked his target, pulled the cord to his cheek, and released. The first death of the day.

The arrow sailed true and found a wiry tattooed man who swung the pole in the lead boat. The broad iron head cracked into his chest, puncturing his bear tattoo, picking him from his feet as if he were a bit of dust being flicked off a woman's dress. His lifeless body splashed into the water after sailing over the two men who sat directly behind him in the canoe. More shouting. More rage.

Our archer, he was the best in the village and specifically selected for this task, took down two more skraelings in this manner before the attackers began to answer with their own onslaught of missiles. Perfect. Now it was time for the second part of our plan and I was confident it would be executed well, for it was the easiest. Our men had to begin to cower behind their shields looking frightened at the oncoming death awaiting them. The bowman stopped his killing and shared a shield with another man. They crouched and ducked behind the shields, poking their heads out occasionally to shout again, coming up with impressively imaginative ways to curse the enemy.

I turned back to Folkvar and gave him the agreed signal that all was ready. He ran off to make the final preparations with Thorfinn and the other men. My gaze returned to the action and I stood, getting prepared to take my own position. I resisted a brief urge to scan the flotilla for Ahanu when one of the twenty defenders took an arrow in his upper arm and was instantly dragged away from the battle by another man. This was not good, yet it was to be expected. It would actually play better into our trap, making it all the more irresistible to the attackers.

Eight ells, that's how close the nearest boat was now. Our archer shot one more man then ran away himself. Then three more men fled, leaving fourteen. Six ells and the first men began pouring over the sides of the canoe, so eager they were for battle and their deaths, I hoped. Simultaneously, another eight of our men took flight. These last men standing at the fjord were brave, and I was proud to be their commander. They stood their ground as instructed. They were the fastest men we had to be sure, but being swift of foot is not much comfort when hundreds of armed warriors are bearing down on you, intent to pull your innards out.

Then one of these last six, Egil, took action I did not expect. He raced forward into the pounding waves to attack the first skraelings approaching land. In truth it was foolish, but it helped us set the trap, and I was delighted afterward when our men sang a battle song around the hearth to Egil's bravery. With some inspiring agility, he avoided an axe blow from a howling warrior and plunged his spear into the man's side. Yet the wind and surf were strong and a particularly powerful wave slammed into Egil's feet, taking him down face first. All attention had turned to him from the nearest boats and within seconds no fewer than six arrows jutted from his back, as he floated lifelessly in the breakers.

Run, I thought, and they did. The last of our men at the beach turned, scattering back toward the village. One of them, Ormr, was slammed headlong into a tree by a heavy spear that pushed into his back through his thick leather mail. He crumpled to the ground on his side and I saw that his chest heaved while he fought to live. His arms scratched at the rocks strewn on the beach; he was alone and could not be helped. I needed to run too, but I hesitated a moment to watch the skraelings pour onto the pebbled shingle, then watched with some horror as the man who threw the spear bent down with a thin knife in his hand and cut the skin and long hair from Ormr's head while he yet lived! While the other warriors flooded around him through the trees that separated the village from the quay, he raised the bloodied mess high above his head and shrieked with such power I dropped back a step from the noise and shock.

Now I had to fly. Grabbing my bow, I ran along the backside of a curving ridge to remain concealed from the attackers down below; my helmet sat atop my head. Even now they would be entering the village in pursuit of the defenders they believed they had successfully dislodged from the beach. Those brave runners were our tempting bait. But the skraelings would be frustrated for the village was empty. We sent the women into a ravine some miles away where they were guarded by ten men. The rest of the men waited to spring the trap.

I ran down the hill, concealing myself at the edge of an open meadow, once again waiting for my chance to kill. You see, all of our runners ran into the village, hiding behind the farthest longhouse. When the invaders came close enough, they would all flee into the forest screaming in terror so that the skraelings would give chase. The screams of panic came just then, so I pulled an arrow from the quiver which hung at my leg, deliberately setting it in place – only moments now.

A group of the fastest of our runners flew past me through the meadow. I was never as fast as these men, even in my youth, certainly not now. Then came another batch, while the last men came singly with larger gaps forming among the slowest of our fast. The cries of their pursuers grew closer and I saw that several of their men, with axes raised, gained on our soldiers. Just as one enemy began a downward swing to crush the head of a Norseman, my arrow tore into the skraeling's right cheek, sending his head spinning, his body skidding across the ground. The dead man's companions ignored the fallen man and jumped over him to continue to gain on our runners. A second man raised a spear to hurl it into the back of our last man, but my arrow found its way into the pit of his arm, burying deep into his body. I reached into the quiver, grasping a missile with which to kill a third skraeling, but like a fat-fingered child, I fumbled with the arrow. Under my breath, I cursed, because the delay gave enough time for a pursuer to successfully launch a spear into the back of the trailing settler.

I moved again, angling away from the trail to the spot we selected for our battle. Time and again, I have been witness to the benefits of choosing the site on which to shed blood. As I panted beneath my bear skin, I hoped it would be so today. At last I made it to what would be the left end of our curving line and ducked down next to Thorfinn amongst the bushes. Despite the circuitous route taken by our swift men, they were arriving in the clearing ahead simultaneously. They paused, resting their hands on their knees to take in gulps of breath while the others came into the clearing.

These vastly outnumbered men did not have to act frightened at the first sight of their would-be killers. They ran en masse to the end of the clearing and began picking their way up an incline with scattered rocks, bushes and trees. Oh, True God, I thought, but this was marvelous. The whole lot of the skraelings ran headlong into the clearing and without noticing the hundreds of eyes fixed upon them, ran to kill our exhausted men at the opposite end.

"Up!" I shouted and the slaughter began.

. . .

Every man with a bow, except for those of us on the far left and right flanks, sent arrows indiscriminately into the mass of bustling bodies. Beneath the red paint on their faces I could see shock taking over the savagery of pursuit. Then it turned to fear as blood from their companions began splattering on their clothes and faces. We had the high ground, with the center of our line among the trees and rocks at the end of low, wide ravine. We had the high ground on each side, standing behind scrub bushes that had produced hearty berries only weeks before. Arrows poured like the showers of spring, a cold front of death brought by our hands. Mayhem reigned in the panicked group of skraelings as they were surrounded on three sides, with a pincer that would quickly form behind them.

Thorfinn, Folkvar, myself, and ten others would close the left side of that pincer, while Arnkell and Snorri would lead the swinging gate on the right side to its close. Both sides were nearly closed by the time the attackers in the back of the skraeling ranks realized what was happening. However, when they did figure out they would soon be trapped like a rat in the bilge of a knarr, they became ferocious. In their eyes, fear vanished. I saw it instantly replaced with cruel fierceness.

They came to us. I did not hear any grand commands from leaders, for their men knew what they must do to survive. The first man I met came at me with a long wooden spear, tipped with jaggedly sharp stone of a light blue color. He was quick, despite his broad shoulders, and he feigned to strike me beneath my shield so that when I moved to stop the blow, he was already bringing the point toward my surprised eyeballs. Only a lucky upward stroke with my saex deflected the blow so that it glanced off my helmet.

He was a very good warrior. But I am writing my story today in my old age, and he is not. I learned from my first mistake, and then I was the better warrior. While he pulled his spear back for another strike, I made a show of dropping my saex. When I saw the flicker of a smile and glint in his eye, I knew he would die. He reached forward with one hand to pull the top of my shield downward so that he could drive the spear into my face or neck. I let him pull it so that it tore away easier than he expected, causing him to lean forward, falling directly onto the blade of my hidden long sword.

The clattering of battle rang throughout the forest. Pain and fear and piss reigned. I saw that we still held them in check while I bent to retrieve my father's saex which had fallen blade-first into the ground. Still bending, a loud clank and pull surprised me as an arrow from my left caught amongst the loose mail at my chest and nearly spun me around. I looked to the direction from which the arrow had come and saw him – Megedagik or Mukki or as he would always be to me, Segonku.

I thought for an instant about rushing him, paying no attention to our line or the danger of his arrows, but I did not. The safety of Thorfinn on my right and Snorri the Elder on my left depended upon me staying alive and in my place. So I stayed, even when my rage and yearning for revenge on the man burned a hole in my soul. He was partly responsible for this, I think. You who now read my words may disagree, but I hated the man. Segonku took away a man whom I could be friends with, hunt with, laugh with, or, more plainly, trade with. He killed Kitchi. He caused two of his innocent friends to attack me, break my arm and nearly kill me, before I killed them. I wanted to drive a blade into his soft flesh and watch him pinch a tear from his eye as his life ebbed away.

A terrible pain awoke me from my insane musings during the battle. Someone had driven something so hard onto my left shoulder that it felt like one of the giants from Utgard had swung an entire mountain down upon it. I fell onto that left side, facing away from my attacker. Without waiting to see what was happening, I gripped my saex tightly with my right hand, rolled toward the skraeling, and stabbed the blade deep into the first makizin I saw, affixing the foot to the ground.

The man, who wore a ring in his nose, howled in pain, but had the presence of mind to bring his round stone hammer down toward me again. I reached over my head and grabbed the shield I had let go, catching the hammer safely against the iron boss. Scrambling to my feet, I drove the shield into his head so that we both toppled over backward, his foot still pegged to the earth. His ringed nose was broken, his ankle and knee looked dislocated and blood darkened his makizin. With two hands firmly gripping the sides of the shield, I raised it over my head, bringing its full force against his twisting face. His struggling halted.

I gathered my wits and weapons, scanning the battlefield. I lost Segonku again. Perhaps another man had the privilege of exacting revenge for me. Then I noticed that the skraelings had fought their way up a slight incline and through a gap they created in our pincer. Many of them were already gone, sprinting to the shore. I saw that Snorri the Elder tried to rally men to close the hole in our line, but to no avail, as the retreat was too massive to halt for so few.

And so they ran. Arnkell led a few men on pursuit, but while still sitting on the dead man's chest, I shouted, "Stop! We'll not pursue them, or we may give them a chance to take us apart piece by piece." I paused to suck in precious air, then added, "We'll stick together and follow them out like a proper army."

Arnkell looked disappointed, but Thorfinn nodded his approval of my plan. In the end, it was just as well, for the survivors in the skraeling band fled straight to their boats and paddled away vigorously.

We had won. We defended Straumsfjord, the village was safe. Nearly fifty of their men, young men of fighting age were dead – there were no prisoners taken. Segonku was not among these dead. But neither was Ahanu, nor Nootau. Eleven brave Norsemen died that day. Another two died in the weeks following from wounds they received that day.

We had won. We had killed. For what? Was it for the safety of Norway? Was it for my king? Was it for the One God?

Was it for profits? Was it for revenge? Was it an act of self-preservation or defense?

I did not know the answers to my questions. We had won.

LEIFSBUDIR

COVE

CAPE

COVE

Leifsbudir

BROOK

TYRKR'S GRAPES

heLgi & finnbogi's Longhouse

BLACK DUCK POND

PART III – Enkoodabooaoo!

1,007 – 1,008 A.D.

CHAPTER 9

Freydis. Freydis with the lines on her forehead and the beginnings of birds' feet at her eyes. Freydis with what was once her thick red curls streaming down her shoulders, that was now painted with swaths of grey and wrapped firmly in braids at the top of her head. Freydis, with the wonderful, large tits, that now sagged a bit more than they once did. Freydis, with hips I longed to grab a hold of beneath our covers long ago, that were now a bit wider than they once were. Freydis with her two children with a striking resemblance to Tyrkr and another child bulging from her pregnant belly due to arrive in the coming months. Freydis the former life-giver to all my dreams, all my lusts. Freydis, like me, had aged and she was here, bringing with her tension, dissension, and eventually murder.

But here wasn't Straumsfjord. I was back in Leifsbudir in Vinland living amongst two brothers from the cold, desolate eastern fjords of Iceland and babysitting Freydis for Leif. Before the tale continues too far afield, I should back my story up a bit so that I tell it in the proper order.

The winter following our victory over the skraelings brought nothing but peace from our enemies. In fact, despite our increased vigilance, sentries standing on the cliffs and probing bands sent into the forest, we saw no sign of them. However, the falling snow brought nothing but discord among our own people.

I have told you that only five women were in our company. I still recall each of their names for each was young and pretty in her own way. There was Gudrid, of course, with her thick blonde hair wrapped under the cloth on her head. I never did see her long hair again after our time when I sent the seed of little Snorri into her. There was also Idunnr, Eir, Ynghildr, and Aslaug. Each of them was relatively young, but each was also married to someone on our journey. The other one hundred forty or so among us were men who had no woman with which to bed. They became resentful and jealous of the men who were husbands while they became lustful toward the women.

As the winter wore on, Thorfinn and I had to pull apart more and more men from tearing at each others' eyes with the brave fingers of ale-induced courage. The men became so wicked that the women were clustered together to sleep huddled next to each other in a single tiny longhouse. I was deemed to be the only one old enough to show restraint and not enter while they slept to ravage one or all of them, so I spent many lonely nights guarding their door. No one thought it important to ask that if Gudrid ever gave me the slightest inclination, I would have taken her as my own, fleeing into the forest. But no one asked, and she did not indicate that it was to be.

As a means of occupying my mind during the cold nights, I did entertain my dreams, allowing them to run, that all five of the women would call to me in the night. That fancy did not happen either. None of our men thought it wise to cross me in the night for I wore my blood-stained berserker coat over top of the well-used mail Olaf sent to me in Vinland, reminding them of the countless deaths I had gifted to men who were much better warriors than any of them.

So I sat there, lonely, most of the winter. I hunted by day when the weather broke then hid inside during the worst of days, reading my two books over and again next to a sputtering oil lamp made from a bowled-out stone, when the wind and snow returned.

I talk about all this disagreement within our band because I believe it helped alter Thorfinn's enthusiasm for developing Hop, Straumsfjord, and Leifsbudir into thriving Norse cities. It was more than altered, actually, for his zeal for the idea disappeared altogether.

He came to the log on which I sat guarding the women from our own men one cloudless night, when the moon shone so brightly that I could hardly see any stars dotting the sky. It was cold, but calm. Our breaths turned into the misty steam of dragons' breath as we talked, encircling us like the smoke of a bath-house fire.

"But we can make this place safe. We can bring women to make the men happy. These will be great lands," I protested at his willingness to abandon our plans of profit while his wife slumbered next to little Snorri and the other four women behind the turf walls.

"I don't think I can take another year of managing the peculiarities of men," he sighed. "I even had to promise a half pound of silver to a group of men if they would just put their lust away for two more months until we returned to Greenland. Then they'll be Leif's problems."

I shook my head, for paying men to do what they ought for free was not a good leadership strategy, but I said nothing on the matter, preferring a different tack. "Women will come and the men will be happy. Even if they can't convince any to enter their longhouse, they'll get to see countless maids as they gather water or scrub clothes in the yard. That will count for something."

Thorfinn spit to the side before listing another reason, "I've thought on this, Halldorr. Straumsfjord and especially Hop are just too far from anyone to profit. Why would I go through all this, travelling for days away from the fjords where we are already welcome?"

"The profits will be ten times those you can earn elsewhere!" I assured him, though in truth I had no way of knowing. I did not really care if the profits were the same or more or even less. I was beginning to think I'd rather not be around other men. Trouble, others just brought trouble.

But Thorfinn wasn't fooled by my claims, "I can make more in profit in frequently travelled waters." Then almost as an afterthought, "I need customers to which to sell. Look around you, no one is here."

I found myself not caring at all about our plan, yet still arguing to maintain it. God, I thought, let me not return to Greenland, surprising even myself for I missed Leif. "They will come. You saw Hop. Settlers came to Greenland in droves and it is frigid, dark, and treeless. What a godforsaken place that is!"

"Well, you weren't attacked by skraelings numbering in the hundreds over and again those first years. When we return to Greenland, what do you think the empty rowing seats will mean for willing explorers?" I opened my mouth to offer another protest, but

Thorfinn continued, "We'll all be in constant danger here. We are too few, too removed from help, not to invite more attacks."

After our battle in the fall, he was right. I shook my head in disgust there in the moonlight at what could have been with Ahanu and his people. "What of little Snorri?" I asked.

"Well, what of the boy? He's growing like wheat that's been sown next to the dung heap, isn't he? Soon he'll pass up his father!"

"Aye, he will," though I thought of my own height, while Thorfinn thought of his. "Shouldn't the boy of a fine trader and explorer be raised here to learn to forge his own way in the world? Why should he go seeking the troubles found in civilization?"

He thoughtfully considered this for some time; so long that it seemed as if he would ignore my questions altogether – or perhaps he judged this argument valid. Then Thorfinn sighed again, "That's it, isn't it, friend. It's about my boy, but I want to settle next to Gudrid and keep her safe. I want to keep Snorri safe. I want to trade and not worry that my family will be slaughtered while I sail." He rested his elbows upon his knees then finished, "I think the woman is with child again. She hasn't bled in two months."

And that was it, wasn't it? He was a good man. He loved Gudrid as I once hoped to do for the rest of my life. He loved Snorri, who would grow to be his boy, never knowing I was his father. I considered returning to Greenland with them when they went, but decided I would just be tortured living so close to them without the chance to live like a family. Leif had his family, was jarl of Greenland, and wouldn't have time to spend with an aging bachelor. Erik, my second father, was dead. Freydis was married and humping the former thrall, my friend, Tyrkr. What would I do there other than be the cause of trouble? I didn't even have Bjarni to kill anymore.

"I'll not be going back with you," I said with a made up mind.

"I knew that already," answered Thorfinn. He saw my confusion so he added, "You're meant to be here among the savages, I think. Leif told me you'd be a jarl, and I suppose you'll be jarl of Vinland, though I don't know who you'd rule. You're really too dangerous to take among the towns."

I ignored his last comment, spent that night and the rest of those winter nights guarding the women, then saw that they dropped me off in Leifsbudir when the days were long enough for them to safely sail back to Greenland. There was no sign of my old friend Thorhall the Huntsman and his nine men who were to sail here earlier. In fact, the longhouses looked the same as the day we left with the exception of additional weathering.

Alone like a hermit for several months I was quite happy. In only one or two weeks I had fixed all that had fallen apart at Leifsbudir in the years since we left. My first task involved killing a family of small hairy beasts who had taken up residence in the main longhouse. Despite their size, they were ferocious, as I rapidly discovered when I marched into the abandoned home upon my return. I quickly noticed several sets of eyes staring back at me perched atop the sleeping platform in the back corner. Shrugging I marched over with my sword to swat them out, but the two largest beasts, with grey-black fur and a prominent black stripe across their eyes, sprang over my sword. Together they clawed and bit at me with more power than I thought they should exhibit. I was so surprised that I fell back into the long-cold ash of the hearth while they tore at me. Thankfully I wore a thick leather jerkin that day because of the chill remaining in the springtime air. It saved me from many painful cuts and scratches. When I finally discovered my wits and footing, I pulled my saex and chased the two creatures all over the longhouse, like an active boy running in the yard. At last, swinging both blades I killed one, then the other. Then I rummaged through the old storehouse, found an old dusty sack, swept the babies into it along with a heavy rock, and tossed it into the creek so that they did not grow up thinking we would share a bunk. I made two very nice hats from the two parents I killed, wearing them with their fancy ringed tails hanging to the side or back for many years.

After the initial excitement and mundane chores, I settled into a steady routine while waiting for word from Leif giving me some type of orders. Most mornings were spent fishing or hunting, while the afternoons were occupied with smoking or salting the meat I did not immediately consume. Within a few short weeks I had much more meat put away for the next winter than I could ever use, but I did not know when relief or others would arrive so I over-prepared. I also gathered grapes and ate of them until my bowels screamed for me to stop. When they did this, I began to dry the grapes for use in winter. Several varieties of wild berries came in and out of season so I never wanted for sweet delights. I should also tell you that Thorfinn saw fit to leave a basket of the delicious walnuts from Hop with me so that I ate better than many a king.

In the evenings, which were short because of the summer sun, I read next to the hearth. Eventually, it got too hot for me to endure sitting so close to a flame, so I began quitting my tasks earlier, while the sun yet shone, in order to get more reading time by daylight. It was on those nights when I was studying the Latin words spread before me on the vellum when I missed Kenna, my wife, most. I missed her company, of course, as well as her body next to mine in our bed. However, that year I remember missing her learned conversation on topics covering an immeasurable number of subjects. Ideas, concepts, thoughts, jokes, politics – anything that used language was commonly discussed around our old hearth. I missed her use of many different languages and realized that some of them were slipping from my memory from lack of practice. Upon realizing this, I vowed to read aloud to at least retain my speaking and pronunciation knowledge of the universal tongue found in my books.

So that is what I was doing one late-summer warm afternoon as I sat next to the seashore to catch a cool, salty breeze, leaning idly beneath a tree while my mind raced, interpreted, and studied the text. A stray gust of wind picked up one of the pages, flipping the leather cord I used for a bookmark off the book into the grass around the gnarled tree roots. When I absent-mindedly leaned down to retrieve it, a curious flash in my peripheral vision caused me to look up with a start.

There on the horizon was the unmistakable sail of a longboat coming from the north on course to enter the shallows around Leifsbudir. My grand silence would soon end, but I was not all that distressed by such a change. It would be enjoyable to see what adventure I would find myself taking when the boat arrived. Dropping my eyes to the page, I took my last few moments of peace to finish reading a passage to myself before carefully setting my bookmark back in its place then gently setting the book closed.

I extended my legs for a moment and realized they had become stiff. In my mind I thought I was nineteen, ready to kill any man or beast in my way. Yet my body was beginning to tell another yarn altogether for I was forty-one years old. I wondered how men of Ahanu's age remain so limber. Now in my winnowing years, I know they just fool themselves into thinking they feel well. Or, the alternative is that they are just fools. When my limbs came back to life, I stood, tucking the book beneath my arm and patiently waited for my friends, whoever they would be, to arrive.

I waved the boat toward me, guiding them with an extended arm around the particularly shallow spot where Leif and I had become beached on our first visit. The sail and men standing in the prow, I did not recognize, but had no reason to fear them. I did not even run to gather my weapons, which still lay leaning against my reading tree.

As they slid the strong keel into the sand, I noticed for the first time that another sail rose far off behind them. "Afternoon friend, how many do you lead to Vinland?"

The man had been smiling at me, lost his smile for a moment when he looked back, but then found it when he faced me again. He sprung over the gunwale with another man who was taller, thinner, but had the same nose and eyes. They were brothers, I could see. The stockier one approached, shaking my hand vigorously as if we were old friends. He had a well groomed beard that was trimmed shorter than mine with dusty blonde hair. I looked down at my own beard for some reason and saw that I now had many white hairs beginning to win the battle for territory upon my face. His brother, who looked to be the older of the two, though at least ten years younger than I, wore a serious expression, not of anger, but rather from stoicism. His beard was longer and darker than the short man's, but groomed nicely.

"Don't fear, Halldorr, friend, we are few," the man answered finally, while grasping my hand. "It is only my brother and me and our small troupe."

"And the other longboat?" I asked.

"Oh, but you are becoming a hermit," he said laughing after finally releasing my hand. "Leif said you'd be a loner." Then he leaned in as if there were listening ears and he had a secret to share, "That man, he knows things. I can't explain it, but he knows things."

I nodded, for I knew that to be the case, "And the other longboat?" I asked again good-naturedly.

"Oh, yes. They are small in number too." He looked to his older brother asking, "Perhaps thirty? At least that's the number we all agreed upon for each boat."

The thin one nodded, then grew tired of our conversation and began to help unload baggage from the boat onto the shore with the help of the others. There were about twenty men plus the brothers plus five women on board. At least four of the men were dressed like thralls, but seemed to be reasonably well treated, for they were not grossly thin.

The boat itself was older, but very well kept. In the past year, she had received several new strakes and a fresh coat of pine tar. The rigging too, was new, with ropes looking unblemished from the weather. Other than these items, she was certainly old, but taken care of as a woman cares for her child. She was clean and strong with a simple serpentine design on her prow.

The stout one saw me looking past him to the boat so he proclaimed, "She was our father's ship. Built in Norway about the time Finnbogi was born. My father loved her before he died, and now we treat her like he would want us to. My brother and I were raised on her."

"What do you call her?"

"*Leidarstjarna*! My father was a master at navigation and would sail on through the night, unafraid of what may come. Ol' Finny and I kept the name," he answered with much deserved pride. Even now most sailors still found a safe cove to tuck in for the night before continuing on.

"Your father sounds like he was a great sailor. He taught you well." He smiled while nodding at my compliment before I continued. "So your brother is Finnbogi. What should I call you?"

"Oh, by God, I forgot!" He extended his arm and we again shook hands vigorously as if we had not done so just a moment earlier. "I'm Helgi. We heard about all the wealth and fortune accumulating to those who went to Greenland, so we left our current homes in Iceland. But when we arrived at Brattahlid, all of Eystribyggo was talking about the riches of Vinland. Sure Thorfinn said he was worried about the skraelings, but I've got good men." Then he added, "And now I've got you!"

I shrugged, for I wasn't sure anyone other than God and the norns "had" me, then bent down, grabbing one of their tightly packed hudfats to lead them to the collection of longhouses. My book was still tucked under my other arm and I was ten or so paces up the beach when I turned to ask, "Who commands your other ship?"

"Why do you ask?" he asked with a change in tone that said more than his words.

"I thought that if the captain is unfamiliar with these waters, I'll have to wave them around the sandbars as I did you and Finnbogi," was my honest reply.

"She's not our boat," he said with a bit of disgust, placing his hands on his hips while facing the sea to watch the approaching vessel. "Truthfully, I did not want to come with her but Leif insisted, so she comes."

I am a fool. You ought to be certain of that by now. When Helgi said that Leif insisted she come, I thought at first that he sent Thorhall who commanded his boat, *Valhalla*, back to Vinland. I was happy for a moment. Then my mind took another step and thought that perhaps Helgi spoke of a woman and not the boat when he said "she" comes. I thought that by some miracle or working of the norns that Gudrid decided to come back to me, bringing our son for a life of bliss for all my days.

I squinted in the afternoon sun reflecting off the sea, but could not clearly view the ship or the passengers, so I asked my new friend, "Leif insisted she come? What do you mean?"

"Oh, that woman. Halldorr, I don't want to speak any more on the subject. Just know I did not want that woman coming here with us." It must be Gudrid, I thought at the time. I could not figure out Helgi's dislike of so fine a woman, though. Then he finished, "You know after what she did to her husband, she's got a reputation, and I didn't want that kind of trouble following my trading."

So it was Gudrid! I found myself bouncing with happiness like a dog ready to go on the hunt. "Helgi, I believe you'll grow to like the woman for she is upstanding, intelligent, and proud, though not too proud."

He laughed at that or at me, I don't know which, saying, "Lord knows I will try to like her. Just like the Lord knows she is proud, but I think he also knows she is too proud. So proud that it's like she's ready to claw at any man for even a sideways glance. Can you believe she is Leif's sister? They are so very different."

"Sister?" I mumbled. "The captain of that boat is Freydis, Leif's sister?"

"Of course it is. What other woman would be commanding a vessel?"

I dropped the hudfat to the sand with a thump and turned to the last passage I had studied before the visitors came, using the leather band to find my page. In the great book of Proverbs, I read, "My son, keep my words and store up my commands within you. . . they will keep you from the adulteress, from the wayward wife with her seductive words. . . Do not let your heart turn to her ways or stray into her paths. Many are the victims she has brought down; her slain are a mighty throng. Her house is a highway to the grave, leading down to the chambers of death."

Closing the book while looking back to the sea at the return of the woman of my dreams who more and more seemed like the woman of a filthy sweating nightmare, I gave a heavy sigh. Turning, I picked up the hudfat and bade Helgi to follow, not caring what happened to Freydis and her boat among the sandbars.

. . .

"These will be my houses, given to me by my brother!" Freydis screamed with intense vitriol. "You will carry your filthy belongings out of them now!" The expensive gold brooches I bought her over twenty years ago still held her red tunic in place over top her dark brown dress. They had a brilliant sheen that afternoon under the bright sunlight as if she had a thrall put a new shine on them just moments before her longboat skidded to shore.

She threw her fit out in the yard of the largest longhouse that Leif and I and the rest built after discovering Vinland. Helgi and Finnbogi had already hauled all their luggage into it before Freydis arrived and now she refused to even enter until they were gone. She had climbed onto the stump I used to split logs into more manageable wood for the hearth while she shouted. I sat some feet away on an overturned crate watching the scene unfold. Freydis, despite her aging features, was beautiful in the most base, lustful sense of the word. And so I chose to watch her for her form because certainly her words were nothing I cared to hear.

The brothers and their party were not moving fast enough for her liking. "I said get out! Why do you linger? Do you not take me seriously? Do you not think I rule here? I may be a woman with tits between which all you men dream to suffocate, but don't take that for weakness." While saying the last, she slipped both hands between her pregnant belly and swollen breasts, hoisting them a touch with a simultaneous jiggle.

Helgi and his crew worked methodically to remove the small amount of items that already found their way into the home, setting them onto the dirt outside the door. Freydis looked at me for an instant and flashed me a smile which softened her features. For a moment, ever so brief, she was the young woman of my dreams again. I saw her freckled nose and her full lips, framed by the two stray curling ringlets of her red hair that escaped her braids and was enchanted like a man a fraction of my age.

Then as quick as it was back, the feeling fled. She had turned her face to more forcefully direct her anger toward the others, "Why do you not answer my questions? Are you dumb? The whole lot of you must be dumb!" All the while, Torvard, her husband since soon after my banishment from Greenland, paced nervously behind the stump, warily watching the earth beneath his feet as if it were preparing him harm. Torvard gnawed on a fingernail. I noticed that all of his fingers had torn nails and dried blood from frequent bouts of anxious chewing.

Her two children scrambled all over the wood pile I had neatly prepared next to the door for the coming winter. Logs rolled off, scattering up against the longhouse or into the yard. I ignored the additional work, deciding that perhaps I could have the children help me re-stack it later. The oldest would be seven if my memory was correct and he did look like Tyrkr, but with the deep red hair of his mother and grandfather. It had been years since I saw children, yet I think he was short for his age. His younger sister was a replica of her mother. It was like I watched a memory of her and me playing the same game many years ago. In fact the girl was about four years old, so they were about the same difference in age as Freydis and I. The only feature that indicated that Tyrkr had been to visit Freydis's bed again was the man's honest, round eyes. I guessed that the child she now carried was again from my old friend's seed because I could not imagine Freydis allowing the cowering Torvard to touch her, let alone leave something in her womb.

Helgi let out a sigh while he gathered his patience, then spoke, "Freydis, we are happy to move and will not do anything to cross your will in any way, but there is plenty of room in the house for our two families. I ask you, if it pleases you, to allow us to stay until we have a home of our own built." Her stare bore into him. I am sure he wasn't used to obliging the whims of even kings, yet here Helgi stood, shrinking to the will of a spite-filled woman. Freydis' stare must have unnerved him because he continued, "I assure you that we all understand that these are your homes, given to you by the jarl of Greenland, your brother, Leif. We further assure you that we will have our own longhouse prepared well before the winter arrives among us."

Still the woman stared. It unnerved even me, and I wasn't looking at her face. At last Helgi grew frustrated, shaking his head while roughly grabbing his woman's hand, pulling her back toward his boat. Finnbogi and his wife followed, carrying their belongings back to the shore as well.

I slapped my knees loudly, stood up, and grabbed more of their baggage to carry it to the ship. I guessed they would spend nights there until they had a proper structure built to shelter themselves from the weather. Helgi, feeling safer from her wrath at this new distance, gained the confidence to call over his shoulder to Freydis who remained fixed on the stump, "Freydis Eriksdottir, we brothers and our crew will never be any match for your ill-will. You have certainly got your way, but I, for my life, cannot understand why you are this way, when your family is such a delight."

Freydis mumbled something that I know Helgi could not hear. I only heard the words, you'll and delight, though what came between them I'll never know.

. . .

I suppose I should have known it would only be a matter of time.

For the first week, I slept on board *Leidarstjarna* with the brothers and their wives, after moving my own goods out from the longhouse the day of Freydis' arrival. Eventually, I grew tired of being awakened by the couples and their nightly humping in the hold so I politely excused myself to sleep, isolated, next to a campfire on the bank of Black Duck Pond far from the sea's shore. Finnbogi so liked the spot I chose that he convinced his brother it would make a good homestead, and they ceased building their longhouse near the brook, moving to my lake.

By day I helped bring down trees along with Helgi's small band to frame the house. Lifa, Helgi's young, tall wife, along with Ketilridr, Finnbogi's wife, made us a mid-day meal over my campfire. They were larger meals than we needed, but no one turned the food away. These two women, who, I learned were sisters raised in the western fjords of Iceland, had a knowledge of cooking such as I had never witnessed. They knew how to combine fish and nuts and herbs into a meal that made my belly moan with satisfaction.

By night, my new set of friends went to their boat to sleep. The others in their band camped along the shore of the sea, behind some large driftwood to protect them from the wind. I stayed behind for the solitude of the pond and my lonesome campfire.

On the fourteenth night of their arrival, a sharp crack of a twig awakened me with a start. My hand landed on the hilt of my beautiful sword before my eyes even opened. It seemed that I was sitting up and looking toward the sound before it fully died away.

The snap came from the direction of Leifsbudir so any fear I had lessened. My eyes scanned the woods finally seeing the movement of a human form. It was Freydis. I know she saw me because I was partially illuminated by the small fire which had died to a low glow. Showing no shame, the woman crouched with her back against a noble tree, hiking her dress up so that I could see her milky thigh. I could not see it, but I heard the tell-tale sound of her urine splashing on the recently fallen leaves beneath her hovering buttocks. While she finished her work, Freydis turned to look at me, giving me a soft, very pleasant smile in the process.

At last she leaned forward and used her hands to crawl up the tree to right herself on two feet. The task was completed with some degree of difficulty; I heard a single grunt from exertion, due to her bulging belly. Instead of showing me her backside and returning to the longhouse she had so desperately wanted, Freydis walked slowly toward me on a circuitous route, avoiding several low areas filled with leaf-clogged water.

And so I thought this was to be her first move to bring her naked body into my blankets. But she calmly found a wooden prop used in the construction process for the brothers' home, set it near the campfire, before gathering several logs and stoking the flames to a bright, lapping glimmer. Then she backed up so her hind quarters leaned against the construction prop, watching the fire silently.

I trusted her not. She was a spy in my kingdom, a traitor searching for co-conspirators to stage a coup against the king, a thief probing for weaknesses in the locks of my house, a villain capable of all means of treachery. I was wary, my senses waited for the chance to accuse her of evil, for the chance to drag her into Leifsbudir, before her nervous husband and shrinking crew, showing her for the seductress I knew her to be.

Yet, the chance did not come.

Freydis stayed there with her ass fixed to the prop, in a trance watching the dancing flames greedily lick their way ever higher, seeking every opportunity to totally consume the new fuel. Her face shone in the fire's rekindled light, and I saw for the first time ever, even compared to when we were young, a barely perceptible introspective sadness in her eyes.

I leaned back onto one elbow still under my blankets to watch the flames as well, preferring not to be the first to speak. It is common among all men and women, I think, to find the undulating blaze and deep orange-red glow of the embers resting peacefully beneath their rhythmic action hypnotic. Many nights I have found myself staring into the fire of a hearth pondering my life while the rest of the longhouse slumbered. Olaf, my third father, used to do this on occasion, slowly pulling his way with his hand down his beard, worrying about those things which bother kings. He thought no one knew of this, I am sure, but many nights I awoke from my place on the floor in Kaupangen in the midst of a nightmare and saw him leaning forward on a simple stool, mesmerized by the fire.

That night with Freydis was similar. I do not know how long we sat there quietly watching. For a long while nothing in particular worked my mind, until the questions rolled upon me like the giant swell in the sea. Why did I find myself in this place with this woman? Where would my wife come from? Leif promised me I had to stay here to find my wife. I was certain she was to be Gudrid, but she was gone, maybe for good, with her husband and my son.

Freydis took in a long breath, letting it out slowly before speaking, "You seem well, Halldorr. Despite the isolation, you truly seem to be doing well. The One God faithfully shines upon you."

I thought of correcting her to my point of view that I believed myself to be cursed most of the time, but did not have the energy for such a discussion. Instead, I said, "Perhaps that is so. You, however, do not seem to be doing well."

She looked away from the fire, toward the blackness of the pond, letting my remark hang in the air. When Freydis turned her face again so that I could see it, she had streaks of tears down her cheeks, but did not beg for sympathy. In fact she half laughed while wiping the tears away with the sleeve of her dress, "Leif tells many stories about you and your adventures with Olaf. He says you would share the harshest, but truest ideas with the king, who would normally kill for such honesty. Somehow you got away with it, and so you will today." Freydis brought her arm back down, shaking her face to clear her mind and the hair that stuck to it briefly. "I am not well. You speak such truths," again with a head shake. "In the years since you've left, in all the years I remember, really, I've treated others terribly. They now expect it of me, and I expect it of myself. So I give it to them, so they are not disappointed." A long pause, then, "I ask myself until I am exhausted, why my life turned out this way."

I said a prayer to the One God right then and there for the woman who was still just a confused angry little girl playing in the icy waters of Iceland, searching for the most perfect smooth stone to hurl at her older brothers. I asked the One God to grant this woman his peace, at least for this moment, and it seemed to work, for without a word from me her face brightened, looking like a weight was lifted from her soul.

I did not know what to say on this subject anymore, so I redirected our conversation to something more factual, less emotional, "What is Thorhall the Huntsman doing back in Greenland? He must be nearly mad without Erik to join him on his famous hunts."

Freydis looked genuinely confused by my question, "I don't know how he is doing. He's not in Greenland, unless he moved himself to the Vestribyggo without my knowledge."

I worried for a moment for my old grumpy friend. "He was to be waiting here, but when he wasn't, I just assumed he went back to Greenland."

"I do not know where he is, but Leif speaks highly of Markland. We passed its many fjords on the way here. Perhaps my father's old friend is killing the deer there."

"You are, no doubt, correct," I said, then thought no more on the matter, instead returned my gaze to the dancing fire.

Soon thereafter, another sigh from Freydis brought me out of my sleepy state. She was walking already, adding a straightforward, "Have a good night," before threading her way back to the village.

My gaze remained fixed upon her while she slowly disappeared into the darkness. I did not understand women, particularly Freydis.

So it was only a matter of time until Freydis came to me. However, I had no idea it would be to share time staring into the never-ending abyss of our pasts through the portal of fire.

. . .

I worked closely with Helgi and Finnbogi during those days. They were good men and I was growing fond of them, especially Helgi. Finny, as Helgi called his brother, was prone to sullenness and perhaps a little too close to my own personality for us to be close friends. But Helgi had the ability to set me ablaze with laughter, so much so that my innards felt as if they would split my belly to burst onto the construction yard.

Despite his years of obvious experience running a successful trading operation, slicing through the highest of rough seas without fear or dread, Helgi was not much of a carpenter. He acknowledged this fact, even poking fun at his own short-comings, endearing him to me even more. Once when we gave him the measurement for one of the main timbers that would support the roof, he cut it far too short. Finny complained about it like any brother would, I was aggravated at doing the same work twice, but Helgi was nonplussed. He just said, "At least for the first time in my life, when someone says that ol' Helgi cut it off too short, it wasn't Lifa speaking about our fun on the sleeping platform." He then began a crafty laugh that I joined when I finally got the joke. Finny shook his head in a loving disgust, while Lifa, who heard our conversation from the cooking pot, used an iron shovel to toss a hot coal at her husband in a high arcing throw. It glanced off his head, singeing his hair, then slipped down his back, causing him great, howling pain. He arched his back inward so that his chest and belly fled as far from the coal as they could get. Helgi jumped about the site trying to decide what he would do. Lifa, who threw the coal in jest, was horrified that she now caused hurt to her husband. At last Helgi did the simplest thing and plunged into the cold waters of Black Duck Pond.

This last act brought a deep, rolling laugh from Finny. Soon the whole crew of workers and thralls laughed at Helgi's expense. When he finally came shivering out of the pond, with his hair matted to his face, and trousers drooping as if filled with the load of a baby's wrap, even Helgi began laughing. I wiggle a little upon my own stool today just remembering that scene from so long ago.

Freydis, too, kept her crew busy elsewhere around Leifsbudir as the winter approached, careful to avoid contact with Helgi's men and women due to the continuing and building tension. Her boat was filled with more than the thirty mouths that the covenant with Helgi originally called for. I did not make an exact count, but it was at least forty, likely more. They worked diligently at bringing down many fair trees, trimming the branches for local use, then dragging the hulking trunks to her longboat which now sat perched on the shore, up from the farthest extent I had ever seen ice and water reach.

By night, Freydis awakened me with her visits. They always began the same way with her pregnant belly making her flee Torvard to urinate in the forest. She would stoke the fire then find a comfortable place to sit or lean while we talked, never within reaching distance. The talking for the first two nights following our quiet stare into the flame was stilted and awkward and, like our actual physical time together in the past twenty years, was separated by long gaps.

Soon, however, we became more comfortable with one another, even sharing stories about our lives spent apart for so long. We talked of my battles and strandhoggs for she still seemed to be as fascinated with power wielded as she was when we were young. For two consecutive nights, Freydis wanted to hear the story of our sacking of Aber Tawe along the underbelly of Wales. She poked about into my past with regard to women, love, and family, but I chose to keep my time with Kenna, Olaf, or anyone else I loved to myself. Trusting her was not something I was willing to do, especially not so soon and in light of her completely disparate moods by day and night. Therefore, I became adept at deflecting her questions with gentle tact to other lines of conversation.

Freydis shared of her many, varied, and sometimes disjointed thoughts. "I don't know why he takes these actions," she said out of the clear night sky.

"Torvard?" I asked.

"No, Leif. I don't know why he does it," she said with some exasperation.

"Freydis, I don't know what you are talking about with Leif."

"When we were young, he seemed like such a man of promise, but now he is just a weakling. He barely touches me when we are in bed and I'm glad of it because he is so weak," she said to the fire.

"Leif comes to your bed?" I asked. "He is your half-brother and he is in Greenland. What are you talking about, Freydis?"

"What are you talking about, Halldorr?" she asked with confusion in her voice and eyes.

"I'm talking about Leif. What are you talking about, Freydis?"

"Torvard. I talk of my weak husband. I cannot understand why you bring my wretched brother into this."

I nodded to her with a sad smile. I have seen some men lose their ability to decipher reality, usually after battle where their brothers-in-arms are sent to a premature death before their eyes. However, I have never seen a woman exhibit such erratic behavior as Freydis did that night. I should clarify; there was once a woman in Dyflin who went from bed to bed for jewelry and silver trinkets from the soldiers or mercenaries. She sometimes confused me when I spoke to her on the streets. She actually frightened me so, that I did not ever choose to join myself to her, but the woman was often at the yard of Kvaran, Dyflin's king, because he had a penchant for young, dark-haired girls. I do not know what ever happened to her.

In any case, shortly after that our conversation became more normal, continuing on quite pleasantly for some time.

Then it came time for her to leave. Freydis's visits ended each night in the same manner. She would sigh and say that Torvard expected her to leave during the night, but that he would expect her back shortly. I remember thinking that Torvard's expectations likely rarely figured into Freydis's considerations, but nonetheless, I let her white lie go unchallenged.

But in time, the brothers' longhouse was complete, and we all moved in just as the weather turned cold. We would be warm with nearly thirty of us sleeping in the small hall. The four thralls who came with Helgi and Lifa stayed with Freydis and Torvard's thralls in the small hut outside my old house. The day we carried our baggage inside the walls of their new longhouse, Finnbogi gave me the choice of where I would sleep, so in jest I said, "Well if it's truly my choice I'll rest my head next to Ketilridr, but I cannot say we'll do much sleeping."

Helgi and Lifa roared in laughter, with the woman giving a sharp elbow to her sister, Ketilridr. Finnbogi became a little flustered but tried his best to send a witty remark in my direction. "I would hate to ask you to go back outside for the cold winter."

"It's a shame that you plan to send your beautiful wife outside for the winter months, but if that is where she'll be, I guess we'll have to find a way to keep warm."

This further frustrated him so that he stopped trying altogether, feigning disgust. Ketilridr smiled sheepishly at all the fun at her and Finnbogi's expense, so I returned the smile and answered, "Finny, I am sorry for having fun with you on this. I know you meant the offer to be taken seriously, and I do, for I will, for the first time in my life, choose a place on the sleeping platform. I do tire of the cold air down on the earth."

As we unpacked everything, Lifa, hanging a black iron pot from a dangling chain over the cold hearth, asked me, "You were raised with Freydis, were you not?"

Here she was again – Freydis. I moved out of the house without being asked because I did not want to be near her. I slept next to the lake to be isolated from her, yet she came in the night to piss and talk. Now I moved in with wonderful new friends, and Freydis was the first topic of conversation. Finding one of the pegs we set into the wall, I hung my belts before answering, "More or less," hoping that was enough.

It was not, "Then you can help us."

Helgi joined his wife, "Aye, she's right. We need help with that woman."

People were stacking items on shelves, bustling about to strike jasper stones in the dry grass between the stones of the hearth for the longhouse's first fire, so I hoped that I could feign busyness by announcing, "I had better gather some of my raisins from the work shed at my old house."

I could not. Helgi answered, "No, we'll send Bedwyr." With a nod of Lifa's head, the Welsh thrall ran out the door. "Now what shall we do to make this relationship work with your sister?"

"She is not my sister, she's not even Leif's full sister. But why do you even care to make this work?"

Finnbogi took up the cause, "We made a bargain with her and our father taught us to honor bargains. We said we would split the glory and rewards for this trip. Everyone who has come back from these voyages to Vinland is renowned. Even if our profits from this journey amount to nothing, we will win future trade because of it. We cannot have this woman speaking ill of us. So the question remains, what will we do about the woman?"

Hands now on my hips, I stared up at the clean timbers of the roof, preferring to study the underside of the turf and wood forming the gable than become further embroiled in such nonsense as this. Helgi grew impatient with me saying, "The story goes that you nearly married the woman, so you know her better than any man who is a part of this house."

"It's only by God's good grace that I did not marry that woman. She and others meant ill for me, God set the results of their actions right. I do enjoy you, my new friends, but I do not want to become involved in childish arguments."

"Halldorr, you must help us work with this woman," pleaded Helgi. "I fear that we could have bloodshed between our bands if we do not straighten this out." He stopped when I scoffed at the suggestion, but continued when it was clear I would say nothing, "You may be right that my concern is unwarranted, but I have seen how some of her men look at us. I've been approached by enough pirates in the marketplace to know when we are being examined for attack. And if you don't care about our welfare, remember the lovely form of Ketilridr. You would not want any harm to come to that." He flashed his charming smile when he finished.

I liked the man and his troupe. I did not want any harm to come to any of them or to any of Freydis' men. "Damn you Helgi, but you make a good argument. But if my plan is to work to my maximum benefit, I ought to wait to offer help until old Finny is underground from some skirmish. That way I get the delights of Ketilridr to myself." All but Finny, I think he tired of our jokes, laughed and then we settled down to discuss a plan.

. . .

The three day Christmas celebration of midwinter was upon us, but there was no hlaut sprinkled anywhere in Leifsbudir for we were universally Christian. We also had no horse or goat or other livestock to sacrifice because none was brought with the new batch of adventurers. I had no man such as Thorhall the Huntsman with whom to reminisce about our old customs and stories growing up with Odin, Thor, and the other mighty gods of the Aesir dynasty. Now the only way to relive those times of my youth was to go to Asgard in my mind.

One aspect of the old days would return this Yule. Our talk on the first night in our new home saw to that. Two weeks ago, I was dispatched like a young messenger to organize games and entertainment with the house of Freydis as a sign of peace. At first my suggestions were greeted with contempt, but eventually Torvard and even some of her ruthless looking men began to support the idea. But I think it was her two children who did the most good in convincing their angry mother that the sport would be a welcome diversion from the winter that settled more and more closely around us with each passing day.

We hosted the first two nights of merriment at our new house on the shore of the frozen pond. In truth, the evenings went very well, certainly better than any of us expected. Even after starting rather ignobly, with stares across the hearth between the two groups, eventually the ale spread cheer among both sets of explorers so that laughter and Yule songs rose to an ear-splitting roar. The hall was warm that night as it was packed with more people than it was ever intended to hold.

Both of the nights, four thin men sat in a corner atop a sleeping platform playing various tafl games on an old, weathered board with simple game pieces freshly carved from oak scraps that had been set aside for kindling. I had played these games many times in my life, and they could be fun. However, I never witnessed them go on very long without arguments breaking out, then escalating. You see, each region, or each man in some cases, had its own rules for the tafl games, even though they were all basically the same. Invariably, one player would try a move that was accepted in his home village, and his opponent would cry foul. When ale or mead flowed excessively as it did during that Christmas celebration, someone ended the night with a badly swollen eye while his counterpart ended the night with sore knuckles. These thin men were no different, and both nights they argued, then fought one another, only to come back together to play again. There was never any danger of their fight catching fire among the entire crowd since they all hailed from Freydis' house. In fact, their scraps helped bring the two parties together as we all cheered them, toasting the man who was successful enough to get a particularly good pummeling in.

The rest of us bore a merry, raucous tone both nights. I adored the hours of watching and participating in glima wrestling. Normally we scheduled wrestling during daylight hours for more room, but we pushed observers up onto the sleeping platforms so they stood three or four deep in places, creating a small, cleared area around the hearth on which to sport. Glima is a particular style of wrestling that emphasizes technique over strength. The crowd keeps the rules sacred as any man who is seen infringing upon them is harshly jeered, with wooden or horn mugs quickly pelting him, inflicting more shame than pain.

Glima is popular among the masses of Norse and our Danish and Swedish cousins. The children love it so much that Freydis' two offspring found a flea-ridden dog whose right ear, like my own, had been damaged in some fight or another, dragging the docile beast into a space under a sleeping platform to practice their own form of wrestling on the dog. The women, too, wrestled each other using the glima style.

Lifa and Ketilridr had a particularly boisterous contest, sending the men into fits as they cheered, secretly hoping that one or more of the women would lose an article of clothing. It was not to be however, as Lifa soon tired and her sister easily sent her falling on her backside. Both of the women's husbands proudly kissed their women after the match, with Helgi happily squeezing a hand on his wife's ass. It was sore from the fall, however, so she let out a surprised shout, slapping Helgi playfully on his chest. He smiled, apologized, then grabbed her rump's other cheek for good measure for all to see. We gave the two young lovers a merry cheer. I liked them very much.

Soon it was not only Lifa's behind that hurt, but her groping husband's as well. After many terrific matches between the men, it was Helgi and I who were left for a championship bout next to the roaring hearth. We were stripped to our waists by that point because of the heat generated by the billowing crowd and nearby flames. The wind howled outside, finding its way into the longhouse through several small cracks that would need sealing and through the larger smoke hole near the roof. I shivered briefly from a cold draft hitting my back at the start of this last fight while bathed in sweat from the previous grappling. But then the crowd called for the start, and we began the stepwise dance.

In glima, the participants must remain standing tall while we circle one another in a sun-wise manner, always moving, which creates many opportunities for attack or defense, preventing a boring stalemate. The objective is to get your opponent to touch a part of his body between the knee and elbow to the floor by throwing him. Once thrown, the pursuer is not permitted to follow or drive the other man into the floor. So the sport is all about leverage and technique, not so much brute strength.

Helgi and I circled one another barking out good-nature taunts as should begin a confrontation. In an instant, the shorter man left a part of his middle exposed with one misstep so I reached in with both hands, grabbed his belt and waist, but my hand slid from his slippery skin. We continued the dance. Over and again we grabbed at one another trying to gain the upper hand. His shorter height was actually proving to be a benefit to him and twice Helgi successfully tossed me, but I used my feet and hands like a cat to catch myself and stay in the match.

At last I successfully latched both hands about his belt securely, but instead of twisting him, pulled him toward me, over my bent left knee. His feet spun out over his head and he landed with a dull thud on his rump, puffing up a cloud of brown dust. The crowd, both camps, cheered. I lent a hand to Helgi to pull him up, and we basked in the small glory of being the champion and reserve champion wrestlers that night. After so much glee, I resolved to plan a water wrestling tournament at the height of the following summer. These matches were pure joy in which to participate and almost as much fun to watch.

As we gathered our tunics, Freydis proposed a toast to all who gathered, even offering a prayer to the One God for sending his son, the Christ to us this day many years ago. After a somber salute and downing of our ale cups, we all lounged while a skinny freckled man in Freydis' company, a would-be skald really, began singing and telling stories of old. His voice, of higher pitch than tenors, could carry a tune better than most men, but he was not among the best skalds I had ever heard for his voice cracked at the highest and croaked at the lowest ranges of the songs. His songs of heroic raids on the weaklings in Ireland and Scotland made me proud because of my part in those actions. In one rambling adventure story, he even told of Leif the Lucky and his drinking of dew from the grass of Vinland when we first set foot upon this island some years ago. Though my memory is not perfect, I thought I would have remembered our pitched battle and subsequent victory over some nasty giants in those early days conquering this land. I noticed that nowhere was it mentioned that Halldorr Olefsson was always at Leif's side saving his hide from one scrap after another, guiding him, advising him, but those gathered in the hall that night knew, and I was something of a celebrity after his songs.

The first night ended with drunks slowly shuffling their way back through the cold forest on the short walk to Freydis' house. I do not remember much after that for I was so exhausted that a dreamless sleep found me as soon as I found my bed next to the dog the children had been playing with. His breath was terrible, worse than my own, I think. When I awoke the next morning, not having moved an inch all night, the dog still lay with his hot panting breath wafting directly into my nose. When our eyes blinked open around the same time, his tongue came out to lick his nose then my nose while he didn't move another muscle.

Soon after waking, I cracked the heavy door open so that he could run out into the snow to chase birds and relieve himself. He ran straight toward his normal residence with Freydis, hopping happily in the light, cold snowfall, pausing briefly to make his mark, then continuing on with a merry bark. I smiled at his simple happiness. He made some man a faithful companion, I thought.

I have spent much time talking about the first evening of our Christmas party that year. The second night of celebration was much the same, again held at Helgi's and Finnbogi's, with ale and gaiety abounding. I have tarried so long on the singing and wrestling because it brought me so very much pleasure. Few times in my adult life have brought that much excitement without any loss of life, and so as I wrote these words in the universal Latin language, I wanted to spend more time reliving the moments. Pardon an old man for wasting time.

The third night, I found, was altogether different, however. This time Helgi, singing dreadfully off tune, but happy nonetheless, led our band over to Leif's former house for the drinking and sport. In truth, the first half of the evening went as well as the previous two, with smashed potatoes and blood sausage served, but midway through as I sat breaking open the beaten down Torvard with conversation, our joy eroded.

Drunkenly confused, Torvard said, "No, Tyrkr seems to be a good man. Even though he is free now, he seems very willing to help our family in any way he can. He is always nearby. I suppose it is from a sense of duty he feels to Freydis from his time as Erik's thrall."

I sighed, "That is probably the case," not wanting to dispel the myth he had weaved in his mind, popping another slice of the blood sausage into my mouth.

"I'm glad you agree because I used to become jealous that he and Freydis seemed to be such close friends. But I soon found that something in their friendship brought benefits to me!"

"What could that possibly be?" I asked, swirling another bit of sausage into my potatoes using my eating knife.

"Each day they spend time together, working in the barn or gathering berries, Freydis comes back to my bed filled with passion, taking my body as she never does." He leaned in as if he were telling me something I did not know, whispering, "My woman knows how to handle herself under our blankets. Then, like clockwork she is with child and soon I have a healthy son or daughter. My seed must be so supreme that I only need one try to form the baby." Leaning back on his stool with obvious pride, he added, "We'll see what it is she carries now. Freydis is so large already that it must be one of these moose of which you talk!"

He was happy in his own way so I let it be. Turning the matter, I said while marveling at a spot of sausage on my plate, "I haven't had blood sausage in years."

"Oh, we had some wonderful blood sausage just before leaving Greenland!" exclaimed the jovial Torvard.

"What did you use?"

"Pork and rye."

"In my experience, the most enjoyable is lamb blood mixed with rye flour and oats stuffed right back into the sewn lamb stomach. Oh, that is delicious!" I said dreaming of the delicacy. "I haven't had that in years, but have lived off this land, which provides enough, I suppose."

"It's a wonderful land at that! I hope to convince that part-sister of yours to stay, to make a home. It seems like it would be lonely at times, though."

"I've had my books to pass any long nights," I said with pride.

"None of us read, Halldorr. Well, the priest Torleik back at Thjordhildr's church does it. Sometimes I've even seen him writing in a strange looking tongue. It all seems magical to me."

"Where does he get the vellum?" I asked.

"The what?"

Disregarding his ignorance, I thought of how I should begin to create my own vellum pages to start penning letters or even the beginnings of this journal. I sat quietly wondering how much success I would have using the hides of my wild game rather than that of our domesticated goats or lambs.

"I am reminded that we have a set of items for you," Torvard said, interrupting my thoughts. He pointed to some hudfats bundled tightly in a pile hidden beneath a red and blue striped blanket at the end of a sleeping platform. After receiving a nod of permission, I leaned over, pulling the nearest sack to me, untying the bag. In an instant I knew what it was.

"Do you know what this is?" I asked with no hidden disgust.

"No, I saw the strange writing. I told you, I don't read."

"Why did you not inform me of this earlier?"

He was clearly drunk because his honesty came easily, "Freydis told me to keep the letters a secret. I don't cross her, you know."

"I know."

From the handwriting using our Norse runes, I could tell they were letters written by Leif and Olaf. And just like the package I received some years before, it contained exotic gifts from my third father as he travelled the Holy Land. Why would she want to keep these from me, I wondered?

Breaking the seal from Olaf's I scanned through the message. It was heartfelt, like the last, imploring me to do good things in the name of the One God, telling many amazing details about the sights and sounds of Jerusalem. He had taken a thrall woman from the poorest section of the city as a wife and was delighted to announce she had a baby. It was a girl, but Olaf's first and only surviving child. The name of his daughter was Abeer which he said meant fragrant in his wife's tongue. I smiled as I read of his success while he hid. Beneath the letter in the hudfat was a small box containing empty places for jewels where some greedy captain or crew member clearly pried them loose on the years-long trip to find me. Nothing in the message or gifts explained why Freydis would keep them from me, unless it was just Freydis acting in her typical inexplicable manner.

Torvard sat watching me with a pleasant smile etched in his completely inebriated face. It made him look quite idiotic. He waved his hands, spilling ale on his legs, encouraging me to move onto the next letter. I broke the blue wax seal of Leif's letter, carefully unfolding it and knew immediately why the woman kept it from me.

The letter began:

> *Halldorr, Jarl of Vinland, Good Steward of all*
> *Properties of Erik and Erik's sons –*

Why did Leif keep referring to me as Jarl of Vinland? When others came, he implored me to serve them. When these Greenlanders left, I ruled Vinland which was a jarldom of one. I controlled no one. I ruled no one. The man could be maddening.

His letter continued:

> *Dear Brother, I am saddened that so much time has passed since I have laid eyes upon you. You are my only brother yet living, and I miss having you about for counsel. Thorfinn told me of Thorvald's death which brings me to tears. Be certain that I will see that his wife is well cared for, though marrying the woman off again may prove to be difficult.*
>
> *Freydis continues to prove herself to be unwilling to exercise even the most basic of our societal norms, preferring to act as a spoiled child. Her anger grows. She brings bitterness to every meeting with every man and woman within the settlement. After an evening of celebration, she brought herself to me, trying to force me to lay with her to plant a child within her womb.*
>
> *I have had to banish my own sister, but I could not bring myself to send her into the unknown, so I have sent this pack with the thrall before you now, Eoghan. He had explicit instructions to carry the pack to you only after sailing with Freydis. Please reward him accordingly.*

*Please see that Freydis and her family are cared for.
Please lend her my home in Leifsbudir, but have her
men build other homes to house them and Helgi and
Finnbogi. She is not to exercise any control over this
expedition, the brothers are commanders, leading the
expedition. You will like them both, especially Helgi.*

*I see little Snorri and see you in his eyes. I smile
when he says something as you would say it. He
grows tall and strong like you and Gudrid both.
Know that Thorfinn cares much for the boy. In my
regard to my references to your future family, you
must stay in Vinland if you ever want the happiness of
a woman. She is to be yours. She will be yours until
death separates you. I can tell you no more without
spoiling the future, for if you know it, it will slip
between your fingers as you clasp tightly about it,
trying hard to hold on.*

Your Brother in Christ, Leif

"Which thrall is Eoghan?" I asked Torvard when I finished
the letter.

His eyes were shiny like the waters on a sunny day. My
voice awakened him from his wide-eyed slumber to say, "Poor
Eoghan, one night on the voyage while we slept, he awoke early to
prepare a small morning meal for our crew. A pitch in the sea sent
him tumbling to the deck onto his own knife, killing him instantly."

"How do you know he fell on the knife?"

"What else could it be?" he asked confused.

"Someone could have driven the knife into him while you all
slept."

"No, that's just not the case. The person at the rudder while
we slumbered watched it happen in the waning moonlight, then
screamed as his blood quickly spread all over the planking."

"Which man saw it happen?" I asked, scanning the crowd.

"Huh?" asked the wavering Torvard. "Oh, yes, it was no man. Freydis saw Eoghan fall that night."

"Freydis ran the rudder?"

"Yes, after we had sailed for a day or two from Greenland, she insisted on taking the rudder. It was hard for her at first, but she did well enough. We're here, aren't we?"

"And Eoghan's body? Did you bury it in Markland on the way?"

"No. Freydis was so upset at the sight that she let go of the rudder while we wiped the sleep crusties from our eyes, causing the boat to turn abruptly. She fought the turn, staying on her feet, while rolling Eoghan's body up over the gunwale. That woman is powerful when she must be."

I had my answer. It was obvious to me as it must be to you. She killed the man who was Leif's messenger.

Clutching the letter in my hand, I rose to my feet and strode to where Freydis stood, leaning heavily on a man I did not recognize. Spinning her around by the shoulder, I shoved the parchment in her face, saying nothing, letting the page be all the accusation I needed.

Her eyes widened in confusion, then darted about it fear, at last narrowing with the hate-filled rage of someone with a complete break with reality. Before I could react, she let out the roar of a bear. "I'll sleep with neither you nor Helgi! How dare you ask me to commit such heinous acts of depravity!" Her voice rose louder as it spewed more potent venom. The rest of the room grew silent as the once jovial crowd watched with unease, games ceasing. "I should have known that you, all of you, would have another motive to share Christmas together. What shame you wish to bring here!"

"I thought it was the ale talking when Helgi made the proposition last evening while I was helpless outside relieving myself. Yet, now I see that all in your house are doomed. You'll all die, and I want nothing more to do with you!" Torvard turned his head all about from his stool while she shouted. He was using every fabric of the wits he had left to try to understand the situation. I wanted to strangle her, to cut off her lies before another syllable rolled out, but I remained in control.

Then Freydis seemed to calm herself, speaking at a normal volume, "Halldorr, I've ignored all of your advances since we came here because I felt sorry that your weak offspring killed your sickly, weaker woman, but I cannot stand for this insult any longer. You'll have to leave with the heathens, Finnbogi and Helgi."

I did not think; my muscles took over, commanding their own actions. In an instant my hands were clutching her neck with my thumbs pushing down on her wind pipe so that her mouth opened, her tongue lolled, her eyes rolling back in her head. It would only take a moment for me to kill her. She needed to die, bitterness followed her everywhere. Freydis fell back to the earthen floor with me on top of her. I did not think of Erik or of Leif or of Freydis, the bastard, nor of her bastard children. I wanted her dead.

But the beatings on the back of my head began in earnest. At first I ignored them, still gripping Freydis by the throat, squeezing tightly. Then many boots, mugs, and dishes and even a hammer, I think, crashed about me, until I collapsed forward into her round pregnant belly in a foggy blackness knowing only that she lived and angry shouts swirled about the party.

I awoke several moments later being carried roughly by four men, one on each arm, one at each leg. We fled through the snowy woods, the unnamed dog barking at our heels. I saw the moonlight reflecting off the ice-covered pond ahead. Vaguely familiar voices hurriedly called all around. I heard Finnbogi barking orders to others, but could not understand his words in my murk, then my head bobbed loosely, and I passed out again.

. . .

Neither party attempted any more interaction for the rest of the winter. To avoid bloodshed, our men hunted and fished in the forest, never crossing an unspoken, unwritten, un-agreed-upon line drawn half-way between our houses. The traitorous dog, that I now called Right Ear, decided to stay with us, and we let him for it seemed as if that simple act could be viewed as a small victory in our dispute.

The men and women of my new house said nothing to me, not a single complaint, about causing all this potential harm with my impulsive action. In a short time, they too had interacted with Freydis enough to know the evil of which she was capable. They treated me as if I had been a brother or cousin, raised on the decking planks of *Leidarstjarna* by their father, traveling from kingdom to kingdom on the open seas, trading as one of them, while bringing wares to those in need. Maybe someday I would be a captain in a fleet of their trading knarrs.

I had to be told the details of the fight that ensued from my wild attack upon Freydis, of course. The man on whom Freydis had been leaning so familiarly at the celebration was called Thorbrand Snorrason. He was the one inflicting all the harm to my head and back when I fell upon Freydis. Thorbrand had grabbed a heavy black kettle, using it repeatedly to strike me down. His action brought an immediate response from Finnbogi who started fighting his way toward me, using his balled fist against any nose or cheek that came into his path. He reached me just as I dropped to the floor, dragging me back toward the door by one leg. The end result was that none of our company was seriously wounded, for which I thanked the One God mightily. Three men received shallow knife wounds on their forearms, before Helgi called for a general retreat.

But all this had been just over three months ago. The days grew steadily longer now so that the sun actually created a bit of warmth by late day. I took this opportunity to flee to the woods, away from the people I had grown to love. These people, my own people, brought love, kindness, laughter, joy, beauty, talents – all gifts that make life worth enduring. Yet people, my people, all peoples, especially those like Freydis, bring anger, jealousy, strife, boredom, irritations – I wanted a respite from this for I felt the burning from her acidic bitterness as if it had settled into the very water we drank.

Helgi offered to come along on my trip, and I thought of bringing him, but only for a moment. He would have livened the trip such that I would need a physician to tend to my sore belly from my fits of laughter. But I declined in a friendly way, saying I would be back to retrieve him for a follow-up journey in a week or two. He heartily accepted my proposal, burying his nose in Lifa's chest beneath their covers before I even stepped out the door on that crisp spring morning.

Right Ear had sneaked behind me to tag along, yelping when I caught his tail in the slamming door. After releasing him, I softly scolded the dog to return to his place beside the hearth inside, but he would have none of my direction, so I let him be. Together we set off along the eastern shore of Black Duck Pond, walking south down the length of the thinner arm of water which pointed almost due north. We walked at an idle pace. I stayed close to the pond, Right Ear darted in and out of the wet grass, gathering burrs in his coat.

For two weeks I was gone, walking farther and farther away from Leifsbudir, taking in the wonder that is Vinland. On the first evening, as a red sun shone in the western sky, I saw a glorious bull-moose traipsing in the cold water of a swampy lake. His antlers were as wide as I was tall, having several plants with bright red berries hanging from them. While he chomped on something, his long brown-grey beard danced beneath his chin. I looked at my own blonde-grey beard and chuckled silently. Right Ear and I chose to sit quietly, watching him for a long while until at last he stomped his way up and out of the lake into the dense forest sitting on the opposite shore. I could have stalked the beast, bringing him down with one of my true, iron-tipped arrows, but I chose not to.

We camped at night wherever we found a soft patch of pine needles on a slight rise of dry land. These places were sparse since I was moving through an area densely packed with lakes, bogs, swamps, and ponds. Water fowl was prevalent, with large, black-necked geese flying in nearly constant motion over our heads, searching for the perfect lake to skid into for a landing. Many nights we shared one of these succulent birds for dinner.

Soon after eating, I would pull my books out from their leather purses to read in the firelight. Right Ear would often grow bored at this point and escape into the night. I would read until my eyes were heavy, eventually laying my head down on the books. When I awoke the next morning, Right Ear was always next to me, sprawled out, in dire need of rest from whatever adventure he had been on during the dark hours.

But one of the nights was different from the rest. I had felt we were watched all day while we hunted, however, I could never put so much as an eye on who stalked us. Ignoring the feeling while being secure in my skill with my father's saex and my sword, I allowed Right Ear to lead us deeper into the wilderness. That evening when I made camp, I chose a spot next to a large, lonely boulder with faces climbing straight up from the ground. This would prevent my retreat if it became necessary, but would allow me to survey only one entry path for attack.

After a dinner of tree nuts and roasted rabbit, I propped my back against the great stone, watching into the night. Sleep did not come to me; I listened, certain I heard the footfall of a man a time or two. Strange birds began calling to one another with a soft coo. I had heard these calls before, but these had the characteristics of a man's voice, coming from a little too close to the ground. Still I did not see anything.

In moments Right Ear was fast asleep, dreaming of some wild hunt as his legs ran at his side. He yipped occasionally, making me smile despite the potential for trouble during the night. But soon even he settled to a peaceful rest with his chest rising and falling with a slow steadiness. He was so rested that in a short time I smelled one of his stale farts wafting around our campsite. It was so foul I was certain my eyes would water and I punished him with a nudge from my boot with just enough force to awaken him from his slumber.

The dog raised his head to see what I wanted, decided he would rather sleep, and so rested his head back on the ground. But then it was raised again and Right Ear was on his feet growling into the blackness. The scruffy brown hair atop his shoulders rose slowly, standing at attention.

I patted his backside gently, while still reclining and said loudly enough for our visitors to hear, "There, there Right Ear. They are friends out playing wood elves in the forest. They mean us no harm." Then I called even more loudly, "Anamikaage Ahanu!"

His soft chuckle told me I was right in my guess of who spied upon us. Then I heard other men grumbling as I saw their faces by the light of the fire while they emerged from the night.

There were four men in all. My friends Ahanu and Nootau led the way, ahead of two younger men, Hassun and Rowtag, who struck Hassun on the shoulder, blaming him for giving their party away.

"Young Hassun, don't let your friend lay the blame upon you for letting me discover your band," I called. "I have been on this earth for many years, seen many battles, with many men keen to kill me. I know when someone stalks me." I did not add that I was really not sure if my imagination ran wild that night. However, once Right Ear noticed their approach, I knew that it must be Ahanu, for a single arrow could have killed me if they meant harm toward me.

I stood and shook hands with all of them, indicating they ought to take a seat around my fire. Nootau and Ahanu did so, but the young men walked some distance off standing guard against something or someone.

"Ale?" I asked, passing them the pot of brew I had stowed within my rucksack.

"Yes, thank you," the men said, with Nootau, then Ahanu taking a sip. It must have been awful to them because they both squinted while swallowing hard. The pot quickly came back to me with no requests for another taste that evening.

"What brings you to me out here in the woods? I have a home, you know. You are welcome there, though I know you've never been."

Ahanu seemed bashful at the moment, but his friend Nootau did not delay, "We wanted to speak to Enkoodabooaoo directly, for you are moderate and fair. We did not want to encounter any of your people and were fortunate to find you out here alone."

"Enkoodabooaoo?" I stumbled.

My friends exchanged smiling glances at their obscure, wickedly-difficult to pronounce word. "It means, 'One who lives alone,'" answered Nootau. "It is what we have come to call you."

"But I do not live alone," I said, confused.

"You do not?" asked Ahanu, eyebrows raised.

I took a drought from the ale, accepting their moniker as descriptive enough then set the pot at my feet with Right Ear quickly lapping at the drink. "You are fortunate, for I am here. Though I would say you would be most welcome among the new arrivals of my people. Welcome in *one* of the houses for sure. Helgi and Finnbogi are moderate and fair as any men I know. The occupant of the other house is best avoided by all men, Norse and skraeling alike."

Nootau looked to Ahanu, indicating with a curt nod that he should speak what he wanted to say. Ahanu's eyes told me he had sad news, but he spoke not. "Out with it," I said. "I'd have my friends treat me with respect and honesty. What do you need to tell me?"

Ahanu looked down at his arm while sliding the arm ring off, played with it while spinning it between his hands, then extended it toward me. "Take this. I cannot keep it."

I was honestly offended, "It was a gift as a sign of friendship. It is yours to keep."

"Your people and my people are at war. My people look on this ring with disgust when I wear it. I cannot accept it."

"My friend, Ahanu, you are wrong on many accounts. Our peoples are not at war, for all those who fought against your village are gone, returned to Greenland. So while many of your best men are dead, you have won, driven the Norse off. I am here, but do not intend to fight anyone. The new settlers will just harvest trees here in Vinland and take them back to Greenland for profit. As far as your people and their anger toward you, I would think an elder such as yourself can tell whomever you wish to eat turds! Finally, you have no choice, you have already accepted the gift. It is yours, what you do with it, is your business, but I will not take the ring back."

He reached the ring a little farther toward me saying, "My chief has told me that I must return this to you, and so I must."

"Your brother? You obey the daft words of your crippled brother?"

"Halldorr, my chief is my chief, whoever he may be. Brother or not, I will carry out his wishes. If this ring is mine to do as I wish, I wish you to take it as a sign of true friendship from me. Wear it around your arm, remembering that we are friends so that hopefully, someday our peoples will be friends." He stood, grabbed my wrist, shoving the ring into my hand. His thin hands were strong, squeezing my own hands around the gold. Ahanu then leaned forward, kissed my forehead, turned and left. Nootau rose said a friendly goodbye and disappeared into the black night.

Years earlier, I would have called Ahanu my fourth father, after Olaf my third, Erik my second, and, of course, Olef, my first. But sitting there in the dark, I finally felt I was old enough, man enough not to clamor for another father. He was not another father to me, Ahanu was my friend, chosen by me. I shook my head, not knowing why the One God would not allow me to even give a gift to a friend. Why did he isolate me so?

Soon my friends were completely gone, the sound of their footsteps grew fainter and fainter. The soft, muffled chattering of Hassun and Rowtag became quiet. When all was again silent, I reached down for a sip of ale, but found that my dog had emptied the bowl. A well-timed ale fart told me he enjoyed it very much.

. . .

By day we marched about without any worries. I feared no man, mostly because there were no men anywhere nearby that I knew of. Ahanu's company was long gone, and I saw no signs of anyone else. But I also feared no one because I had become quite proficient in the language of these Vinland peoples, and so I knew I could speak peaceably and passably to anyone I met. If they chose to approach me in anything other than a friendly manner, I had the confidence that comes with experience and age to know without a doubt that I would prevail in whatever maliciousness a young man, eager to make a battle name for himself, could plan.

These two weeks did much for my mood. I was already becoming something of a hermit, or enkoodabooaoo, I could tell it in my soul, and so I would need to resist such leanings. But I did look forward to seeing my friends again; sharing with them my stories of the sights I had seen and the game I carried upon my back. But such joy was never to be had.

Right Ear was ahead of me as we approached Black Duck Pond. He had been chasing a squirrel, determined to catch it then do what, I am sure he did not know. I called to him often while he ran after the tiny, fluffy-tailed creature, taunting him for his lack of pursuit skill. The creature taunted him too, because it chose not to flee up the trunk of a tree, but instead ran along the ground from rotting tree trunk to clusters of rocks. The chase had gone on for several harrowing moments before Right Ear caught the tip of the animal's tail, spinning it up into the air. The squirrel hissed, swinging a small clawed paw at Right Ear who yelped from nothing in particular, causing the squirrel to drop to the ground and at last skitter up a tree.

I laughed heartily at the scene which seemed to drive Right Ear ahead in shame to the lake. Moments after bursting through the brush to the water's edge he began barking loudly in such a way that said he was not playing. Then I began to hear faint sounds, like screams of pain or terror in the distance, being carried to my ears on the wind. Clutching my pack and my bow just a little tighter, I jogged to the shore.

Helgi's home was nearly an English mile away from me now, so I could not see anything other than the roof and wispy smoke from the hearth trailing away from the hole. But the openness of the pond allowed a terrible screeching sound to roll all this way without losing its power. God help us, I thought, a skraeling attack. That is why Ahanu and Nootau were about. My Norse friends were dying.

Without thinking, I dropped my pack and game to the ground in a rumpled heap and ran toward the battle. I noticed my formerly injured leg throbbing, but the excitement of confrontation so near allowed me to run like a man half my age. In minutes, I was close enough to see men surrounding the longhouse. The screaming continued, but it was an isolated screech now, like some of the war cries I had heard from skraelings. Our men seemed to be loitering about, yet they were all dressed for war with spears standing tall, swords in hand.

Still I ran. Now I was close enough to see that the men's leather and chain and blades were covered in blood, fresh blood from a recent battle because it was still crimson red not brown. It still dripped wet from their articles of war, running down their helmets or faces. I was also close enough now to know that it was Freydis, not a skraeling warrior, who cried like a woman possessed by the evil one himself. I could not see her, but it sounded as if she were on the far side of the longhouse with the men looking on at something she did. They faced me, some still panting from the exertion of battle.

Something was wrong. Obviously, the blood and screaming told me that something was amiss, but something else was terribly wrong. I could tell it as my feet pounded closer to the screaming. Amidst the shrill cries, I heard an occasional whimper or feeble weeping that would be abruptly cut off after a dull thud. Then I noticed that the men surrounding the longhouse were Norsemen, of course, but each one hailed from Freydis's camp, none from that of Finnbogi's and Helgi's house.

These men noticed me approaching, but none of them moved to stop or attack me or welcome me. Instead they leaned further on their spears, watching me come with an air of total disinterest. I doubled my efforts until I came around the longhouse among them.

Horror. I do not know what else to say about the dreadful sight which greeted me. I have seen morbid, disgusting sights in my life. Men do terrible, repulsive acts to one another in battle. But this shock was more than I could take. Sadness unleashed itself within my soul, taking over my entire being. A few of the men chuckled behind me when I went to my knees in the yard, tears welling up, rolling out of my eyes like those of an infant with an empty stomach and wet backside.

Each man in Helgi's household lay splayed out before me. Dead, all of them. Hacked down without being given the chance to defend themselves. None of them carried a javelin, spear, or sword. Defenseless, they were cut down by the men who now surrounded me. I could have spun and killed three or four, perhaps more before I would have been killed myself. But I did not. I kneeled there watching the remnants of the carnage, hoping for a flinch of life so that I could swoop in and save someone. I knew it would not happen.

I kneeled there with tear-obscured eyes watching Freydis in what was an unbelievable sight, even when I consider Freydis. She strode among the bodies of men, wearing a bright green dress under a simple brown tunic with white details along the edges. The tunic and skirts of her dress were soaked in blood as if she had washed them in the stuff. With two hands she carried a sword that was just a bit too heavy for her so she tripped and struggled. Next to her on the ground were the bodies of the women, all apparently killed by Freydis. Freydis screamed again. She was a mad woman, shrieking. Then she took a step to the side while drawing the sword high over her head, blood dripping into her red hair.

Lifa, Helgi's lovely young wife, yet lived. She kneeled in a defeated position with blood splattered across her dress, cradling her dead husband's head in her lap, lovingly combing his hair out of his content-looking face with her trembling fingers. I firmly planted a single foot into the ground to rise myself up, to make the short sprint to kill Freydis, but my strength faded when she brought the blade down onto Lifa's peaceful head. I fell from my own weight as the leg buckled beneath me.

As I rolled onto my back, looking at the bright blue sky, I heard the assembly begin to disperse. Right Ear finally found me, sniffed my face and tucked his own into my armpit as if to console my intense grief. I lay there frozen, unable to move, not wanting to ever move again. Why should I ever move again, I thought?

Then the shadow of Freydis fell upon me. The sun was blocked by her face so I could not see the expression she wore. Blood, more blood, dripped from those curling ringlets I used to love, onto my face, spattering. I moved not. I glanced at the heavy sword she had dragged over to me with one hand, scratching a path in the earth behind her. Drive it into me, I thought. I would have spoken the words, but all power was gone from me. How I managed to breathe and see, I do not know.

I write this by my own hand in my extreme old age, so you know that Freydis did not kill me that day. Perhaps she killed a part of me years earlier, making me resigned to whatever life thrust upon me. Yet I wished she would do it then. Plunge the thing into my heart, cracking my ribs. Or even hack at me, as many times as it took. Whatever she did would be better than what I was experiencing at that moment. She did none of this, for even in her insanity, she is wise. Freydis knows how to torment a man more than he knows himself.

Freydis began laughing at me. The laughing went on for some time while the last of her men left the clearing, until she said, "You are a helpless weakling, and you will always be a helpless weakling." She finished her thought by spitting at my face. I saw the ball of phlegm approaching my eye, yet I did not even try to close it. The wad splattered there, as if it were an exclamation to finish Freydis' own thoughts.

She dropped the sword, letting it clatter down among the dead men next to me and walked back to her longhouse by the sea.

. . .

The brothers' thralls survived the brutal attack by the house of Freydis, but soon found they had new masters, considerably harsher than the last. Shortly after that day, I spoke to one of them, Bedwyr, the Welshman, who carried out a full, sloshing dung bucket from the longhouse occupied by that woman and her band. He was nervous, in a hurry to return lest any ill come to him or the other recently acquired thralls, but Bedwyr took a few moments to tell me of the events of that terrible day.

Early in the morning Freydis came alone to Helgi's home, knocking courteously on the heavy door, calling aloud for a truce in the pent up hostilities. Bedwyr was fixing a small fishing net behind the longhouse and so heard the entire exchange. The men of the house welcomed Freydis gladly, saying they would be relieved to move on and begin to work together to build Leifsbudir into a respectable village. With that, the short exchange was done, and the men went back inside to finish their morning meal. Bedwyr saw fit to peek around the corner of the longhouse because he began to immediately hear mumbling from Freydis once the door slammed shut. She was speaking to herself in a loud voice, walking unsteadily with her boulder-sized pregnant belly protruding some distance before her down the walking path. Bedwyr followed.

When she was a safe distance from Helgi's, Freydis began to scratch herself with twigs and sticks. She ran her face into the trunk of a large tree with jagged bark, creating an open swollen wound on her nose and left eye. The thrall was confused and worried. At first he actually considering running and offering help to her. But he did not, for he was frightened of the woman, and rightly so. After generating terrible scrapes all over her face and arms, she at last dropped to the ground, rolling in the forest debris. Eventually climbing to her feet with much effort, Freydis looked as if she had been in a battle, attacked, maybe even raped. Leaves were stuck in her hair; her dress and tunic were torn and soiled.

Bedwyr secretly spied upon her the entire way back to her home. In the last ten steps she began weeping, sobbing loudly, limping with an air of tremendous weakness. Torvard and some other men came rushing out of the house at her sounds, quickly steadying her, setting her down to rest. After some time, Freydis struggled to explain that she had been ambushed in the woods by Helgi and some of his men then left for dead.

That was all it took. In moments Torvard had organized the entire household into battle dress, armed with every weapon they brought with them. Bedwyr ran ahead to warn Helgi, but arrived only a short time before the war party. The rest of the events are self-explanatory except that after cutting down all the men, Freydis' husband and the others refused to kill the women. Freydis had no such misgivings, grabbing an axe, then the sword I saw, chopping them down one at a time.

I lay on my back for the rest of that awful day with their bodies surrounding me. Right Ear eventually grew tired of me, running off into the forest. I heard his barks echoing many miles off as he chased some type of prey. Even that was not enough to bring a smile to my lips. I lay there on my back throughout the darkness, not rousing even after relieving myself sometime in the night, moving at last when the sun rose brightly bringing with it a sweet spring breeze. The air itself was a gift from God for it brought life into my muscles, and I began the task of cleaning up what remained of my friends.

It was two full days of digging, dragging, lowering, praying, and covering before I was done. Not a soul from Freydis came to investigate or to help. I worked in isolation and was glad of it. I placed the women in their graves first, thinking that I owed it to them to see that their faces remained pretty in my mind, before the mottling stink and rot of death enveloped them. I have buried everyone I have known, outliving all, but those days, with one friend after another getting their bodies pushed beneath the earth put a profound sadness within me I do not think I have ever shaken. I still feel it in my chest and belly today, a tightness seizing hold. My breathing becomes labored while I lean in next to the flickering light in my house, just thinking of their faces, the ghastly, contorted pain frozen for eternity.

Men and their women, that woman, we are terrible, awful creatures. So much evil from which so much good is possible. My own life has been filled with countless evils done by my own hand, but I am confident from my reading that the One God's son has done the hardest work for me. Why is all this so? I know not. Why is it all so confusing? I know not. I only know that I have failed much, but, despite those failings, found courage to wake up each day to kill or love as the case may be. Whether the strength came from within or from God, I know not. In fact, it exhausts me to complete fatigue to even ponder the question.

I found that I was in no danger from Freydis and her men. Moving about wherever I wished, they ignored me more than ever. Some days I wished that they gave me some notice, for it was worse that I created no menace in their minds. I do not know why I never even considered donning my bear skin and killing the lot of them in one swoop or by claiming one life at a time with great stealth, finding one in the forest with his pants down about his ankles, or finding another ambling to gather kindling. I did it to Bjarni, but that was years ago, for an injustice done even further back. I only know that I did not consider revenge. Was it maturity or laziness? I do not have answers to these questions either.

I only know that I don't regret letting them live, for in some strange, perverse way, Freydis had a purpose to serve in my life. Her actions, which were yet to come, would indirectly bring about the most joy I had experienced since leaving the service of Olaf.

. . .

The clack and song of axes, which had usually brought reminders of so many fine times, rang throughout the forest as Torvard led his men to harvest more trees. I watched them clean the tall trees and drag them all the way to *Leidarstjarna* for stacking in the hold. It was clear that Freydis meant to load Helgi's dead father's ship as if it was her own, to take the badly-needed timbers to Greenland for even more profit. Her blatant thievery, which was of course nothing to her murder, stirred anger within me, but I again chose to ignore it. Helgi and Finny would have no need for the ship any longer, rotting as they were beneath their barrow mounds.

A certain resignation set in, and I developed idleness during these days. Three weeks after the killings, I sat beneath my tree at the shore reading the book from Olaf, once again doing my best to ignore the comings and goings of Freydis, until she plunged out of the brush next to me, looking as large as the ark of Noah with her round, swollen, pregnant belly. By the One True God, she was enormous.

"You stole my dog," she accused while standing there looking uncomfortable in her own skin.

Still looking at the words spread across the parchment before me, I set a hand upon Right Ear's head, patting it lightly, while saying, "You may call him. If he comes to you, he must truly be yours."

In a mocking tone she sweetly called, "Halldorr, come Halldorr. I named him Halldorr because of his ugliness and grotesque ear." Thankfully, Right Ear didn't move. Instead, he cocked his head to the side as dogs often do then bolted for another adventure, this time in the rolling surf.

Trying to overcome the defeat, Freydis said, "We'll profit handsomely from these two loads of trees. I plan on selling them to Leif for a price just under what they cost from Norway." I nodded absent-mindedly, for it sounded like a reasonable plan. "And I trust the men I send back with them. They will do my bidding and return to me for more trees in the autumn."

I looked at her. It was the first time I looked into her face since she was obscured by the shadows created as I lay on my back in the killing yard. I saw her self-inflicted wounds were nearly healed – they must have been awful the day Bedwyr watched her in the forest. I pushed the thoughts of that day from my mind. "You mean to stay behind?"

Almost startled by my question, Freydis answered, "Of course I intend to stay. This is my domain, my kingdom, even though I don't intend to allow Torvard to reign in any capacity, certainly not as king." She chortled at the thought.

Her kingdom. Her domain. God, I prayed silently, please let her be mistaken. Please see to it that this woman and her band leave Vinland and never return. "Et quodcumque petieritis in nomine meo hoc faciam ut faciatis laus Patri Filio" from the gospel of John formed in my mind at that moment, lending comfort. This was my domain. Leif declared I would be its steward, to rule over it. I did not mind that I ruled no man, but felt powerful having Vinland, the land, under my control. I returned to my book, trying to dispense with Freydis once again.

Freydis said some more words to me, which I chose not to hear, before she, thankfully, tired of me, finally trudging off awkwardly through the sand to oversee loading more logs into her stolen vessel. It made me ill to think of Freydis and her wretched family, and some bodyguards, I was sure, to be a constant burden on Vinland, my Vinland, for much longer.

But then an idea popped like a spark from a log on the hearth. It was a scheme I thought I had previously discarded altogether. But since the image was now bouncing in my skull, I had clearly been mistaken. With only a handful of men surrounding her, I could avenge Helgi, killing the entire bunch at will. I was a killer, a warrior, the God willed me to be a weapon. They were not. Could I kill the children? I asked myself this question. I had killed Bjarni's rodent son and felt no guilt. Yet, he was a pig, like his mother and father. I asked myself again, could I kill the children of Freydis? Spending my youngest days in Norway, I witnessed infanticide many times, especially of female babies. But as a practice, its use was waning with our new faith demanding so. Yet, it could be done; I could do it, I could kill the children. But then I thought I might take her children as my own, raising them to be sane rather than the miscreants they were likely to become.

Freydis and Torvard, choosing to stay behind as they had, clearly did not fear me. They should, or would, rather, I thought, before an evil, curling smile formed as I tenderly closed my precious book. I would take my revenge.

. . .

But I killed no more Norsemen or women. I kidnapped no children – though I am confident I would have done both the killing and stealing, feeling no remorse. The canoes came instead, finally giving Freydis an opportunity to do something which would be of benefit to me and many others even though the impulse of her actions was rooted in the same insane selfishness I had come to expect.

It was morning – a morning where the air was as fresh as I ever recall. The spring breeze came off the salty sea, filling my nostrils with its very own vigor, making me believe that with the passing of a few short days, my vengeance could begin. I was alone on the shore, walking with Right Ear, who was now my nearly constant companion. He followed me all over Vinland, even bothering me when I stretched over the dung hole.

That morning I threw bits of drift wood out into the rolling surf for him to chase and retrieve. With each successive toss, I sent him further into the sea so that he eventually had to paddle his paws instead of running on the sandy bottom. Despite planning a certain amount of evil, choosing to withdraw from my reading for the past few days so as not to be accused of iniquity through the Word, I was light hearted, allowing myself to focus on the happiness of the moment. The repetitive nature of walking and throwing brought me a sense of peace.

On my longest throw so far, I saw black dots forming far on the horizon. A pod of whales, perhaps, I thought. But they did not appear and disappear like the bobbing beasts of the sea. Instead these dots I watched were constants, moving up and down with the waves. Right Ear had the stick again and was jumping on his hind legs, rubbing my chest with his front paws, poking the stick into my face to encourage me to continue the game. I took the stick, but hurled it toward the trees which caused the dog some confusion until he heard it rattle down against branches to a crunching stop on the underbrush. Right Ear ran after it, not returning for much of the day, obviously side-tracked by some scent.

The dots grew in number and soon turned into blobs, finally becoming bark canoes paddled by menacing-looking warriors. I chose to stand on the shore for a time while they came closer and closer. A quick count gave me an estimate of eighty or more men. Still I remained, watching them come. None stood in the bow yet swinging a wooden pole, for they were too far away.

I prayed that when they did stand, that they circled the pole in a sunwise direction so that I was sure they came in peace. There was no doubt in my mind they came from the village of Kitchi, Ahanu, and Nootau. The canoes looked of the same construction, and many of the men had similar dress as the many times I visited with them in Straumsfjord. Their faces were too far away for me to recognize anyone.

I stood alone with my hands upon my hips when it occurred to me that I had no allies if we were to fight. Why should I fight with Freydis and her band of animals? And if I chose to fight with them, would they have me on their side? Or, would one of them seize the moment and plunge a spear into my back, later blaming a skraeling?

But if I did not fight with my own people, for whom would I fight? Did I stand a chance if I retrieved my weapons, for I was weaponless that morning, except for my saex which never left my belt, then waded to the nearest canoe to offer my services? No, I would be cut down with countless arrows before I uttered a single word of friendship.

Perhaps I should fight for or against neither. Instead I should run into the forest like my dog and hide, waiting for a victor by one side or the other. Like my dog! Huh! If I ran into the forest, I would be like a dog, cowering from the stern hand of God or man as the case may be. No, I would stay and fight.

But I held out hope, for there is always hope. When nothing is left, there is hope. When we were surrounded by Sweyn Forkbeard and his innumerable allies while we sailed *Long Serpent* there was hope. Even when all of our own number was dead, save three, there was hope. If there was no such thing as hope, or if it was just the dream of simpletons, I would not have been standing on the shore that day. Hope, even though I discount it much at times, hope brought me there. So I hoped that their leaders in the bows would soon stand and rotate those wooden rods sunwise.

They were closing, and I saw hand signals and heard indecipherable shouts. These were followed by a stirring of the men in the prow while they steadied themselves to stand in the rolling waves. Soon I would know if blood would spill this day, or if we would celebrate around a table of merriment, eating cheese and trading red cloth.

One boat pulled ahead of the rest and the man in the prow stood wide-legged so as not to fall. I squinted to get a better view, even bringing my hands to my eyes to shade the sun's reflection. The man was bending at the waist, reaching to pull something, probably a pole, out from the canoe. He shouted something back at the men behind him, sounding like a good scolding, but the words were muffled. When, at last, he raised himself again to his full height, bringing the rod with him, I knew we would have blood.

Standing at the front of the lead canoe was Segonku, Megedagik, or Mukki. His other names meant nothing to me, he would always be Segonku. It didn't matter what direction he spun the pole I knew he wanted blood, and I intended to give it to him.

Calculating all the possibilities of battle and success, I decided to dash off to Freydis' longhouse to rouse the men. I could be there and back before any of the skraelings landed for home was close by. I ran.

In short order I burst into the longhouse where men lounged about eating a breakfast of smoked fish and cheese. Freydis sat uncomfortably on a sleeping platform with a light dress and tunic and no shoes. Her feet looked swollen and fat, her toes uncomfortable. "Skraelings attack us. Get your weapons and come to the shore. They are upon us!"

Freydis began berating me already, "Oh, Halldorr you act like a child. Why. . ."

I cut her off, "Freydis, you should choke on your own tits, God knows you've shoved them on the rest of us enough! Now shut up." I pointed to the nearest man, "Give me your bow and a quiver." Though confused, he dutifully handed them over to my extended hand. I was half-way out the door when I again shouted, "You can either die in here when they attack or try to kill them in their boats. Now come!"

I raced to the shore, not knowing if they followed, but soon had the answer to my question. They came. At first two or three arrived, still strapping their belts about their waists. Then the rest came in a large bunch. We were less than forty. Only half or so had a shield. Some had spears, some had swords. We were a ragtag bunch with no hope of killing many of them, let alone prevailing. Most of us, all of us really, would likely die.

We were wholly unprepared for battle, and so the only hope we had was to frighten them into not landing, turning back to the sea. I began screaming curses at them, encouraging others to join me. When they began to carry on the chorus, I felt into the quiver for an arrow, grasping one, setting it in place on the taut cord. I aimed for Segonku, hoping to kill him with one draw. There are those who say there is no honor in killing a man from such distance. These men say that you must look into your opponent's eyes to see his fear, to smell his piss in his pants. They say you must give your enemy a chance to properly defend himself. To these men I say, "Eat pig shit!" These men, these "they" are wrong. They have never stood in a shield wall with death surrounding them on every side, with their best friend's blood stinging their eyeballs from the arrow that sliced into his neck – bowels, arrows, and bladders loosened everywhere. These "they," they are fools. I would kill Segonku from across the sea if I could.

I pulled the cord back to my ear. It felt strange for it was not my bow, and when I released I knew I missed. It sailed badly off course, plunging into the sea three or four ells ahead of Segonku's canoe. I cursed, but reached into the quiver for another arrow, laying my hands on it, setting it in place, drawing the missile, adjusting my aim, releasing. I thought it would kill him, but it slapped into the curved prow of his boat. One more, I thought, one more, and I would have him.

I reached into the quiver a third time, reached deeper, felt all around, then pulled it up to see that it was empty. Who is so careless as to have a quiver nearly empty? "Arrows!" I shouted. "Who has more arrows?"

I looked down our line of disheveled defenders and saw that none other had brought a bow. Not a single arrow was to be found. In a fit of rage, I took the quiver from my waist and threw it into the sea where it landed gently atop a wave, soon bobbing up and down like a piece of driftwood. All I had was my saex.

We were one warrior with a child's blade and a group of cowardly killers inexperienced in real battle with an ensemble of unsharpened weapons. Our group would have been perfect as bait in our battle at Straumsfjord, but we were not perfect today in Leifsbudir. We were the bait and prey. We would all die if we stayed.

So as much as I wanted to kill Segonku, to stay and kill and die, I called, "Retreat! We must retreat to the forest!"

Their faces turned to my own, showing me the fear they felt. Torvard looked pale and sickly. Skraeling arrows slapped two or three shields, then one ripped into Thorbrand Snorrason belly. He tumbled back, gasping, dropping his sword straight down into the sand so that it jutted, pommel up, ringing back and forth. He heaved in death throes for an instant then died when a heavy rock was launched into his head from the approaching canoes.

That was enough. Killing the defenseless family of Helgi was effortless for these cowards, but true contest and battle was more than they cared to endure. They broke and fled. I shouted behind them orders on where they should go so that we could regroup and somehow, with hope, prevail. But they did not hear or care to hear. They ran in all directions like scattering horses, some plunging into the forest, some running to Leifsbudir, others fleeing down the beach to follow the brook.

Perhaps what I did next is not heroic, but it is what I did so I must tell it. I looked over my shoulder and saw that Segonku was mere feet from landing. Thinking for a brief moment of confronting him, I hesitated, placing my hand upon my saex. Then I too, broke and ran. I planned to run to my home, gather my weapons and then head into the forest to survive on my own, killing him at a time and place of my choosing – the way of an old warrior, not a rash, young, dead warrior.

Then I saw the ambling, struggling pregnant Freydis finally arriving at the beach. She swore, cursed, and shouted, wincing with her swollen bare feet, their skin stretched entirely too tightly. I ran right past her while she continued on to the shore. I remember thinking that perhaps she would die so I and the world would finally be rid of her. I decided to witness her death so I skidded to a stop, turning to watch Segonku or a stray arrow cut her down. I would still have time to run to my home, I told myself.

The wretch Segonku jumped out of the starboard bow of his canoe where the surf was an ell deep. He gave a high-pitched war cry while pulling an axe from his belt. His red-painted face was frightening, even to me where I stood. Freydis would be terrified, I snickered, when she met her death.

But still Freydis marched forward. She cried to no one in particular, "Why do you flee such miserable opponents? Why are the men around me cowards, looking to me to be capable of killing these beasts off like sheep? If I had a stick between my legs, like the limpest of you all, I would fight better than any of you! If I had a weapon, any weapon, I would fight better and kill more than any of you weak, powerless ball-sacked, dung-splattered deserters!" Freydis cursed more and more, piling obscenities on the old gods and the One God. Her arms flailed about while Segonku closed in on her raising his stone axe high to crush her face. But her hand fell upon Thorbrand's sword which danced in the sand, a lone soldier ready for action. Without looking, her hand clasped the hilt, swinging it up to her own chest.

Segonku paused when he saw the weapon and then watched in amazement as did I. Freydis did not attack the skraeling, instead she used the sword to slice her tunic and dress off at the shoulders, baring her large, milk-swollen breasts. She then used the fuller or blood gutter of the sword to slap one of her breasts, lifting it with her other hand. "Do you see this, you skraeling dog? These give me more power than anything your wilted stick can give to you."

I was mesmerized by the scene, my feet planted in the earth while I watched. The other canoes were captivated as well. They stopped paddling, just watching wide-eyed at the crazed flame-headed female demon before them. Their boats bobbed uncontrolled in the waves. Segonku, too, was spellbound. He lowered his axe to his side, examining Freydis with wonder, mouth agape. Then in one swoop, Freydis lunged with the sword, slicing through the full front half of Segonku's neck. For a split second, he looked simply like he would be nauseous. However, a thin red line formed across his neck, then blood like water pouring from a bucket spilled down his chest.

Segonku's body fell straight down into a heap on the beach, and with two hands Freydis gripped the sword, hacking, hacking, hacking the remains. She shouted more, "I know you watch me Halldorr! I know because you want nothing more than to be like me, to be in me. But you will never be in me again. You are timid, running away today as you fled the skraeling battle at Fridr Rock. I loathe you!" She hacked.

The skraelings looked horrified at the loss of one of their princes at the hand of a flaming, fire-breathing woman. At first they looked from canoe to canoe, not sure what to do. But then they began shouting back and forth, finally settling on a course of action. One by one, they turned their canoes, paddling away with such haste it was as if they were pursued by the ghost of some underworld god. In our stories of the old gods, the world was formed from the icy depths of Hel. It would end in a fiery death following the end of the gods, or Ragnorok. While, perhaps, someday in the future a volcanic demon would scorch us all, I was thankful for this day, the life of Segonku met its ruin in the form of Freydis, complete with searing curses, burning hatred, and blood splattering madness.

CHAPTER 10

My death was likely to be slow and painful, maybe torturous. Strangely the notion did not concern me at the time. It was a fact like the warmth of the sun, the feel of a woman, or the grip of a sword hilt. Nor does it weigh upon my heart even today in my old age. My contact with my countrymen was likely to be forever broken; I was alone, by choice – the Enkoodabooaoo. Leif, whose predictions were always so accurate in the past, the Thing, my return to Greenland, was wrong this time – I would not find a wife in Vinland.

The entire band of Norsemen left Leifsbudir just days after Segonku was chopped down on the beach. Freydis, too, and her family set sail with their tree harvest and stolen boat, bound for Greenland, but not before Freydis freshened with two new bastard pups. She gave birth right there on the beach next to the hulking mess of Segonku's remains, letting out a massive screech while the skraeling canoes fled. At first I thought she was letting out her rage vocally, but then I saw her dress darken below her ass and she toppled to all fours, panting.

Soon Freydis rolled over to her back, slapping the sand while swearing at the One God. No one else was close by, so I sauntered over to the woman, standing above her in a reverse of how she towered over me the day she killed Lifa and the others. She didn't notice me at first for her eyes were clenched tightly in one of the massive bouts of pain that come with childbirth. I remembered my Kenna for a moment. I even saw her perspiring face with its fine features as it flickered in my mind. I remembered the pain and joy we felt those days. For a moment I felt nothing but sadness and pity for Kenna, for myself, and even Freydis. I recalled the supreme ache that welled in the hidden depths of my being. Why did Freydis live with all these bastard children, when my own Kenna died after the birth of one baby? I knew the answer, it was those wonderful hips. Those lush hips that drew me to Freydis when we were both young, allowed her to spring forth baby after baby and live. Kenna was too narrow in the hips, but she was wide and deep in knowledge and life.

I was lost in my thoughts for these moments, even looking out to the sea as the canoes fell further away. Freydis howled again, bringing me to my senses. I looked down just in time to see that she swung the sword at my legs. I hopped out of the way, but she caught me below the knee, cutting my trousers and drawing a bit of blood.

Anger steamed inside me like the steam that rose from the rocks of Iceland. I could kill her here and not a soul would know I had done it. I would say I killed the Segonku after he had killed Freydis. My hand even went to my father's saex, gripping the hilt so that my skin made a squeaking sound against the handle. Revenge against this woman would feel sweet, certainly lightening the burden that was Freydis from the shoulders of entire world. I would not be blamed; here was my opportunity. Even Leif would be relieved upon hearing the news.

The saex blade was halfway drawn from its scabbard when I hesitated. I don't know why I stopped, I just did. Freydis saw what I had done and laughed between the swelling pain attacks, "I've known you to be a coward your whole life, you bastard!" She panted heavily, ignoring the fact that she too was a bastard. "I lay before you, weakened, and still you do not kill me!" Freydis tossed the sword into the rhythmic surf, "There, kill me now you feeble simpleton. I am completely defenseless."

She was so right, Freydis would die. I again began to slide the saex out, but again I halted. I looked at her sweating, gasping bare chest, heaving from exhaustion. I scanned the area behind me toward the village and forest. I scanned the sea again. Freydis laughed and laughed.

Then I slapped the blade back into its resting place, stepped toward her face and crouched down, still standing upon my feet in the sand. I took my right hand and raised it high into a balled fist. Freydis laughed but instinctively closed her eyes to cover them from the blow.

But, of course, the blow never came. Her laughing died. She slowly opened her eyes while I carefully brushed her wild hair back behind her ears, dabbing her forehead with my shirt sleeve. Her confused countenance was worth many times more than her empty dead face would have been. I leaned down and kissed her forehead tenderly.

It was many minutes before any other man came down to the shore. In the intervening time, I helped Freydis give birth to the two bastard pups, using what I had learned from Sif, the midwife who swore and assisted Kenna all those years before in my home in Kaupangen. They were both healthy, strong boys, both with piles of red hair matted on top of their heads. They both had many of their features from Freydis and Erik before her, but they were not Tyrkr's children. I did not recognize them, but whoever bred the woman, must have had fun for there were two of them, and must have been of some importance for Leif to banish her.

But that all happened several months ago. Within a week Freydis announced that she and her family would go back to Eriksfjord with the rest, preferring to leave me behind to deal with the skraelings and hopefully die here alone. I did not intervene with her escape by suggesting that Leif intended for her to be banished, never returning. Instead, I preferred to allow them go. Freydis would be my adopted brother's problem once again.

So like Thorfinn before her, the tide came in, her boats crept up from the sand, and the lot of them rowed away, leaving me to my own devices. Right Ear sat at my side scratching at a flea that bit at his damaged ear, thumping the sand with his rear leg at each pass. A man and his dog, I was the Enkoodabooaoo Ahanu proclaimed me to be.

Throughout the summer, I harvested the bounty of Vinland, from her grapes, to her berries, to her roots, and animal life. I gave no thought to when or if I would ever return to Greenland or my people or any people. My giant moose antlers that hung in Freydis' house soon hung in my own, for I claimed Helgi's home next to the pond for me, deciding that to live where that woman lived would guarantee bad fortune.

Twice that summer I know I was watched by skraeling. They were quiet, skilled trackers, finding me whenever they wished, but I was as adept at discovering them. A small band of them could have cut me down, carving off my scalp as I had seen them do in battle. Yet they did not. Their men did not even try to talk with me. I paid no attention to them, simply strapping on my belts and weapons each day as I tread upon my land. At night I slept soundly, secure in the fact that Right Ear would warn me of their presence and that if attacked, at least three of them would be killed before I drew my last breath.

With time, however, the solitude became too much for me to bear. A day, a week, a month, I had been alone for even longer times, yet I grew restless. At last, one morning as I walked through the forest to the place where Tyrkr first discovered grapes while thinking of my friend Ahanu, I realized how close in proximity he really was to me. Why should I force myself to be alone?

I would go to them, I decided. They could view my coming as an affront, or worse, as an attack. Then my death would be certain – but perhaps not. Perhaps Ahanu could talk sense to his brother, the chief, and I could be welcomed as an ally. I had killed several of their men, but I was sure that they understood the difference between war, battle, and murder. They were good, honorable men if Nootau and Ahanu were at all representative.

How would I get to them? I had no boat, and if I did, I had no crew. I could build a boat as I had done twice in Kaupangen, but that would take years without the aid of other strong backs. Then I thought about my skraeling friends and their canoes, those bark covered boats I admired so much for their near weightlessness. I could take what I learned from Skaffhog about a boat's dimensions, its length and width, and apply that to what I observed in the birch bark canoe.

That was a mere three days ago.

I hurried back to my longhouse, pulling out my woodworking tools, nearly jogging with excitement back out to the nearest stand of birch trees. I was comfortable with skinning a birch tree while she still stood proud, for we used birch bark layers under our sod roofs many times to make them waterproof. Done properly, the tree would survive to produce more bark in the future.

Once to the stand I hastily lashed together a ladder from small saplings, propping it up against a broad, straight birch without any low branches. The tree would already have its winter bark and so peeling it would be more difficult than if I had done it in early summer, but with that trade-off came a higher quality, durable bark. I scampered to the top of my ladder, scoring a horizontal cut around the circumference of the tree, climbing up and down two or three times to move my ladder around the base of the tree. Because of my excitement I had forgotten to cut the lower horizontal slash, so had to lumber down to do make it. Then I climbed to the top again, finding the vertical section that would score the easiest and began the long upright etching.

By the time the mid-day meal came, I had peeled off the bark, taking the long rectangular section, spreading it upon a soft bed of pine needles, outside up, keeping it flat with rocks I set gently on top. In no time, I built a lightweight frame of cedar to form the bottom of the canoe's shape. I made two stems, one for the bow and the other the stern, and the gunwale out of the same species, suspending them about an ell over the bottom frame with stakes.

I had seen the skraelings used spruce roots to lace the pieces all together, so even though dusk was fully upon me, I waded into the nearest swamp that had a grove of spruce surrounding it and pulled the roots up that lay upon the floor, cutting them off with my saex. Sopping wet, I marched back to my work site with my quarry, resting upon a rock while I split the roots into a mounting pile of cord. It was only Right Ear's whimpering that reminded me that darkness now surrounded us and we had not eaten. We camped there next to a warm fire for the night, careful not catch the needles and my new boat ablaze, sharing small portions of the dried meat I carried in my rucksack.

It rained the next day, with a bit of thunder and lightning, but I stayed on task in the dripping forest, stretching the bark up around the bottom frame to the gunwale. I soon discovered my original bark section would be too short on its own so I found another tree, using its bark to create patch strips above the waterline to piece up the sides. To form the bark in the shape of the canoe, I cut vertical gores in the bark, gathering the two sides of the cut in an overlapping manner.

Now I was ready to lace it all together with the split spruce roots I had harvested the previous evening. By now Right Ear was so terrifically bored with my task and miserable in the rain that he ran off. I found him the next day chewing on a half-eaten squirrel outside the heavy, closed door of my longhouse. Yet despite the tedium and repetitious task on which I toiled, poking the bark with an awl, threading and tying the roots over and again, I was energized by the thought of being on the waves again, even though I would be paddling a canoe and not commanding a fantastic longboat with blowing sails, flapping banners snapping in the wind. For dinner, I ate a literal heap of wild mushrooms warmed by the glowing coals of the fire.

It stopped raining sometime during the night which further invigorated me and my mood. I remember feeling this much excitement when I was a very young man on the eve of Erik's journey of exile from Iceland while I wiggled my feet beneath my hide covers on the floor of his longhouse. We left the next morning for the unknown. Erik said only that we would go west, to the very edge of the world. I did not worry then, as a child, just as I did not worry as a grown man, about the unknown. I slept beneath the tree canopy on the damp soft needles next to my nearly-finished craft.

My spirits were so high that I ignored the ominous fog lying thick like fat upon the back of an old bull well past his days of glory when he would mount every heifer enclosed in his pasture. With my lacing completed, I ran, or jogged rather, to Helgi's home, found Right Ear and his squirrel, snatched a large black kettle with its lid, some stray iron, a sac full of smoked cheese, a pot of ale, and quickly returned to my project next to my unlimited supply of trees.

The kettle and iron, I set in a neat stack while I used my whetstone to sharpen my axe, eating cheese and drinking ale like the ravenous hound I was. Right Ear pounced with his dirty feet all over my lap until I shared most of the food and drink with him. He made me laugh out loud many times, and I recall to this day that after eating the rich cheese, the dog had a blinking look on his face that was as clear as if he said, "I don't think I'll shit for a week." I laughed joyously, patting his head.

Soon my axe brought down a small cedar tree. She split easily as I used all the techniques Skaffhog taught us in the oak grove on the gentle hillside outside Olaf's Kaupangen. I worked diligently, breaking only to sharpen or re-sharpen my axe. The chilly fog did not stop me from sweating profusely, so that even though it had been over twelve hours since it stopped pouring on me, I was still wet. Just after mid-day, when the sun finally began burning through the mist, I had cedar sheathing and ribs neatly stacked in two piles between my fire and the canoe.

Since I forgot a bucket, I had to carry the kettle to the nearby swamp, lugging the massive beast back, filled with water. Above the flames, I hung it from the iron rods I drove into the ground with the back of my axe head, stoking the fire, stacking the excess cedar around the pot. The arrow-straight cedar ribs were set into the quickly warming water, still jutting out the top, with the lid set awkwardly on the rim to hold in steam and heat.

While they cooked, I set the sheathing in place, lining the bottom and sides of the boat up to the gunwale, holding them in place temporarily with bending twigs wedged between the walls. Several of the plank linings required trimming to fit snugly which added enough time for the boiling water to perform its duty on the ribs.

When the boat was properly lined, I took my outer tunic off to use it like a potholder, grabbing one of the hot ribs from the boiling kettle. Working swiftly, I bent the wet board around a nearby tree to get the basic shape then drove it down into place in the canoe, trimming just a bit off one end so that it could be wedged beneath both gunwales. One after another I pulled a rib, bent it, drove it down against the sheathing, fitting them all securely in place. Only one snapped from a knot I had not seen while splitting them earlier.

She was nearly done. The pot bubbled with steam, and water spurted out, creating hisses as it hit the burning embers below, and I nodded to no one with self-satisfaction. She was going to be a beautiful boat, slicing through the waters. She was better suited to rivers, ponds, and lakes, but I would try her on the open sea. I thought about my trip, vowing to leave tomorrow regardless of the weather.

I hiked her over my head, piling as many of my tools as I could into a sack slung across my shoulder. The canoe was light as I anticipated, but even I, someone who had grown used to possessing massive strength all my life, became tired by the time I reached my home. The dog happily nipped at my heels the entire walk back which made him uproariously cheery, but made me quite angry. Rather than kick him like I wanted to do, I just let him continuously knock my rearward foot into the back of my forward foot's ankle, causing me to nearly fall and the boat to crash to the ground more than once.

I set the boat upside down between two stacks of firewood for it to receive a heavy coat of pitch from buckets we had gathered and stored some time earlier. This time the dog brought laughter to me again. He ran again and again under the canoe, brushing his back on the sticky pine tar. When Right Ear finally noticed what was happening to his back, his fur was packed and matted into an uncomfortable mess. He attempted to fix the situation by twisting his face to gnaw at the jumble, but received at mouthful of repulsive filth. This caused him to recoil, smacking and pulling his lips back, his tongue lapping everywhere. Right Ear tipped over to the earth while he struggled, rolling his back into the dirt, picking up heaps of broken grass, wood chips, and muck. As I said, I laughed and laughed at him, feeling a little sorry for his troubles, but avoiding offering any aid nonetheless.

That night, after gathering all of my implements from the forest and while sitting next to the blazing hearth, I carved a paddle in the style I had seen used by Ahanu's people. I made a monumental fire, needing to thaw or dry out my bones from so many hours in the damp chill. Several times, I had to inch my stool even closer to the flames to capture warmth even though I had endured much colder temperatures most days in my life. A quick batch of oil from my supply of walnuts, coated the blade, then I was off to sleep, staying on the floor next to the hearth for extra warmth. Three times Right Ear nudged me with his nose to curl up next to me, but I demurred, preferring to not become glued to the beast and his pine-tarred back.

We slept in, catching up on much needed rest. When I did open my eyes, returning to my senses, I saw that it rained in a miserable, steady downpour. But I would not be dissuaded from my adventure. Rising to make us a hearty breakfast before our travels, I scowled at the hair on my left harm which was matted with pine tar from Right Ear who had at last stealthily managed to lie next to me. I took out a supply of smoked fish and refried it in seal fat, salting it with salt I gathered from pans of evaporated seawater during the summer.

Then after puttering back and forth to the shore several times with the canoe, paddle, food supplies, navigation equipment such as my notched stick and a sunstone, weapons, blankets, et cetera, Right Ear and I latched closed the doors of Leifsbudir then hopped aboard the canoe for its maiden voyage. Did the skraelings name their ships, I wondered. While this was not a ship, but more like a rowboat we would have stowed aboard one of our longboats, I considered it my own ocean-going vessel, absolutely name-worthy. I pondered the question while I learned the subtleties of the craft, how she handled waves or wind, how she responded to different movements of my paddle, how she sat in the relatively calm water now that she was laden with goods. I was so pleased with her performance that day that I decided to call my new canoe *Sjor Batr*, which means, quite simply, sea boat. I have always had a gift for giving vessels a proper name.

So I paddled, taking my time, conserving my strength for the long voyage on such a small craft. I paused after a short time to cover Right Ear from the rain using a portion of an old sail that had been left behind in Vinland. The new warmth allowed him to stop his whimpering and fall into a peaceful sleep, lulled to boredom by the constant slap of raindrops on our supplies. I paddled on to what I thought would be either a delightful short visit, or an immediate death. Despite the uncertainty, peace welled inside me while I hummed an old song from the old gods while simultaneously thinking of the mysteries buried in my books, themselves now buried safely in their leather purses deep within my pile of supplies, about the One God.

So I paddled.

. . .

I paddled down the west coast of Vinland for several days, camping on the shore at night next to a small fire started with jasper, until I reached the southwestern-most corner of the island. After resting there and gathering two flat sticks as spare oars in case of an emergency, I struck off straight southwest toward Kjalarnes and Ahanu's people.

The going was difficult. The rain stopped on the second day of our voyage, and I thanked God truthfully. But as we pushed toward Ahanu, the wind came into our faces, making my light boat like a sail pushing us backward. I had to strike the oar through the waters three or four times just to move the distance normally traveled with just one pass. So I thanked God's Providence again when, after paddling all day and all night without ceasing, I saw a cragged shoreline looming in the morning light. While it was not my destination, I fell down and kissed her granite rocks after pulling *Sjor Batr* out of the sea.

Right Ear and I stayed on that island for two straight days while we waited for the wind to change directions or at least fall. It was a truly isolated, small island without any wildlife other than a myriad of seabirds. I sent the dog running into the flocks of birds to scare them away while I gathered their eggs for each of our meals. It had been some time since I had eaten eggs, for the chickens we raised were all taken by Freydis back to Greenland. They were delicious.

After resting long enough that I had forgotten about the pain in my shoulders, we set off again despite the still-present wind.

In a short time, with joy, I called out to Right Ear that I already saw Kjalarnes where Thorvald buried the keel years before. The monument was long gone, but the beach remained. I gained strength at the sight. Right Ear became so excited that he jumped out of the canoe which caused many tense minutes while I shouted at him above the wind-driven waves to paddle back to the boat. Even when he finally did, I remembered how difficult it was to retrieve someone from the sea in a small boat. With strength, patience, and luck I eventually hauled the dripping dog back into the boat, being blown nearly the full way back to our island respite.

Again I paddled. The wind was stiffer that day, blowing bits of seawater into my face so I had to blink constantly, and sending the waves taller. I realized my error after one or two hours, but could not bring myself to simply turn around, allowing the wind to hasten us back to the safety of the island. Instead, I remained stubborn. Young men are supposed to be stubborn, for they are certain in their inexperience that they are right. Yet I was not young. I was forty-two years old. Forty-two! My, but I paddled with my sore, burning shoulders thinking about how God-awful old I felt. It was the first time in a long while I thought that I should have been sitting next to a great hearth with my feet upon a stool and a woman, some years younger than I carrying my child while preparing a bounteous meal. Yet I was stubborn in my age, embarrassed to admit a poor decision even with no one around to know. I paddled. I struggled.

For the rest of the day and that night, I toiled against those waves. It was not until the late morning of the next day that I skidded the canoe into the fine sand, dropped the paddle, and toppled over the side fully exhausted. The waves lapped all the way up to my waist so I used the last bit of strength I had left to pull the boat to safety and collapse onto the dry sand. I slept.

In my sleep, I dreamed. This dream warrants a telling because of how truly vivid it was. I lay there, passed out, sleeping in the sand with my wet face and hair gathering any stray grain they touched when my friend the One God came to me as a gentle friend. When my eyes flickered awake, I saw him crouching next to me gently nudging me to consciousness with a soft push and even softer words. He beckoned me to follow him and when I rose, I found that I was at full peace, rejuvenated, feeling no pain or regret or sorrow or any of the things which pang at a man's deepest thoughts. I was sated. The One God walked up from the rolling surf, his clean priestly robes catching traces of wind, flickering at the ends. At the edge of the beach where the sand met the forest sat a simple wooden throne. He seized a single piece of carved, smoothly sanded wood and affixed it to the chair. I realized it was not the One God before me, but his carpenter son, the Christ Jesus. He made his own throne from the trees of the forest by the work of his own hands like he had done on the cross many years before. The last piece he set in place was the armrest for the left side, and it fit snugly without any pounding or nails or wedges. I watched silently, impressed at his craftsmanship.

When he finished, the Christ stepped back admiring his work with his hands upon his hips. Then he pointed at the throne, and I, without a word, knew it was for me. So I walked to it and though I was confused, still felt at ease as if receiving a visit from a dear friend who brought the gladdest of tidings. So I sat, awaiting his eloquent words.

But Jesus, the Christ, simply sat himself. But he chose a mangled, dry section of driftwood that teetered a little when he put too much of his weight on it so that he had to keep his feet firmly in place on the ground to steady it, working. Jesus pulled out a small knife and picked up a stray piece of wood, unable to refrain from exercising his carpentry skills. I thought we all must be like those pieces of wood to him, on which he needed to continually work. In mere moments he had made a flute or whistle. I noticed the Christ's hands at that moment. They were muscled with strength like the biggest man I had ever seen. His hands were calloused from constant shaping, squeezing and moulding, yet they were impeccably clean. Not a smidge of stray dirt soiled his light sun-bronzed skin.

While finishing the whistle, he spoke, "Halldorr." When he said my name a profound happiness grew within me. "Halldorr, you are a faithful reader of my Word. Do you remember Abram?" Jesus looked at me, his long Norse-like hair blew across his face from the ocean breeze.

It pleased me that I knew the answer, "Yes, he was a righteous man from Ur. The Father God made a covenant with him and he became the father of the nations."

Jesus smiled broadly, "True enough. And his children?"

"The One God promised they would be as numerous as the stars in the heavens," I answered, proud of myself.

The carpenter's simple answer was, "And so it will be with you." He set the whistle down and went to work carving a spoon from another scrap.

But my response was not the righteous response of Abram. Instead I reacted more like Zechariah when, from Gabriel, he learned that he and his wife would be the parents of John the Baptist. "How can this be? I am already old. My woman is dead. I have no wife. I am alone."

Thankfully, Jesus, the Christ, is merciful, more so than Gabriel to be sure. The Christ chuckled, finding great humor in my answer. At last he sighed, "It is always the same with my children. But you should know that I have said the words. It will be so with you."

Then he put the whistle to his lips and played a merry tune. He smiled behind the instrument, bouncing and bobbing his head to the music. I tapped my feet and hands even though I did not recognize the song. Christ got up from his seat and slowly walked away down the length of the beach, still blowing his tune. I did not follow for I knew my time with him was done. Even though he grew further and further away, the sound of his music seemed to grow and still I danced in my chair. Then he was gone out of sight and the music became louder and louder. Then the music was so loud it was not in any way pleasant. The tune was gobbled up by the volume, and it pierced my ears, creating great pain. I winced with scrunched eyes, tried to cover my ears with my hands, but I could not. My arms were exhausted again and I could not move them.

A sting shot through my back and I fell out of the throne, hitting the sand again. Extreme bouts of pain stabbed my back and sides. I rolled down the beach, back to the spot where the Christ found me. Then my eyes popped open again.

Chaos reigned in my corner of the sand. Several ells away Right Ear growled, howled, and barked angrily. Closer, I saw the makizin feet and legs of at least four skraeling men. The feet alternated going up out of sight and back down to the beach. Each time another foot went up, I felt a new bout of pain in my back. I know now they kicked me, but at the time, confusion ruled my mind. The men made shrill war cries as they beat me.

My muscles would not respond to command. I did not even curl up to protect myself, instead lying there flat to receive the full brunt of the punishment they dealt. Then they rolled me onto my back and I thought would begin the process of beating my face, chest or stomach. One or two bent to punch me in the cheek, but they were merciful, grabbing me by my arms, dragging me.

I spoke some words in their tongue to them about friends and Ahanu and peace, but they ignored my pleas. I mentioned Nootau and visit, but another swift strike upon my brow brought a welcome respite from my pain for I fell into unconsciousness.

The next memory I can recall is that I awoke with an old woman standing over me with some type of shovel. She cackled like a crow as she drew the shovel up into the air over her head. I thought she meant to strike me with it and that I would surely die at the hand of the hag, not able to defend myself. However, it was then that I felt a searing pain upon my chest. All the strength left in me marshaled at once, and I rolled over, spilling hot embers off my bare chest. Where my jerkin was, I do not know. A crowd had gathered around me, all laughing, jeering. Right Ear or some other dog barked nearby.

I admitted my grave mistake in coming, resolving to endure the torture for only a moment longer while I prayed for renewed strength. I rose to all fours to slowly crawl away between two birch bark homes, but the old hag kicked me in my ass and I tumbled onto my face. Then powerful hands clasped around my belly, heaving me into the air. In an instant, I hung upside down like a limp bundle of hay. Then whoever held me began spinning, at first slowly, then ever faster. I saw the villagers in blurs. I saw flashes of sunshine, shadows, and cooking fires. Then I forced my eyes shut to keep control of my nausea, but it was too late. I vomited while still spinning, with my stomach contents running up my nose and into my eyes and hair. Soon I was sure I would die with my intestines pushing into my mouth from the spinning.

When my tormentor became dizzy himself, he halted and I thought I would survive, but a compatriot took up the task, spinning me faster yet. I vomited again, but the contents were just the acrid yellow juices from my belly. Laughter and shouts greeted the torturer when he, at last, dropped me into a heap, head first. Through my blurry vision, I saw his stumbling feet walking in the dust next to me. I pictured his smiling face, wanting to snuff the life from it.

For a moment, I was forgotten as the group celebrated its gaiety. I would stand and flee to the forest now, but when I gathered all power, the only thing that happened was that my arms and legs flailed like a fish cast upon the deck planks of a longboat. This only called attention to me again, and I felt my limbs seized by four men. They lifted me from the ground, swinging me back and forth until they began counting. One, two, three, then each of them released me at the same time so that I crashed into the hard earth on my back which had been so badly beaten earlier.

I couldn't breathe. I prayed, not for escape this time, but for death. Please God, command this torture cease. They clutched my limbs again. "God!" I cried out as they hefted me into the air. The men laughed at what they likely thought was a funny word. Then I remembered their name for Jesus and called, "Glooskap!" This time one of the men looked down into my eyes. I thought I saw a moment of pity, but his glance went to my *Charging Boar* tattoo. He pointed it out to his friends as if he was noting an interesting rock formation – just something of a curiosity.

They began their counting again. One, two, three. I did my best to prepare for the extreme pain that would arrive in a moment.

"Stop this!" came a high-pitched scream from a woman. I could not see her through my blurred vision. The men briefly halted, but then started swinging again in order to drop me. But whoever she was, she shouted again, "Stop torturing this man!" The voice was closer this time, right behind the man who held my right hand. I think blood came from my eyes, mixing with the vomitus on my teetering head.

They stopped swaying my limp body, holding me while one of them answered, "Who are you to tell me what to do? You know you are nothing but a woman?"

"I am but a woman, but I know my chief's will. You are like the porcupine, blustering up to appear bigger than you are. You are a fool, assuring that you will never hold any power among our own people. You will stop harming our visitor at once!" Her tone was powerful, demanding, but was conveyed with a calmness that spoke volumes of self confidence.

"Visitor? He is one of the foreign invaders! He is likely a spy."

"A spy who came in broad daylight to our village with a barking dog? You are more foolish than I thought." Several chortles from the assemblage said that the woman struck a nerve.

"What would you have us do?" asked my torturer.

"I would have you set him down and walk away. I will then tend to his wounds."

"And then who will pay his ransom?"

"If he is a captive, the chief will pay a ransom to keep you and your warriors from attacking him. If the chief wishes it, that is. If he is not a captive, there is no ransom to pay, you simple-minded tree."

He and the other three men quickly debated her words, then the leader said, "It will be as you say. The chief and council will decide." But instead of setting me to the ground gently, the men dropped me one more time onto my aching back. Again consciousness fled.

. . .

There was no position that would be comfortable, though the woman did her best to decide on what would likely be the least painful. I awoke inside one of the birch bark dwellings when the sun had already fallen outside. A diminutive fire lit the small space where I lay on my belly, the bare wounds from the old woman's embers on my chest nearly made me swoon in pain as they dug into the soft fur of a pelt on which I sprawled.

Moving only my eyes, I scanned my surroundings. Jagged wooden poles formed a frame on which the bark had been set. From those poles hung all sorts of items, pots, various herb bundles, several strings of wood and bone carvings, small cutting tools made of stone, and weapons. A spear was tucked neatly, adjacent to a main support pole. A quiver of arrows hung next to it. Even a bow was available. I slowly lifted my head and saw that I was completely alone in the home. I would confiscate the weapons and fight my way out of the village. Just another moment to regain strength was all I needed, at least that is what I told myself. But the moment turned into many minutes while I struggled to even move my hands up from my sides, bracing them to push into the ground.

Footfalls outside told me someone approached so I let out a groan, pushing myself up, locking my elbows straight. I was exhausted; I could move no more, my breathing was labored. The footsteps entered the low door behind me and my savior, the kind woman who rescued me said, "You're not able to go anywhere. So lie down and conserve your strength."

Unquestioningly, I obeyed, dropping my weakened body back to the hide. She fiddled with some of the herbs, crushing a handful into a bowl she brought in. The woman then came to the fire, sitting next to it and me, pulled out a spoon-like utensil of some sort, and began dabbing it on my wounds. I looked at my naked arm, the only part of my body I could see, and saw that she had already cleaned the dried blood and vomit and was now applying a green paste to my abrasions.

I followed the movements of the spoon as it sprang smartly from bowl to my skin and back again. I noted her slender, though not thin, fingers gripping the utensil. They were fixed on the ends of young hands, certainly not those like the old hag who attacked me earlier. In the distance I heard the rolling surf hit the shores where Thorvald had killed the skraelings under the hide boats years earlier. The green paste stung the wounds for just a moment, then my skin felt soothed, cool.

My eyes wandered further up her bare arms. They were strong arms, developed from years of working for her people, somewhat tan in color. She had no sleeves, for her light brown tunic was cut off at the shoulders, running straight down her sides. The dress was simple with no designs at all except for the fringe and beads that encircled the neck. She wore a single necklace with a triangular-shaped bone carving affixed at the end. Dizzily, I looked down past where her breasts pushed out at the fabric. If I hadn't been in such pain, I have no doubt my glance would have lingered there for a time.

Her bare knees faced me while the woman sat with her ankles crossed in front of my nose. On her feet she wore plain leather makizins, cinched at her ankles with a tight leather thong. Beyond her shoes, I could see into her dress where I saw the parts of her that could delight the men of her village, hidden by her thick black curly hair. I looked there for a long while and it pleased me. The woman hummed a song that was foreign to me.

I had already seen between her legs and decided I should finally gaze upon her face, so I turned my head more so I could peer up. A shot of pain almost blinded me, causing a quiet groan to rumble from my throat. The woman whispered, "Shhhh shhhh shhhh shhhh," setting the bowl down and petting my head with her free hand.

I looked at her face from below. I believe I fell in love with the woman at that moment. Her hair was black like the hair of all her people. It shone like the shining coal cliffs I had seen on my travels. She had the long locks pulled tightly into a horse's tail, tied securely by a cord at the nape of her neck. The hair was smooth and beautiful. Her nose and cheeks were strong, broad and long at the same time. Above those cheeks she had rich brown-black eyes. Enormous eyes. Beautiful eyes. I have said I loved her instantly. I found her enchanting.

I guessed her to be about ten years younger than I was at the time. Some skraeling warrior of influence would be under a blanket with her tonight which explains why she felt powerful enough to save me.

Footsteps came into the home behind me. A young man's voice said, "Word comes back. The party will return in two suns."

The woman looked toward the young man, nodded, saying, "Thank you. I will be to the mamateek shortly. Off with you." He left without another word. She went back to her humming.

In their language I groaned, "Your son?"

A little surprised at how well I spoke their tongue, she said, "Yes. Fourteen winters he has seen. Normally he would have gone with the others this time, but our chief allowed him to stay behind to help me."

"And your husband, is he with the other men?"

The woman's look turned stern and strong. Sad, but not angry. "I have lost two husbands to your people. I have no husband. No more talking."

She adjusted her position to apply her salve, and we were both silent for some time. I wanted to apologize for her suffering for her losses. Maybe it was my own sword that brought her men down. But my energy was nearly completely consumed. I think I slept then.

When I felt and heard her stirring to leave, I woke up, saying the first thing I thought to say, "Thank you for helping me."

The woman walked over from the other side of the home, bending down to me. Again she patted my head with its sweating, matted hair. "The chief and his council will decide your fate. You may yet be tortured and killed when they return in two days." No malice. No sadness. She spoke with the assuredness that comes with facts. No opinion. No worries. She spoke like a woman who had gained experience by living, receiving gifts and loss. She was a woman resigned to fate. The striking woman patted my head once more, rose to her full height and left through the open doorway.

And I lay there, immobilized, a man resigned to the Providence that would be mine. A man who would be sentenced to a hideous death by the father of Megedagik, the chief of Ahanu's people.

THE END
(Dear Reader, See Historical Remarks section to help separate fact from fiction.)

HISTORICAL REMARKS

My goal while writing this tale was to make a compelling story, but also keep as true to history as possible. If you've read *The Norseman*, Halldorr's first yarn, you know that much of the action takes place in Europe, Ireland, Wales, England, and Norway to be precise. It turns out that such geographies made it quite easier to find ample volumes of recorded events of the time.

Not so with *Paths of the Norseman*. Many of the events in this work were only recorded in *The Greenland Sagas* or the *Erik the Red Sagas*, collectively known as the *Vinland Sagas*. You will see from the discussions below that these two distinct works record many of the same events, with broad differences that can only be expected from histories written down separately from oral traditions two hundred years after the fact. Since the Vikings did not have a written word tradition and neither did the peoples with which they came into contact in their new world discoveries, we are left with no other documented verification of the events.

However, the reader should not fret. We are not left with fun, heroic stories of an allegorical nature only! Archaeology, especially in the latter half of the Twentieth Century, confirmed many of the accounts which the sagas discuss. Where there is disagreement, I made my best attempts to note them below and to make them make sense in Halldorr's story. Characters such as Erik, Leif, Thorstein, Thorvald, Thjordhildr, Freydis, Gudrid, Thorhall, Bjarni, Thorfinn, little Snorri, Helgi, and Finnbogi were real people. Putting feelings and action to the cold facts of history bring them alive for me and hopefully, allow you to feel a closeness or better understanding of lives they and their peers led.

Our hero, Halldorr, is a fictional character, meant to not only follow the action of the famous characters written in the sagas, but also to embody the Norse spirit of adventure, to show the confusion any of us would have endured when a new foreign faith is thrust upon us, when we have comfortably followed our old gods for generations. His ability to read and speak multiple languages makes him an enigma to be sure.

Leif Eriksson is famous for making his way from Norway all the way to Greenland in the first nonstop transatlantic sea journey in history following his stay with King Olaf. Leif paid a visit to the king, shortly before Olaf fought the overwhelming sea battle of Swoldr which was portrayed in *The Norseman*. King Olaf so liked Leif that he gave him two Scottish thralls, or slaves, as a gift so that the travelling Greenlander could more easily spread the newfound Christian faith among his countrymen. Please read *The Norseman* for a more complete understanding of Olaf and his faith in the One God.

Leif was bestowed the name Leif the Lucky after rescuing a band of stranded men on a rock in the icy waters of the seas surrounding Greenland. The good fortune that followed Leif wherever he went allowed him to successfully convert the Greenlanders to the new faith with ease, because like many of us today, his people wanted to follow a god of affluence and luck, answering to our whims. The sagas say that Leif rescued the men on a return trip to Greenland from his Vinland travels, but I had to move the event to his transatlantic crossing so that Halldorr could be in the right place at the right time in order to record it.

I have been unkind to Bjarni Herjolfsson. In the sagas, he was not shown to be traitorous and was not, as far as anyone knows, among the dead in the mass grave at Thjordhildr's church. The idea for Bjarni as a cowardly villain came to me as a lightning bolt as I read the account of his initial voyage to Greenland. How could a man be in such dire straits and still not stop in to the foreign shores for a respite? I still shake my head at his obtuse view today. If you are interested in the account, read *The Norseman*.

Next to the ruins of Thjordhildr's Church in Greenland, a mass grave was discovered in the 1960s, containing the bodies of twelve men and one nine year old boy. No women were in the original grave, but were in the grave in my tale. All the individuals had been buried at the same time and were completely disarticulated with their crania arranged neatly in a row on the grave's eastern side. The scene when Halldorr boiled the bodies and bones of Bjarni's family members was meant to be horrifying, but conveys a bit of historical insight. Many archaeologists surmise that when their comrades fell on foreign shores far from home, the Norse Greenlanders would boil the remains to make transporting them back for burial more convenient. The sagas themselves confirm such events.

Erik did become despondent following his youngest son's death, and so Leif badgered him to again go adventuring or a-Viking. He was on his way down to the boat on the day they were to leave when he was thrown from his horse and badly injured. Erik, who never converted to the new faith, viewed the injuries as a bad omen and refused to go along. He withdrew further into his shell and Thjordhildr's decision to withhold sex from her husband until he converted likely hastened his bitterness.

Helluland is the name Leif Eriksson gave to the first land he came to from Greenland on his famous journey of exploration. It is commonly thought to be Baffin Island and I have kept with tradition but chose to be more specific in my selection. I chose what is now called Resolution Island which is at the southernmost tip of Baffin. It made the most sense to me given its proximity to Eriksfjord and given Bjarni's description of an island that he and his men were able to circle in short order. Baffin itself is just too large, extending far north of the Arctic Circle and its pack ice, to think that they circumnavigated it.

Markland is thought to be part of today's Labrador, Canada. Since Leif and his men did not tarry there, we do not have any archeological evidence to corroborate this inference generally. Neither do we have evidence of the specific location. I described an area that is known as the Okak Islands today. The reader should not assign any special significance to the place with regard to Leif Eriksson as I selected it based purely on its position on a map.

Even though the Norse did not build any shelters, permanent or temporary, in Markland according to the sagas, we must assume that for many years after Leif's voyage, Greenlanders came to the shores of Markland to harvest timber. Its proximity to Eystribyggo made it an ideal location, certainly better than either Norway to the east or Vinland to the south.

Leif's ship did find itself beached with the falling of the tide when they were discovering Vinland – a rather ignoble beginning to a European's first settlement in the New World. Today Vinland is a rather barren, cold place, wind-swept from the surrounding sea, but 1,000 years ago the conditions were quite different. The Medieval Warm Period was in full swing allowing for many of the journeys and conditions written about in the sagas. Forests and swamps covered Vinland, today's Newfoundland.

I am clearly not an American-Indian anthropologist, archaeologist, or historian. My research tells me that the most likely inhabitants of the Vinland at the time of Leif Eriksson were the Beothuk peoples. However, the last surviving member of the tribe died in 1829 and so as a people, they are officially extinct. They were never a people who existed in great numbers, perhaps several hundred at most. Their demise came from the encroachment of Europeans after Columbus's rediscovery of the Western Hemisphere, but also their cultural isolation. They did not interact nor form many alliances with other Native American nations and so adapting a thriving trading culture with the scores of bearded European sailors proved too difficult.

Four vocabulary lists, totaling approximately 400 words were written down in the Eighteenth and Nineteenth Centuries. However, there is no example of connected Beothuk speech and those who made the wordlists did not use any consistent method of recording what they heard. Therefore, deciphering the sound system of the Beothuk language is a daunting task. Since the 1860's it has been suggested that the Beothuk language was related to Algonquin, one of the Algonquian languages. Therefore, any references to speech I used for the Beothuk peoples in this work were Algonquin, itself only spoken by a few thousand people in the entire world. I offer my apologies for any errors noticed by any linguists or native Algonquin speakers in my reading audience. Please forgive me.

The sagas disagree on who gave Kjalarnes its name. The *Greenlanders' Saga* proclaims that Thorvald named it after repairing his damaged keel and burying the old one in the sand. The *Erik the Red Saga*, which is very complimentary of Thorfinn Karlsefni, says that Karlsefni came ashore and discovered the buried keel, thus naming it Kjalarnes. Comparing the two works, I thought it most likely that Thorvald buried and named the land. Thorfinn simply found the land later on, after Thorvald's death from the arrow of a skraeling. Thorvald, Erik's oldest son, was taken by his new faith, and as he died requested a grave marked by two crosses.

In my telling of a small portion of Thorfinn Karlsefni's tale, I have been liberal with the histories. In Halldorr's quest to find a woman and settle down, he had to once again see Gudrid, Thorstein Eriksson's widow, and become a father to the first European baby born in the New World, Snorri. The sagas are clear that Thorfinn and the widow Gudrid were Snorri's parents, this scrap of Halldorr's tale is presented with artistic license.

As with much of the history of the period in which our story takes place, scholars disagree on many of the particulars. In their readings of the sagas, some have come to the conclusion that the discussions of Straumsfjord and Leifsbudir (literally meaning Leif's booths or homes) actually refer to the same physical location. Other researchers say that they are two different sites as a simple reading of the texts suggest. I have read the reasons for both accounts and find each to have its merits and each to leave unanswered questions. Ultimately, it should not surprise the reader at this point that I do not have the same requirements as my learned historian counterparts. As has been my preferred method, I have chosen the simplest explanation and put the two settlements in two separate places.

Our explorers had an exceptionally difficult winter in Straumsfjord with hunger throughout. Thorhall, who, like his old friend Erik, never converted to the new faith, left the encampment to offer a prayer to his old gods. Rescuers found him mumbling as described in the novel and soon thereafter discovered a whale that had washed ashore. Their troubles were answered, with no more discussions of scarcity in the sagas. It was after that terrible winter that Thorhall and nine of his men left the company of Thorfinn, but I will leave the details of what became of Thorhall for another book.

There remains much disagreement among learned and amateur scholars alike as to the location of Hop as discussed in the

Vinland Sagas. For a host of reasons I have chosen to assume that Hop was somewhere in what is present day New York, specifically the Hudson River. In *Vikings: The North Atlantic Saga*, Gisli Sigurdsson contributes a chapter which, in my mind creates a logical argument for this location. However, the reader should always remember that as of this writing, the only archaeological evidence of a Norse civilization in North America remains at Leifsbudir on the northern tip of today's Newfoundland.

Thorfinn and Halldorr's trip south all the way to the Outer Banks of today's North Carolina is pure fiction. However, no one knows how far south along the coast of America the explorers traveled. They were, by their very nature, adventurers and so I merely attempted to show that as they spent the summers exploring around their main encampments, there is a very good chance that some of their longboats sailed further than many scholars give them credit. The archaeological evidence does not support such trips, but the human element, I think, does.

Thorfinn's encounters with the skraelings are well documented in both of the *Vinland Sagas*. The natives would come to them in the mornings swinging wooden poles while standing in their canoes. The two peoples had modest success for a short time trading for cheese, red cloth, and hides or ivory. Unfortunately for everyone, misunderstandings involving the trading of weapons in general and a frightened, bellowing bull in one instance did precipitate bloodshed.

Soon thereafter, the skraelings attacked in a larger number and were summarily beaten back after they chased the Norsemen into a clearing in the forest. My story assumes that this was all part of the battle plan. The sagas are less clear, though they tell of Thorfinn's worry and preparations for a response from the skraelings.

Eventually, Thorfinn took his small family, Gudrid and Snorri, away from Vinland. They returned to Greenland, eventually settling on a farm called Glaumbaer in Iceland. Many years later, following Thorfinn's death, Gudrid became famous for making a pilgrimage to Rome, even being called Gudrid the Wide Traveled in the sagas. Their offspring had in their lines, many men who served as bishops of various Norse or derivative settlements through the years.

The sagas speak on Freydis' foray into Vinland with the brothers Helgi and Finnbogi with an air of condemnation and bewilderment. Her husband's name was actually Thorvald, like her older half-brother who died at Kjalarnes, but to simplify the story and make it slightly easier for the reader to follow I changed his name to Torvard. You're welcome.

The character of Freydis is quite fascinating, likely among the most interesting in all of the Vinland Sagas. She caused much enmity among the inhabitants of Greenland and so her half-brother, Leif, the new jarl did not seek to prevent her from leaving. Freydis and Helgi agreed to populate their crews with thirty men each, but from the start Freydis broke the bargain, taking more along. We may never know if she had evil intentions from the start. The brothers, Helgi and Finnbogi arrived at Vinland first, having enough time to unload their goods into Leif's house, but when Freydis came, she sent them away. Helgi responded by saying they would never be a match for her ill-will. He could not have known how correct he was, for even after the brothers arranged games and entertainment over the winter, the parties began arguing, splitting further apart.

Freydis went to offer peace, but beat herself up on her way back, convincing her husband and his men to kill the brothers and their household. When none of her men would kill the five women, Freydis said, "Hand me an axe," one-by-one cutting the defenseless women down outside their longhouse. She took their longboat as her own, stocking it with all the goods that Vinland had to offer, taking them back to Greenland. Leif soon heard stories of her wicked actions, even torturing some of her men to get the truth of all that happened while she was away, but could never bring himself to order her death.

Before leaving for Greenland, there was another skraeling attack with which to deal. However, this time the Norse chose not to fight. In my tale, I assumed it was because they were unprepared or badly outnumbered, though the true reason escapes me. The sagas do, in fact, state that while the Norsemen retreated away from the skraeling warriors, a man named Thorbrand Snorrason was killed with a slab of stone to the head. A very slow and pregnant Freydis shuffled out toward the attackers, picked up Thorbrand's sword and stripped to her bare breasts. According to the sagas, she did slap her breasts with the sword, all the while accusing her men of weakness and cowardice. The skraelings were afraid of her actions and fled. Segonku or Megedagik was a fictional character, but I used his death to help explain why they took flight.

One of the last major scenes in this work involved the torture of Halldorr at the hands of his skraeling captors. While the events are fiction, I used the memoir written by John Gyles, a hostage beginning in 1689 of the tribes of what is today Maine. While they were likely a different clan and a different tribe altogether, easily separated by hundreds of years, I appreciate the first-hand account for its honesty. The simple methods also appear to be more legitimate than the elaborate torture techniques devised for film. Mr. Gyles witnessed each of the methods I describe and more.

Halldorr has many more adventures to experience, many more peoples to see. I hope he is able to escape his current predicament! We will find out by following Halldorr's tales which come to us from his mythical memoirs. He has a woman to find who will bear him children as the soothsayer Leif and the Son of the One God have told him. I hope you enjoyed this part of his story and are willing to follow along with his further escapades in his next book. Turn to the "About the Author" section to see what you can do to ensure that there are more novels to come.

ABOUT THE AUTHOR

Jason Born is the author of the first two volumes of *The Norseman Chronicles*, *The Norseman* and *Paths of the Norseman*. He is an analyst and portfolio manager for a private Registered Investment Advisory firm in the United States. Jason lives in the Midwest with his wife and three children. He loves learning in general, especially history. If you enjoyed this work and would like to see more, Jason asks you to consider doing the following:

1. Please encourage your friends to buy themselves a copy – and read it!
2. Go to his author page on Facebook and click "Like" so that you may follow information on the next book.
3. If you think the book deserves praise, please post a five star review on Amazon and/or a five star review on Goodreads.com.

Thank you!

Printed in Great Britain
by Amazon.co.uk, Ltd.,
Marston Gate.